The Secret of the Abbess of Assisi

Vlastimil Vondruška

ISBN: 978-1-7392249-3-6

Published by Handshake Press

To my wife Alena

CHAPTER I

I n the year of our Lord 1186, the seven-year-old King of Jerusalem, Baldwin V, died and was succeeded by his mother, Sibylla. When she then stepped aside in favor of her husband, Guy of Lusignan, all hell broke loose. The new King of Jerusalem had no interest in living peacefully alongside the Muslims. He immediately banished the former regent, Raymond of Tripoli, to his fiefdom in the north and abrogated all the peace treaties concluded by his predecessors. At issue for him wasn't religion, but adventure. He liked war, enjoyed waging it and reaping the spoils. And so the years of relative peace in the Holy Land were over.

Guy of Lusignan had the support of dozens of knights who had come to the Holy Land with the same goal in mind – get rich. Perhaps the most ruthless and reckless among them was the Count of Antioch, Renaud de Châtillon. He was already an old man who lived only for killing and looting. Even controlling a fleet of pirate ships on the Red Sea wasn't enough for him. In the name of Christianity, he set off to attack the island of Cyprus, which belonged to the Emperor of Byzantium. He massacred the defenseless population, completely unconcerned by the fact that they were also followers of Jesus Christ, if in the Eastern manner. His deeds were of such cruelty that the entire Christian world preferred to remain silent about them. No one was happier to see Lusignan sitting on the throne of Jerusalem than Renaud. On the very day of Guy's accession, he renewed his attacks against Muslim caravans in the Jordan Valley. The sand along the trade routes was soon again stained with the blood of worshipers of Allah. The outbreak of war was inevitable.

Although Saladin had unified the Muslim world by this time, his reaction to this provocation by the Christians was at first restrained. He demanded an apology from the King of Jerusalem and the return of all captives and stolen goods. Only it never occurred to Guy to hold Renaud to account. He believed he would win this war and so immediately began making preparations. In the spring of 1187 he raised an army, something which no other King of Jerusalem ever had at his disposal. Even the exiled Raymond flocked to his banner, for he understood, as did most of the moderate knights, that keeping the Holy Land in Christian hands was at stake. They didn't agree with Guy, but that didn't mean they were willing to stand idly by in the face of Muslim attacks. They were, after all, Christian knights.

The troops pulled out of Jerusalem after Easter.

Saladin's forces were waiting for them at Lake Galilee. Soon they were just a day's march away, but the actual distance between the two armies was nearly insurmountable. The path to the lake led through dry, hilly terrain. Continuing on without adequate supplies, in the dust and along scorching rocks with the sun overhead, wore not only the men out, but also, importantly, the horses. To survive the high plateau only to land into the hands of the enemy was the same as marching off to defeat. Like Saladin, the King of Jerusalem was well aware of this trap, so he called the Christian army to a halt.

They set up camp not far from a small river and started to do what was normal for such situations. The knights and their attendants forayed into the surrounding countryside in search of loot. They fought off boredom by occasionally skirmishing with advance units of the Muslim force. Both armies had engaged in dozens of similar skirmishes before, but they usually ended in a truce. Then, after waiting in vain for some decisive battle to take place, they would head home.

Despite lacking overwhelming numbers, Saladin was in no hurry for a quick truce. Not this time. The Christians had committed too many outrages and acts of violence. But he was not ready to risk a march across the arid highlands. He therefore opted for the closer and more secure goal of attacking the city of Tiberias, which lay on the hillside of Lake Galilee. By coincidence, the command of the city's defenses fell to the wife of Raymond of Tripoli. Her husband, however, did not feel compelled to risk an attack across the highlands. On the contrary, Raymond publicly announced that it was better to lose one city than the entire army and Jerusalem. He knew that at heart Saladin was the same caliber of knight that he was. Nothing would happen to his wife. At the most, he would have to pay a ransom for her if Tiberias fell. He implored the King of Jerusalem to stay put and not do anything provocative. But Guy used the attack on Tiberias as an excuse to continue the war. He conferred with his most trusted advisers until nightfall, but they too admitted an attack would be too risky. Reason had prevailed. But sometime during the night, while the soldiers slept, the Grandmaster of the Templars came to Guy in his royal tent to persuade the King not to lay his sword aside. "You must proceed like the first Crusaders did when they reached the Holy Land! Their position was worse than ours is now, but still they attacked the infidels and won. God is with us!" he shouted, raising his right hand with the sacral sword of his order firmly in grip. He persuaded Guy to join battle the next day, and in doing so decided the fate of Jerusalem and that of Oldrich of Chlum.

The trumpets sounded at dawn throughout the Christian camp, calling the troops to arms against Saladin. Raymond came up to Guy, insisting he call off the march at the last minute, but Guy refused to see him. Running between the tents, the supporters of the King of Jerusalem enticed wavering soldiers with thoughts of plunder waiting for them in the Muslim camp. They were also busy calculating, based on the reports of their scouts, how big a force they would be facing in Saladin's host. The army set off before sunrise.

It was a hot day in July. The plain on which the Crusaders marched was totally barren, without shade anywhere for shelter and rest. For months the scorched earth hadn't seen a drop of rain. Their water supplies, carried in leather pouches, were gone before noon. The helmets on their heads were so hot they were nearly impossible to touch, but removing them only made matters worse. At noon the first man died of exhaustion. Still, no one gave the order to retreat. They staggered along, their heads hanging listlessly, trying not to think about what lay ahead. Such was their life, the life of a Christian soldier.

"Keep going!" the knights called out to the men in their companies. "We will reach Lake Galilee by evening. You can drink it dry if you like. The water is cool, clean and sparkling..." But a few hours later not even they had the strength to keep up the encouragement. The army had slowed to a pathetic crawl. The men began to stumble and many horses collapsed. Dusk arrived and still the lake was nowhere in sight.

"Let's halt here! We must rest for a while," implored the Grandmaster of the Templars, his parched tongue sticking to the roof of his mouth. He and his Templars were having the hardest time of all, and their horses even worse. Finally the King of Jerusalem agreed. The army camped in a shallow depression near the village of Hattin. They pitched no tents, constructed no fortifications, not even temporary ones. Nor did anyone post a watch. They were too exhausted. They fell to the ground and begged God to make the sun go down. There was only one well in Hattin, with little water in it. Renaud de Châtillon's men seized it for themselves.

The camp was surrounded by the Muslims during the night. Despite their exhaustion, the Christian knights couldn't sleep. They had to be on guard. Saladin could attack any time during the night, but he didn't. He waited till morning. The Christians suffered from cramps, and thirst made them claw at their throats as if they were suffocating. Barely a soul felt the same grace of God that had stirred them to take up arms. Instead, they were overcome with despair.

In a fit of anger, Raymond cried out at Renaud, "It's your fault! You provoked this war. You're not a knight! You're just a common brigand!"

"It was the King's decision to set out against the Muslims," Renaud replied wearily, without any of his usual haughtiness.

"And the will of God," added the Grandmaster of the Templars, his voice no longer inspired. He knelt in front of his sword, which he had stuck into the earth as if it were a cross. He placed his hands on the hilt and prayed.

At the first light of dawn several thousand foot

soldiers lined up in ranks. They had already decided during the night to no longer obey their knights, and Guy didn't have the strength to stop them. These soldiers set off in the direction of Hattin in an attempt to make a breakthrough for Lake Galilee. All of them yearned for just one thing. Water.

Without the support of knights on horseback or any field command, the infantrymen were easy prey for the Muslims. They were all butchered without mercy. To the last man. Meanwhile Saladin's cavalry fell upon the core of the army. Although the Christian knights were at the end of their tether, they succeeded in turning back the first assault. Still, they had lost the majority of their foot soldiers and without them they could not maintain an effective battle line. Once their horses began to panic, there was no longer any hope of maintaining an effective battle formation.

"We're all going to die here!" wailed an elderly Knight Hospitaller, whose eyes had become so inflamed from the sun that he could barely see.

"I don't want to die here!" a young soldier cried out in anguish. He had arrived in the Holy Land only a few weeks earlier.

"God will protect us," said the King of Jerusalem, trying to reassure them in a firm and steady voice. He then looked around at his knights, who were waiting in silence for him to make a decision. He knew they wouldn't obey him anyway. In order to give some appearance of royal authority, he muttered, "I absolve you of your vow to my crown. Let every man, God willing, try to break through the siege as best he can! Save yourselves!" It was as if he had announced he was giving up. The battle was lost.

Just off to the side, Raymond was sitting on his horse, surrounded by his men. He glowered at Guy. He was already planning to do as the King of Jerusalem suggested. They had no choice but to attack. He flashed a smile of encouragement at his knights, many of whom he had known since childhood. "We shall be the first of our noble brothers to die. I thank you all for your faithful service!"

He drew his sword and charged in the direction of the hilltop where Saladin's green banners were flying. It was not an attack in accordance with knightly tradition. Only with great effort did his company manage to stay together. Before them gleamed the shields and helmets of the Muslims. A charging knight usually summoned up his courage by shouting out, only this time they lacked all vigor and enthusiasm. They were happy just to stay in the saddle. They would save their last bit of vitality for the heathens.

The enemy, however, was silent in the face of their advance. To the surprise of the Christians, they did not unleash a volley of arrows against them. In fact, the Muslims began to open up their ranks. Raymond reined in his horse and stopped. He searched for Saladin in the distance and found him easily, sitting on a beautiful black horse beneath a canopy. His beard was short, his face swarthy and deeply lined. They knew each other well. They had often fought together, even more often negotiated. Always in good faith.

Saladin grinned and gestured to the opposing force with his hand that they should continue. Whenever he was content, he knew how to be magnanimous. Raymond bowed his head ever so slightly in a sign of thanks and saluted him. He then spurred his horse forward. As soon as his company had passed through the open ranks of the Muslims, the circle closed tightly again behind them. In addition to Raymond's men, the son of Renaud de Châtillon also managed to slip through the encirclement.

The battle immediately started, but didn't last long. Only two other companies were able to break through the lines. One of them was commanded by Balian of Ibelin and the other by Reginald, the Count of Sidon. The Muslims knew that both of them belong to Raymond's moderate faction. They considered them brave and honest knights. They would never slaughter defenseless merchants or villagers, unlike those who were now cowering in the valley around a single tent, over which the banner of the kingdom of Jerusalem limply hung. But no great effort was made to prevent even these combatants from fleeing.

When Saladin's soldiers broke into the camp, they found the King of Jerusalem in his tent with several trusted followers. They were lying on the ground, too exhausted to get up. The Muslims had to haul them away to their own camp.

Waiting in a great tent, made out of black silk, was Saladin. He had scored a spectacular victory and knew that the Battle of Hattin would firmly cement his position in the Muslim world. Having seized power only recently, he had to prove that he was the best among Allah's warriors. There would be no doubt about it after today. He wasn't so foolish, however, to think that this was the end of it. He had an even higher goal. He yearned to conquer Jerusalem back. That's why he conducted himself graciously with Guy of Lusignan. Diplomacy was always better than empty boasting on the heels of victory.

He offered the King of Jerusalem a cup of crystal clear water, wonderfully cool thanks to the containers of ice carried there by his slaves. In Saladin's world, handing a cup to one's guest was a guarantee of safety. In other words, the life of the King of Jerusalem was in safe hands. But he must act accordingly and acknowledge total defeat.

Guy drank eagerly from the cup and handed it to Renaud, who was standing next to him. It did not occur to him to act otherwise. As a Christian, he wanted to share with his neighbor.

Saladin furiously screamed at his interpreter to tell the Christians that he had offered the cup only to the King of Jerusalem. In other words, he was offering no guarantee to the lives of the others.

Renaud de Châtillon may have been a plunderer, but he was no coward. He had lived his whole life in a harsh and uncompromising manner, even when it was at stake. He snarled contemptuously and growled something so impertinent that the interpreter was reluctant to translate it.

But Saladin understood. With wrath and determination in his eyes and lips, he drew his sword in a flash and chopped Renaud's head off. He knew from the expressions of the frightened Christians that this man was the main culprit behind the war, on account of all the atrocities he had committed. He therefore deserved to die. The others deserved it as well because they had allowed this villain to unleash his evil.

The Grandmaster of the Templars knelt next to Renaud's corpse. He picked up his severed head and joined it to the stub of his neck. He closed his eyes and stroked him as if bidding him farewell, but was in fact conducting a discreet body search. Then, terrified, he crossed himself.

Saladin turned his back on him. He had had enough of the Christians. He ordered them to be taken away and given drink. He later conveyed his terms to them.

The Grandmaster slyly edged up to the King of Jerusalem and whispered, "He doesn't have it with him!"

"What?" asked Guy wearily.

"The holiest secret of our order."

"For the love of God! How did he get it?"

"I gave it to him during the night. I thought I was going to die," explained the Grandmaster in horror. "He swore he would give it back to our order after the battle."

"You fool!" snapped Guy. "You should have given the box to me."

"Yes," said the Grandmaster, humbly lowering his head.

"This is a complete disaster," said the King, crossing himself. He wasn't speaking about the defeat at Hattin, rather about something in Renaud de Châtillon's possession that had somehow vanished.

Two months later, on October 2, 1187, the last garrison commander of Jerusalem, Balian of Ibelin, surrendered the city and the tomb of Jesus Christ to Saladin after a short, furious defense.

CHAPTER II

I t wasn't until evening when the procurator Oldrich of Chlum returned with his troops to the administrative court which had been converted, in the King's name, out of nearby Lipa Castle. He was angry, tired and suffering from a gash on his face. He had spent two days on the trail of the brigands who were waylaying merchants on the way to Zitava, but they had again eluded him. He suspected that the leader of this band was Adalbert of Jestrebi, but he had to catch him before he could bring him to justice. Lately he seemed beset only by tragedy. First his wife had died in the spring. Then he angered King Ottokar despite securing the condemnation of the murderer of Dobrej, one of the King's judges. He also fell out with the highest noble in the land, Burgrave Vilem of Landstein, by declining the hand of his daughter Svetlana. And now here at home, in North Bohemia, the lords of Duba and Wartenberg were doing whatever they pleased, as if they were trying to prove these domains were theirs and therefore they didn't have to take any orders from the King's representative.

Ottokar II was now in the second year of his reign, and while he had showed himself to be a forceful and resolute monarch, he was inundated with problems. If only he had to deal with the ones in the Czech kingdom! His father Wenceslaus I had married him to the fifty-year-old heiress to Austria, Margaret Babenberg, who in terms of age was more like Ottokar's grandmother. Together with her hand, he acquired the Austrian lands, and that was enough, at least according to Wenceslaus, to secure a happy marriage. The Czech king had thus become the most powerful ruler north of the Alps. An old adage of his ancestors held that the more family one had, the more problems he had to deal with. And was it ever true. Ottokar had so many problems abroad that he had nothing left for the petty, bickering nobility of North Bohemia.

Maintaining law and order around Lipa fell upon the shoulders of Oldrich of Chlum, and that's why he was in a sour mood now that the highway robbers had eluded him again. He was greatly fond of this hilly and wooded part of the Czech lands. For the first time in his life he actually felt at home somewhere. He had been happy here while his wife was alive. Now he felt consumed by only responsibilities. But there were things of higher value in the life of a knight than mere fleeting happiness. The Lord had given him a sword in order to protect the meek. As the procurator, Oldrich put his entire soul into this task. At the cost of incurring the wrath of the King, the church, and the most powerful nobleman in North Bohemia.

As he passed through the gate, he could see his squire waiting for him in the courtyard. Ota of Zastrizly was a curious fellow. He had recently become a knight and, although an adult, still referred to himself as a squire. And so it stuck. He was also single, despite all the attention he received from more than a few girls. Not to mention a married woman or two, the local chaplain once noted with displeasure. Ota smiled and informed him that if God had destined him for holy matrimony, he would have led the right girl to him. The chaplain indignantly reminded him that it was hard to find the right one when he was too busy sinning with all the rest.

"You don't understand," countered the squire. "How am I to decide which one is the right one, according to you, unless I get to know as many of them as possible first?"

"Of course you should get to know your future wife. But in a devotional way, like when praying in church," retorted the chaplain.

"You think I'm looking for a nun? I prefer to meet women under circumstances which, I hope, will occupy my future wife and me more than prayer."

There was nothing the chaplain could say to that. He sometimes complained about him to Oldrich, who would then upbraid his squire. His reproaches, however, were never more than a little halfhearted. He knew his squire was set in his ways and, besides, he liked and appreciated him. He was the most faithful of servants, always ready to stick his neck out for his master, and as he himself once laughed, the heart will not be dictated to. Ota added in jest that a man being faithful to his master and to his wife were not the same thing because men choose their masters, and not their women, for life.

Ota may have made light of his romances, but he never actually hurt the feelings of any of the girls. He usually chose those who were also looking for a bit of pleasure on a whim. He could certainly offer it. A good-looking lad with his fair hair curled in the German style, he was tall and strong, yet moved about nimbly and gracefully. Despite the care he took in his looks, there was nothing effeminate about him, unlike most of the other youths of his rank. Sneers could be heard around the courtyard that these lads spent more time in ladies' chambers than they did on the tiltyard. Ota claimed to be an honest exception, inasmuch as he could be found in both arenas.

"My lord," Ota urgently called out to Oldrich as he entered the courtyard. "There was a messenger here today from the King."

"What did he want?" asked the procurator, leaping out of the saddle and handing the reins to a groom waiting to lead his horse to the stables.

"He brought a letter. Apparently it's very important but that's all he knows. It has something to do with the exalted aunt of our still more exalted King. The exalted Abbess Agnes."

"Enough with the exalted already," Oldrich reprimanded him. His good mood was slowly starting to return. "Agnes of Bohemia is no longer an abbess in case you didn't know. She gave up the office as a token of humility. Now she prefers to be called an older sister."

"That doesn't change anything. With nuns, there are still only problems. We're expected to undertake a pilgrimage...," said the squire, breaking off in midsentence. Oldrich gave him a knowing look and growled.

"You read the message, didn't you?"

"The messenger said it was important. We're expected to leave soon. You see, the seal on the paper was done very poorly and, well, it came undone. I read the message only to make sure we did not neglect our responsibilities," explained Ota, trying to affect a guilty look.

"So the message is unsealed?"

"Not quite. I lightly heated up the bottom part of the seal and stuck it back. I realized you would not look too kindly on me sticking my nose into your affairs, my lord. But of course, thanks to my precautions, I know where our exalted King is sending us to."

"As if I didn't have enough to worry about here," Oldrich sighed as he headed for the still unfinished court. "So where will it be now? No, let me guess. We just passed the anniversary of St. Wenceslaus. To Stara Boleslav by chance?"

"Much further, my lord."

"To St. Vojtech on the Sazava? No? Somewhere in Moravia?"

But Ota only shook his head.

"Don't tell me the King wants to send us to Austria?"

"No, he's sending us much further. Practically to the end of the world. To Galicia. On a pilgrimage to St. James at Compostela. The older sister has decided to go there."

"What? Are you talking about Agnes of Bohemia?"

"Yes, the former abbess, now just an older sister," observed Ota innocently. "We are going to accompany her there."

"It would be better if you referred to her as abbess. 'Sister' from your mouth sounds like some wench. Still, the pilgrimage to Compostela is the most famous in the Christian world. I've never been there before myself. But it's going to take several months. I'm supposed to have so much time for such an undertaking? I'm the King's representative in North Bohemia," said Oldrich, shaking his head. "Why me? The King has plenty of knights at court who are quite useless. Being an escort would suit them just fine. Why doesn't he send one of them? Who's going to take care of matters here?"

"It says in the message that for the duration of the pilgrimage the Pope plans to declare *Treuga Dei*, the Truce of God, throughout North Bohemia. Should the lords of Duba and Wartenberg try anything against the King, they would be excommunicated by the church. They will think twice about stirring up trouble. And Captain Divis will easily take care of the rest."

"That's complete foolishness!" growled the procurator in disbelief. The Pope declared a truce of God only to protect the property of Christians who had accepted the cross and left for the Holy Land to fight the infidels. Oldrich had once studied at an ecclesiastical school in Magdeburg and was almost positive that the Pope had no such authority merely on account of an ordinary pilgrimage. But he stopped short of criticizing the decision of the Holy Father in Rome. He had once criticized a decision made by the Bishop of Magdeburg and it almost cost him his life. It was also the reason why he never became a prelate and instead entered the service of the Czech king. Although not a member of any important clan, he had gained Ottokar's trust while the latter was still heir to the throne. He eventually rose to important positions thanks to that trust.

For Pope Innocent IV to bestow such unusual protection for Agnes of Bohemia was an indication that something extraordinary was at stake. He was incredulous that it was simply about an ordinary pilgrimage to the tomb of Apostle James. What reason could the Pope have to protect a single pilgrim, even one of royal blood? Oldrich sensed fear and uncertainty, which was usual whenever he was confronted with a difficult task. It was almost as if God had given him the ability to foretell danger that lay ahead.

But his fears weren't simply founded on some irrational feeling of foreboding. Plain logic told him that the whole situation was rather strange. Why would the Pope extend protection to Agnes unless she was in danger? Swarms of pilgrims flocked to Compostela and nothing ever happened to them. For a truly devotional pilgrimage, a small company of knights should suffice. But the King had entrusted his beloved aunt into the hands of Oldrich of Chlum. Apparently he was worried about something. And the Pope too.

Ota was carefully observing his master when it occurred to him why he was hesitating. So he added, almost as an apology, that the message contained nothing more. Just something about the Provost of Vysehrad, Wilibald Odo, also accompanying them.

"The further we go then, the better," sighed Oldrich. He knew the Provost of Vysehrad well and they didn't like each another at all. Wilibald Odo was the sole member of the King's council who opposed him when he was investigating the death of Dobrej, the King's judge. The provost was a conceited blockhead. Oldrich inquired of his squire whether he might have come across any good news in the message.

"But of course," declared Ota. "The message said we have to be in Prague the day after tomorrow, at the latest. So I ordered the cook to bake a blueberry pie."

How Oldrich loved blueberry pie. Naturally, no one knew how to make it as delicious as his late wife did. No matter how hard he tried not to, he dwelt on her practically all the time at home. He knew it wasn't good. Everything in life needed some limit, even memories. A long trip might finally help clear his head a little. It was actually something to look forward to. He loved new adventures. He had never been so far away from home in his life. A smile flashed across his face. Of course, he had no idea of the test of his Christian faith that awaited him.

* * *

Had Oldrich of Chlum assumed they knew more about the pilgrimage in Prague, he would've been greatly mistaken. The King wasn't even there. Last year, immediately after Ottokar II ascended the throne, Bela IV, the King of Hungary, attacked Olomouc with his Cuman tribes. He was joined by Otto, the Duke of Bavaria, and, as usual, the Poles. Olomouc was able to fight off the attack and the conflict was quelled through the intervention of Pope Innocent IV, but peace had not come to the eastern frontier of the country. And so Ottokar was again leading his army into Moravia.

Agnes of Bohemia received Oldrich, but obliged him with only a few polite words after mass in the Church of St. Francis. The only thing he was able to learn was that the leader of the expedition would be

Jacob de Vries, a Knight Commendatore of the Templars. The commandery for the Czech province was located in the Church of St. Lawrence in the Old Town section of Prague. It was only a few steps from the Church of St. Francis, so he stopped there. But he missed the commendatore.

He soon returned in a lousy mood and went to the inn At the Golden Wheel, where he was staying with his squire. Ota still wasn't there. Oldrich sat at a table in a corner by the window. This was his favorite spot. He could see the courtyard outside while sitting next to the fireplace. It was October and uncomfortably cold as dusk was setting in. He ordered a mug of warm mead and sulked about what he could expect over the next few days. Hearing the sound of hooves, he turned his attention to the window and saw a rider entering the courtyard through the open gate. He immediately recognized him. On the horse sat Burgrave Vilem of Landstein. He ruled over the country in the King's absence from Prague Castle.

Up until that one particular case of betrayal, Vilem had always been protective of Oldrich. The procurator could no longer be sure if the burgrave was as favorably inclined toward him as before. He had declined Svetlana's hand and, moreover, the position of king's judge, which he had done in order to save the life of an insignificant knight. The fact that Vilem was now there in person was quite extraordinary, as if the King himself had stopped by this inn in Old Town. Perhaps it meant that everything was forgotten and he still considered Oldrich a favorite. It could also mean that Vilem forgot nothing and wanted him to experience the full weight of his authority. This powerful official had plenty of reasons in either case.

"Damn Abbess Agnes!" Oldrich swore under his breath. He stroked the short beard on his chin, which he was in the habit of doing in similar situations. He was relieved to notice that Vilem was accompanied by only two soldiers and they remained in the courtyard. Their meeting would be private. This probably meant he wasn't going to be arrested. Finally something! He drank from his mug and waited wearily.

The doors of the tavern flew open and in walked a tall, older man with an imperious air, wearing a frock made of blue velvet. A dark cape interwoven with gold, five-leaf roses, the symbol of his family's coat of arms, was flung around his shoulders. Wrapped around his waist was a magnificent silver belt adorned with violent amethysts. He did not bother to close the door behind him. He simply took off his helmet and headed directly to the corner where Oldrich sat at the table. He knew exactly where to find him.

The fat innkeeper obligingly closed the door and followed him to the table. He politely offered him a chair and asked, in a silky voice, which wine to bring him. He had only the best, including two flagons from Thessaly brought to him by way of Venice. "Alexander the Great himself drank this wine," explained the innkeeper, his ingratiating tone belying all the money he was hoping to make on Alexander's account.

"What are you drinking, Oldrich?" Vilem asked, friendly enough. "Mead? Bring me a mug of it as well."

"Only mead?" Creases appeared in the innkeeper's fat face, but the burgrave paid him no notice. Oldrich sat up in his chair. He knew Vilem wasn't one to bestow favors without getting something in return. Now here he was smiling at him graciously. What could he want?

"I see you're still loyal to this tavern. This is where you hid Christian that time, right?" the burgrave continued most amiably.

"That's in the past," Oldrich replied politely but firmly. Christian was the innocent knight he saved from being executed.

"Of course," Vilem concurred. He took the mug of mead brought to him by the innkeeper and toasted Oldrich. "What's past is past. But you know what's really interesting? The King wasn't angry at you at all for helping a condemned man to escape. I would even say he respects you all the more because of it. And then there's the matter of my daughter."

Oldrich knew that it would be at least polite of him to inquire how Svetlana was. But he didn't. Vilem waited in silence. There was a bit of a twinkle in his eyes, as if he knew exactly what the procurator was thinking. The burgrave was a very shrewd man. He had studied at the renowned college in Basel. He was not like most of the other nobles. Although a knight, he prized learning. It was another reason why he wanted to see Oldrich, now a widower, at the side of his daughter. Basically he liked him, in his own calculating way.

Oldrich preferred to change the subject. With a wrinkle of concern in his forehead, he lamented, "I'm troubled by the assignment the King has given me."

"No reason to be," said the burgrave, shaking his head resolutely and drinking from his mug. It was evident in his lips that he was enjoying the mead. "None of the responsibility will be yours. You don't even have to be a part of the escort for Abbess Agnes."

"Then why in heaven's name do I have to go to Compostela?" Oldrich asked sullenly. He was starting to suspect that the undertaking was going to be even more difficult than he originally supposed.

"Perhaps because you have sinned. The King wants to give you the chance to redeem yourself for being stubborn by making this pilgrimage," Vilem laughed. Oldrich took it as a provocation, so Vilem clasped his hands together and humbly added that it was something quite different and would, moreover, be enormously beneficial for his soul.

"I have been to Compostela," the burgrave went on good-naturedly. "An unforgettable experience for any Christian! I still often think of that journey."

Oldrich never once heard the burgrave mention it.

"You know my daughter," he continued. "She's a lot like you. Also very stubborn. When she gets something into her head, there's no use trying to dissuade her. She's like a mule. I guess I must've talked too excitedly about the pilgrimage to Apostle James, I don't know, but the result is Svetlana now wants to go to Compostela too. She's already talked three girls from the best Czech families into joining her. Some of them may even want to enter Agnes's Order of Damianites later on. That's why she's letting them go with her. Of course, she told them they would have to provide for their own escort. The journey there is long and who knows what can happen along the way. But the King has given her his support."

Vilem of Landstein paused and raised his eyebrows slightly. Let's see, what else? Oldrich of Chlum clearly understood. It had been a long time since he felt such fury inside.

At that moment the doors to the tavern opened up and Ota the Squire sauntered in. He walked up to the table, politely bowed and excitedly began to tell Oldrich that he had some wonderful news. Among the pilgrims accompanying Agnes to Compostela would be a group of maidens from the nobility. The journey was therefore not going to be as boring as he originally feared.

CHAPTER III

It soon became clear that the departure from Prague was nowhere near as urgent as the message had suggested when it was first received in North Bohemia. They were supposed to set off in four days' time. Oldrich of Chlum decided to use the lull to learn as much as possible about the journey ahead of them. At dawn he headed for the Vysehrad Chapterhouse. The writings contained in the scriptorium there were mostly by church scholars on the Christian faith, but it owned several scientific works as well. And while the St. Vitus Chapterhouse had more books, Oldrich knew the Vysehrad librarian, Emmeram of Greifsfeld, and admired his rather prim erudition. If there was anybody who could help him in this matter, it was him.

"You're the third person who has shown interest lately in the pilgrimage to St. James," the shaven-headed librarian, wearing a monastic frock, genially nodded. A sleepless night and toothache had left dark circles under his eyes. Whenever something bothered him, he looked even more gaunt and withered than he actually was.

"That's probably because Abbess Agatha is making this journey to Compostela," said Oldrich. The bony librarian frowned and admonished him, with all due severity, that the highborn Agnes was not an abbess, only an older sister in the service of Jesus Christ. He opened a chest and took out four codices bound in white pigskin.

"I have everything ready. Would you believe it, Sir Procurator, that our own provost wandered in here by mistake?" He didn't even try to hide the sarcasm in his voice. The Vysehrad provost, Wilibald Odo, was a Norman by birth. He had lived in the Czech kingdom since his youth, but had never properly mastered the language. He was tall and muscular, had beautiful flaxen hair, light eyes and a bellicose temperament, just like his Viking forebears. The librarian hated the provost because Wilibald Odo knew only a few basic Christian tenets and was convinced they were quite enough. By some mysterious twist of fate, he had become the confessor of Agnes of Bohemia. He disdained learning and preferred the sword as the testament of his faith. He also despised Emmeram and let him know it.

"At least Wilibald Odo now knows where to find the library in his chapter," chuckled Oldrich. He knew exactly how to get to the skinny monk.

"Yes. Miracles are possible even today," Emmeram scornfully observed. "But only that he was able to find the library, because our most distinguished provost got no further than the door. Rather he stood there and ordered me to write down only the essential information on parchment. He didn't open a single book! He said he didn't have time to read all the nonsense that somebody else wrote way back when. If only you could have seen how he looked at me! He knows that I'm writing a treatise about the life and work of St. James. He knows how to belittle people, but you've probably already observed it yourself. He might be a servant of Christ and therefore our brother, but he enjoys humiliating people just the same."

"Tell me, brother librarian, what did you note of importance on the parchment?" Oldrich asked with undisguised interest.

"You can have a look for yourself. He still hasn't sent for it," replied the bilious skeleton, fishing a scroll out of the chest. He unrolled it and handed it to his guest, who read: "James the Greater or Older (there was another disciple of Jesus named James, referred to as the Lesser). He was the younger brother of John, the evangelist and another apostle. He was present for the Transfiguration of Jesus Christ after his resurrection. He was one of the leading apostles. He preached the Gospel in Hispania, was the first of the twelve to die a martyr's death in Jerusalem, after which his disciples put his remains in a boat and set it adrift. Led by the hand of God, the craft made it all the way to Hispania, where local fishermen found it and buried the remains where Santiago de Compostela stands today. Be careful, brother Provost – the place is called Compostela, not Santiago (Santiago is Hispanic for James)."

Oldrich rolled up the scroll and handed it back to the librarian. He observed, somewhat amusingly, "Unusually accurate, but then every monastic novice knows this story."

"The provost ordered me to write only the main facts," Emmeram grimaced. "That I did, as you can see, because I'm not sure whether that Viking pirate even knows as much as your typical novice. I will consider it a miracle if he reads my scroll all the way to the end. Besides, why should I even have bothered? He ordered me to go with him. If he needs something, he will ask."

"You are going to Compostela with us? That's good news," smiled the procurator, but the quarrelsome librarian cut him off to say it wasn't good news at all. He had a lot of work to do, plus a toothache, and on top of all that he hated riding on horseback. He suddenly checked himself, as if he started wondering whether the procurator was here just so he could hear such complaints. He crossed himself to ward away the thoughts that stood in contradiction to his monastic humility, and asked Oldrich how he could be of service.

"I would like to find out as much as possible about the pilgrimage to Compostela. But just so we both understand, I'm only interested in the journey itself. With all due modesty, I can say I already know quite enough about James."

"And whatever you don't know, I will be happy to explain later. There will certainly be plenty of time for disputation along the way," Emmeram gladly offered. "Otherwise, I must apologize that our codices have little to say about the way there. Just some Benedictine monk inscribed a few remarks about his pilgrimage on the lifted pastedown of the Gospel of John. Naturally, he wrote them in Occitan. Even though it is the closest language we have in the Christian world to Latin, you probably wouldn't understand everything. I would have to translate the text for you. But even that wouldn't help you very much. The monk wrote down only tripe. Where to find a good inn or river to ford or how to get around the mountains. But what prayers to say on arrival, not a single word. Fortunately, I know them. The venerable Isidore of Seville wrote many illustrative treatises on the spiritual importance of the pilgrimage. Unfortunately, we don't have them here in our library, but I know them practically by heart. And then..."

"I would nevertheless be grateful to you, brother, if you would translate the text of the lifted pastedown of the Gospel."

Emmeram nodded with a sigh and opened a thick codex. The book side of the back cover contained a description in small letters of the journey from Constance to Besançon, and from there by boat on the Doubs and Rhône Rivers to the sea. Then it was walking across the province of Languedoc to Toulouse, then on the Garonne River to Bordeaux and finally by boat along the ocean shoreline to the harbor below Compostela. According to the Benedictine monk, this particular way was longer than on foot but much quicker. It only took him a little more than a month to reach it, because it was all downstream and the progress was therefore rapid. Oldrich thanked the librarian and asked to borrow the codex from him. He studied the text on the pastedown.

He knew the way from Prague to Constance. The monastery in Melk in lower Austria wasn't far away. From there it was possible to go on the Danube to Sigmaringen, then only one or two days in the saddle to Lake Constance. That was, of course, if you were traveling in spring or summer. Here it was already October and he could feel a chill on his neck. He couldn't understand why Agnes had to make her pilgrimage during the worst months for traveling. But whether she was being guided by reason or not, he had no doubt they would take the more comfortable way.

Agnes of Bohemia had to be at least fifty but looked young for her age. She was thin and ever restless, having long subscribed to the maxim of St. Gregory that the devil finds work for idle hands. Although an adherent to the asceticism of St. Francis of Assisi, she would have found it difficult to choose the less comfortable route to St. James. Being longer, they would reach the tomb later, and Oldrich suspected that Agnes was in a hurry to leave so she could celebrate Christmas in Compostela.

The librarian slipped his arms into the sleeves of

his monastic habit and quietly observed him. He tended to judge the souls of Christians by the way they treated books. Oldrich turned the pages with an attentive and dignified solemnity. Quite nearly the same as Emmeram of Greifsfeld.

Oldrich gently closed the codex and secured it with metal clips to prevent it from accidentally opening. At that moment the door hinges creaked to announce the presence of the Vysehrad provost in the library. Surprised to see Oldrich there, he growled, "What are you doing here? If you are indeed the learned man they say you are, Sir Procurator, you have no need to be snooping around in libraries. You would already know everything beforehand."

"My learning is certainly no match for yours, venerable provost," Oldrich calmly declared. "You have no need to read any books."

"I have prepared these notes for you here," said Emmeram, handing the provost a parchment scroll. The prior snatched the roll from him, quickly opened it and bemoaned the fact that it was so long. With a parting glance around the musty library, he blessed them and left.

"Did you hear that? And this man is the provost of the Vysehrad Chapter! When King Vratislav founded it, it was supposed to be a seat of ecclesiastical scholarship," sighed the pitifully thin librarian. "Now he fills this place with monks whose only advantage is they come from noble families. Otherwise they are lazy and stupid. And do you think, good sir, that the situation is different elsewhere? The church is deteriorating, and it's all the fault of those begging orders. All this living in poverty and filth and ignorance and declaring that it's the only true path to salvation. But where will it really lead in the end?"

"It doesn't look like Wilibald Odo is suffering from poverty," the procurator observed ironically.

"That's for sure. He prefers a lack of education for his deprivation. Well, what can you expect from the offspring of pirates? The Normans once burned our farm on the Rhine and nearly murdered my entire family."

Oldrich politely bowed his head and clasped his hands in a sign of prayer for the salvation of the souls of the librarian's deceased family members. He quickly counted up the events of which he was speaking and figured they had to have occurred at least two hundred years earlier. How he must really hate the provost!

* * *

Meanwhile Ota, who had not received any special task from his master to fulfill, decided to try and find out something about their expedition. He was particularly interested in learning which young maidens would be accompanying them. He thought about paying a visit to Svetlana at the burgrave's palace within the confines of Prague Castle. Ota had once saved her life, even though she was convinced that his master deserved most of the credit. And while she smiled sweetly at him whenever they crossed paths, he didn't think it was very tactful to be asking her such questions at this moment. She might chide him for taking too much interest in women before setting off on a holy pilgrimage. Svetlana could be very spiteful when she wanted to and Ota could never imagine her becoming somebody's meek and submissive wife, much less a nun.

As he strolled along the broad road leading to the Old Town market, he pondered how he might find out more about that little matter of interest. In the end he decided that the most reliable sources, as always, were those in the know, in this case the army of nursemaids and cooks that attended the nobility. And so by noon, he had discovered the names of the three girls who would make up Svetlana's retinue of highborn maidens.

He did not personally know Jana of Blatna, nor could he remember ever catching a glimpse of her or even hearing of her at court. His recollection of Katherine of Gutstein was also rather vague, for he had not seen her in a long time. He knew, however, that a friend of his, Michal Kekule of Stradonice, was aiming to win her hand. Frankly, he could not imagine it ever happening. When it came to the fair sex, Michal was without doubt the clumsiest and most bashful of knights. Finally there was the third name, and it gave him cause to worry.

Zdena Berkova of Sloup belonged to a branch of the aristocratic clan from Duba. In spring, after one excellent feast in Lipa, he became rather more intimate with her than church doctrine would allow for chaste behavior. They had not seen each other since that time, but Ota wasn't sure how he should act when he met her again. He wasn't exactly her first lover and they exchanged no promises when they parted ways in the morning. But it had to have meant something. That was the difference between girls of noble birth and ordinary ones: that which went unsaid might just as well have been said, and then try to argue with them in a reasonable manner!

The easiest solution would be if a knight from North Bohemia wooed the hand of Zdena Berkova. It would take her mind off him and everything would go back to normal. But in all likelihood he would learn that Zdena had no suitor, which he could not understand because she was both pretty and rich. He was starting to worry about the complications he was going to face on the journey. And he didn't even want to think about what would happen if Agnes insinuated herself between them. Her other passion besides piety was arranging marriages for the daughters of aristocratic families.

"So what?" he told himself. "I've been through worse things. What's the point of organizing a defense when there's no enemy at the gates?" He knew just what to do. The stupidest thing would be to avoid Zdena. At the first opportunity he would try to speak to her in seclusion. He considered it more honorable to tell her right off that what had transpired between them was over. Or better put, it had never begun. Better to have it out in the open at the start than to endure nasty reproaches or expressions of love and tears. His friends often envied him his success with girls, but if only they knew how much work went into dumping them honorably.

He was aroused from his thoughts by a shrill voice speaking in German. "Are you Ota the knight, from Zastrizly?" It was a man of small build and sharp features. His unmistakable foreign accent indicated he wasn't German. Ota had been so preoccupied that he didn't notice him following him all this time. He was swarthy, wore the chain mail of a warrior, and had a black cape draped over his shoulders. He didn't have a sword with him, but a dagger, with a beautifully polished handle adorned with brown topaz, hung from his belt.

"At your service," Ota bowed politely but warily.

"A grown man but still a squire. Isn't that rather odd?" the stranger jested. "I might know how to change that."

"What if I don't want to?"

"Only saints want to live in poverty. And you're no saint from what I've learned. If we were to go around the taverns of Old Town, the wenches in at least half of them would recognize you. Not bad, I would say!"

"Surely you exaggerate," laughed Ota. He was curious to find out what all this was about and so adopted the same friendly tone. "I would wager that only a third of the wenches at most would remember me. The rest is just gossip."

"Such tastes still don't come cheaply. Perhaps you might need this?" smiled the rough-hewn stranger as he reached under his dark cape and pulled out a pouch stuffed with coins. He pressed it into one of Ota's hands. If it was really full of denarii, there would have to be at least ten times threescore silver coins in it. More money than he earned in an entire year.

"You're wasting your time," Ota sneered. "I don't need to buy any wenches, especially with somebody else's money."

"Money is always useful! A long journey awaits you. When you get to French lands, you will be amazed what the tailors there can make. And from what material! You won't know what to look at first in the markets. Moorish weapons, Byzantine perfumes, Venetian lace. Treat yourself to a little luxury. Life is too short, noble knight from Zastrizly," the man said in all earnestness and bowed. Stepping back, he added, "No need to thank me. Perhaps we shall meet again." He left the purse in Ota's palm, then turned and quickly headed in the direction of Judith's Bridge.

"Hey, wait a minute," Ota shouted and ran after him. He grabbed him by the hem of his cloak and attempted to give him the money back, but the stranger folded his arms across his chest. Sternly looking at Ota, he scolded him. "Kindly remove your hand. It wouldn't do for us to grapple on the street like two people in the market. But should you be so foolish as to call for help from, say, that cross-eyed bailiff who's been watching us from around the corner, I shall deny that the money was ever mine. Have a safe journey to Compostela!" With that, he pulled himself free from Ota's grasp and briskly continued on to the river.

CHAPTER IV

The commendatore of the Templar order in the Czech province, Jacob de Vries, came from Flanders. He was a strong man, middle-aged with chiseled features to his face. He had blue eyes, a wide, slightly flat nose, and tight, narrow lips, all lined by a well-groomed red beard. The lush locks of his hair were the same color and hung down to his shoulders. He was dressed in the attire of his order, a gray cloak with a red cross embroidered across the chest. He knelt humbly before Agnes of Bohemia, but with a fury in his face to match his pretense to humility.

"Forgive me, older sister Agnes, but I simply cannot agree. I am the leader of the expedition. I am responsible for the safety of the pilgrims and therefore cannot countenance the presence of this man with us. Oldrich of Chlum does not have a good reputation. He does not venerate the sacraments, he interprets church dogma however he sees fit, and he recently posited himself against the King himself. I would say nothing if he joined us as a penitent dressed in plain robes, but he is to make the pilgrimage as a knight. Why?"

"Enough!" said Agnes, wearily stretching out a white, manicured hand. She had a magnificent gold ring on despite the coarse garments she wore as her sign of humility. She may have been the representative of the Damian order of impoverished sisters, but she was also the daughter of a Czech king.

"Your objections are groundless, Commendatore. King Ottokar himself chose Oldrich of Chlum to accompany us. Unlike you, he thinks his administrator for North Bohemia is a faithful servant. And I have doubts about this insinuation that he is not a good Christian. I dare claim there would be less wickedness in the church today if all prelates were as honest as he is."

"So why doesn't he lead the expedition then?" de Vries fumed. "It would seem he is a paragon of Christian virtues even though his battles for Jesus Christ have gone no further than wielding a goose quill. Meanwhile, I have been shedding blood in the Holy Land for ten years fighting the infidels."

"No one is disparaging your services. And what matters is God is well aware of them. He will reward you for them when the time comes. But you would do well to remember that pride is a sin. Did you raise your sword against the Muslims to liberate the tomb of Christ or only to promote yourself over other believers? Worse is the one who cannot control his sword. It was the King who ordered Oldrich of Chlum to join us. He will look after a company of four virtuous maidens. If you are indeed so well informed about the lack of virtues of the gentleman from Chlum, then you certainly know he has recently enjoyed the attentions of the daughter of the burgrave in Prague. He was therefore chosen to accompany the noble Svetlana. Enough about it already!"

"Fine. I am a humble servant of the church and will obey," he said, with apparent effort. He looked at the floor. "But there is one more matter, older sister. Much more serious!"

"Well?"

"Are we really going to Compostela to pay homage to Apostle James? I have received a letter from our distinguished Grandmaster in Acre. In the name of the order of the Templars, he has entrusted me to ask you whether our journey is not somehow connected to the death of Count Renaud de Châtillon."

Not a muscle in the face of Agnes of Bohemia twitched. Only her eyes flashed angrily. Still, she answered him in a calm voice. "My dear Commendatore, a moment ago you expressed your doubts about the true faith of Oldrich of Chlum. But you can be assured he would never doubt my pious intentions. His faith is strong. Why does your Grandmaster suspect my intentions? What reason does he have? If my soul were suddenly consumed by anger, I might say something foolish like I was not in Jerusalem when it was conquered by the infidels. But your Grandmaster and his order were. You can go now!"

Jacob de Vries rose, shaking with fury.

* * *

Although the pilgrims were not supposed to begin their long journey until the Monday after the feast of St. Havel, Oldrich left Prague with his squire Ota on Saturday. The reason was simple: some members of the expedition, it seemed, had already left Prague Castle. Svetlana, the daughter of the burgrave, had sent word to Agnes that she and the other maidens were going to wait in Landstein, the seat of her father's dominions, since the pilgrims would have to pass close to the castle there anyway. Several knights had left with them. Oldrich, moreover, now understood that with the exception of the King, no one supported his presence among the pilgrims. It therefore didn't matter whether he departed alone or with the others.

"And when I discovered that the Bishop of Prague was planning to celebrate mass on Monday for the benefit of the pilgrims," he informed his squire, "I decided it was better to leave immediately."

"I would do the same," agreed Ota. They were in the saddle galloping along on the road to Benesov, which was broad in width to accommodate the trade traffic. It was a beautiful autumn day. The sun felt warm and the road was lined with a wall of brown and yellow-colored woods. "What's the point of waiting in Prague anyway? Keeping company with virtuous maidens is far more agreeable than with virtuous prelates. It's better for us to start off in Landstein."

"You're wrong on several accounts," Oldrich chuckled. His mood much improved once they passed through the gate and left the dark fortifications of Old Town Prague behind them. He loved the open countryside. "First, none of the prelates on the expedition is virtuous. Second, none of the maidens you associate with is virtuous. So it's all the same who we keep company with. And third, we're not going to Landstein."

"I suppose now you're going to tell me we're not even going to Compostela," sighed Ota. "It's no easy task to serve you, my lord."

"If you're referring to that stranger's offer, I won't stand in the way of you and fortune," the procurator taunted him. Ota had, of course, informed him about the suspicious encounter he had had on the street. When he tried to hand over the purse filled with silver coins to his master, however, Oldrich refused to take it. He couldn't help thinking out loud at the same time that the man who gives is a fool, but the one who doesn't take is a bigger one. Ota got the money without having to promise anything for it. So he can keep it. For now anyway. Who knows what good it might bring them on the way.

"Are you dismissing me from your service?" Ota immediately protested. Of course, he knew his master was joking, but he still felt a twinge of resentment.

"I do hope you're not expecting me to list all the reasons why I can't do without your services," said Oldrich in a conciliatory tone. He reined in his horse. The road began to wind and climb a steep hill.

"You can if you want to. It's nice to hear such things sometimes. Besides, there's nothing else to do. By the way, where are we going if not to Landstein?"

"We are going to Landstein. But we're taking the long way, so there will be plenty of time for me to list all your good qualities. And your bad ones while I'm at it. Of course, I will need more time for them, so let's start there first. Zdena Berkova of Sloup to be exact."

"How do you know about her?" Ota sheepishly asked.

"My dear Ota, am I not the procurator? The best in the Czech kingdom according to our most gracious sovereign. It's therefore only logical that I know about you two."

"I guess so, my lord," Ota replied with a radiant glow in his eyes. He was clearly enjoying himself. "You are indeed an excellent procurator, while I am only a humble lover. The best in the land according to several girls. It's therefore only logical that they court my affections." He was cut short by a blow from Oldrich, which he managed to dodge at the last moment. Ota spurred his horse on and since they were at the end of the climb, he dashed off ahead at a rapid gallop.

* * *

They spent the night at a wayside inn in Olbramovice and reached Milevsko the following day after lunch. Although it was a Sunday, the superior of the Premonstratensian priory eagerly welcomed him. Abbott Quido was a young man with a goodhearted expression. Oldrich had once proved very helpful to him when he was just an ordinary monk, but he never had the opportunity to repay him. He was all smiles as he made Oldrich comfortable in his magnificent hall and offered him some excellent Burgundy wine, which he had brought from the mother convent in Premontre.

"I'll begin by telling you why I've come here," said Oldrich after they clinked glasses. "I am accompanying Agnes of Bohemia to Compostela."

"Yes, I heard she was planning to make a pilgrimage there," nodded Quido. "To be honest, I was a bit aggrieved by the news. When I was in Prague this summer, she promised to spend the Christmas holidays in our monastery. We're trying to find money to repair the Cathedral of the Virgin Mary and she would certainly know how to persuade the King on our behalf. Of course, there is nothing we can do now except wait for our venerable abbess to visit us another time."

"There wouldn't happen to be a monk in the priory who speaks not just French, but also Occitan? Perhaps even Hispanic?"

"I have two here who come from southern France. They must certainly know Occitan. But whether

Hispanic...I'll find out. Would you like to take one of them with you on your journey?"

"Yes, but not just for interpreting purposes. He should also be a virtuous and trustworthy man. Well, he needn't so much be a man. Important is that he's virtuous."

"All my brothers are virtuous," the abbot replied with a friendly wink. "Should his virtue take on any particular form?"

"Of course. I don't care if he's self-indulgent, proud, penurious or stupid. To a certain degree. But he must abide by the sixth commandment and not entertain any sinful ruminations or intentions in the company of women. I would like him to serve as confessor for the four maidens who will be in our party."

"I can see you do not want to entrust this task to your squire. One of the brothers I mentioned a moment ago is well-suited to serve in this capacity. I cannot guarantee he won't entertain any sinful thoughts, but I can vouch for his lack of sinful intentions. He is simply not capable of any. He suffered an accident once and since that time he's been missing that which is necessary for such intentions. He is a very good man. The name he took after arriving here in the monastery is Hyacinth. But please, don't ask him anything about his past. From what I know, his parents were burned as heretics during the Inquisition in Languedoc because they were Waldensians. He knows excellent Occitan because it's his native tongue. But in spite of all he went through as a child, he's a fervent believer. He has been living in our monastery for several years. I'll call him for you."

Oldrich was satisfied with brother Hyacinth. He was a tall, handsome man of about forty who spoke, notwithstanding the physical impairment touched upon by the abbot, in a beautifully deep voice. His eyes, however, betrayed a kind of girlish delicacy and, as could be expected, a fragile soul. Despite his manly appearance, loud noises frightened him. He was also clever and obliging, so there probably would be no problems with him on the journey. After he was told what was expected of him, he humbly bowed his head and quietly added that he served God wherever it benefited the order, the trials and tribulations of which he had accepted. And to do everything to make brother abbot satisfied with him.

For a moment Oldrich hesitated to accept the abbot's invitation to stay overnight in Milevsko, but finally agreed. "It would not do to travel on the day of our Lord," Quido earnestly argued. "Brother Hyacinth must say farewell to the other brothers, go to confession. Also, the steward must prepare a bit of food for him for the trip, some money, a change of clothes, a bowl and so forth. Do you think it will be easy for me, a servant of God, to make our steward break the Ten Commandments and work on Sunday? And what's more, it's been a long time since I last saw you. Do you think I will just let you go and calmly wait several more years for you to appear again? Nothing doing! I will prepare a feast and we shall spend the evening together."

"Even if today is the day of our Lord?" Oldrich jested.

"Listening to your pious Christian wisdom would be nearly the same glorification of this day as reading sacred books," said the abbot with a smile. He then quickly crossed himself and added that God would certainly forgive him these words because they were spoken with honest intentions. He suggested that Oldrich rest up for a while and they would meet again in the evening. He called for his prior and ordered him to prepare accommodations for him and his squire in the almshouse for guests.

* * *

They didn't leave the priory in Milevsko as planned the next day. Abbot Quido led Oldrich to the library and proudly showed him four large shelves filled with thick leather-bound codices. Oldrich originally thought he would take just a quick look inside the scriptorium out of courtesy, but then he opened the treatise of Isidore of Seville and began reading it. The librarian was eager to please and soon brought him another codex containing a commentary on the Gospel of St. John. It also included a major historical essay by Jarloch, another abbot at Milevsko, on the events that took place in the Czech lands a century earlier. Oldrich eagerly turned the large parchment sheets, embellished with neat script, and all of a sudden it was already afternoon.

"We'll leave tomorrow," Oldrich told his squire, a bit apologetically. "I completely forgot about the time."

"You see, my lord, it can even happen to you. Sometimes when I'm forgetful and arrive late, you scold me as if I were a child."

"My dear Ota, I forgot about the time because of books. You, on the other hand, are inevitably late on account of skirt chasing. There's a difference, don't you think?"

"Perhaps. But the question here is which delay is the more agreeable. I hope you're not planning to stay here tomorrow as well because of a few books? I thought I would die of boredom today. I spent half of it with this Friar Hyacinth. Absolutely the most boring holy man I have ever met in my life. The fact is I don't really care for virtuous maidens, particularly when they're in a group, but Hyacinth...he really has no interest. Poor Svetlana. Good thing she'll have you by her side!"

"One more word and I'll have Hyacinth accompany you on this journey! I will be nice to him and he will be my basilisk. But let's be clear! Svetlana is no joking matter here. Of course, it's my fault. I should have given you something to do. Whenever you're idle, you think of only foolishness. Next time I'll be sure to keep you busy!"

Oldrich scrutinized his squire while he admonished

him. He had told him nothing about the physical deficiency of Hyacinth. He didn't consider it important. In his mind, a Premonstratensian friar was no more boring than most other monks, but Ota's sixth sense apparently suspected that something wasn't quite right with this particular monk.

"Surely there was nothing I just said to warrant such a threat," Ota breezily defended himself. "I wasn't loafing around. I was thinking about our journey. And you know what is truly odd? Everyone seems to prefer we didn't make the journey. All with the exception of our noble King. Perhaps his aunt Agnes won't be happy to see us either, even if it will be our task to protect her. She was quite curt with you back there. What was that all about?"

"She rarely is cordial. But there's something worse here. I have the feeling that this expedition isn't entirely religious in nature; rather it's being made for reasons which, unfortunately, I'm not familiar with. Three months ago she promised to spend the Christmas holidays here in Milevsko. And now all of a sudden she has changed her mind and decided to go on this pilgrimage to Compostela. No one makes a decision like that on a whim. If somebody wants to make a pilgrimage for its own sake, why the rush and leave at the beginning of winter? Any rational pilgrim would wait until spring. The anniversary of Apostle James is celebrated in summer. It's the time when all pilgrims gather in Compostela. I learned about it in an essay written by Isidore of Seville, which they have here in the library. So you can see that the time spent here wasn't a total waste."

"It's a pity the codex didn't answer the question why anyone would make a pilgrimage to Compostela for reasons other than religious. It would certainly facilitate further inquiry into the matter, my lord," said Ota, rather smugly. Even though he was trying to be funny, he felt a little uneasy. A feeling he was not too familiar with.

"Who said anything here about an inquiry? No crime has been committed. Not yet anyway. Also, I always thought you prefer to look for answers anywhere other than in books. Perhaps that group of virtuous maidens knows something. There's an opportunity for you! Zdena Berkova of Sloup is a very sharp young woman."

"Now who's the basilisk here," mumbled Ota, but Oldrich heard him. He laughed and added, "You will soon get your opportunity. I already arranged everything with Abbot Quido. We leave tomorrow morning right after mass."

CHAPTER V

The weather changed overnight. The sky was overcast, a steady wind was blowing and light rain falling. Trees that only the day before had been covered in autumn colors were now practically stripped of their leaves, which were tossed hither and thither by the wind. Friar Hyacinth was riding a small brown horse and pulling a much larger one behind him burdened with supplies bundled to its back. They were heading across the rolling landscape towards the Vltava River, where they planned to take the Gmünden trade route to Landstein. Since the beautiful weather had held out until yesterday, the way was still relatively dry and they were able to make good progress. They reached Sobeslav before nightfall, where they forded the river, and reached their destination the following evening.

Oldrich of Chlum had never been to Landstein, but heard that it was the most heavily fortified castle on the Austrian border. As they left the forest and stood on the plain before the castle, he could see why it had such an impressive reputation among knights. High above their heads on a rocky promontory rose two massive rectangular towers joined by a majestic palace. To reach the first gate, they had to pass through a large embankment before taking a wooden bridge across a moat carved into the rock. Beyond that gate a narrow path wound beneath the ramparts along the edge of a rocky cliff, leading up to the second gate. The watch waved them through the stone arch and at last they were in the courtyard.

As a groom rudely relieved them of their horses, a man suddenly appeared, out of breath, with a sword dangling from his belt. He wore a tunic with the crest of a rose on the chest, a sign that he was a servant at Landstein. He bowed and asked Oldrich to follow him. His masters had already grown impatient. He brusquely told Ota to take the baggage to a bedchamber in the main tower and shouted to a buxom maidservant to show him the way. He then ordered her to lead the squire and friar to their sleeping quarters among the servants.

Ota turned to Oldrich with dismay, but all he could do was shrug his shoulders and quietly reassure him. "We're only guests here. We can't be giving the orders just yet. But don't worry. I'll arrange things. You won't have to sleep with the servants."

Accompanied by the caretaker of Landstein, Oldrich walked across a stone ramp and through a low arched portal that led to the palace. They passed through a dark entrance hall and climbed a set of wooden stairs to the first floor, which consisted entirely of the Great Hall. At the far end of the room was a huge fireplace and at that particular moment there were several men and women sitting in chairs next to it. As soon as the caretaker formally announced the presence of Oldrich of Chlum, the company around the fireplace grew quiet and curiously turned their attention to him.

Oldrich immediately noticed Svetlana. She was wearing a blue dress embroidered with silver, and her blond hair was cropped short in a boyish fashion. She was slim and very attractive. Sitting next to her was her brother Jost of Landstein, whom he already knew. He recognized the face of the other knight there, but couldn't recall his name. He could easily guess that the three girls with them were members of the retinue of noble maidens preparing to accompany Agnes of Bohemia on her pilgrimage. The elderly, slightly scruffy-looking prelate was certainly the castle chaplain. But the last member of the party he couldn't place. He was a tall, swarthy man in a plain green brocade cloak with no coat of arms on it. The ingratiating expression he wore on his smoothly shaven face softened his rather dull blue eyes.

As soon as she saw Oldrich, Svetlana jumped up out of her seat and ran to him. This alone exceeded the bounds of courtly courtesy. But the daughter of Vilem of Landstein never worried her head about what she was or wasn't permitted to do. She had a provocative nature and gladly did whatever was prohibited to her. She took Oldrich by the hand and, with an air of intimacy, led him to her party. Large beech logs were crackling in the fireplace. The heat from the fire felt good. There were several goblets and two flagons of red wine on a small table next to the chairs.

"How do you like Landstein?" she eagerly asked.

"I have to admit that it's quite imposing," he answered politely. "We have no such castles in North Bohemia."

"You see, it could have been all yours if you hadn't rejected me," Svetlana quietly reproached him. Her brother Jost overheard and was amused. He stood up and embraced Oldrich as a sign of welcome, adding in a whisper, "Don't believe her, Sir Procurator. I shall inherit this castle after our father's death. Svetlana will only get a small one near Slavonice. And some money. She will be a well-endowed bride. I could imagine you as my brother-in-law, but because I also respect you, I wouldn't wish her on you. Even if Landstein was her dowry!"

"What are you whispering there?" she sternly asked her brother.

"Nothing," he said, shrugging his shoulders and winking at Oldrich. "I'm only reaffirming to the procurator what a great catch you would be." He poured two goblets of wine and exchanged toasts with him. The caretaker with the rose crest took on the responsibility of herald and introduced the other members of the noble party.

The girls were of course part of Svetlana's retinue. The rather ordinary-looking prelate was Wolf, the

Landstein chaplain. The second knight was named Peter and was the nephew of Vok of Prcice. He had recently begun to refer to himself as Rosenberg, the location of his new castle. The caretaker left the man in the green brocade cloak for last. He took a deep breath and solemnly introduced him. "And this distinguished gentleman is Cardinal Tiberius of Mantova, a legate from the Pope."

The prelate rose with all due dignity and it was then that Oldrich noticed that the cardinal had a small shaven tonsure on the crown of his head, confirming his ordination as a priest. Tiberius of Mantova raised a white, carefully manicured hand and, with a lavish gesture, blessed him. But his narrow lips were pursed in anger, as if they had just been discussing something not to his liking.

They were hardly back in their seats when Jost decided to confirm if what he had heard about Oldrich was true. "You are the best judge in the Czech kingdom. Perhaps your opinion can settle our argument. What do you think about confessions obtained under torture?"

"There are several ways to prove a criminal's guilt," Oldrich answered cautiously. "Some inquisitors rely on torture, but I prefer reason and logic. I wouldn't claim that I'm the best judge in the kingdom, but I will say that the means I use to discover the truth are more Christian." He didn't know what the spat was about but it was always good to be on guard in the presence of a papal legate.

Jost triumphantly looked at Tiberius and noted, most satisfactorily, "Did you hear that, your eminence?"

"The procurator can be excused if he hasn't any idea what our disagreement is about," the cardinal replied stiffly. "We are not discussing secular law, rather applying the hammer to a heretic, noble sir! Two years ago the Holy Father gave permission to the Inquisition to use the right of torture specifically for the purpose of protecting Christians. You cannot apply logic to the heretic. The devil resides in their souls and must be driven out. With a hot iron and sharp sword!"

"Of course," Jost began. He liked discourse. As the eldest child, he had been expected to become a knight, but like all members of the family he had also managed to acquire a thorough education. "But how can you apply torture if you do not know, at the beginning anyway, whether the person before you is a heretic? Torture should only be used when the guilt of the interrogated is obvious."

"Only heretics are brought before the tribunal, and the guilt of those who stand accused by the Inquisition is naturally obvious!"

"But what if it happens that one of them is innocent? Surely we can allow for that?"

"If something of that nature was to happen, and I, of course, entirely exclude it, because the Inquisition is under the authority of the Holy Father and he, as we know, is infallible, then we must remember what St. Columba said when he ordered the destruction of an entire village of heathens. One of his soldiers hesitated, worried that an honest and virtuous person might also be killed in the carnage. Columba advised him not to worry. God would most certainly accept the souls of the dead and raise the innocent to his throne as martyrs."

Jost scoffed at his remarks but before he could dismiss them, the cardinal jumped up angrily. "I am going to sleep! I have accepted your hospitality with pleasure and therefore do not wish to provoke a confrontation. But believe me, honorable sir, you must be firm with heretics! Weeds must be pulled out by the roots. I spent my youth in Languedoc and fought against the Waldensians there. It would be easier to try and cut the throat a wolf, which by the way I find of more agreeable disposition then these hideous French heretics. May God give you a peaceful night!" He turned and quickly left.

"Why do you provoke him so?" Svetlana sullenly asked her brother. She finished her wine and yawned.

"Why? You could see for yourself how humbly he appreciates our hospitality. And this afternoon he asked the chaplain here about how we are dealing with heretics in our domains."

The chaplain started to protest but Jost snapped at him not to make excuses for the legate, because he was standing in front of the chapel doorway at the time and overheard them. He then coldly continued: "Understand, there will be no Inquisition in Bohemia! Do you even know what Languedoc was all about? It had nothing to do with religion. The King of France wanted to subjugate the Count of Toulouse and add the whole of his region to the crown. He had women and children murdered, and for that they call him Louis the Pious now."

"That's too simple a way of looking at it! You can't deny that the King of France has been a good servant of the Christian faith," objected Peter of Rosenberg. "How many years has he given in the struggle to liberate the Holy Land?"

"He returned home in the summer," noted Oldrich. He thought the same about the Inquisition as Jost did. Even though he had not been a party to the dispute, he decided to support Svetlana's brother. "Of course, without any success. The Muslims defeated him. Louis's intentions were indeed pious, but God denied him victory just the same."

"What are you saying?" hissed Peter.

"What?" smiled Oldrich. "I only wanted to point out that any just and righteous conduct requires more than just pious intentions. The King of France certainly had good intentions when he set out to liberate the tomb of Christ. Perhaps he had the same pious intentions when he set out to suppress the heresy in southern France. You understand what I mean, don't you?"

"All too well," thundered young Rosenberg as he slammed his fist on the table. He rose and left without saying goodbye.

"Good that you made him leave," chirped Svetlana.

"He's a boring and pompous fool. Now we'll finally get a chance to talk. Would you believe they have been arguing nonsense for three whole evenings? In front of noble maidens no less! A knight in the company of such ladies should try to entertain them, not prove how intelligent he is."

Jost stood up with mischief in his eyes. "It is apparent that I am among those knights who, according to my sister, do not know what topic is appropriate for the company of noble maidens. Since you, Oldrich of Chlum, are more adept in this matter, I have no doubt that in your hands they will finally get to experience something chivalrous. I've had enough of them for the whole day. Goodnight!"

Oldrich was clearly annoyed by his posturing, but what else could he do except stay? He asked the chaplain to fetch his squire while he attempted, a little stiffly to be sure, to make small talk with the maidens. The arrival of Ota at the top of the stairs relieved him of the burden. The chaplain was nowhere to be seen.

Ota headed for the fireplace, politely bowed to each girl, and took a seat. He looked from one to the next and then, as if picking up the threads of the previous discussion, asked provocatively: "Did you know that in Languedoc they burn not only heretics, but also people who engage in indecent behavior?"

"Why are you telling us this?" Zdena Berkova of Sloup snapped. She glowered at him in a manner that could only suggest she was less than thrilled to see him. "Or perhaps you would like to humbly admit that if you lived in the south of France, you would be a pile of ashes right now?"

Ota was not so easily provoked. He raised his goblet and sipped from it judiciously. He smacked his lips with satisfaction before taking aim at her: "I should clarify my statement. Usually both are burned for indecency. The man and his mistress. It is often said that the unlucky pair embrace each other to the very end."

"How do you know?" Svetlana asked tiresomely. It was clear she didn't much care for this topic either.

"The Premonstratensian friar who came with us told me. He was born there," said Ota with a grave expression on his face. "But if I may just add to the quarrel you were having beforehand, I would also be against an Inquisition in this country. What crabby moralists call indecency, I prefer to think of as love. And who can be sure that you won't be called a heretic because of it?"

"You used to be more fun," lamented Zdena. She yawned and announced that she was ready for bed. She and the other two girls rose and headed to the staircase. Ota was pleased to notice that Katherine of Gutstein, whose hand was being sought after by his friend Michal Kekule of Stradonice, had grown into a beautiful girl. And also that she cast a discreet glance at him before leaving the room. That brightened his mood.

"And what about you, Ota?" Svetlana asked. "Don't you feel like going to sleep too?" There was no mistaking the suggestion in her voice that he should make himself scarce. She would be able to handle Oldrich by herself.

Ota looked to his master, whose morose expression made it clear that he was in no mood for joking around. Contrary to Svetlana, he thought his squire was exactly where he should be. He had no desire to flirt with her. When they said goodbye in Prague several months ago, they did not hide the fact that they weren't suited for each other. Nothing started between them and nothing ever would. Still, he was worried what Svetlana might do now. When it came to love, even knights were prone to break their promises. What could he expect from a girl born to high nobility?

Ota let out a mighty yawn. Svetlana beamed with satisfaction. "I would like to go to sleep," answered the squire with affected modesty. "But as a knight, I cannot leave you alone, dear maiden. It is my master who must leave. A man is waiting for him in our quarters. He arrived just as they were closing the gate. He says he must speak with the procurator forthwith."

"I'm not falling for that," Svetlana retorted. "You're a liar, Ota! And if you're trying to protect your master, then you're a double-edged liar."

"Come with us and see for yourself," Ota calmly shrugged. "That is if you're not worried the papal legate might find out about it. The daughter of Vilem of Landstein going into private quarters with two knights after nightfall. Terrible to think about it. Even a hundred Lord's-prayers couldn't rectify such a lapse!"

"Now you're a triple-edged liar. You really expect me to believe such nonsense?" Svetlana angrily finished her wine and stood up. The three of them proceeded to take the stairs to the upper floor, where the quarters for noble guests were located.

"She could see right through that," Oldrich admonished his squire but not so that Svetlana could hear it.

"Should I have left you alone with her?" Ota asked innocently.

"Not for a minute!"

Svetlana stopped before the door that led to the quarters assigned to Oldrich of Chlum. Her hand was resting on the handle. She gave Ota a contemptuous look. "I thought you were cleverer than this!" she crowed as she abruptly opened the door.

Inside, sitting on a small table next to the window, was an elderly man wearing a dusty cloak and holding a wayfarer's staff in his hand. His chin was covered with gray stubble. He stood up and addressed Oldrich. "You are the king's representative for North Bohemia? I must speak to you urgently. In private!"

Ota solemnly bowed to Svetlana and offered her his arm so that he might escort her back to the hall. Svetlana glared at him but took it. As she led him down the hallway, she hissed, "I can't sleep now after all the boredom of this evening. As punishment for what you've just done, you will keep me company. But you'd better amuse me or else I will say such nasty things about you that no decent maiden will ever speak to you again."

"None have complained so far," said Ota. "But I'm sure I will survive any attempt to sully my reputation. I don't much care for fair maidens anyway. And the others know what I'm capable of, so they wouldn't believe you anyway."

"You know what's funny here?" she laughed. She was never one to fret over courtly conventions, which perhaps was the reason why she was still unmarried. Her parents loved her, and her mother had gone so far as to say she could choose her future husband herself. "Every squire is always a little like his master. But not you. Too bad Sir Oldrich has to always be so serious."

They returned to the Great Hall and sat down again by the fireplace. Ota poured two goblets of wine and clinked with Svetlana. He then started to explain the way he saw things. "I don't quite agree with you. In fact, I'm just as shy as my lord. And serious too, at least in my soul. Of course, unlike Sir Oldrich of Chlum, I learned to overcome this shyness in the company of beautiful girls. That's because I respect the duty of every knight to entertain girls of noble birth, as you rightly noted, my dear Svetlana. I have actually spent my entire life doing nothing except discharging this duty."

"In this case, I would advise you to take a respite from your knightly duty during our pilgrimage. There will be no need to overcome any shyness and you would do well to exercise restraint with regards to my retinue, as your master shows me. Understand?"

"Just to be sure I know exactly what you're saying," said Ota, comically feigning ignorance. "You would like me to understand that I should avoid them? Well, I'm not against that. Of course, I would like you to ask the same of Zdena Berkova of Sloup. I will avoid your retinue and she will leave me in peace."

"That much I won't do," she laughed. "You made your bed, now sleep in it." It would seem she knew about their nightly trespass. Her good mood had returned. She finished her goblet, had him refill it, and asked him to tell her what his master had been up to in the past few weeks. Ota obeyed, but now and then surreptitiously cast his gaze towards the staircase. He wondered what the stranger wanted from Oldrich.

The tête-à-tête with Svetlana was most agreeable and they went to sleep just before the midnight trumpet. Both had drunk quite a bit and when they took their leave, Svetlana gave him a friendly goodnight kiss. She then added, quite seriously in fact, that she had yet to thank him for saving her life back in the spring, but perhaps she would compensate for it on the way to Compostela.

Ota headed for the servants' quarters and fretfully thought about this latest wretched turn of events. When it came to girls, he knew he could always count on his master to save him from the altar. With one exception, and if he managed to get himself into a pickle over Svetlana, Oldrich would gladly stick him with her.

He crossed the bridge and silently walked along the outwork to the building where the servants slept. He tried to kick a chicken that wandered into his path, but it cackled and dodged his foot.

CHAPTER VI

Ota woke up early the next morning and couldn't go back to sleep. Not that he was curious about the stranger who came to visit his master, rather the fact that he had to sleep in the servants' quarters. The whole night the place reverberated with snoring, wheezing, creaking, whispering, giggling, swearing, and footsteps. If someone asked him that morning to describe what purgatory was like, he would finger the servants' quarters in Landstein without hesitation.

Outside, he splashed some water from a stone trough in his face, and then hurried to the upper gate. He found his master still in his chamber, fast asleep. Oldrich opened his eyes as soon as he heard Ota walk in. He stretched and marveled at the fact that it was already morning. Apparently he had slept like a log. Never in his life did Ota feel like strangling his master as he did now. The day was off to an absolutely miserable start.

"Why didn't you come up during the night?" Oldrich inquired of him, pointing to a low bed in the corner with a quilt on top. "I had them bring it in for you."

"I didn't want to interrupt you," said Ota as he ran a hand through his hair.

"Don't tell me on account of that stranger. Did you think he was planning to bunk here with me? But I'm sure Svetlana was more agreeable company than me anyway."

"We only talked in the Great Hall," snarled Ota. He spied something in his master's eyes that he didn't like at all, almost as if Oldrich was ready to hug him for joy if he said he had spent the night with Svetlana. Unintentionally, Ota added rather provocatively, "I didn't come just in case the noble Svetlana had decided to drop by. She spoke only about you the entire evening."

Oldrich the procurator stared sternly at Ota the squire. He knowingly nodded and announced that for this particular lie, his penance would be to spend the entire day with Svetlana. "The problems with one stubborn girl," he laughed. "At least I have just this one to worry about. But you and your flock! I certainly don't envy you. Now for more serious matters. Mass is about to begin and I hope you're still enough of an aide to want to know what transpired in my chamber last night?"

"That's why I'm here," nodded Ota. Several jokes about what could have transpired were on the tip of his tongue, but this was clearly not the right time or place. Opening the trunk, he listened inquiringly as he helped his master get dressed.

"That stranger who called upon me last night is actually a nobleman, even if you couldn't tell from his dirty cloak and the staff he was carrying," said Oldrich. "He claims he's from Compostela, a courtier from Alfonso, the King of Castile. Now in case you didn't know, the King of Castile is a cousin of King Ottokar. He told me he has a letter for Abbess Agnes. He went to Prague to give it to her, but he just did miss her. Instead he spoke to Burgrave Vilem of Landstein, who told him to hasten here. Apparently he only stopped to change horses."

"But why did he come to you?"

"It would seem my fame has reached as far as Castile," scoffed Oldrich of Chlum. "Vilem advised him to seek me out, claiming that I was the right hand of Agnes of Bohemia and therefore could be trusted as if he spoke directly to her. He gave me the letter and a long message to deliver in person. Too bad the letter is sealed though."

"Can I have a look at it?" Ota asked. Taking the letter in hand, he carefully inspected it and reported, "The seal, my lord, has become unglued here. It could fall completely off. Shall I fix it? I will carefully unstick it and re-glue it."

Oldrich gave his consent. "Sure, that will be best. How much time do you need?"

"A while at least."

"Then let's leave it until after mass. Maybe in the afternoon when there's more time."

"Tell me, my lord, what did the Castilian knight tell you?"

"Better to wait until you've fixed the seal to talk about it," chuckled Oldrich and headed for the door of his chamber.

* * *

The castle chapel was quite small. It was located on the floor beneath both rectangular towers. The nobility were assembled on the tribune, the servants and castle hands below. Despite being jammed in shoulder to shoulder, several still had to wait on the threshold and peer into the chapel from the wooden porch in front. They were all looking at the apse, where a stone mensa was standing. The mass was supposed to be celebrated by Cardinal Tiberius of Mantova himself. Chaplain Wolf was up at the crack of dawn, running around the castle and eagerly telling everyone that a service from the Papal legate would bring them much more of God's grace than from an ordinary priest. It was even possible he would grant indulgences to sinners at the end. That's why no one should miss it. The chapel had never been so full. Most of the servants usually found a compelling reason to avoid mass, but not today. If the enemy were to strike at that moment, he could walk through the gate without any difficulty.

To give the mass a celebratory tone, Wolf asked Hyacinth to assist him at the altar. To his surprise, the

Premonstratensian friar outright refused. He said that since he still hadn't received higher ordination yet, he had no right to be there. Oldrich overheard the dispute and was certain that the monk was lying. He had a shaven tonsure on his head, which he shouldn't have if he really wasn't ordained.

Lying to a cardinal wasn't quite the same thing as lying to a chaplain, and in the end brother Hyacinth had to stand at the altar. Of the three prelates, he was easily the best singer and his rich voice completely overshadowed the other two during *Te Deum*. Oldrich was amused by the frown on the cardinal's face, certain that he was angry with himself for having forced the friar up to the altar in the first place.

After mass was over, the cardinal blessed everyone and announced that the Pope had given him permission to grant indulgences, which he would declare at some mass or other until the venerable Agnes of Bohemia reached Landstein. Disappointment could be observed in the faces of the servants as they began to leave.

Still in the chapel, several girls descended upon Hyacinth with the request that he sing them something else. They offered to attend to all his needs after their work for the day was done. Their eyes betrayed more than just a desire to hear him sing. The monk turned red with embarrassment and clumsily tried to free himself from their grasp. He was saved in the end by Zdena Berkova, who was just then coming down the narrow stone staircase with the rest of the nobility. She haughtily ordered the girls to leave and be quick about it. The monk breathed a sigh of relief, but before he could thank her, she grabbed him by the arm and began singing praises to his voice. As with the girls, this new attention caused him to stutter again, but she paid no notice and commanded him to come to the Great Hall in the evening so she and the other maidens could enjoy more of his company. Speechless, he bowed and tripped over the chapel threshold, nearly falling flat on his red face.

Svetlana saw everything and started to giggle, but she quickly put one hand to her mouth after she noticed Peter of Rosenberg glowering at her and indicating, in the strictest terms, that they were still in the house of God. But she didn't let him spoil her mood. She came up behind Katherine of Gutstein and snickered: "Did you see him? He liked to have died from shame. A little like your betrothed..."

"Michal Kekule of Stradonice is not my betrothed," Katherine objected. She then sighed and added that maybe someday he would be. Of course, she considered Michal even more timid than the monk. And being a knight, he had no reason to be. Ota, who was standing behind them, had to agree. He ducked his head and walked through the stone portal to the porch. The weather was still cloudy, but a bit warmer.

Jost stopped his guests in front of the chapel and eagerly announced that hunters had sent him word that a stag had been cornered in the woods not far from them. He ordered his horse saddled up so he could join the hunt. Other members of the nobility received the news with excitement, perhaps none more so than Cardinal Tiberius. He called out to Jost to wait for him, that he had to first change clothes and pray.

"I'm not going," Oldrich excused himself. He didn't like hunting and would rather have a look around the castle anyway. At home he lived in an ancient and none too impressive court close to Lipa, but was hoping to build a strong royal castle in North Bohemia soon. He had already chosen a hill for it halfway between Lipa and Boleslav, known by the locals as Bezdez. It was nearly cone-shaped and offered a view of the entire surroundings. He was therefore curious about the construction of Landstein.

"What about you?" Svetlana asked Ota. "Are you going on the hunt or staying with your master?"

Ota looked at her inquisitively and quickly considered his options, which should naturally suit his master at the same time. But the answer was obvious. He was just a servant, so he courteously asked Svetlana if she desired him to accompany her on the hunt.

"I would be most grateful," she answered, suggestively.

"Off you go then," said Oldrich, only too willing to oblige her. "We'll take care of the seal in the evening."

The hunting party set off. All guests with the exception of Oldrich were participating, including knights, prelates and noble maidens. But they had hardly left the forecastle for the woods when Svetlana slowed up. She was waiting for Katherine to catch up so she could tell her something. Glancing over his shoulder, Ota reined in his horse and stopped. "What's wrong?" he shouted out to the girls.

Katherine then turned the reins of her horse loose and galloped towards Ota, but Svetlana turned around and was slowly going back to the castle. Ota clucked at his horse, pressed his calf into its side, and turned it around just as Katherine reached him. Slightly flushed in the face, she explained that Svetlana was all of a sudden not feeling well. Saying she didn't want to spoil the hunt, she was asking him, Ota, to keep her, Katherine, company in the woods.

He nodded in absent-minded agreement and took one more look over his shoulder. He could see Svetlana looking at them from the bend in the road. When it became clear to her that Ota was going to continue on the hunt, she sat up in her saddle, waved at him and mischievously stuck out her tongue. She then quickly galloped back to Landstein.

Ota had to laugh. She had outfoxed him, but he wasn't worried because his master would have no cause to blame him. He looked at Katherine long and hard. She had long, coal-black hair, a symmetrical face with an ever so slight snub nose and large, doe-eyes. Unlike the thin and springy Svetlana, she had a full figure in all the right places. She looked very fetching in her dark leather pants and hunting blouse. Having caught his eye, she spurred her horse on as if she had suddenly been startled. But Ota easily overtook her.

With unfeigned modesty, she asked if he wouldn't rather keep company with the maiden from Sloup. Ota realized that Zdena had boasted about their nocturnal adventure to everyone in her path.

"You are much more beautiful," he answered without thinking. He considered it best to use hackneyed phrases in such situations.

"Do you say that to every girl?"

"No, only to those who deserve it."

"I wouldn't know about that. But they say, and I mean no offense, that you prefer girls who can offer you more than just polite company. I'm nothing like Zdena Berkova!"

"May I confess something to you?" he asked rather secretively. "I'm really not the type of person they talk about. Most of what they say about me is false. Knights like to boast about how many men they kill in battle, while noble girls like to exaggerate about the number of knights in love with them. Well, supposedly I'm popular, so perhaps it's modern among highborn girls to boast about having been with me. But I swear to you, practically none of it is true!"

"Really?" she asked, quite surprised. She was a gullible girl and there was no helping it. She looked at him curiously for a moment and sighed: "It's a pity!" She quickly galloped on ahead and it took Ota some time to catch her. On the way he noticed Zdena having a rather intimate chat with Peter of Rosenberg.

* * *

Oldrich was at that moment studying the foundations of the large rectangular towers when he heard footsteps behind him, followed by Svetlana's voice. None too pleased, he turned and asked what was wrong.

"You don't look excited to see me," she reproached him with a wagging finger. "Didn't I tell you yesterday that I have to talk to you? In private, just between us."

"So that's why you lured my squire into the woods, where he's at the mercy of demons and wolves. Just like a fairy tale," he wearily sighed.

"I didn't leave your squire at the mercy of wolves, rather beautiful and wellborn maidens."

"I don't find that reassuring in the least."

"I know," she laughed merrily. "Shall we go somewhere to sit for a while? It's cold and damp here. I promise to be nice, so you don't have to act like a condemned man on his way to the block. Am I really so disagreeable?"

"Of course not," he shrugged and tried to smile. "But you know me, and what I think about our relationship."

"Yes, and I happen to think the same thing. The two of us could never live together. I haven't changed my mind about that. I have no ambition to become your lover, much less your wife. There, I hope that much has been settled. Otherwise I still like you."

"I like you too in my own way, Svetlana. So what's

this about?"

They reached the palace and climbed the steps to the Great Hall. It was empty. The fire had died down and the stone walls inside were as cold as the dungeon underneath the tower. Svetlana called for the caretaker and firmly advised him to get the fire going at once and bring them some hot mead.

The beech logs in the fireplace had barely begun to crackle when she sat down next to Oldrich. The look in her face was serious. "I wanted to talk to you in private because it's about the pilgrimage of Abbess Agnes. You've probably already suspected as much, but quite a few things have happened in recent months which you have no idea about. They upset the King so much that he ordered you at the last minute to undertake the pilgrimage as well."

"Your father hinted at something similar. Apparently he was the one to kindly recommend me."

Svetlana laughed heartily. She was pretty with an unusually sensual mouth. "He told you that? He wasn't even at Prague Castle when the whole matter was discussed. The day before King Ottokar set off with the army to Moravia, he was visited by the new provincial judge. He then immediately summoned me and I will tell you exactly what he told me as an introduction. Dear Svetlana, because Oldrich of Chlum loves you and you are quite intelligent, I shall entrust you two with a very special task."

"Wait a minute!" Oldrich cut her off and commenced to stroking the short beard he wore on his chin. "A proverb from our wise forebears advises against trusting women. Especially young and beautiful ones. Are you sure our noble monarch didn't say it somewhat differently?"

"Like I said about not being suited for each other! I couldn't bear to have you by my side as a husband. Now what displeases you? That the King said I was intelligent?"

"I don't doubt he said it, or that I love you according to his conviction. We have your father to thank for that. You know yourself that he even prevailed upon the King to order me to marry you, and I am sure the King would never entrust the two of us with an important task. Just to me, as the law dictates."

"What difference does it make? Not for all the money in the world would I ever live with you. But you'll never learn anything if you insist on interrupting me."

Oldrich humbly nodded. A steward appeared in the hall and poured goblets of warm mead for them. He lustily drank from his and savored the bittersweet aroma.

Svetlana grinned as she observed him. He was the only man she was willing to submit to, and that was precisely why she couldn't love him. She was too used to bossing others around. But this wasn't about her anyway, so she quickly quashed any further such thoughts. She picked up her goblet but waited until the servant had left before she got back to the point.

"The King told me he had to set off the next day with the army but was worried about his aunt. He tried to dissuade her from undertaking the pilgrimage but she refused to listen. He was only mollified when he learned of the Pope granting her his personal protection. He even promised to send his legate to accompany the delegation."

"It's clear from the presence of Cardinal Tiberius that he fulfilled that pledge," Oldrich interjected. There was danger inherent in every pilgrimage. Ottokar's fear for his aunt's safety was understandable. While Oldrich did not see any cause for worry this far into the tale, the Pope's interest in this particular pilgrimage was indeed unusual.

"Up until that point everything was all right and the King had not yet summoned me," said Svetlana. "But then two peculiar events occurred right before his departure for Moravia. One was that Michal of Cimburk was to lead the expedition of pilgrims. He was an experienced diplomat."

"Yes, I knew him. He was also a great knight," Oldrich nodded, "but he died a few days ago after some unfortunate accident."

"That's true but it was no accident. Supposedly he fell from a horse, but the healer who attended him insisted to the King that he had also been struck in the head by someone. It was murder. Of course, it could have been done by anyone for any number of reasons. Perhaps none connected to our journey. So the King immediately named a new leader. But that same evening another knight – his name is not important – was killed. It happened close to Porichsky ford. He was found with five arrows in his body."

"It would seem that someone is committing these murders in order to ensure that a certain individual is appointed to lead Agnes's pilgrimage. I understand that a commendatore of the Knights Templar is the new leader."

"Yes, but the King had in fact entrusted the mission to the Margrave of Wartenberg. But he asked to be relieved of this duty because he was injured in a skirmish with the lords of Duba and had to spend several weeks in bed. That was the first incident that unsettled the King. The less serious of the two."

Oldrich twisted the side of his mouth in a gesture of complete bewilderment. He knew nothing about this, and no one, not Abbess Agnes, Commendatore Jacob de Vries or Provost Wilibald Odo had mentioned anything to him. It was also true that all three had spoken to him in a curt and offhanded manner. Obviously they were all in agreement to keep him in the dark, perhaps because they were afraid of something.

"And the second incident," continued Svetlana quickly, as if she wanted to get it over with. She was an incredibly impatient person by nature and was already beginning to find their conversation tedious. If any further investigation required similarly long discussions, she would happily leave everything in the capable hands of Oldrich of Chlum. "The King received a message from a certain prelate who works for him in the Roman curia. I don't know his name but I suspect he must be someone very high up in the clergy. The message was brief. Basically this prelate had learned by chance about Agnes of Bohemia's journey and there were signs that she would be murdered on the journey."

"Did he show her the message?" Oldrich angrily shouted. Nothing bothered him more than the intrigues of church officials, which had nearly cost him his own life on another occasion.

Svetlana shook her head as if apologizing on behalf of the King, adding, "She probably wouldn't have believed him, and besides it might endanger his man in Rome. He thinks his aunt is sometimes hopelessly naïve in matters of faith and can imagine her sitting down and writing a letter to the Pope asking him if it was true that somebody wanted to kill her. But I think he underestimates her. Agnes is not so foolish. But it doesn't matter now. It was this message that made him decide to call upon you. On the face of it, you are there to watch over me and the other maidens but in reality you will be guaranteeing the safety of Agnes of Bohemia and your head may well depend on it. I'm serious. I'm telling you exactly what the King told me. There are certain situations when you can trust a woman despite the half-witted utterances of our otherwise wise forbears about female perfidy and ignorance."

CHAPTER VII

The only one in the party who chased the stag with any real passion was Jost of Landstein. The others had joined in more or less to get out for some fresh air. Anything was better than sitting around bored all day long in the castle. Besides, they were expected to hunt. The aristocracy had to find some ways to amuse themselves.

Ota rode at the side of Katherine and attempted to engage her in conversation. He felt attracted to her, if only because he also felt she misunderstood him. Most of her replies were nothing like he thought they would be, and that intrigued him.

"When I told you that I was not the sinner everybody said I was, I didn't mean I was a saint," he explained with downcast eyes, pretending to be ashamed to admit it.

"Your confession has upset me very much," she answered gravely.

"So what do you want to hear? First, when you thought I was a sinner, you glared at me. Then, when I tried to defend my honor, you still glared at me. Now when I tell you I'm neither sinner nor saint, you say you're upset. So what do you suggest I be?"

"Isn't it all the same? And what Zdena Berkova told me about you...is it true? Or did she make it up?"

Before Ota could decide how best to answer, they heard angry shouts. They spurred their horses onward and encountered Cardinal Tiberius and Peter of Rosenberg behind the bend in the road. They were sitting on their horses facing each other with their hunting knives drawn in a menacing manner.

"I shall not tolerate any such thing!" young Rosenberg shouted.

"You dare not oppose the Holy See!" the papal legate shouted back in kind.

They fell silent the minute they heard the clatter of hooves.

"Noble sirs. We are pilgrims, walking in the footsteps of Jesus the Crucified One for the greater glory of Christendom. Here is not the place for it," Katherine rebuked them. But Ota knew this girl well enough to know that she wasn't driven by faith to settle their quarrel, rather because she was a sensitive soul who could not bear to watch people argue.

Mantova and Rosenberg put their knives back in their sheaths, muttered something vaguely, and each headed off in a different direction. At the next clearing they encountered Zdena. She was alone and looking quite sore.

"Are they still arguing?" she asked sulkily.

"No," Katherine smiled. "Do you know what it was

about?"

"About me," she answered proudly.   Katherine grinned and nodded, while Ota detected a bit of malice in Zdena's lips.

As soon as they were alone again, Katherine said, "I believe you when you say there was nothing between you." Although Ota had said nothing of the kind, he hypocritically nodded. Katherine continued, now with indignation in her voice. "Young Berkova thinks she is irresistible and the whole world is at her feet. What nonsense! A cardinal arguing over her! When she told me that you spent a night together, I foolishly believed her. She probably tells similar fairytales to everyone she meets. Next she will claim even the cardinal had erred with her. Does she really think it's something to be admired for? Well, I have nothing to be ashamed of. I have never violated the Ten Commandments and shall remain chaste until the day I get married. How can anyone boast that they have sinned! Do you understand it?"

"My friend is lucky that he has chosen you," said Ota, evading the question as graciously as possible.

She stared at him as if she had something she wanted to share with him but in the end she said nothing and galloped ahead. The riding party was waiting for them just beyond a row of bushes. They had just brought down the cornered stag.

Ota was now convinced he had lost too much time with Katherine. Initially he had found her naiveté charming, surprised by some of the things she said, but now it had grown tiresome. Ever since their encounter with Zdena, she spoke only of morality.

He rode behind her and, out of boredom, observed the silhouette of her figure in the saddle. It made a very good impression on him. He therefore decided that talking to her would be only a partial waste of time. If he had to choose, he would say that Katherine was much prettier than Svetlana or Zdena and he took immense pleasure in knowing this.

Of course, every sin committed on a holy pilgrimage was a hundred times heavier to bear than one committed at home. It was absolutely inconceivable for a pilgrim to engage in an unbecoming manner with another. Moreover, he promised to conduct himself honorably, at a time albeit when it looked like an easy promise to keep. He would have to keep any sinful thoughts about Katherine to himself. He believed her when she said she was determined to preserve her chastity for her future husband. He was also developing a most unflattering opinion about Zdena Berkova. All the more reason to avoid her. But Svetlana worried him because nothing was sacred to her. Yesterday she was very sweet to him and he enjoyed being with her. If Svetlana got it into her head that she wanted his attention and favors, then pilgrimage or no pilgrimage, she would have them. And Ota simply couldn't allow that to happen. He wanted to be a virtuous pilgrim and do everything not to cause his master any shame or embarrassment.

* * *

Agnes of Bohemia and her entourage arrived at Landstein in the afternoon. Their numbers were surprisingly small. In addition to the Vysehrad provost Wilibald Odo and his librarian Emmeram of Greifsfeld, she was accompanied by Friar Gregory of the Minorite order and Prech of Michalovice, who was leading the company of knights. The commendatore of the Templar order, Jacob de Vries, was missing.

Inasmuch as the hunting party led by young Jost had not yet returned, Svetlana had to assume the role of hostess. "My humble apologies, gracious elder sister, we did not know that you would arrive so early. We were informed that you would come at the end of the week."

"It was my original intention," Agnes replied. "But in the end we left Prague earlier. Show me to my chambers, dear girl, I'm tired. I would like to rest up before the evening mass. Has the papal legate already arrived? I need to speak with him."

"He's here. But he left with the rest of the hunting party."

Agnes nodded in silence and began walking toward the palace. Svetlana led her to the best chambers in the castle. They were normally occupied by her father, but he had to spend most of the year now at Prague Castle discharging his duties as burgrave.

Oldrich knew Prech of Michalovice quite well,

because his castle stood not far from the administrative court of North Bohemia which he presided over. They were roughly the same age, but when Oldrich was younger and regularly took part in jousting tournaments, he defeated Prech several times. They amicably greeted each other and headed for the forecastle, where there was a rather decent tavern. Only servants and members of the garrison went there, but the beer was good and the oven hot, which made it pleasantly warm inside on this cool autumn day.

"Has something happened in Prague?" asked Oldrich, getting right to the point. "Abbess Agnes seemed subdued. Didn't smile at all. It can't be because she's tired from the journey. Why did she leave Prague earlier than planned?"

"Maybe it has something to do with the death of the Templar commendatore."

"What's that? Jacob de Vries is dead?"

"Yes. He was murdered, his body found outside the city walls. Somebody put a couple of arrows in him and then split his head open with an ax. They might not have been able to identify him had he not been wearing the attire of his order. A heinous murder it was. Naturally the murderer also robbed him."

"I have never encountered a case where the robber shot his victim with arrows. These thugs have no military training and cannot hit anything from five feet away. Did you see his body? Where was he struck? Were you able to determine how far away the killer was by the depth of the arrow in his body?" the procurator inquired.

Of course, he instantly thought of what Svetlana had told him before lunch. This was now the third murder connected to the pilgrimage of Abbess Agnes. If Oldrich had suspected that Jacob de Vries was behind the first two murders in order to assume leadership of the pilgrimage on behalf of the Templars, that hypothesis would now have to be reconsidered.

"I'm no investigator like you. I cannot help you here, friend," Prech shook his head. "I didn't see the body of the commendatore because the Templars immediately took it away. Why should I want to inspect it anyway? I wasn't supposed to journey with Agnes in the first place and only after it happened did she personally ask me to take charge of the expedition. And we left that same day. Sunday afternoon. She didn't even want to wait for the ceremonial mass on Monday. Of course, I thought that was strange, but I had to get the soldiers ready and she didn't tell me anything more. Also the prelates with her were staring at me with pure disdain. I didn't bother myself with them at all."

"But you had to have overheard something that could help me," Oldrich suggested. "What about the soldiers in your outfit? Don't tell me they haven't been talking about the murder!"

"Of course, they have," countered Prech and shouted to the portly tavern keeper to bring him some smoked meat and potato cakes. "They were as upset as I was. Started cursing like heathens, so much so that Abbess Agnes made them do penance as punishment. Originally a group of Templars and their commendatore were supposed to set off on the pilgrimage along with a couple of the hofmeister's cavaliers. But the commendatore was murdered and Burgrave Vilem quickly decided to send another military attachment with Agnes. I think it was he who advised the honorable abbess to leave Prague immediately."

"So none of your men knows anything," he sighed disappointingly. The tavern keeper placed some smoked ham on the table in front of Oldrich, but he declined, telling his friend that he had just dined. He stood up and apologized that he had to get back to the castle.

"You never rest, not even for a minute. I was telling you I don't much care for the prattle of prelates, but I do remember this one sermon which preaches that only fools rush in." And with that admonition, Prech dug into his food.

Oldrich hurried to the upper gate, pondering about how to stay alive. His head was on the line for the safety of Agnes of Bohemia. True, it was a good thing that the military attachment was being led by his friend, but the abbess and her prelates were making all the decisions about the pilgrimage itself. None of them held him in any high regard. He wasn't one of them and Ottokar had to insist on his participation over the objections of his aunt. He couldn't hope to be included in their councils. Abbess Agnes acted haughty and contemptuous whenever something displeased her. She was a Přemyslid and not even her habit could cloak that fact. The one person who could perhaps tell him more was the Vysehrad librarian Emmeram of Greifsfeld.

He found the scrawny man sitting on the wooden railing of the walls together with the chaplain. They were taking in a magnificent view of the winding river and wooded hills below, beyond which lay the border with Austria. He was following the movement of the chaplain's hand as he described the region before them.

"May I join you?" Oldrich asked.

"We've been waiting for you actually. Even though you are a good Christian, you are primarily a procurator and are not joining us on the pilgrimage simply out of faith. This should be of interest to you. Brother, say it once more," said the librarian, turning to the chaplain.

But he started excusing himself on the grounds that he didn't know anything for certain and would be most unhappy to commit a sin by slandering his neighbor. Emmeram cut him off. "Brother Chaplain, I understand your hesitation. I promise not to tell anyone what you have confided in me. In order for me to fulfill this promise, I ask you to repeat it to the procurator yourself. Believe me, he will keep it to himself. It is your eternal duty to protect Christendom everywhere, is it not?"

The chaplain nodded and crossed himself. He nervously looked around, wondering how to begin. Still reluctant, he finally ventured forward. "Very well! It has to do with something that worries me. Two things in fact. Brother Hyacinth, that Premonstratensian friar you brought here, is not, noble sir, a good Christian."

"What makes you think so? Because he didn't want to attend mass?" asked Oldrich, knowing full well that this wasn't the reason. He wanted to prompt the chaplain a little.

"Partly. He mainly wanted to avoid the papal legate. I noticed how he stared at him at the altar. I think he hates him."

"I also quarreled with his eminence last night," Oldrich remarked. "You heard our argument about the Inquisition. But it means nothing here."

"A quarrel is one thing, but to hate somebody with all your soul is another. And it's not a matter of opinion here. Brother Hyacinth is completely different with him. It's personal, and I'm not the only one who has this feeling. I overheard, and hesitate to say it, but I overheard brother Hyacinth praying to God to summon the legate and judge him."

Oldrich merely nodded. He knew what it was about. He learned from the abbot that Hyacinth came from southern France, where his parents were burned as heretics. The legate was most probably an inquisitor in his youth and ardently supported the persecution of the Waldensians there. Their paths have therefore already crossed. Since the Premonstratensian friar was still a child then, he didn't know the legate but could probably remember his face. And there was one more crucial detail that Oldrich noticed. The chaplain constantly talked about the cardinal only as the legate. Not once did he refer to him otherwise. Not by name, not by the title that denoted his high position in the Church. He realized it had something to do with the second order of business that was bothering the chaplain. That's why he didn't want to talk about it; so he decided to challenge him outright. "And what is so strange about the papal legate..."

"You too?" the chaplain erupted. He breathed a sigh of relief and started to explain that he had once been with Vilem in Rome. They were there as messengers bearing a letter from Abbess Agnes to the Holy Father. While there he caught a glimpse of Cardinal Tiberius of Mantova. Although it had been a few years, Chaplain Wolf swore that the man in the castle now was not the same Tiberius of Mantova. With that, he excused himself and fled.

Before Oldrich had the chance to ask the librarian for his opinion on this entirely suspicious matter, a noise could be heard emanating from the gate. The hunting party led by Jost was entering the courtyard. A gamekeeper was strutting along behind them with two brush beaters carrying a pole on their shoulders. Dangling from it was a magnificent royal stag.

* * *

Agnes of Bohemia did not appear from her chamber that afternoon. She had the evening meal brought to her and invited only Wilibald Odo and Friar Gregory for discussion. She declined to include Oldrich of Chlum. That suited him just fine. He still had the sealed letter for her from the King of Castile and this way he could attend to it through the night with a clear conscience.

Oldrich discreetly continued his inquiries into the evening. Naturally he didn't learn anything from the librarian about the death of the Templar commendatore. He pondered whether to speak with Svetlana about the suspicion that the papal legate was not the same person he claimed to be. Then he thought better of it. He didn't want to give her the notion that they would be making inquiries together, especially since it involved an extremely thorny issue. That man may indeed not be the cardinal, but the Pope still probably sent him. Even if it was somebody else, it didn't mean he didn't enjoy a high position in Rome. His appointment had been confirmed by a papal bull which he carried around with himself.

There was always the possibility that he had gotten a hold of the bull through theft, perhaps had even killed the cardinal and not only stolen the bull but also his clothes and other items. But on first glance it all seemed highly unlikely. If he had robbed the real cardinal, why put on this ridiculous show? Also, his manners were indicative of a high primate. He spoke perfect Latin, celebrated mass without a single mistake and had, according to Jost, who welcomed the papal legate several days ago and had already held several discussions with him, a deep knowledge of not only theology, but of other sciences as well. Most likely what had happened was that another important member of the Roman curia had assumed, with the Pope's blessing, the identity of the honorable Cardinal Tiberius. A highly unorthodox situation to say the least but Oldrich was determined not to hastily mention it to anyone until he had spoken with Agnes first.

Oldrich informed his noble company that he was tired and retiring early. He told Ota in front of everyone to move his things, including his straw mattress, to his chambers. By way of explanation he added that there were several beautiful girls residing in the castle at that moment, all of them highborn and, as maidens, were innocent, inexperienced, and pure. Everyone would therefore sleep better if he kept his eye on him.

"Many thanks for that," Ota scowled after they were in Oldrich's chambers. "Do you realize what you have done? Stirred up even greater interest in me among members of the fair sex! No offense, my lord, but in matters of the heart, you behave like these maidens you aim to protect. Innocent and pure, only most of them have already forfeited their virginity. I guess I will have to somehow deal with it. I shall armor myself with a firm faith and drive them away with tenacity!"

"Here I wanted to help you and you're angry at me," said Oldrich, amusingly. "Imagine, someday a chronicler will write about us. Oldrich the knight, served by the most successful seducer of highborn maidens in the Czech kingdom. Or something like that. Of course, assuming the chronicler in question isn't a prelate. He would have another name for you, no doubt." Having said his piece, he gave Ota the sealed letter and indicated that there were more important matters at hand.

"I'm on it," said Ota. He briefly held the seal over a candle flame, taking care not to damage the parchment. Then, very carefully, he used his dagger to separate the seal from the paper. "There," he said, relieved that it was over. He put the seal aside and handed the parchment to his master.

"Come closer, I will read it to you. I only hope it's not written in Hispanic. But then Abbess Agnes wouldn't understand it either," Oldrich whispered. He opened the letter and was happy to see it was in Latin.

" 'My dear and venerable...' and so on. Not interesting... 'Greetings to my royal cousin...' Nothing special there... 'God helped me to conquer Cadiz...' Good Lord, why did he even send this? Here it is, finally, all the way at the end. Listen, Ota! My heart rejoices that you want to visit Compostela. Your venerable companion Clare of Assisi also visited. That was at least forty years ago. She was still a girl then, accompanied by her teacher, known today throughout the entire Christian world as Francis of Assisi. That you may follow in her footsteps. As far as we have learned, she spent several months in the nearby village of Bertarimans. I can also recommend it to you. As always your...' and so on. What do you think?"

"What I think, as a sinful squire and all, is that Clare was a saint accompanied by a man who was also a saint."

"Not the time and place for such remarks," Oldrich reminded him stiffly. "They lived together as brother and sister. The monastic order of St. Francis included both men and women in the beginning. They spent evenings and sometimes whole nights together meditating about the sufferings of Christ. According to the original Rule *Forma Vivendi* of 1216, the women were supposed to rely only on that which their brothers had begged for them. It was a religious community of the poor and humble. But three years later the Pope issued a new Rule called *Privilegium pauperits* that separated the men and women into different branches. Only then did their cloisters begin to form in the Benedictine tradition, meaning secluding the sisters from the world of men."

"Quite interesting from a historical perspective," said Ota. "Of course, it logically confirms my irreverent and profane remarks. Why should the Pope want to separate them with a Rule if they were living together in chastity, as you say? No, don't tell me that saints can also sin. Especially if she fell in love with her saint. That probably wouldn't be a sin..."

"The papal legate would agree with you, but I should like to point out that there is, of course, a big difference between the platonic love of two hearts suffering for Christ, and lustful squires and lascivious daughters who have forgotten that they belong to noble Christian families. But we are not here for that."

"If I remember correctly, the King of Castile also sent a confidential verbal message. May I ask, my lord, what he told you?"

Oldrich leaned back in his chair and stroked the beard on his chin. He wondered what words to choose. Until then, he had thought about the message in a completely different light because he did not know the contents of the letter.

"He said only a few words," he said, weighing his own words. "They could mean anything. I am supposed to tell Agnes that the Pope knows nothing about Clare's visit to Compostela. Furthermore, there is no one still alive in Bertarimans who can remember her visit. And the most peculiar is the last one. Among the treasures in Compostela is a thick candle which Clare gave to the church together with St. Francis. There is an inscription on it, but the messenger explained that the King of Castile has no idea what it means. The inscription says, 'The Legacy of Apostle James'."

"Abbess Agnes might know what it means."

"Perhaps, and if she won't tell us, as I suspect, she'll be playing with fire, because she's certainly not the only one who knows what it means and a couple of people have already died on account of it. She could be in great danger, but for now there's nothing we can do about it."

They tried to piece together the evidence they had so far, but it was pathetically small and they were not able to make any sense out of it or construct a hypothesis. They weren't even able to determine the direction to proceed in.

"Might as well leave it to faith for now," uttered Oldrich. "Maybe something will soon happen that will provide us with another clue."

Precisely, and it happened that very night. In the morning they found the papal legate murdered in his sleep.

CHAPTER VIII

The legate's body was discovered by Chaplain Wolf, who had come to his chambers after he failed to arrive at the morning service in the chapel. He found him lying on the floor in a pool of dried blood. The several dozen stab wounds on his body suggested he had been the victim of a frenzied attack. His trunk was also open and his cardinal's apparel strewn all about the room.

When the chaplain returned to the chapel with the horrible news, Agnes of Bohemia shrieked and nearly fainted. Jost turned pale, but instantly dashed down from the tribune where the other nobles had gathered and blocked the exit. He ordered that no one was to leave without his permission.

"You have no such authority," shouted the Vysehrad provost Wilibald Odo.

"Yes, I do!" Jost shouted back. "The papal legate has been murdered in our castle. Unless we find the murderer quickly, the Pope will place all of our domains under interdict. I have to do whatever is necessary to prevent that from happening. Do you understand?"

Peter of Rosenberg and Zdena Berkova were among those to voice their support for the provost.

"You will obey him!" the abbess suddenly declared in a shrill voice. "This is my pilgrimage. Young Landstein, have Oldrich of Chlum, the procurator, find out what happened."

Standing not quite three steps from her on the tribune, Oldrich was blindsided. Up until that point, she had pretended as if he didn't even exist. But the woman before him now had sunken eyes and a quivering mouth. Her attempt to maintain the dignified composure of the ruling class couldn't hide the fact that she was on the verge of collapse. He bowed and gave her his solemn word that he would do everything in his power to bring the murderer to justice. His promise did little to reassure her, not if the flicker of fear he noticed in her eyes was any indication.

He and Landstein had just left the chapel when Jost, now more in control of himself, said, "I hope we can lay this terrible crime to rest. Fortunately I know who the murderer is."

"You saw who did it?"

"No, but I know the reason why the legate is dead. Yesterday you spoke with our chaplain, so you know too. Revenge. Did not Friar Hyacinth pray for his death?"

"Whoever wants somebody dead doesn't pray for it. He does it. Our monk put his revenge in the hands of

God. Christians pray to God that he may help them do something they can't do by themselves."

"Christians maybe... But Hyacinth was a heretic. Didn't you know?"

"And how do you know, Sir Jost?"

"That's not important. Only that I know."

Jost felt vindicated when they walked into the chamber and saw the body on the floor. "Look, Sir Procurator, at these stab wounds. It wasn't enough just to kill him. Brother Hyacinth must've stabbed him like a man possessed."

Oldrich bent over the body of the papal official, lying face down, and carefully examined it. As he turned it over, he felt his own sense of vindication.

"Look for yourself, Sir Jost. He has stab wounds all over his body. Front and back."

"Like I said, a man possessed."

"Think about it. The killer starts stabbing like a madman and when he's finished, he turns the body over and continues stabbing? Doesn't that strike you as strange? Whoever killed the legate wanted it to appear as if the murderer acted out of hatred and revenge. This murder was more cold and calculating, executed to cover up the real reason behind it, and it has nothing to do with hatred or revenge."

"No? Who do you think did it then?"

"We'll find out sure enough. First we must question everyone. And look at all these things scattered about. Another sign that this was no frenzied attack. The murderer was looking for something and perhaps found it."

"I have an idea. Follow me," said Jost, leading Oldrich from the palace to the servants' quarters. There they asked an old man who had spent his entire life in the castle where the young monk was staying. The man pointed to a plank bed in the corner. Underneath it was a leather pouch.

Jost pulled out the pouch and untied it. There at the top was another pouch full of silver coins and embossed with the coat of arms of the Roman curia.

"What do you say about that?" Jost crowed, taking the smaller pouch out.

"That it was planted here by someone without much imagination. Only a fool would fall for this trick!" retorted Oldrich. But Jost had no intention of arguing with him any further. Without a word, he left the quarters and started heading back to the chapel, with Oldrich reluctantly following him. On the way Jost presented his plan to him: "It's a good thing the monk is involved. Nobody can blame my family and the church will have to resolve it alone. The Bishop of Prague finally got his immunity, so he will have to judge the monk himself and answer for it to the Pope. It's out of our hands and yours as well. I will have Hyacinth sent to the diocesan court in Prague and we'll have peace and calm here again."

"He had these things with him when we left Milevsko, including money the abbot gave him for the pilgrimage. More than what's in this pouch. Why to kill for a couple of silver coins? And where's the rest?"

Jost suddenly stopped and muttered, "What rest?"

"Do you think the legate was carrying around only one half-empty pouch? If Hyacinth robbed him, where's the rest of the money? And if it was only robbery, why the furious attack? Was the motive revenge or robbery?"

"That's for the diocesan court to find out," Jost growled. Oldrich looked him straight in the eye and the young knight stared straight back, but then turned away. He bit his lips, turned and headed quickly for the upper gate. After a few of steps he stopped to wait for Oldrich.

"Fine! I'm not as simple as you might think," he declared indignantly. "I know there are inconsistencies. But understand that an important member of the Roman curia has been murdered in our castle. The Pope will take advantage of it. Can you imagine the fine he will impose on my father? It could destroy our entire family. The only thing that can save us is if the murderer is a church official. Do you understand?"

"But you have no authority to charge Friar Hyacinth," Oldrich argued vehemently.

"Why not? Let the Bishop of Prague worry about it now. Perhaps he will come to the same conclusion as you, namely that the monk is innocent. But at least our family will be absolved!"

"You must have a poor opinion about me if you think I would agree to such a plan?" scowled Oldrich. "I have sworn to make a proper investigation and find the real murderer."

"When?"

"Whenever!"

"Agnes of Bohemia wants to depart tomorrow. If you don't find the murderer before then, I will charge the monk!" Jost brusquely declared and shouted to the guard at the gate that no one was to leave the castle without his expressed consent.

* * *

"And that was the verbal message of King Alfonso," said Oldrich after he told Agnes everything and had handed her the letter.

"Why didn't you give it to me yesterday?" she asked, the anger rising in her voice.

"I had asked you for an audience and you refused. I couldn't say what it was about in front of the others," he courteously defended himself.

Agnes nodded, then looked at the seal and broke it. As she opened the letter and read it, Oldrich noticed that her hands were trembling. She was nervous.

"May I respectfully ask why you entrusted me with the investigation?" Oldrich ventured to ask after she had finished. Agnes had brought him into her chambers immediately after leaving the chapel with the others. She was sitting in a chair by the window, her hands clasped and her eyes closed as if she were praying. The letter was now lying in her lap.

"Because my nephew believes you are the best

investigator in the Czech kingdom. I know you are an honest knight and therefore I also hold you in high regard."

"My dear abbess... older sister... forgive me, I didn't mean to address you so," Oldrich apologized. He needed to buy time, because nothing Agnes was saying made any sense in relation to the events of the past few days. He decided he would talk openly with her.

"I am most gratified by your approval. But up until now you have treated me most dismissively, giving me the impression that you do not want me to accompany you on the pilgrimage."

She smiled, somewhat ruefully. "Not even the best investigator can know everything. And sometimes shouldn't know everything. Just before his death, Commendatore Jacob de Vries insisted that you not be allowed to accompany us to Compostela. I sharply rebuked him and insisted that you were coming. I have not given you this audience just to be dismissive of you, as you men enjoy complaining, rather to protect you."

"I could understand if there was some danger, to me and perhaps to you. Please, what is it that you fear?"

Agnes raised her clasped hands to her lips, still in a sign of prayer. She thought for a moment and nodded. "All right, you should know more. It's obvious that my hasty decision to leave on this pilgrimage has had many clever people wondering the reason for it. But it wasn't taken simply on a whim. In August of last year my teacher and beloved companion Clare of Assisi died. Prior to that, she had written me a letter asking me to immediately set out for Compostela. It is my Christian duty to fulfill the last wishes of a dying person. As fate would have it, someone waylaid the messenger and I did not receive the letter until nearly a year after her death."

"But she did not ask you to undertake the pilgrimage, did she?"

"You needn't concern yourself with the rest of the letter's contents! It concerns a spiritual mission," she answered sternly. A moment ago she was speaking openly, as if she wanted to confide in him. That now suddenly changed and she was again conducting herself in a haughty manner. Even though she was at the age considered old by her sex, her face still retained the unmistakable charm of the Přemyslid women.

"I believe the Pope himself visited Abbess Clare two days before her passing and confirmed the Rule of the Order of San Damiano," Oldrich began.

"To the immense joy of all the sisters in our order," Agnes readily confirmed. "The mother superiors of all the convents governed by these rules shall soon meet. Clare had designated her order as Damianite in honor of the Church of St. Damian, where she and her sisters lived. We would like to change that now and call ourselves Clarites in her honor. And we would like the Pope to canonize her. To a certain degree my pilgrimage is connected to that end."

"Is that why Pope Innocent provided you with special protection for the period of the pilgrimage?"

"There is one matter you have not been precisely informed about," Agnes mentioned dolefully. "The Pope did indeed rush to Clare at Assisi. He approved her rule for the monastic life, but she could not rejoice in her earthly life, for she was already gone by the time the Holy Father reached her bedside. The problem was she wanted to give him a certain relic. It was very important to her that her part of the agreement be fulfilled, so she asked me to do it for her. This relic is supposed to be in Compostela or nearby."

"Are you saying the Pope approved the rule for her order of high poverty in exchange for this relic?"

"I didn't say that," she snapped. "I only said that Clare had promised the Pope something before her death and wanted it to be fulfilled. Nothing more. Don't be so impudent!"

"My apologies for being presumptuous, but I can at least presume that it was behind the murder of the men in Prague who were supposed to accompany you. And now the legate has been murdered during the night, also on account of this relic."

"You could very well be right. But I again repeat this is a high church matter."

"And it could be that the murderer is someone in high church circles because no one else would know about the connection to Clare of Assisi. And it would also have no value to anyone else."

Agnes was now glowering at him, but during her

long life she had learned to always proceed pragmatically. Since she had resolved to let Oldrich in on part of her secret, she couldn't just throw him out in the hallway. First, there would be nothing to gain from it, and second, he was probably right. Moreover, he was the only one who knew about the message from the King of Castile. She not only needed him to keep quiet about it, but suspected that her life would indeed be in danger over the coming weeks.

"Jost of Landstein conveyed to me his suspicion that the Premonstratensian friar killed the papal legate," she said calmly and grew silent. She looked at Oldrich as if inviting him to pick up the thread and the procurator gladly obliged.

"And did he tell you about my doubts? I don't believe the monk did it. Certainly not in connection with the matters we are speaking about. He wasn't even in Prague last month."

"No, he said nothing about your doubts. But since you have spoken about criminals in church circles, do you have anyone in particular in mind?"

"Broadly speaking, yes, but for now I have too little evidence to charge anyone. We can presume, however, that the person who committed the murders in Prague is also our murderer here in Landstein."

"Your reasoning is theoretically sound, Sir Procurator, but it has a basic weakness. The prelates who journeyed with me are above suspicion. The Vysehrad provost Wilibald Odo has been my confessor for many years. He has no reason to kill. Then there is his librarian. A chapter monk of no importance. And I am willing to swear on my soul for the innocence of the last of them, brother Gregory. The other monks, whether the local chaplain or that unfortunate Premonstratensian, were not in Prague, as you mentioned."

"May I ask what you are suggesting?"

"That there is more than one murderer. Certain circles have various people to protect their interests."

"Whose interests? The Pope in Rome?"

"Nonsense! Ach, if only you knew more," she sighed like a mother chastising a dull-witted child. "There's nothing more I can tell you. No, trust me. These murders are not being guided by the hand of Rome. Not in this case." She lowered her head and was silent. Clutching her palms, she at last decided to unburden herself.

"Sir Procurator, it is the Templars I suspect! And I have my reasons for it."

"That also occurred to me, but it doesn't explain who would kill their commendatore in Prague." Up until that point, everything between him and the abbess had been about religion. Now he could see she was quite capable of discussing worldly matters as well. A true Přemyslid.

"Did you see the body of Jacob de Vries? I didn't. The Templars had it removed to their commandery immediately after it was discovered. Apparently his face had been beaten to a pulp. Maybe it was the commendatore, maybe it wasn't. When he and I had that argument about you, I told him in no uncertain terms that I would not listen to him any further on the matter. Perhaps he decided to look for other means to get his way. A dead enemy always gets his way in the end!"

"Were you not by chance an investigator or judge in your youth?" Oldrich flattered her and bowed. Naturally he thought the same thing when he was told of the condition of the commendatore's body. Unfortunately he was not able to learn more from the head of the military unit, Prech of Michalovice. He had therefore dismissed the hypothesis about the true identity of the body. Too convoluted for the time being.

The abbess returned his compliment with a wry smile in her otherwise serious and pale face. Perhaps Ota was right about one thing. She was both a saint and a woman. "Whatever happened to the commendatore, doesn't explain who committed the murder here at Landstein? I again have to repeat that brother Hyacinth did not do it."

"Why shouldn't the Templars have their own little helper here?" she noted heatedly. "I have in fact taken on the robes of an investigator lately and have come up with two hypotheses. Peter of Rosenberg has been secretly trying to join the Knights Templar. Jost of Landstein fought in the Holy Land and spent some time in Acre, the seat of the Templar Grandmaster. And last night the papal legate had a visit from Jana of Blatna. That poor child is the ugliest of the maidens in our company. It's hard to imagine any rendezvous had to do with sins of the flesh. Do not underestimate the good taste of prelates! They look at women the same as other men, if more reverently. But I will offer another explanation. Jana's father is a trusted friend of the Grandmaster of the Knights Hospitaller, who resides not far from their seat in Strakonice. What if both orders are helping each other? Women can kill just as easily as men. And not only Jana of Blatna. There are plenty of servants working here in the castle. No doubt a few of them are willing to kill their own mothers for a bit of money. So why not the papal legate?"

"You still say papal legate," Oldrich observed almost as an aside. He didn't have to say more. As if on cue, Agnes continued: "Of course, you already know that the dead man is not Cardinal Tiberius of Mantova. The Holy Father had informed me about the ruse, even though I have no idea why he decided on this course. That person, whoever he was, was a very important figure. In the Roman curia, he was the cardinal charged with defending the faith. Perhaps he went under an assumed name because he had many enemies. It seems he was one of the clerics responsible for the initiation of the Inquisition."

CHAPTER IX

After lunch Ota appeared in Oldrich's chamber tugging Wolf, the Landstein chaplain, by the hem of his frock.

"I have him, the villain," he declared. Ota's riding boots were caked in mud, so too was the chaplain from head to toe, and his face had a fresh, bloody gash on it. His hands were bound by rope and a cloth stuck in his mouth. Pointing to the gag, Ota explained that the chaplain kept voicing his disgust so loudly that he felt compelled to shut him up.

"Better then leave it in while you tell me what happened," said Oldrich.

His interrogations had ended only a moment ago and he was in the process of writing up his remarks. The only interview worth notice had been with Agnes, but even that one was hardly satisfactory. Given the circumstances, he could understand her refusal to explain many things or else offer him only vague hints. But he had the sneaking suspicion that she was not being entirely truthful with him. Perhaps she was hoping to lead him in a direction of her own choosing.

In particular, he found her insinuations against the Templars not very credible. Was he supposed to believe that the entire order would stake itself on a crime committed by one of its own? On the other hand, he had the feeling that the abbess was determined to protect the reputation of the Roman curia at all costs. The only thing clear so far was that a church secret was involved. And it was always difficult dealing with the church. They could be terribly secretive about the most trifling matters, and yet harbored other secrets so terrifying that just thinking about them made the flesh crawl.

Examining the remaining members of the nobility turned out to be a waste of time. None of them wanted to get involved in a case involving the murder of a papal legate. As such, all of them claimed to have seen nothing, to have remembered nothing. Peter of Rosenberg even denied arguing with the legate while on the hunt the day before. He insisted they had merely been talking in loud voices about nothing in particular.

The only examination of value came from the noble maidens. They had forced brother Hyacinth to sing for them in the Great Hall, delighting in his discomfort and tormenting the poor fellow all the way back to the forecastle. They even accompanied him as far as his bed. Oldrich naturally asked the guard at the second gate whether the monk had returned to the palace during the night and he emphatically denied it. That alone proved that he did not murder the papal official.

The killer had to be someone who was moving about in the palace after twilight.

"So, Ota, what did the chaplain do?" Oldrich asked his squire.

"Well, I was thinking about the legate's missing money," Ota began, clearly proud of what he was about to say. "You said it had to be more than what you found in the monk's pouch, so it occurred to me that the person who stole it was probably the one who entered the dead man's chamber first. Of course, there was no time to haul it all away, and what's more he could run into somebody in the palace. There was only one thing to do with the other pouches. Throw them out the window! Like all dry moats, the one here is full of rubbish. Nobody would notice several small leather pouches among it."

"Just you, Ota," smiled Oldrich. How great it was to have such a smart and reliable aide by his side. Only a fool surrounded himself with fools in order to shine. He knew plenty of crown officials who subscribed to this approach, including the Bishop of Prague.

"I went to look right after mass and found them there. The guards told me that they walk through the moat every afternoon on their watch, so that meant the thief had to hurry. I hid myself in an alcove and waited. The chaplain here eventually comes for it and I nab him. He confessed to throwing the pouches out the window after finding them on the legate's body. He then rushed into the chapel with the news of the murder."

Oldrich stroked his beard and thought for a moment. Another suspicion was bothering him. Burgrave Vilem had helped him out many times at court, and even though he had tried to marry him off to his daughter Svetlana, he was an honest knight. It pained him to think he would be in danger of losing his Landstein dominions all on account of the stupidity of his son Jost. But he was the procurator and justice had to be meted out equally, to the Prague burgrave, the Premonstratensian monk, the castle chaplain, to Oldrich of Chlum. And of course to the victim.

He turned to Wolf and removed his gag: "Do you admit it? Is everything as my squire says it is?"

The chaplain hung his head and quietly nodded. There were tears in his eyes and his hands trembled from fear.

"But it's only part of the truth, isn't it?" Oldrich continued in a stern tone. "Now tell me about the one pouch that you didn't throw out the window!"

"How do you know about it?" the chaplain burst out in horror.

"It was rather peculiar that Jost knew right where to go after the murder. The right place to look. He led me from the legate's body straight to brother Hyacinth's belongings. That's where you hid that one pouch, isn't it?"

The chaplain cowered even more. He clasped his hands together, dropped to his knees and prayed through a hail of tears for God to forgive him.

* * *

"It's time to speak the truth about the murder," said Oldrich sharply. He was standing in the castle chapel, where he had summoned Jost and his sister Svetlana to join him. In the apse of the altar waited Chaplain Wolf, his head still hung low, being watched by Ota. A cross had been erected on the stone tabernacle, with one large candle burning on each side of it.

"My squire figured out what became of the legate's pouches and found them in the castle moat. He also figured out what became of the final pouch, the one you had placed in brother Hyacinth's belongings so you could accuse him of the murder," Oldrich continued in an official manner.

Svetlana glared at her brother but said nothing. Oldrich was surprised. He presumed she had nothing to do with the crime but nevertheless expected her to immediately and vehemently protest her innocence. She did nothing of the kind, only betrayed disappointment in her face. She kept her silence probably out of love for her brother.

Jost, on the other hand, lashed out, insisting he knew nothing about it and if the chaplain claimed otherwise, he was lying.

"A lie like that in the chapel will prey on your conscience," warned Oldrich. "How do you know it was Chaplain Wolf who threw the pouches from the window? His name didn't even come up. He's only standing at the altar because that's where he normally stands. You are a knight, Sir Jost, and should know when you have met your match!"

Svetlana turned red from the humiliation of it all. Her brother noticed it, bit his lip and turned away. He clenched the fist of one hand with the other and if they had not been in the chapel at that moment, he might have drawn his sword and hurled himself at the procurator. He had lost all sense of self-control.

"My office is satisfied that you and your chaplain are guilty," Oldrich continued in a firm voice. "This afternoon I shall publicly exonerate brother Hyacinth of any suspicion of murder. And now I want the truth! Remember, we are standing before an altar. Who killed the papal legate? Did you, Sir Jost?"

"How dare you? In my castle! I am lord here!" shouted Jost almost hysterically. He turned around and stormed out.

"He always was a hothead," Svetlana said softly as she restrained Oldrich, who had started after her brother. There were tears in her eyes. "He's done a terrible thing. I'm sorry on account of him. A true knight should not behave so. Only most knights do today. They, the church, the King. The ends justify the means. I don't mean to make excuses, but that's how our fathers taught us to behave. Please don't think badly of him. I know him; he's not wicked. He only meant to protect our father and his domains. Is that so terrible? But I swear he did not kill the legate."

"Let's talk about it then," Oldrich nodded and with

his head gestured to Ota to take the chaplain elsewhere. Once they were alone, they sat down on a low pew placed against the back wall and next to the stairs leading to the tribune.

"We are in the house of God, Svetlana, and you say you can swear on the innocence of your brother. At least in the matter of the murder. I believe you. Now, what do you know about it?"

"I wouldn't say anything under normal circumstances, but now I must. First, I would like you to swear, in the house of God, that you will never tell anyone what I am about to tell you! Don't worry; it's no trick on my part."

Oldrich briefly looked her in the face and quietly promised to keep it to himself.

"Very well," Svetlana nodded and began rubbing her chin in the same fashion as he was wont to do. If the situation weren't so serious, he would've broken out laughing. King Ottokar had charged Svetlana to help with the investigation and here she was unwittingly assuming the mannerisms of the investigator.

"Last night I visited the legate in his sleeping quarters," began Svetlana with a sigh. "My intention was to examine him. As a woman, I have certain advantages over you in certain situations. You send your squire to examine women with the same thinking in mind. Why should you hold back from sending me? And since the legate made indecent overtures to Zdena Berkova during the hunt, I knew my chances were good to learn something from him. I am, in my own humble opinion, prettier than she is, don't you think?"

"We are in the house of God. Don't ask such questions here!" he shrugged her off. Of course, she was right, but he knew that confirming a woman's humble opinion about herself was akin to opening the gates to the enemy.

"Never mind," smiled Svetlana. "I'll wait until we are in a more appropriate place to ask you again. I'm not mentioning it to force you into something. Don't worry. I was only reminded of it by way of explaining what happened in his sleeping quarters. Or rather what didn't happen, to be more precise. The papal legate acted very cold towards me. Did not show the slightest intention of becoming familiar with me. You can understand how displeased I was."

Oldrich nodded. That was another mystery of the Christian world. Astronomers were able to determine the movement of planets and create a calendar based on them, even though it seemed practically impossible. But not even the greatest mathematician in the world could give a reasonable accounting of the way women thought. Time and again he was amazed by them, and none was more capable than Svetlana.

"At least he was willing to talk to me," she continued, unknowingly engaging in the utterly feminine gesture of making sure her short blond hair was in order. "I informed him at the start that I was not too familiar with theology and so did not come there to argue liturgy or the Inquisition with him. I said I was only there on account of the pilgrimage to Compostela, because I was leading a company of noble maidens and felt responsible for them. I simply wanted him to tell me something about the pilgrimage. Mostly about the difficulties that await us."

"I suppose he told you to learn the right prayers and study the work of Isidore of Seville," said Oldrich, recalling his recent conversation with the gaunt librarian of the Vysehrad chapter.

"How did you know?" she asked surprised, but then returned to her story. "Finally he gave me a bit of useful advice."

Oldrich discerned irony in her voice and wondered what bit of advice an important member of the Roman curia could have for an entourage of young women.

"We should wear comfortable riding boots for one thing. He also recommended we wear short pants underneath our skirts while in the mountains. To prevent a pilgrim from catching a glimpse of us should the wind happen to lift up our skirts while we are climbing a steep slope. Imagine that, short pants! He said we should wash sometimes during the journey, but when one of us is in the water, the others should stand watch on the bank to make sure some man doesn't appear out of nowhere. He emphatically warned us not to sing, dance, laugh or talk with young men. We're also not supposed to talk with men who look lustful. So as you can see, I know exactly how to behave during the pilgrimage."

"Amusing, but what does any of this have to do with your brother?"

"I was there quite a long time. When I finally left, I caught a glimpse of Jana of Blatna tiptoeing along the wall and sneaking into my brother's chamber."

"According to Abbess Agnes, she visited the legate."

"That's what Jana made her believe. Agnes also caught her in the hallway, but didn't see which chamber she disappeared into. She couldn't really tell her that she went to see my brother," Svetlana patiently explained.

Oldrich remembered one more small detail that he had to mention. It was Agnes's opinion that Jana was the least lovely of the noble maidens. He didn't think so, nor did Svetlana. She immediately began to defend her.

"I don't mean any offense but how can a mother superior from a begging order, where the sisters all walk around dirty and in rags, know about feminine beauty? Abbess Agnes thinks only emaciated girls with no hips or breasts, who do not arouse a man's fancy, are beautiful. She said so herself. But the Lord himself endowed Jana with more than enough. Unlike me," she added dolefully, but Oldrich saw through her veil of humility.

Svetlana frowned when she realized she wasn't going to get any persuasion or comfort that one might expect from a knight. She lowered her eyes and looked at him inquisitively, and then all of a sudden she grinned and said, "You're as hard as stone. I suppose, though, because we're in the chapel."

"Not just in the chapel. You know me," he replied.

Svetlana sighed. "I know...back to the matter. In the morning I quietly observed my brother's chamber and saw Jana slipping out just after sunrise, before mass commenced. I made sure to ask Jana about it after the body of the legate was found. She swears she was with my brother the whole night and didn't leave him for one moment."

Despite his promise, Oldrich eventually told his squire everything in brief. He had learned that Ota's help was invaluable during an investigation only when he knew everything. Otherwise they got nowhere with their search.

"So you see, my lord," said Ota, shaking his head as if outraged by the villainy inherent in mankind. "A Christian should especially avoid the sins of the flesh while on pilgrimage. But here, the nobility do it freely and I have to tighten my belt."

"And tighten it even further," Oldrich sternly warned him.

CHAPTER X

In the afternoon Oldrich of Chlum was summoned by Agnes of Bohemia. She was nervous and in no good mood at all.

"Tomorrow morning we are leaving Landstein," she announced brusquely. "That means everybody and everything must be ready to go. Spiritually as well. It will not do to imprison the chaplain in the dungeon because we will celebrate mass in the evening. I also heard that you plan to have him escorted to Prague to the diocesan court. Surely his trespass is not so great that he cannot join us on the pilgrimage to Compostela. On the contrary! A pilgrimage is meant to absolve one of sin. Release him and I shall speak to him."

"As the procurator, it is not my office to judge the means used to punish clergymen," he shrugged. "May I go?"

"No! There is also the matter of Jost of Landstein. He came to me to beg forgiveness and I find him most worthy of it! He honors his father and mother and only wanted to protect their estate, as the Ten

Commandments proclaim."

"Forgive me, venerable older sister, but the Ten Commandments also prohibit bearing false witness and..."

"Leave the interpretation of the Ten Commandments to those appointed by God. He did not murder the papal legate; we are all in agreement about that. I therefore do not wish that he repent before the others. The Premonstratensian friar will also not be imprisoned and will make the journey with us. The others know he is not guilty. I believe that should suffice!"

"It's a rather cavalier way of dealing with him."

"There is nothing cavalier about protecting the honor of a knight! My nephew the King warned me that you are an excellent investigator, but lack humility. He was right! I will pray that this pilgrimage opens your eyes and you come to realize that pride of intellect is a grievous sin. Faith, not erudition, is what a Christian honors most, Sir Procurator. I have already spoken with brother Hyacinth and he agrees. I therefore consider this entire matter closed."

Oldrich bowed, if ever so slightly, in acquiescence to her command, but he was still compelled to ask, "None of that addresses our basic problem. Who murdered the papal legate? Certainly the Pope will not be satisfied with the news that one of his cardinals is dead. Murdered in fact. He will want the guilty people punished. All we can be sure of is the murderer is among us. Moving about in our company and together with us on the pilgrimage to Compostela."

"So it is, unfortunately," she said stiffly. "God will watch over us and protect the faithful. I thank you for your efforts to find the murderer, but I forbid any further investigation during the pilgrimage! From this moment forward we shall all conduct ourselves as penitents. We shall pray and think only about Apostle James! I relieve you of the authority I granted to you in this matter."

"Is something wrong?" he asked anxiously. Such reversals didn't just happen.

"You shall henceforward concern yourself exclusively with the safety of our entourage of noble maidens. It was your original assignment for the pilgrimage, if I'm not mistaken."

"I'm afraid you are mistaken," Oldrich retorted. He was beginning to tire of this difficult woman. He understood that she was burdened by worries she did not know how to cope with, but why should that be his burden? Whatever game she was playing, she was doing it most unskillfully. Of course, she did not know how to proceed in such matters. She came from a royal family, was raised a princess sought after by the most distinguished husbands of the Christian world. But in the end she became the abbess of a convent founded by her brother King Wenceslaus. It provided her with no experience to guide her now. She was unquestionably clever and resolute, but also naïve to claim that her faith was enough to find the killer. She didn't have the slightest clue about the world of ordinary people, much less criminals.

"You are mistaken," he repeated. "Our majesty the King entrusted me with more than looking after the safety of the maidens. He explicitly ordered me to see to your protection. And that I will do whether it pleases you or not!" He bowed and headed for the door in a huff.

"One moment," she weakly commanded. She was not used to such defiance. "We have still not spoken about another important matter. Do not say any word about Clare of Assisi and the letter from the King of Castile! Now you may go!"

* * *

The entire company broke up immediately after the evening service. Normally it was the custom to celebrate such a long journey with a feast, only nobody was in the mood on this particular occasion. Ota brought a mug of hot mead to his master in his chamber and together they sat and discussed, as was their habit, their latest findings to see if they might be able to draw some conclusion. Only here, no matter which way they looked at it, everything came to a dead end.

"What we have here is a triangle," ruminated Oldrich. "Clare of Assisi, the Pope and possibly the Templars. Of course, their role in these crimes is not certain. Even if Abbess Agnes is convinced of it."

"More like she confirmed it," Ota reminded him.

"You yourself said she was incredulous, and her attempt to point suspicion at the Templars is in itself very suspicious."

"That's true. This case is not going to be easy at all. The person who killed the papal legate is not working in the interests of Holy See, and if it's not the Templars, it must be somebody else. But that's not important. Let's just keep them in one corner of the triangle for now. Time will tell."

"If it is indeed a triangle, I don't understand why to put Clare of Assisi in one of the corners," Ota asked politely. "She's dead. For more than a year now."

"Why? Because I'm courteous," Oldrich smiled. "We could easily put our venerable older sister Agnes in her corner instead. I'm not saying she's mixed up in these crimes. Definitely not! It's just that Clare turned to her before her death and she is acting in the interests of her departed companion. Or perhaps in the interests of their entire order of sisters of the most high poverty. You know how much she desires the Pope to approve her Rule and she is as much a founder of the order as Clare was. And all this about the letter from the dying Clare getting lost and not reaching her until over a year later strikes me as a fabrication. Do you know what persuaded me so?"

"The letter from King Alfonso of Castile," said Ota. "In it, he is clearly responding to a question she had sent him earlier. It's obvious from his answers that his officials were already investigating the case. Had Agnes received Clare's letter only two months ago as she claims, she could not have received an answer from Hispania so quickly."

"Correct. And if she declines to speak truthfully about such a seemingly insignificant detail, how can we be sure she's not trying to deceive us about something far more important? I think she is willing to lie in the name of her order and faith. And possibly...," Oldrich suddenly paused, quite surprised by how far he was venturing. It unnerved him, until finally he shook his head. "No, it's nonsense!"

"The abbess claims that Clare promised to give the Pope some relic. Supposedly the legate told Jost that when he left Rome, Pope Innocent was dying. Perhaps he's already dead as we speak. What if Agnes's departure for Compostela just now is somehow connected to the death of the Pope?"

"Quite intuitive," nodded Oldrich. "Let us suppose that Clare obtained documents that could discredit the Pope. She promises to return them and in return he officially approves her order. No, no, it's nonsense! What could be in such documents that could upset the Holy Father so much? From the things they say about the papacy, you can hardly discredit it even more. What's more, if the Pope approved the order of Clare of Assisi but did not receive that which he was promised, he could have canceled the order after her death. He could have declared it a heretical order and obtained the documents through the Inquisition."

"Assuming that the sisters in Assisi knew about them after Clare's death," Ota demurred. "But what if they don't know about them? Of course, Agnes of Bohemia does. They are hidden away in Compostela and that's why she's going there. If the Pope could not get them from Clare, then he will try from our Agnes. Perhaps he will also approve some monastic order for her. But it's all so suspicious. Nothing given in advance. Everything exchanged from hand to hand, like buyers in the market. So that's why we are in a rush and leaving in winter. Why else would Abbess Agnes have asked the King of Castile whether Clare had been to Compostela?"

"Never mind that this hypothesis is an outrage against the beloved aunt of our gracious monarch. It also lacks any logic. A lot of it," said Oldrich with a look of dejection. "Whatever the merit of our case is, it's probably lying hidden in Compostela. If Clare of Assisi owned something so important and compromising that it forced the Pope's hand in approving her order, she would surely make sure no one took it from her. She would never let it out of her sight, or, most probably, hid it personally, somewhere no one would look for it. Compostela is an ideal location. Of course, Clare visited it only once, and that was forty years ago. We can assume from that that the article was compromising for a pope long dead, not for today's pontiff. But it begs the question why Innocent would even care if it does not involve him? Even on his deathbed. It's absolute nonsense!"

"But what if this thing discredits not just one pope in particular, but the entire papacy?"

"There are scores of legal documents challenging the existence of the papacy and nobody cares about them. No, that's another wild goose chase."

"What about discrediting the whole of Christianity? The entire religion?"

"My dear Ota, we need to stand on firm ground here. What you're suggesting smacks of heresy! What could possibly discredit Christianity? That the Virgin Mary wasn't a virgin? Or Christ didn't rise from the dead and name St. Peter as his successor?" Oldrich immediately crossed himself. What he had just said, in the heat of the discussion, was incredible blasphemy. Although no avid believer, he never doubted the basic tenets of the religion. And as a judge, he knew that rules, order and procedure were based on indisputable facts. Justice was for law what dogma was for faith.

"Perhaps you are right," admitted Ota. "But what else could it be about?"

"You're forgetting the triangle we established as our working model. Now we are talking only about two points. We have hypothetically placed the Templars in the third corner but otherwise we haven't given them much thought."

"That's because we don't know anything about them."

"Exactly," yawned Oldrich. "And now we're talking so much nonsense that an inquisitor would gladly start rubbing his hands as he prepared a nice fire for us at the stake. Let's go to sleep."

He rose, drank the rest of the mead straight out of

the mug, unbuckled his sword and placed it on the trunk. At that moment there was a knock at the door, but before they could say anything, it opened to reveal Svetlana standing at the threshold. She took a quick look around the hallway before darting in and closing the door behind her.

"Can I speak to you?" she asked in a muffled voice.

"Should I sleep in the servants' quarters tonight?" Ota asked innocently.

This time it was Svetlana who snapped at him for being so foolish. "Can't you ever think of anything else? I don't even know what you're doing involved in this case. Why don't you go make yourself useful?" she upbraided him.

Ota retorted, in not the most affable terms, that he was able, unlike her, to investigate and still maintain a pleasant and agreeable disposition.

But Svetlana wasn't through. She sneered, "Really? So what do you know about Peter of Rosenberg?"

"Are you just coming from him? That's why you have your night garments on underneath your coat."

"Enough already!" ordered Oldrich, before they really got into a quarrel. "What is it, Svetlana? But be quick. I'm tired and want to go to bed."

"Peter of Rosenberg secretly left the castle a moment ago. But you're probably not aware of it because your squire is too busy noticing what I'm wearing under my coat. You would do better to have him watch what's going on in the palace! Fortunately I'm more mindful of these things."

Insulted, she turned to leave, but Oldrich grabbed her by the arm. "Wait. Ota didn't mean it. He will apologize to you."

Ota mumbled something to that effect. It was not comprehensible at all but Svetlana felt vindicated. She proudly began to tell what she knew: "I was lucky to catch young Rosenberg leaving. My brother was still awake at the time so I sent him after him. Jost can track anything and anybody down. A knight on horseback the easiest of all." She grew cross when she suddenly noticed the look of skepticism Oldrich gave his squire: "My brother really has atoned for what he did. And wants to help the same as I do."

"Does that mean I now have a third aide? Ota and you and now your brother?" Oldrich asked, wholly indifferent by this time.

"No, not at all," said Svetlana, fervently defending herself. "My brother wouldn't listen to you anyway. It was the King's wish that only I help you and Jost is helping me."

"Now there's a plan," waxed Oldrich enthusiastically. "What about you, Ota? Don't you want somebody helping you too? Perhaps Zdena Berkova? She might like to join our investigation as well."

"Why must you always belittle me?" Svetlana moaned and sat down on the edge of the bed. She put her hands in her lap and looked at the floor.

"Because I like you and Ota here and don't want anything to happen to you," he replied with a tinge of gentleness. "This is not a game here! There is still a murderer among us, here in the palace. What do you think he will do when he finds out that it's not just Ota and I looking for him, but now you and your brother are involved as well? What if you really discover something important and he discovers it? He would kill you in the wink of an eye. The more people who get involved in this investigation, the bigger the risk that the perpetrator will flee. That has been my experience. Numbers here are not an advantage."

Ota nodded in agreement, although he had never heard his master talk about any such experience. During a recent investigation in the Old Town part of Prague, he even heard him telling a local magistrate who had turned to him for help that the bigger the posse, the faster they could catch the criminal.

"I appreciate your help immensely, Svetlana, but I am responsible to the King for Agnes of Bohemia, and to your father for you! Before it was just a thrilling adventure. But that's over now! Here in the castle we have an advantage, but the perpetrator will have it once on the pilgrimage. We will not have these walls to protect us. We will be in a foreign land among strange people. Dozens of unexpected things can happen, which he can use against us. Or he can contrive them himself. Starting tomorrow our lives change. We are the ones who will have to be on guard. But I promise to keep you informed about the investigation. And as soon as I think it's safe, I will ask you for help. But you will undertake nothing by yourself. Promise me that!"

Svetlana hesitated for a moment, but then sighed and nodded. She didn't like to promise anything. She even wondered in her soul whether she would feel the same before the altar if she had to promise her husband to be faithful. Most definitely.

"Can I at least stay with you for a while?" she asked, trying to effect modesty. "I told my brother to immediately come here and tell you whatever he found out. I would like to be here for it." She noticed that his mug was empty. Before he could stop her, she grabbed it and ran out.

"Do you think, my lord, she took any of it to heart?" asked Ota.

"Certainly," nodded Oldrich. "But she'll keep her word for one, at the most two days. I was overstating the advantages of the perpetrator a bit, but it doesn't change the fact that this thing is getting hairy! But Svetlana was right about one thing. From this moment on, I forbid any more silly comments about love. We are on a pilgrimage. We should not be quarreling, which may or may not be a mortal sin, but in any case no more silly jesting. Is that clear?"

"Quite, my lord," Ota nodded most obligingly. "But just for clarity, what constitutes silly jesting? How to distinguish it from its clever brethren? And is clever jesting permitted about matters other than love?"

Before Oldrich could answer, in heat no doubt, Svetlana ran into the room, breathless, carrying several mugs of mead. Still at the threshold, she began explaining in whispered tones that Rosenberg had returned to the castle. From a window in the kitchen, she spied him passing through the gate, lit by torches, and noticed that he was wearing a new gray cloak over a tunic with a red cross drawn across the chest. Jost wasn't with him, but she expected him to appear at any moment.

Svetlana handed them each a mug and apologized for the mead inside not being warm. "So, what shall we drink to?" she asked.

"To your obedience," Oldrich proposed.

She glared at him but took a sip from her mug. In the hallway they heard brisk footsteps, followed by the arrival of Jost of Landstein. He bowed only slightly.

"You already know from my sister what she got me into here. Will this girl ever come to her senses?"

"That's not important! Did you find anything out?" Svetlana asked impatiently.

"Rosenberg left the gate and headed for the woods. He got as far as the first clearing, where two Knights Templars were waiting for him. He dismounted, walked up to them and knelt. They dressed him in a tunic with the Templar cross and handed him a sword. He kissed it, stood up and headed back to the castle. Not a single word passed between them. I stayed behind for a moment. The two Templars got on their horses and left. That was all. And now I'm going to bed, Svetlana!"

"What do you suppose it means?" Svetlana thought out loud, showing no intention of leaving.

"Your obedience," Oldrich repeated, picking up his mug and taking a sip.

She bit her lip but bowed in acquiescence. She stood up and left with her brother.

"Well, our triangle finally has its third point," Ota noted with satisfaction.

"Do you think so? If that were true, then I understand nothing. And the Christian world would be beautiful if it were logical. Only it usually isn't," Oldrich yawned and informed him that he was going to sleep.

CHAPTER XI

In the morning the company was greeted by a steady drizzle and cold wind blowing down from the mountains as it made ready to leave Landstein. Delivering a fiery speech about the pious importance of the pilgrimage, the Vysehrad provost Wilibald Odo got so carried away in his earnestness that he confused the names of the apostles, much to Oldrich's amusement. On the other hand, librarian Emmeram of Greifsfeld frowned the whole time, probably from his aching teeth.

Peter of Rosenberg appeared wearing the red cross of the Templars across his chest. He proudly told everyone around him that he had always wanted to become a knight of Christ, and now, just before the pilgrimage, God had answered his wish and he was admitted to the order. Oldrich asked him if he didn't by chance know who succeeded Jacob de Vries as the new Templar commendatore in the Czech province, but Rosenberg insisted he didn't.

"You probably don't know how it works when somebody becomes a Templar," he announced with an air of importance. "Everything, of course, is agreed to in advance. Contracts are signed, gifts to the order are arranged. But the actual ceremony takes place in silence. I had no opportunity to speak with the brothers, so I don't know. But you can be sure they will select a commendatore who will protect our interests with dignity."

"He looks good in his Templar tunic, doesn't he?" Jana of Blatna prodded Zdena Berkova, but she didn't answer. Yesterday on the chase it looked like Zdena was quite enamored with young Rosenberg. Now this! He had told her absolutely nothing about his intentions. If there was anyone in the church who obeyed the command for physical restraint, it was a member of the knightly orders. Zdena was seething. All the smiles and secret glances she doted on him over the past few days, and nothing. Absolutely nothing. She looked over her shoulder. Ota was on a horse next to Katherine of Gutstein, enjoying a friendly chat.

"Oh no," she mumbled to herself. "I must have a knight for this journey. Actually it wasn't so bad with Ota that night." She steered her steed towards them.

"Ota, can we talk for a moment?"

"Gladly," he smiled. "But later. Right now I'm talking to Katherine. I'll come looking for you when we finish." Zdena Berkova noticed Katherine beaming with a look of triumph. She reined in her horse and let them go ahead of her. She bit her lip and fumed, "I'll show you, you wench!"

Oldrich was riding next to Svetlana. Not that he wanted to, but somehow it ended up that way. "Does Rosenberg becoming a Templar mean anything for your search?" she asked curiously. She made sure to emphasize the word "your". Oldrich noticed it and grinned. Of course, that made Svetlana throw her head back in utter defiance. No, she had no intentions of being obedient for the rest of her life.

"It depends on what Rosenberg did or promised he would do in order to gain entrance into the order," he explained in a low voice. The entire expedition was riding two abreast and naturally he didn't want the others to hear what he was saying. "He didn't mention anything about his plans before then? You were here together in Landstein for several days."

"Not a word. But he did always seem to be siding with the prelates over the knights. No matter what we were discussing, he was constantly preaching that we should believe in Jesus and behave morally. I think he must believe with all his soul in his mission as a warrior for Christ."

"That, of course, can make him all the more dangerous," Oldrich pointed out, now in a whisper. "Should you ever become involved in another investigation, never forget that a person who commits a crime for money is never quite as dangerous as a fanatic who does it in the name of a higher calling."

"I'll remember that," she said. "Does this mean you might find some use for me in your work later on?"

"May I remind you that last night you reproached

my squire for always thinking about the same thing?"

"Excuse me?" she asked indignantly, her face somewhat flushed from embarrassment. "It's hardly the same thing."

"It is and it isn't," he shrugged. "I would only like to impart that apart from these unusual circumstances, I don't see us spending many days together in the future."

"What about nights?" she asked with an innocent look. "Investigations happen at night as well, don't they?"

"And may I, only for completeness, quote your brother Jost? When will this girl ever come to her senses?"

"Never!" she laughed out loud. Agnes of Bohemia, riding ahead of them, turned and glowered but said nothing.

Bringing up the rear of the expedition, snaking along the road in two long columns, were Wilibald Odo and Emmeram of Greifsfeld. The scrawny librarian turned out to be an excellent horseman despite all his complaints about becoming exhausted easily in the saddle. He was the type of person who simply complained, no matter what the occasion. Whenever they stopped to eat, he felt the food was either too meager or too much, never of such quantity that he might rub his belly and thank the Lord, adding, "I feel great."

"Keep your eyes open," Wilibald Odo ordered him under his breath. "The procurator claims that the murderer of the papal legate is among us."

"You fear, Brother Provost, that he may even harm us?" the librarian shrieked and quickly crossed himself.

"Silence, you fool! We must find the killer."

"So you can punish him?"

"Ach, you'll always be an idiot! Can't you see there's something to be gained here?" the provost sneered haughtily. "We must discreetly hear the confession of everyone here. Someone will surely say something. That's my experience." He then spurred his horse forward because the librarian was beginning to bore him.

"Your experience!" Emmeram scoffed. A moment later the Landstein chaplain rode up to join him. As a penitent, he was wearing a long white shirt over his garments with a rope tied in a noose hanging around his neck.

* * *

Despite the less than ideal weather, the party made rapid progress. The trade route, winding through deep forests and across hilltops and shallow valleys, was in good condition, and they were able to reach Gmünd early in the afternoon. The Lord of Kuenring was waiting for them at his castle. On top of the tower the banner of King Ottokar was fluttering in the wind, and the windows and entrance to the palace were decorated with garlands of dry flowers. Abbess Agnes all but ignored the faded ornaments.

"She didn't want to pass through here," Svetlana whispered to Oldrich. "But the King insisted that we stop. That's why we went through Landstein first. You probably know why Agnes has that look of disgust on her face."

"I heard something," he said none too excitedly. To him, adultery was as despicable as betraying the code of chivalry. But whenever he tried to discuss it with his squire, Ota would argue, "You can be unfaithful only if you choose your wife and you love each other. In the case of the King, he didn't choose Margaret Babenberg. His father arranged the wedding for him. The King is as young as you are, my lord, and the bride was about fifty. But the dowry was worth it. All of Austria. But it's surely no marriage based on love. It's a political deal, so it's only logical that Ottokar would quickly acquire a mistress. Why to judge him so? Do you know what they are whispering now? That it was his wife herself who put Agnes of Kuenring in his bed."

Whether it was true or not, Oldrich understood Agnes of Bohemia's misgivings. Agnes of Kuenring resided there in Gmünd and during the summer had given birth to an illegitimate son of the King, Mikulas. His first child. The king was as happy as a little boy himself. The dry flowers around the palace were the remains of the decorations put up for the baptism of the royal bastard.

Agnes of Kuenring was a slim girl with short red

hair. She resembled Svetlana a little, not only in appearance but also in character. She was independent, loathed manual labor, and acted like a mischievous child when on horseback. Because of her hair, cropped in the fashion of a page boy, she was given the nickname Palcerik.

She came to welcome them in the courtyard. Walking gracefully behind her was a plump wet nurse holding an infant wrapped in soft linen. Agnes of Kuenring showed no sign of having recently given birth. Agnes of Bohemia embraced her coldly and blessed the child with even colder hands. She then asked for her chamber, saying it had been quite a long journey and she was tired and needed to rest. She was after all an old woman. They would see each other at the evening service.

"It will be a short one today," her namesake announced amiably but firmly. "I am holding a banquet in honor of our son Mikulas. He is exactly ten weeks old today."

"I beg to differ. The mass will not be shortened. Praising our Lord is much more Christian than praising another bastard," Agnes the abbess sniffed.

"He is the son of the Czech king," Agnes the mistress retorted stiffly. The two women seethed as they stood facing each other. The small slender girl with short red hair, clad in flowing robes cut from blue-green brocade, and the tall, aging abbess in a black monastic habit. They could easily be mother and daughter.

"His illegitimate son!" replied the abbess icily.

"At his baptism our noble king publicly proclaimed him to be his son," said the consort, refusing to give in. She then assumed a hostile glare and added with undisguised irony, "Not every Czech king was conceived in the conjugal bed and they went on to rule! The blood of these bastards circulates in every Přemyslid. You and my son are no exception. Besides, I fear Queen Margaret is no longer capable of giving the King a son."

"What is that your concern?" hissed the abbess. "A woman who bears a child not conceived in the conjugal bed is worse than a whore. It says so in Scriptures."

"Really? Supposedly there are some sister-brides of Christ who have not abided by them. In fact..."

"Silence!" Agnes of Bohemia demanded, aghast by what she was hearing. "For the love of God, I beg you to be silent!"

Only now aware of what she was saying, Agnes of Kuenring closed her mouth and bowed. She then lifted her head and proclaimed in a sonorous voice, "With joy in my heart, I welcome the pilgrims to the tomb of Apostle James. Our venerable older sister Agnes of Bohemia will spend this evening in prayer while the rest of you I invite to a banquet in honor of the son of the Czech king!"

* * *

"There wasn't much Christian love and forgiveness in that, was there?" Ota observed. "It was more like a meeting between two enemies on the eve of battle."

"Very impolite enemies, you mean, because knights understand how to kill each other with grace and elegance," Svetlana pointed out. "I feel sorry for Palcerik. She loves the King and never wanted anything from him. Only his love, of course."

Oldrich disagreed with both of them. He had his own opinion about the King's extramarital excursion, but it wasn't important at the moment and no one cared anyway. There were many things he disagreed with in the Christian world, but knew he could never change them. Let the prelates preach morality; his job was to prosecute crimes. And to love one's king was no crime. But there was one point in the wrangling of the two women that intrigued him. "Did you hear what Palcerik said at the end of their argument? She looked the abbess in the eye and said nuns also have illegitimate children. She even had a name on her lips, but Agnes stopped her in time."

"She was probably thinking of sister Kveta, one of her nuns. She became pregnant and left the order. Supposedly the father was a Minorite monk," Svetlana explained.

Oldrich quietly nodded, even though he was not quite satisfied with that explanation. After Ota left, he asked Svetlana about her relationship with Agnes of Kuenring. He was interested in knowing whether they were close enough to ask her something in confidence.

"I think so," she answered. "We've known each other since we were girls because our castles are only a day's ride away. We've even worn the same hair since that time. But that's a long story. Why do you ask?"

"Could you ask her for the name of the nun she was about to reveal in the courtyard? I don't believe it was some insignificant sister from Prague. Didn't you notice how white Agnes became?"

"I could try, but the problem is I promised not to get involved in your investigation," she said, throwing her arms up in a pretense of frustration. "I said I would be obedient."

"What I'm asking has nothing to do with the investigation. I'm only encouraging you to have a chat with your childhood friend."

"Stop! Lying during a pilgrimage is a particularly serious sin!"

"Forget it then," he replied indifferently and bowed. He turned to leave.

"Never, never would I have you for a husband!" she fumed, but called out after him that she would try.

It still wasn't dusk outside when mass was quickly and quietly said inside the chapel. Afterward most of the party gathered in the Great Hall, leaving only Agnes of Bohemia to pray at the altar in the company of the Vysehrad provost, Friar Gregory and the new Knight Templar, Peter of Rosenberg.

Waiting for the rest in the Great Hall was not just a fabulous feast but also entertainment in the form of the famous minnesinger Ulrich von dem Türlin. Agnes of Kuenring was an attentive hostess and it would never occur to the uninformed observer that this merry band of people were Christian pilgrims on their way to Compostela. But the days of the first Christian pilgrims were long past. Penitents no longer made the journey barefoot, in a white shirt with a noose around the neck. Even Chaplain Wolf had forgone the ritual for the evening's festivities and was now dressed in secular clothes. The instructions given by the prelates on how to behave during the pilgrimage were more religious ideology than reality. All the talk about submission and humility was out the door the minute they left church. That went for commoners as well as the nobility.

Oldrich was bored by the courtly amusement. He knew that Ota could easily fulfill the social commitments for both of them, so he went off to sit next to a window in an alcove and ruminate.

"May I join you?" Emmeram asked in a slurry voice. His eyes shined with wine and he could barely stand up straight. Oldrich was curious about the argument he had with his superior earlier in the afternoon. They were shouting so much it was a wonder they didn't go for each other's throats. So he made room for him, saying that back in Prague he had promised they would have a real chat and now was their chance. As they clinked goblets, Oldrich asked offhandedly what the argument with Wilibald Odo was about.

"He's a conceited, uneducated fool," the librarian grumbled. "Don't you think there have been enough unfavorable signs already? God is warning us not to continue. When I tried to explain that to him, he mocked me. Can you believe that?"

"What signs are you talking about, brother librarian? The murder of the papal legate?"

"Not only that one. The other ones too."

"I don't know much about them because I wasn't in Prague," Oldrich humbly excused himself in an attempt to get him to talk more about them. "Were they also murders?"

"What do I know?" Emmeram muttered. "But one thing I can tell you: Whether these men died by another's hands or not, it was a warning from God. He's summoning home all those leading the pilgrimage. He didn't want our worthy older sister Agnes to leave Prague at all."

"What would bother our Lord so much about a pilgrimage undertaken by devout Christians?" asked Oldrich, now quite clearly interested. Since he had never considered the sequence of events in this light, he was curious to know what a prelate thought about them. He suspected a clergyman was behind the recent crimes, so an interpretation of the events from the viewpoint of faith might prove useful.

"It's not about a pilgrimage," Emmeram railed, finishing his goblet and taking another one from a servant wearing a leather doublet. "It's about St. James! It's obvious God does not want us to stand before his tomb."

"You are the greatest expert on his life that I know

of in the Czech kingdom," Oldrich bowed courteously. "You probably understand this problem much better than I do. Myself, I understand that every saint rejoices when pilgrims visit his final resting place. Why should Apostle James be bothered by us, a group of pilgrims from Bohemia?"

The Vysehrad librarian drank long from his goblet and hiccupped. He was quite drunk, but not so much that he wasn't aware of what he was saying. Pursing his lips, it was clear he was struggling with something inside. Suddenly he slammed his fist into the stone wall next to him and began spewing forth. "Do you know why we shouldn't go there? Because we're not going there to glorify him, but to disgrace him. The same that Clare of Assisi did long ago."

"Clare? How could a saintly virgin disgrace St. James?"

"Forget it," Emmeram hiccupped again. "James the apostle only encountered misunderstanding wherever he went. Did you ever study the Gospels?"

The last thing Oldrich needed now was a change in topic. He had to somehow compel Emmeram to get back to Clare of Assisi, so he answered, "Yes, I studied the Gospels. But I have no idea what you mean now."

"Every Christian knows there are four of them. Every Christian except our provost, of course! There's Matthew, Mark and Luke, which are very similar and contain roughly the same events. That's why we call them synoptic, because you can place them side-by-side and compare them. They also have the names of the twelve apostles in them and always in the second or third position you find James the Greater."

Emmeram lifted his goblet and again drank greedily from it. A trickle of wine ran down his chin because he was too drunk to press it fully to his lips. But he was still able to talk coherently.

"The Gospel of John is different in many details. Our church fathers teach that John used sources unknown to the other evangelists. But none have noticed the thing that worries me the most and it's why we shouldn't go to Compostela! John the evangelist names only some apostles and nowhere is there any mention of James at all. Isn't that strange?"

The librarian started wagging a finger in front of his face.

"Why isn't he mentioned? He was his brother, after all! One of the senior apostles. Why not a single word about his brother? I don't care if he had some other sources. James was his blood brother! There's something bad here, but nobody, nobody seems to notice it."

He stood up erect and tried to embrace Oldrich, who had to grab him to keep him from falling on the floor. Emmeram rested his head on Oldrich's shoulder and with tears in his eyes kept repeating, "Why didn't John mention his own brother? Why?"

Next he mumbled something unintelligible and fell asleep. Oldrich carefully propped the librarian up on the bench in the corner of the alcove and there he began to snore.

"I'll take care of him. We're sharing the same chamber," he was told by an unamused Wilibald Odo, who had appeared out of nowhere. Apparently the provost had had enough of the meditation in the chapel. He now picked up the librarian and tossed him over his shoulder like a sack of oats. He then headed towards the exit of the Great Hall, maliciously adding that here was a clear case that too much poking around in books was a waste of time. What good was it if it didn't teach a person how to drink?

CHAPTER XII

By morning the rain was coming down in torrents. The dreary and unpleasant weather was reflected in the mood of the pilgrims. Most of them had hangovers after last night's banquet, some with dark circles under their eyes, and Emmeram had wrapped a cloth soaked in cold water around his head. He looked for all the world like the Last Judgment was upon him.

Svetlana was among those with a hangover and she blamed Oldrich for it. "It's your fault! I did what you asked me to and tried to find out from Palcerik about the illegitimate children. I thought if I got her a little drunk, she would tell me more. What I found out is she knows how to drink more than me. I ended up falling asleep."

"Did she tell you anything at all?"

"Maybe. I just don't remember," she whined. "Don't talk to me right now!"

Abbess Agnes ordered everyone to prepare for departure. All the pilgrims were wearing a broad riding cape with a hood over their heads. The outfit was stitched out of thick serge cloth, forcing the water to drip off as if hitting a wall, thereby lowering the chances of somebody catching cold during the journey.

It took some time for Wilibald Odo and company commander Prech of Michalovice to assemble everyone in the Great Hall, where Palcerik was to officially say farewell to them. The soldiers meanwhile were waiting on horseback in the courtyard. It was then, before the servants had handed out goblets of hot wine, heavy with the aroma of precious spices, that a member of the armed retinue ran up to Prech.

"My lord, something terrible has happened. This morning Merry was missing from our sleeping quarters. At first we thought he got drunk and passed out somewhere. So we went to look for him and…"

"And what?" the commander barked.

"Is something wrong?" asked Abbess Agnes angrily. She was anxious to leave. Just being in the presence of her namesake made her irascible. "If he's asleep somewhere, let him be. He'll have to catch up with us later."

"He can't, venerable older sister," answered the soldier, politely bowing. "He's dead. Murdered. We found his body in a narrow gap between the palace and chapel, beyond the range of the courtyard. Someone stabbed him with either a knife or dagger. It must have happened during the evening or later at night. He's completely stiff. We found this in his hand," the soldier said showing them a brand new silver coin. "We found two more trampled in the mud."

"God punished him," Agnes of Bohemia declared implacably. "He should have stayed with us in the chapel after mass and devoted his time to contemplation. His death does not change our mission at all. He was probably playing dice with somebody; they argued because he was of course cheating. Let the castle bailiff investigate the murder. He should find out who did it with no problem. We will not delay our journey on account of it."

"As you wish," Prech said with a bow, but the moment they left the castle in Gmünd, he rode up alongside Oldrich. He quietly began expressing his concern that the noble Agnes was wrong. Merry never played dice. He was a penny pincher to the point of being stingy. If he lost even a copper piece, he would be a wreck for a week.

"But there's no denying the silver coin in his hand," Oldrich added. "Could it be that he saved up some money and somebody was out to rob him? Surely the other men in your company knew about his stinginess."

"I have another explanation," posited Prech in a low voice. "Merry was on watch in the palace at Landstein the night the papal legate was murdered. When we questioned him, he swore he saw nothing suspicious. But what if he did? He could have seen the murderer. Maybe started to blackmail him. He was greedy, remember. The murderer promised him some money in exchange for his silence. Last night he takes advantage of all the commotion and invites Merry to that empty place behind the palace. He gives him the money and as Merry starts to count it, he stabs him."

"Exemplary work," Oldrich praised him. "Please, say nothing about your suspicions to anyone."

"Haven't I been telling you I'm fed up with all these prelates?" the knight grumbled and rode on ahead.

The expedition was now moving along much more slowly. The long snake of riders had become so protracted that huge gaps were growing between them. Riding in the lead, Prech would stop now and then to give the company time to draw up ranks.

"What are you afraid of?" Agnes asked crossly. The rain was still coming down hard and the inclement weather was making her knees ache, which of course made her grumpier than usual. "Do you think brigands will waylay us here? Even without God's protection, I can't think of a safer region than this one."

"I'm not worried about brigands. I'm worried someone will get too far behind and end up lost. We're surrounded by deep woods," said Prech, defending his decision.

The decision whether to wait for the stragglers or not eventually led to a sharp argument between them. But the knight held his ground, which only made Agnes even more bad-tempered. The lousy mood was something shared by the entire expedition. The rain was incessant, a cold wind was blowing, and the way was so muddy that the riders had to take care their horses didn't slip or become bogged down. Most of the party felt drained after the sleepless night. Both knights and noble maidens were apt to close their eyes and drift off, so they had to do everything to stay alert in the saddle. Nobody felt like talking.

Ota caught up with his master. The road was now somewhat wider. They were able to ride side-by-side comfortably. "Have you ever considered, my lord, that indulgence can sometimes prove invaluable for the Christian world?" he began in all seriousness. His eyes, however, beamed with irony.

"Most of the people here would disagree with you today. The difference between them and me is I have to listen to such stupid observations all the time. So what's this latest one supposed to mean?"

"That people often lose control of themselves when they drink and have a good time. You can meet the real person once he's drunk a couple of goblets of wine. Last night's banquet turned out to be quite beneficial for our manhunt."

"The last I saw, you were orbiting exclusively around the noble maidens."

"Not entirely. Jost spent the whole time dancing with Jana of Blatna and Svetlana was drinking with Palcerik like two boozers in a village tavern. They were laughing over every little trifle and seemed to really enjoy themselves. At one point I overheard what they were giggling about, and you know what it was? Whether you or our exalted king is manlier. I was curious to see how it turned out."

"Can't you get to the point?"

"Of course. So, having taken your advice to heart, I was determined to avoid Zdena Berkova."

"There you go again. I did not advise you to avoid her in particular. I remember ordering you to tighten your belt when it came to the charms of the young girls in our retinue. No exceptions."

"I must have misunderstood you then," Ota apologized with feigned humility. "But it was thanks to this misunderstanding that I was forced to devote my attention to Katherine of Gutstein. She was the only one left available. That made Zdena so furious she stalked up to her and they proceeded to have a spat similar to the one between our venerable abbess and Palcerik in the courtyard."

"What about? With you, it's always like pulling teeth, and I'm in no mood for a long story in this downpour."

"Zdena let slip that on the night of the murder of the papal legate, she had also visited him in his chamber. Probably before Svetlana. Supposedly they arranged a rendezvous during the chase."

"And?"

"That's all. You wanted me to be brief."

"That's all? Indulgence has no value for Christian society, as you claim, because it already suffers from too many impoverished souls. You use too many words to put together long and difficult sentences without the benefit of any clever ideas. As the Bible says, let your words be as clear as the flame on Moses' staff. Now kindly flesh out your impoverished thoughts!"

"Zdena boasted that the legate tried to get intimate with her, forcing her to flee into the hallway where she ran into Peter of Rosenberg. She complained to him about the legate's improper conduct, and he declared he would go in there and protect her honor. I let her go on bragging in that vein, and once she left, found out the truth. Rosenberg didn't go to see the legate, so he obviously wasn't too concerned about the honor of Zdena Berkova. Katherine confirmed this, because he went to her instead to ask questions about life among the Templars. And now, to prevent any further criticism of my superfluous elaboration of events, I shall only add that Katherine's cousin also became a Templar not too long ago. That was news to me. She's told nobody about it yet."

"Good work, Ota."

"Glad you see it that way, my lord. Katherine thinks the same. We had a wonderful time together last night. We danced and she even let me kiss her hand. She said our exalted King did well when he entrusted the care of her and the noble maidens to us."

"Just to be clear, he entrusted them to me," Oldrich corrected him. He meant to look stern when he admonished him so, but couldn't quite pull it off. In the end he laughed and observed that Ota should not have been born the page of a Christian knight, rather a wealthy Muslim with a huge harem.

"Not for anything in the world," Ota insisted, crossing himself. "A Muslim? I could tolerate Mohammed's faith, but ten wives? Never!"

Lunch was in the woods under a large elm. They ate the potato pancakes, cheese and fruit prepared for them at Gmünd. The rain had stopped, but the cold wind continued to blow. Their progress was much quicker in the afternoon.

There was still plenty of daylight left when they reached the Danube. As they proceeded along the rocky bank, they could see the majestic castle of Melk looming large against the gray sky ahead.

It had been built by Leopold Babenberg, whose descendents grew dissatisfied with it and moved the seat of the Eastern March to Vienna. They gave the castle to the Benedictine order, which turned it into a monastery. Of course, it was a very unusual monastery given that the monks, unlike their other brethren, were living in a castle, in circumstances that made it difficult to abide by the strict code of the monastic rule.

Before Melk came into sight, Agnes blissfully announced they were going to spend the night in a monastery, where each pilgrim could contemplate the devout purpose of their journey. Those who had sinned the night before were recommended to do their penance, their meditation, in the church.

The way along the river was unpleasantly cold, but they made good progress and in no time had arrived before the huge gates of the Benedictine monastery.

The castle palace was decorated with garlands of fresh flowers, and servants were anxiously moving about in the courtyard. A smiling abbot came out to meet them. He rejoiced in the fortune that had brought them the unexpected visit of the venerable and renowned older sister Agnes.

"We are extremely pleased to have you and your pilgrims with us today," he said beaming from one corner of his mouth to the other. "Tonight we shall have only a short vespers because I would like to invite you to a banquet. Tomorrow is the thirteenth of October and we are celebrating the feast day of Saint Coloman, the principal patron of our monastery. You will see that when it comes to a feast, the Benedictines in no way lag behind our exalted knights here. Already plenty of the nobility from the surroundings have arrived. I have also invited a most superb minnesinger to entertain us. I believe, older sister, that you will be quite amused."

"I am not passing through here to be amused," she replied, definitely unamused. "In case you haven't noticed, Brother Abbot, I am on a pilgrimage."

"Are pilgrims not allowed to celebrate vigil feast days of important saints and martyrs? If I'm not mistaken, Pope Honorius even recommends such religious gatherings while on pilgrimage. And I must say, older sister, I would be very offended if you claim that our patron St. Coloman is not an important saint. Certainly he deserves a feast, don't you think?"

Agnes reluctantly agreed. "With faith in your piety,

Brother Abbot, I trust the feast will be modest given that it's taking place in a monastery."

"But of course, older sister," the abbot sagely nodded. "And whoever thinks our modest hospitality is much too generous may gladly forgo it. The rule of our order is every Christian must know his limits." He then blessed everyone with a dignified sign of the cross and left for the kitchen to oversee the preparations.

"I like this man," Ota whispered to Svetlana.

"I only hope I don't have to question him like I did last night. I would bet that this pious abbot could take a flagon of wine and drink even Palcerik under the table."

* * *

Oldrich paid a visit to the cloister library, famous throughout the land, before dinner. Although it had nothing to do with Clare of Assisi, he still couldn't stop thinking about what the drunk Emmeram had told him the evening before. He was well familiar with all the Gospels, but it never occurred to him to find out which apostles appear in them and which didn't. He had always accepted the Gospels in the spirit of church teachings, much the same as the news about redemption through Jesus Christ. He never considered them to be historic chronicles that described actual events.

He asked Emmeram if he wanted to accompany

him, but the librarian declined, his voice barely audible. The minute he dismounted in the courtyard he went straight to sleep in his chamber, which he shared with his provost.

"Of course, we have several copies of the Gospels here," the obliging local librarian explained. "I can even offer you a magnificent manuscript illuminated by brother Heribert of Graz. It is worth a look, believe me. He had a fantastic imagination. You will be amazed, noble sir, when you see his depiction of the Revelation of St. John." Apparently the librarian wasn't too interested in the preparations underway for the evening's feast.

Oldrich was indeed impressed with the illuminations in the manuscripts. He eagerly leafed through the thick book bound in whitened deerskin. The text had gilded edges with blue and red borders. It was a splendid book, but the illumination of the Revelation of St. John did not captivate Oldrich in any special way. On the other hand, the Resurrection of Jesus Christ was quite unusual. Kneeling at the side of the coffin, over which Jesus Christ was depicted, was a figure in a Roman toga identified in the small print as Pontius Pilate. In no other Gospel was he present at this miracle.

Oldrich continued to leaf through the manuscripts until nightfall, making notes on parchment as he went. He was so caught up in comparing the texts, as if it was a chronicle after all, that the librarian had to remind him that the feast was about to begin.

"And the mass?" he asked distractedly, closing the book.

"That we already missed, noble sir," the librarian good-naturedly reported. "But we shouldn't miss the feast. Was our library able to help you in your search?"

"Immeasurably," Oldrich politely bowed. "I envy you for the treasures in your care."

He waited for the ink to dry on his parchment, then rolled it up and hid it away. He had written down a lot, but there was one particular note that left him more unsettled than the information given to him by Emmeram. In the Gospel of John, Jesus Christ was crucified on a Thursday and not on Good Friday, as the other Gospels claimed. John also makes no reference to Jesus' Sermon on the Mount of Olives, and nowhere is his brother James mentioned at all.

"Just one more question, brother librarian," said Oldrich as he was leaving. "The illuminator, what was his name...Heribert of Graz, correct? Had he ever been to the Holy Land?"

"Of course," replied the librarian, much pleased by his curiosity. "That's why his illuminations look so lifelike. In fact, the Temple in Jerusalem is supposed to look exactly the way he illustrated it. You know that before he joined our order he was a servant of the Knights Templar."

CHAPTER XIII

In the morning the entourage of Agnes of Bohemia boarded a large boat lent to them by the abbot of Melk, who claimed they would need a miracle to find any other boat anywhere because most of them had already been put away for winter. Fortunately, the monastery's boat was still tied up on the river. Their party was now joined by two Benedictine monks who had experience with navigating on the Danube. They insisted no pilot was necessary, that they could manage it alone. Once the pilgrims were ashore at Sigmaringen, two men would hire the craft and sail it back to Melk.

The soldiers exchanged their horses for oars and the party settled in on the hard planks for the ride. The rear of the boat was covered with a flimsy canvas that nevertheless provided some protection against the wind and rain. Space on board was very limited, so the knights and maidens had to sit packed in like sardines. They tried not to get in the way of the soldiers, who needed a lot of room to maneuver the oars. Although this part of the Danube was wide and the current not too strong, the going was nevertheless slow. The relentless rain created endlessly intertwined circles on the murky surface, giving it the appearance of chain mail. As the day grew warmer, a whitish mist rose from the river, at times so thick that it hid the shore from view.

Ota sulked off to sit by himself near the bow, wearing a wide brown hat that he had bought in the market in Gmünd. He wrapped himself up in his cloak so as not to get wet and quietly observed the boat as it plowed through the water. He felt dejected, although he wasn't quite sure why. The only thing for sure was he was decidedly unhappy with the course of this bizarre investigation, if it could even be called that.

Then there was the courtly romance of noble maidens, which struck him as being just as dumb as the investigation. It was courtly love that was neither courtly nor love. Like the rest of this pilgrimage, nothing was going the way it should. As much as Oldrich of Chlum tried not to show it, Ota could see he felt the same way and so understood why he was in a sour mood all the time. But whatever his master thought about the journey to Compostela, there was still the danger that something could happen to Abbess Agnes, and he would have to answer for it. But how was he supposed to protect her if she didn't make it any easier for him to?

"May I?" he heard a soft girlish voice ask behind him. He didn't have to turn around to know it was Zdena Berkova, but her voice was lacking its usual spitefulness. It sounded tender and, as could be expected, tired. The abbot wasn't lying. The feast had been a fabulous occasion, with many guests still singing and laughing in the refectory as he saw the pilgrims off in the morning.

Ota moved over to make room for her. She nudged up to him in a bid for warmth and he obliged by opening up his cape and drawing her close underneath it.

"Why did you just take off?" she quietly asked, looking at the river. She didn't have to elaborate more.

"We didn't make any promises," he replied sullenly. He knew that "the talk" was finally upon him. Her timing was impeccable. He had no chance to escape.

"Do you have any idea how I felt? Like a girl from a brothel. You took what you wanted and disappeared."

"You're wrong. A girl in a brothel does it for money, but you wanted it as much as I did. No one forced you to! I promised you nothing, not then or afterward."

"I was curious to see what kind of lover you are, that's all," she admitted with a blush.

"There you are, and that's the way it is," he nodded and furrowed his forehead like a wise man dispensing wisdom. "If I was to write some poetic nonsense like the minnesingers do, I would serenade that you were curious about the body but had completely missed the heart."

"That sounds terrible," she sighed. Both were quiet for a moment. Then, grabbing his hand, she lowered her voice. "I swear on my soul, your heart is safe with me. But I don't want to be alone on such a long pilgrimage. I admit that I'm spoiled and perhaps selfish too, but I have the right to have a knight by my side to protect me. And to tell me something nice now and then and comfort me when I'm sad. It's not a sin or anything bad. I was a fool to think that after you came to Landstein, Rosenberg would be my knight on this journey. That's why I was so unpleasant to you. How was I to know that blockhead was planning to become a monk?"

"A knight who takes the cross is not a monk."

"Still good for nothing," she retorted. "Do you know how embarrassed I feel now? I've never forced myself on anyone. I don't want much. Just to spend some time with you, that's all. Like now." She gave him the faintest of smiles, then rested her head on his shoulder. They sat quietly next to each other, watching the fog above the muddy surface of the Danube drift by their boat.

Ota was even crankier than in the morning. So many things bothering him and now he had to deal with this. It didn't matter whether Zdena was serious or just cleverly dissembling. He couldn't refuse her in any case. He was from North Bohemia, where there was an unwritten rule to help one's neighbors. Just as his master felt responsible for Svetlana on account of the most powerful member of the nobility, so he felt the same for Zdena because he knew her parents and respected them. He made up his mind quickly. He would look after her only in matters of honor and in all propriety. As a knight. He put his arm around her shoulders and she snuggled up to him. Ota noticed how her breathing became soft and almost purr-like. She fell asleep.

* * *

To have even the appearance of privacy on a pilgrimage was difficult, but on such a small craft was quite impossible. The highborn members of society were sitting clustered under a canvas and whatever one of them said, the others heard it and answered at the same time. Prior to departure, Prech brought two skins of sweet, but diluted wine on board. They were drinking it now from one goblet, passed around from hand to hand.

"At least two knights named by our most illustrious majesty to command this expedition were murdered in Prague, venerable older sister," began Emmeram.

"And the papal legate was murdered in father's castle," Jost continued. Sitting next to him was Jana, who decided she would claim him for warmth and protection after watching Zdena cuddling up to Ota on the bow.

"Nor can you deny the unease we feel over the murder of one of our soldiers," added Prech.

Agnes was perched on a low stool in the middle, dwarfed by the other pilgrims sitting around her on the benches that ran along the sides of the stern. She was nearly imperceptible among them, but it was the only place where water didn't drip down from the canvas overhead.

"You're all conspiring against me!" she raged. "Death is a part of life. Our lives are in the hands of God and he may summon us at any time. That's why we should live our earthly lives in anticipation of that moment; to abstain from sin, especially on a pilgrimage!"

"You're avoiding the subject," Oldrich spoke up. He was in agreement about nothing with the others, but this particular conversation suited him just fine. "God in his mercy gives us different signs to express his will. Don't all of these deaths add up to some kind of divine warning?"

"If they are indeed a sign from God, then it can only mean one thing: the Lord is testing the firmness of our faith," she replied firmly. "He is telling us not to succumb to doubt. Every Christian should be ready to give his life for Jesus at any time, for then he shall be saved. That is why Jesus died on the cross and rose from the dead. To show us that life on earth is only the beginning of eternal life. Yes, God gives us signs and says only the righteous shall find a home in the kingdom of heaven."

"But there are also divine signs that warn us believers," the Minorite monk chimed in out of the blue. Brother Gregory was a taciturn man. He didn't shun conversation but only rarely had something to add to it. He mostly sat next to Hyacinth, comparing notes as it were on the comings and goings around them. He had gleaming eyes with sharp, deep wrinkles around his mouth. "How can you be so sure, venerable older sister, that God is not warning us?"

"What reason would he have?" Agnes snapped.

"Probably because there is a murderer among us, and God doesn't want his feet to desecrate the holy ground where his beloved apostle James is resting," the Minorite said softly. "Didn't you notice during the mass at Landstein how one of the altar candles blew out? Or the body of the dead bird lying in the road as we left Gmünd? Are these not clear signs?"

Hunched over, Agnes cried out, "What do you want me to do?" There was no missing the hysteria creeping into her voice.

"We should go back! In Prague we will purify our souls with humble prayer and contrite confession. Once the murderer is found, we will set off again for Compostela. Purified before God," Wilibald Odo duly proposed.

"And in better weather," added Prech, hopefully.

"No!" Agnes shrieked with tears in her eyes. She was shivering now, as if a fever brought on by the recent cold weather had gripped her.

"Perhaps there's another solution that would please the Lord," said Svetlana. She slid off the bench and knelt on the deck next to Agnes, holding one of her trembling hands. "If the procurator finds the murderer and we hand him over to the court for punishment, it will be the same as if we returned to Prague. We will prevent the criminal from stepping on holy ground and will please the Lord with our piety."

"You are a good girl," Agnes said wearily, raising her hand and placing it on Svetlana's head in the manner of baptizing a child. It was clear from her pursed lips that she was weighing the best way open to her.

"With your agreement, venerable older sister, I would prefer to take over the investigation myself," Wilibald Odo grandly proposed. "I can humbly inform you that I have some experience in these matters. I'm on the King's council and am the highest ranking member of his Majesty's court from among all those accompanying you. And if it happens that the criminal is somehow connected to our holy Church, which my pious soul, of course, fervently doubts, then as a prelate I have the right to be involved. And don't forget that I'm also your confessor!"

Oldrich noticed the derisive but at the same time appalled look on the face of Emmeram, who turned to him and shook his head as if to proclaim that it would be the worst thing that could possibly happen to everyone during the pilgrimage.

"I certainly don't want to interfere in your decision, venerable older sister Agnes," said Prech with firm resolve. "But Sir Oldrich of Chlum was the only one able to prove the murder of Dobrej, the King's judge. Unlike the venerable Vysehrad provost here, who, despite his undeniable experience, protected the actual murderer up until the very last moment. From ignorance, no doubt."

"That's none of your business!" Wilibald Odo sharply rebuked him. "You would do better to worry about your men. Three of them were missing from mass this morning. That should be your concern, not to mention ordering them to row faster. We're floating along like carrion in the water."

"I agree with the knight from Michalovice," announced Jost. "My father, the highest burgrave in the land, says that Sir Oldrich of Chlum is the best procurator the Czech kingdom has ever had."

"I respect the gentleman from Chlum," Agnes of Bohemia solemnly declared. "But only in secular matters. We are a company of pilgrims and the opinion of an experienced cleric will certainly be more valuable and dearer to our Lord. And so I hereby charge Provost Wilibald Odo to take over the investigation!"

* * *

In the evening they moored alongside a small pier newly built before an inn that stood on the shore of the river. According to the monks of Melk, it provided the best accommodations for those traveling on the Danube in this direction. The spacious tavern contained a large fireplace that radiated endearing warmth. The company sat on wooden benches around the fire, warming their bodies numb from cold and drying out their clothes. Everyone went to sleep early. The wind grew stronger and rattled the windows of the building during the night.

When they rose in the morning, Prech discovered that someone had chopped out a huge hole in the side of the boat with an ax. It had taken on a lot of water and might have sunk if it hadn't been along the shallow bank and firmly moored to the pier. Agnes nearly flew at him for not having the good sense to post a watch by the boat.

"Forgive him, venerable older sister," one of the Benedictines instantly spoke up in his defense. "Nothing like this has ever happened here before. This river is safe. We are a party of pilgrims and every Christian is obliged to help us, not hurt us. It has always been like that. We have accompanied dozens of similar expeditions. Surely no one from his village could have done it. It had to be one of you. Yesterday I heard what you were talking about. Somebody apparently wants you to go back."

"How long will it take to repair the boat?"

"At least a week. Probably longer. But I know a better solution," the Benedictine continued. He had a broad smiling face and calm blue eyes. With a gesture of his hand, he summoned the innkeeper, who bowed deeply and offered to lend the company his boat. It was even larger than the abbot's boat and more comfortable. The Benedictine friars would repair the damaged one and return it to Melk. The innkeeper would send his son and two servants with the pilgrims to act as guides on the river. He then grew serious and added, "Altogether it will cost three talents of silver."

"We are pilgrims," Abbess Agnes objected. "It's the custom to help pilgrims in their Christian undertakings for free."

"Certainly," said the innkeeper. "But that goes for monasteries. Here you have to pay for your room and board and I have already put my boat away for the winter. Let me know when you decide if to have it made ready for you. But it will not be free!"

"One moment," she peevishly stopped him short. "Have the boat put in the water immediately. I will pay! But remember, the Lord will reckon it a grievous sin come the Last Judgment."

The innkeeper did not reply to her threat. He merely shouted to his son to get to work.

CHAPTER XIV

The pilgrimage continued over the next few days without any problems or delays. Every night a soldier stood watch over the boat. The rain stopped and the wind died down, so traveling became much more pleasant. Nights were cold, however, and morning would see a thin layer of ice along the banks of the river. Everyone was praying it would be warmer in France and were eager to reach the shores of Lake Constance.

Provost Wilibald Odo was constantly asking members of the party about things he considered important for his investigation. He insisted that the soldiers not only guard over the boat but also the baggage and individual pilgrims who wanted to leave the company even for a moment. He threatened to hold Prech responsible if anything should happen.

Oldrich found it amusing when the provost decided to question each pilgrim individually in the bow of the boat, presumably so the others wouldn't overhear. He didn't realize that because they were rowing into the wind, everything that was said could be heard with remarkable clarity back aft. The others were sitting there under a canvas similar to the one on the abbot's boat and alleviated their boredom by listening to what was being said up forward. And because everyone except the provost knew that the others could hear them, they made sure their answers did not insult or offend anyone in their party.

Meanwhile Emmeram struck a secret agreement with brothers Gregory and Hyacinth that they would assume the most reverential and humble expression they could muster up for Wilibald Odo and ask him whether he had made any progress in the case and if he had any suspicion who the killer might be.

When they stopped for a late lunch at an inn in a small Bavarian village, Gregory again innocently asked the provost whether he had learned anything from his interrogations and would he finally share that information with them. Wilibald Odo exploded, shouting that that was the final straw, that he had his suspicions, and once he had something to say about them, he would say it. Catching a killer or quail were two different things, he reminded them, and if someone asked him anything more about it, he would hit him upside the head with a mug and kick him in the rear for good measure.

At that moment the doors opened up and Agnes walked into the inn. She walked up to their table and with an anxious look on her face asked the provost how much progress he had made with the investigation.

The three friars tormented the provost until well into the evening over the question of whether it was proper for a high prelate to leave a promise go unfulfilled. Exasperated, Wilibald Odo gave up the questioning.

Oldrich was amused by the antics. He knew that the pilgrims were bored and would try anything to amuse themselves. As much as he enjoyed the exploits of the clerics, his squire was starting to worry him. Ota was sulking most of the time and only ventured occasionally to joke around with the girls, which was very worrisome indeed. Whenever he caught sight of him explaining something to Zdena Berkova, he always had a grave expression on his face. And Svetlana was also causing him concern. It seemed as if she was avoiding him and if that wasn't indication enough, she was constantly paying attention to Peter of Rosenberg. He was afraid she was secretly taking the investigation into her own hands.

* * *

They arrived in Regensburg. A few years earlier Emperor Frederick II had elevated it to the status of a free imperial city, but Agnes of Bohemia refused to accept it. She had no intentions of calling on the city council even though it was considered polite for pilgrims from the upper class to do so. She declared she would meet the Bishop of Regensburg instead because in her mind he was the only legitimate ruler of the city. They sailed under the stone bridge and moored next to the shore. It was said that Regensburg was one of the most beautiful and richest cities in Germany and their first glimpse confirmed that viewpoint.

The party of Czech pilgrims parted company here. The knights and noble maidens, along with the soldiers, were accommodated in a comfortable farmstead not far from the water while Agnes and her prelates were welcomed by the bishop in his palace, located near the Cathedral of St. Peter. Rosenberg wanted to accompany them based on the fact that he was now a member of the Templars, but Abbess Agnes harshly rebuffed him. He had not undergone any ordination, she proclaimed, and therefore she didn't see any reason why he should consider himself to be a member of a spiritual order.

"You are a Christian knight," she continued somewhat more charitably. "God shall glorify you for that. But a knightly order is not the same as an anointed servant of the church and I want to discuss spiritual matters with the Bishop of Regensburg." She dismissed him.

That night Rosenberg got drunk in the tavern. He cried out that he wasn't going to put up with this pompous Přemyslid anymore, that he would show her what the Templars were all about. Svetlana was sitting next to him, caressing and comforting him like a child. He eventually went to sleep with his head on the table.

"Oldrich, will you help me carry him off to bed?"

she asked, disgusted with the sight of the drunken knight.

"I don't like what you're doing," he reprimanded her sternly.

"What, are you jealous?"

"Nonsense! I don't like the fact that you're looking into this case on your own. Did you at least find out something?"

"Nothing," she sighed. "But I swear he knows something. Once he almost let something slip out. From what I understood, he didn't just join us by accident. He was boasting that he had to take care of something important in Compostela on behalf of the Templars. But then he started speaking quickly about something else. I couldn't get anything more out of him. But we have time."

"Be careful," Oldrich warned her. He knew she wasn't going to listen to him if he tried to forbid her from continuing, despite the promise she made him a couple of days earlier. Together with Ota, they grabbed Rosenberg and hauled him across the courtyard to the bunkhouse behind the tavern.

* * *

The next morning the sun managed to come out from behind the clouds, with no great brilliance, but it lifted the mood of the pilgrims. That day they moored near the city of Neustadt, where a dilapidated wooden bridge served as a gangplank for them to reach the shore. As they walked across, Agnes jaunted up to Oldrich and quietly asked him to join her in her chamber after evening prayers. But nobody was to see him.

The wayside inn in Pförmig was quite impressive, most of the structure having been built out of stone. There was a bakery and small brewery in the courtyard just behind the inn and the pilgrims noticed at least a dozen merchant wagons parked underneath shelter.

"There's always good food wherever merchants stop over," bemused Prech.

The sound of the evening entertainment was already dying down before Oldrich decided to call on Agnes. He stealthily made his way along the walls of the hallway and deliberately walked past her door as if it was his intention to visit one of the noble maidens. Once he was sure he wasn't being followed, he retraced his steps and quickly slipped into the corner chamber, which was the best the inn had to offer and why Agnes of Bohemia had chosen it.

"You took your time," she mumbled after seeing him. She was kneeling next to a wall where a simple wooden crucifix hung. She crossed herself and stood up. She sat on the edge of the bed and indicated with her hand that he should join her.

"Is something wrong?" he asked concerned. He was slowly getting used to her fickleness, which there was nothing he could do about anyway. Besides, he couldn't very well act like an offended party if he was supposed to be protecting her. Obeying the Czech king was sometimes difficult; listening to his aunt much more so.

"Perhaps you're angry because I'm right?" asked Agnes politely. She was still whispering out of caution.

Oldrich didn't answer, only shrugged his shoulders. He was waiting to see what would come next. For all her irritability, the elderly abbess had been mostly in a good mood that day.

"I want you to understand that I didn't take the investigation away from you because I don't trust you. I needed to restore calm in our entourage," she explained proudly.

"And you believe that entrusting me to continue would not put the others at ease?" he protested vehemently. He had no clue where this conversation was going. Certainly Agnes had not invited him there simply to soothe her conscience for behaving so wretchedly towards him.

"Perhaps it would," she smiled guardedly. "But there's something else at stake here for me. Do you know the expression 'to put a square peg in a round hole'? That's what I am trying to do here."

"Do I understand you correctly? You suspect Wilibald Odo?"

"For a long time now," she nodded. "As my confessor, he knows everything. The papal legate had an order with him from the Holy Father removing Wilibald Odo from the post of Vysehrad provost. With the understanding, naturally, that my nephew gives his consent. I'm sure Ottokar would have done so after our return from Compostela."

"Did the provost know about the papal order?"

"Yes. The papal legate officially informed him of it in my presence after we arrived at Landstein. Of course, the document has disappeared since the murder. The killer most probably took it. That's why all the things from his trunk were scattered about."

"But what would Wilibald gain from killing him? The Pope can simply draft a new order."

"He can't. Innocent is dying. He will probably be dead by the time we return from Compostela. And the new pope will have other worries to deal with. Who knows who will be sitting on the throne of St. Peter's then, and Wilibald Odo has just as many friends as enemies in Rome. He knows his way around there."

"Why didn't you tell me about this sooner, venerable older sister?"

"I wasn't sure. Anyone could have stolen the document. Like the Landstein chaplain, that fool who took the silver coins. Not until yesterday did I become sure of it. Look," said Agnes reaching for her pillow. She pulled out a folded piece of parchment. "I found this the day before yesterday in my bedchamber. Read it."

Oldrich unfolded the parchment. It was quite short and contained no official salutation or signature. It stated only that the pilgrims must return to Prague. Should Agnes of Bohemia fail to obey, another member of their entourage would not reach Constance alive. She should consider whether she wants the life of a Christian on her conscience.

"It's a threat," growled Oldrich. But what Agnes had just told him didn't make much sense. If Wilibald Odo was the killer, he would not want to return to Prague just yet. On the contrary, he would want to draw out the pilgrimage as long as possible in order to make sure Pope Innocent IV was really dead.

"According to this letter, I have a couple of days to think about it. We need at least another week to reach Constance," the abbess continued with undisguised pride in her sound judgment. "That's why I insisted on spending the night with my prelates in the palace of the Bishop of Regensburg. I asked the bishop if he would occupy the other members of my retinue while I searched the provost's baggage. Notice how unusual the parchment is, how soft it feels. I remembered seeing something similar to it in the Vysehrad chapterhouse. And I found ten clean sheets of the same parchment in the provost's trunk. So he's the one who wrote this threatening letter."

"Do you want him imprisoned?"

"No. I want to catch him trying to commit another murder. That way his guilt will be beyond doubt. That's why I summoned you here. You should discreetly warn the others. But no one should mention a word of this around the provost! None of the pilgrims should be alone from this moment forward. They must go everywhere in twos. And when I say everywhere, I mean everywhere. And each pair should be guarded over by one of our soldiers. Discreetly, naturally. We mustn't give the provost any opportunity to act. The closer we get to Constance, the more nervous he is certain to become. I have no doubt he will attempt to fulfill his threat. But if we don't give him the opportunity, he will lose his nerve and make a mistake. I leave his capture in your hands!"

"Forgive me, distinguished older sister, but why tempt evil? A well construed plan can thwart his intentions just as well. The criminal always has the advantage in such situations, because he can choose the time and place where to strike. Wouldn't it be better to simply charge the provost, convene a court, and challenge him with all the evidence?"

"No! We don't have enough time for that. My plan is good. If something goes wrong with it, it will be due solely to your negligence. I have no doubt we can be on our guard against Wilibald Odo. You can go! I only hope that our journey will finally start to become a true pilgrimage. Would you believe I was beginning to lose faith in it? But the Lord helped me recover it."

* * *

Oldrich left the abbess and returned to the bedchamber he shared with Ota. They talked long into the night about what to do. It was soon obvious it wasn't going to be easy to carry out Agnes's instructions.

"If we warn the others about the provost and at the same time warn them to keep the secret to themselves,

I'll bet my soul that Wilibald Odo finds out about it within an hour," a grumpy Oldrich predicted.

"Agnes likes to give advice but we have to be smarter than that. I have an idea. You will talk to each person in private and inform him that you know who the killer is. And that you know that for some unexplained reason he also wants to kill that person. Of course, you promise him that you will watch over him if he does what you tell him to do. The first condition is he must keep silent; otherwise you can guarantee nothing. In addition, some people we can trust will always be close by to protect him. That could work."

"When people are afraid for their lives, they know how to hold their tongues for a couple of days," Oldrich agreed. "But I haven't got a clue how to organize everything in pairs. I have no use for this part of the plan at all. Agnes thinks she's devised something really clever here. Who else but her would think like a Christian about other Christians? I would never put the lives of innocent people at risk for some manhunt. Whenever we set a trap, we always do it so that at most only the two of us are endangered. We can put ourselves at risk. That's our job. But why to put the noble maidens at risk as well?"

"The biggest problem will be with the girls," Ota added. "Even in pairs they wouldn't be able to handle the killer if he struck. I also don't think we should divide up the four of them into pairs. It would be better if the actual pairs consisted of one girl and one knight."

"You know how to use everything to your advantage," Oldrich chided him. By morning, however, he was convinced his squire was absolutely serious. When Jost was informed of the danger, he adamantly declared he would not leave the side of Jana for an instant. Katherine said she would rather die than have to look at Zdena from morning to evening. For her part, Svetlana was of the opinion that she would feel safest with Oldrich. And Rosenberg refused to be paired with anyone because as a Templar he knew how to protect himself.

Agnes was beside herself with anger when he reported to her in the evening. She claimed she had once had a better opinion of Oldrich of Chlum and would now tell her nephew about his indolence. Furious, she ordered him to "do it differently now! Have at least two soldiers watch over the provost day and night. Only so that he doesn't notice it! Moreover, you will watch over Wilibald Odo yourself. Your head will depend on him not killing any more of the pilgrims. I will see to it from now on that you share the same chamber at all our stops."

* * *

The weather took another turn for the worse, only the rain was replaced by sleet and sometimes snow.

"Winter's coming damn early this year," muttered Prech. "If the rivers freeze over, we won't reach

Compostela until spring."

"It couldn't be any worse," Oldrich shrugged. "I tell you, this is the lousiest mission I've ever been on."

"The same here, if you can believe that. Why must I always get stuck with such bad luck? The King has organized at least a dozen expeditions this year. One left for the wedding of some princess in the Rhineland, another to Castile, a couple of divisions left on a punitive expedition against the heretics or to do battle with the King of Hungary. Good times all around. But I have to accompany Agnes of Bohemia and her prelates on a pilgrimage where the pilgrims are killing one another. Oh merciful God, why doth you punish me so!"

"Just take care that his Majesty doesn't punish you if our prelates start butchering each other," Oldrich warned him in a friendly tone. "We have to figure out some way to divide up your men to keep the provost from killing anyone else."

"Do you think he's the killer?"

"I'm yielding to the authority of our venerable abbess. Agnes has pronounced him to be the murderer and I obey. But just between you and me, I have my doubts the provost is involved. Just for assurances, you should have your men keep a watch over the noble maidens."

"At least something good here," Prech smiled approvingly. "My men will certainly enjoy that more than watching the provost."

CHAPTER XV

Nothing connected to the recent crimes occurred on the way to Ulm. It was almost as if leaving the Czech kingdom had removed the threat of the unknown assassin. Still, Oldrich rarely saw any of the Czech pilgrims alone anymore. The nobles stuck together nearly all of the time now, amusing themselves by telling jokes that would give moralizing clergymen pause to consider their Christian meaning. The maidens gave the knights a good run for their money with their own ribald stories, and the mood of the pilgrimage had become, in general, quite agreeable and relaxed.

After several days the weather took another sharp turn and the snowy conditions gave way to late Indian summer sunshine. Oldrich knew of a famous workshop in Ulm where the best parchments north of the Alps were produced. As soon as they were ashore, he borrowed the threatening missive from Agnes and went to see Master Heidenreich in his shop.

The tawer had coarse hands stained by the lye he used to soak the animal skins in. He fingered the parchment, looked at it against the light and even sniffed it. He proudly smiled and confirmed that it did in fact come from his workshop.

"But one thing you are wrong about, noble sir," he explained politely. "I supply parchments to only one place in the Czech kingdom. The Vysehrad chapterhouse. As far as I know, the court of the King buys them from the monks in Waldsassen. Their work isn't bad, but certainly not as good as mine is. Would you like to buy some?"

"I'm still considering it," he replied, also politely. "But I do have one more question: Did you ever make similar parchments for the Knights Templar?"

"No, never. Don't forget that their Grandmaster resides in the Holy Land. There he can get much better quality from the infidels. I don't know why the Lord God has decided it so, but Jewish and Muslim craftsmen make much better things than we do. I cannot understand it and every day I pray to the Lord that he gives us the same skill."

Oldrich thanked him and left. He walked along the road, disheartened by the news. He had expected Master Heidenreich to say something to the effect that other Czech scriptoria could also have the same parchment. But that clearly wasn't the case. Only Provost Wilibald Odo bought this particularly soft and white material. Only in his trunk was it discovered by Agnes. As he continued along the Danube, Oldrich decided to make it his task to discreetly go through the personal effects of the other pilgrims. But nothing similar turned up.

The investigator in him lived by the principle that a hypothesis was only good until something refuted it. Experience had taught him to keep other avenues open, to not focus exclusively on the provost. The other pilgrims should also remain suspects, but there was no escaping the conclusive testimony provided by Heidenreich.

"And why can't the provost be the killer?" he asked himself. He headed to the nearest tavern and ordered a mug of hot mead. To his immense disappointment, a buxom woman in a shabby green skirt informed that they didn't carry the beverage.

"You won't find it in Ulm," she kindly continued. "Maybe in Prussia or further east in the pagan lands. We're a Christian city here and drink only beer and wine."

"Hm, and which of the two is the more Christian?" he asked brimming with sarcasm. As expected, she answered that wine was and immediately produced a not too big mug of strong, mulled red wine with a tempting aroma.

Oldrich took a drink and smacked his lips with delight. He had plenty of time. He was in no hurry to get anywhere. Although the tavern was noisy, it seemed like his first peaceful moment in a long time. It wasn't easy to live in a company of pilgrims. He was constantly surrounded by people, and making matters worse, each of them was completely different, had different interests, and talked about different things.

The knights, maidens, prelates, and soldiers. There was nowhere to escape, nowhere to hide from them. They were crowded together on the boat from morning till evening. Most of the inns where they stayed at for the night had only one or two bedchambers and they were occupied by Agnes and the girls. The rest of them had to sleep in a large bunkhouse, all crammed in together. Whatever he said, a half a dozen other people heard it, including those with no invitation to. He and Ota hadn't been able to have a decent chat between them for at least a week, and there was no time to think in quiet. He suspected that was the reason why he had yet to pick up the right trail in this investigation. Now he finally had the chance to make amends.

He leaned back, stretched out his legs underneath the table and warmed his hands by gripping the rough, rounded side of the mug. The first thought that came to his mind was Ota's observation that the right girl should have nicely rounded hips, in the shape of a mug. He sighed. He wasn't going to make any progress like this. He took a drink and told himself to concentrate.

His thoughts turned back to the Vysehrad provost. What Master Heidenreich said refuted his presumption that it was illogical to suspect Wilibald Odo. Why would he want to hurry home if the Pope was intending to remove him from his lucrative position as the head of the chapter? The safest thing for him to do would be to keep a low profile and wait for the storm to blow by. Especially if he had gotten his hands on the missing document. But then something else occurred to Oldrich that he hadn't thought about before, and he hadn't because he didn't have the quiet that he was used to elsewhere.

He immediately started to formulate another hypothesis. Abbess Agnes told him that the papal legate had brought with him an order dismissing the provost from his post. She did not, however, say that she actually saw it. What if it was not in the possession of the legate at Landstein, that he only spoke about it? He could have already posted it earlier to the Bishop of Prague, the chapterhouse or to the King himself. If Wilibald Odo were the killer, he would still have no clue about its whereabouts. Not until he had killed the legate and gone through his things would he realize that he didn't have the document with him. That would be the most logical reason why the provost was in a hurry to get back home. He had lots of important friends in Prague ready to intercede on his behalf. Of course, he would have to act quickly before the King returned from his military expedition to Moravia. That all made sense.

But there was one more disturbing factor bothering Oldrich. He had allowed himself to be influenced by Agnes and her suspicion that the Knights Templar were behind these murders. The result was he kept searching for clues anywhere their name turned up. But what if it was a dead end? More to the point, what if the murders that were committed in Prague had nothing at all to do with the ones committed on the pilgrimage? If someone else carried out the first murders, the others would then point to the provost.

The new hypothesis was simple. The provost had killed the papal legate in Landstein because he was carrying with him the dismissal order. The soldier had caught a glimpse of him in the hallway during the night and figured out that he was the assassin. He started to blackmail him and that's why the provost killed him at Gmünd. He then started to do whatever he could to force Agnes to return to Prague. If this were indeed the truth, it was clear that he was as determined as ever and would fulfill his threat. Oldrich would not let that happen.

He finished his mug and ordered another one. He started considering the person most likely to fall victim next to Provost Wilibald Odo. It would have to be someone who was close to Agnes, whose untimely end would affect her deeply. Of course, it would also have to be someone whose passing wouldn't affect the provost in the least. He immediately ruled out librarian Emmeram. He meant nothing to the abbess and the provost would be hard put to find a similar librarian in his chapter. He also ruled out Jost and Svetlana because their father sat with the provost on the king's council. No matter what he thought about the provost, he was no cold-blooded killer able to freely meet with the father of his victims for the rest of his life. Gradually he began excluding one pilgrim after the other until there were just two names left.

Both of them were possible. The first was the Minorite monk Gregory, who Agnes was very close to because they belonged to the same monastic order. But he was a prelate, and that's what made the second name more probable. Oldrich of Chlum.

Considered from a detached viewpoint, this scenario was absolutely logical. His death would demonstrate the killer's determination to stop the pilgrims at any cost. The murder of Oldrich of Chlum would certainly make the abbess shudder. Wilibald Odo could moreover settle a score that had been festering since spring, when Oldrich investigated the murder of Judge Dobrej. The probability of this hypothesis gave him no pleasure at all. He was used to sticking his neck out, for sure, but there was something distinctly different about facing an enemy with sword in hand and letting him stab you in the back.

This scenario did offer a certain advantage in addition to the danger, namely the chance to catch the provost in the act and therefore prove his guilt beyond measure. Of course, under the assumption that Oldrich was faster and survived the encounter. He grew sullen as he thought about it for a moment, realizing that Clare of Assisi, the Holy See, and the Templars had now completely disappeared from consideration. Everything was hinging on the singular issue of whether to turn around and go back to Prague or not. Something was wrong here. In the end, this hypothesis was no more convincing than the others.

He paid and walked out on the street. Dusk was falling, high time for him to get back to the city dock. There the entire expedition was spending the night at lodgings belonging to the Church of Saint Nicholas. As he approached the marketplace, he noticed a burgher house with the sign of a large pair of scissors hanging over the entrance indicating that it was a tailor's workshop. Some skirts were displayed on a wooden stand placed in front of the entrance. Katherine was looking through the goods while just a few steps away from her stood the provost, yawning out of boredom.

Even though the suspicions about Wilibald Odo formed just one hypothesis, Oldrich was not at all happy to see them together. A few days before he had explicitly ordered the pilgrims not to get separated. He could not publicly identify the provost as the culprit and so had to imply to the others that they were not to inform him about this precaution. But it would never have occurred to him in his dreams to make sure they understood they were not to be left alone in his company.

"What are you doing, noble maiden?" he asked with a polite bow.

Startled, she answered, "I lost my comb. I need to buy a new one and master provost here kindly offered to accompany me."

"That I did," Wilibald Odo spoke up, failing to hide the sarcasm in his voice. "But I never guessed we would be going from shop to shop. We haven't even come to the combmakers yet. We probably won't either if we continue to linger like this."

"Don't be so disagreeable," Katherine said ruefully. "One merchant had combs but none of them pleased me."

"Perhaps. But I see only skirts here," the provost protested, throwing up his arms in a show of helplessness. "I could have said twenty Lord's-prayers in the time it has taken you to look through them."

"Perhaps I will also need a skirt," she replied unconcerned, wrinkling her nose for good effect. She went back to looking through the goods on display.

The Vysehrad provost trained his sights on Oldrich and began to bitterly complain. "Supposedly it was you who ordered that nobody was to leave our company alone. This girl claims we're in danger somehow. How is it that you never told me about it?"

"Because this danger mostly threatens the secular members of our party," Oldrich answered, quickly realizing that this excuse didn't sound very believable. He immediately added that he had gone to the city precisely to verify this danger and discovered that not only was it true, but the prelates were also at risk.

"What kind of danger?" the provost demanded to know, markedly pointing out that Agnes had entrusted him with the investigation.

"And what have you found out?" Oldrich rejoined smoothly.

"I answer only to God. And our venerable older sister Agnes," snapped the angry prelate. "Now talk!"

"I also only answer to God and the venerable Agnes

of Bohemia," Oldrich countered in a friendly tone. "But there is one thing I can tell you. I fear that there is someone out to murder you. I can say nothing more. But don't be afraid! I shall not leave your side for a moment."

"Me? Why me?" asked Wilibald Odo, starting to get upset. His haughty self-confidence was no longer in evidence.

They continued to linger behind Katherine in the marketplace. Once she had finally chosen a bone comb and bought it, Oldrich turned to her and quietly asked why she had not taken Ota with her instead.

"Because he hasn't moved from Zdena's side," she answered indifferently. "But it's only fair he should take care of her because he dishonored her. And provost Wilibald was kind enough to offer to accompany me."

* * *

The carefree mood deserted the company as they approached Constance. Oldrich contributed to the change by constantly reminding them of the threat hanging over them. He was convinced it was better to spoil their fun than let someone lose his or her life due to a lack of vigilance.

"Do you know what's interesting?" asked Ota when he was able to have a moment alone with Oldrich. "During all of this time not one of the pilgrims has complained about wanting to go home."

"I'll tell you why," smiled Oldrich. "They're afraid of being accused of being the killers. It's all logical. Whoever the killer is wants the expedition to turn around. Ergo, whoever declares that he wants to go back is the guilty party."

"Of course, they would have to know about the threatening letter."

"Of course, they know about it. Abbess Agnes is your typically naïve woman," he indignantly remarked. "No doubt she told the Minorite about it under a vow of silence. According to the rules of their order, he is her brother and therefore she should not keep any secrets from him. He certainly told the other prelates and one of them our knights and they in turn our maidens. It would've been the same had Agnes officially announced it during church service."

"Surely you're exaggerating, my lord."

"Hardly. Yesterday Svetlana came to me with a mysterious expression on her face and offered to let me in on a secret. She then recited the threatening letter practically word for word."

"And you think she doesn't care about you!"

"Ota, since we are talking about the maidens, how are things between you and Zdena?"

"I'm watching over her. Like all the girls you have assigned me to."

"What, you think I don't have eyes? You're jumping only around her. And you know how it looks? It looks like you had violated her and are now working off your sins."

"Katherine told you that, didn't she?" Ota angrily asked. "She's constantly reminding me of my sins. What does she get out of it? She's got a fiancé. She should leave others alone! I'm not jumping around Zdena; it's just there's little space and we always happen to end up sitting side by side. But I haven't laid a finger on her. I mean during the pilgrimage. I swear on my sinful soul. But you know what's interesting? There's something bothering her. She has changed quite a bit since we started off. Whether we like it or not, she's from North Bohemia like we are. We should help our neighbors. Even if they do belong to the Duba clan."

"That is indeed noble of you," Oldrich sneered in agreement. For the first time he had the feeling that he and his squire were not in complete agreement about everything. Above all he didn't believe this claim that he was solicitously looking after a girl simply because something was bothering her. Then it immediately occurred to him that his squire had been hit hard by the terrible boredom of the past few days. Horseback riding was enjoyable, but rowing up a river was worse than listening to one of the chaplain's sermons.

CHAPTER XVI

They finally said farewell to the river at Sigmaringen and settled with the innkeeper's son. After he and his helpers turned the boat around and started for home, the Czech pilgrims left to spend the night in a castle set on a cliff high above a bend in the river.

Oldrich hadn't slept well over the past few days. Following Agnes of Bohemia's instructions that he share sleeping quarters with the Vysehrad provost, he lay awake through the night, eyes closed, listening for every suspicious sound in the dark, expecting Wilibald Odo to jump on him at any moment. He tried to catch up on sleep during the day by dozing off on the bench at the back of the boat, but his nerves were on edge, even reaching the point where he was actually praying for the provost to make his move.

But even their night in the castle at Sigmaringen was a quiet one. Immediately after the morning service, which took place in a grand chapel with high windows, they set off on horseback towards Lake Constance. It was a great feeling to be back in the saddle after two weeks. The weather remained warm and dry over the next couple of days despite the gray clouds rolling in. The horse hooves kicked up mounds of dust as they proceeded along.

While the merchant traffic usually began to taper off this time of year, they still encountered laden wagons and trains of mules on the route. To the displeasure of the knights, custom dictated that the pilgrims stand aside and give way to any merchant caravan coming up from behind. In this territory, commerce had priority over nobility.

"Tomorrow night we'll be in Constance," said a relieved Jost. "Hopefully we'll be done with this stupid waiting around once and for all."

"I pray you are right," said Agnes, looking at Oldrich but saying nothing.

"I found out that from Constance we can again go part of the way by boat," declared Prech. "We will take the Rhine to Basel and go from there on horseback to Besançon."

"Not me," protested Rosenberg. "If you go by boat and I stay in the saddle along the bank of the river, I guarantee you I will be in Besançon no later than you."

"We've had enough of the river," said Svetlana, speaking on behalf of the other girls. "We also prefer to go on horseback."

"It was only a suggestion," shrugged Prech. "When we get there, we'll decide what suits our venerable older sister Agnes best."

Ota rode quietly alongside his master. He waited

until they were out of earshot before letting Oldrich know how he didn't like what he was doing one bit. Why was he freely sticking his head into the lion's mouth?

"My duty is to protect the others," he explained wearily. "Besides, it's not as dangerous as you think. The provost would have to be a complete fool to murder me while we are alone together in the room. He would be the obvious suspect then and have a hard time trying to talk his way out of it. If he wants to kill me, he'll have to find another place and means to do it. Sleeping in the same room has definitely complicated the situation for him. Assuming that he's the one, of course."

"Just to be sure, I won't let him out of my sight during the day," offered Ota. He then paused and added, somewhat reflectively, "That is, if I can manage to take my gaze away from some of our lady pilgrims. Have you noticed how good this trip has been for some of them? They've become more beautiful. A poet might say they look like roses on the verge of budding."

"Oh, stop it, Ota!"

"My apologies. I suppose I'm also acting foolish now."

"Also? Who else do you have in mind? Me, for instance?" laughed Oldrich.

"Everybody. Don't you find all these suspicions about the provost rather foolish? I've wanted to talk to you about my doubts that he's our killer. The most serious objection, I think, is the uncertainty that he wrote the threatening note. If he did it, he would have to be unbelievably stupid. And while Wilibald Odo is arrogant and maybe a fool in some cases, I think he's a crafty and clever fellow."

"What's your opinion about the note?" Oldrich asked. He was also troubled by the same doubts. Failing to size up the situation correctly could lead the entire expedition to a disastrous conclusion.

"I will come to that in a moment," said Ota. "The basic problem here is this hypothesis that the provost killed the legate and the assumption that since he didn't find the Pope's letter on him, he now wants to get back home. If this were the case, he would need to get to Prague as soon as possible. Time would be of the utmost importance to him. So why does the entire expedition need to go back with him? He could easily find hundreds of reasons why he must leave alone. He could get ill or injured or simply disappear. But let's allow that he's afraid Agnes will spurn him if he did leave; why write the threatening note on his own personal parchment and then give her so much time to turn around and go back? Why not write that we should go back immediately instead of waiting until we reach Constance? He loses several more weeks this way. No, something here just doesn't make sense."

"Logically, you're right, of course. But I'm afraid we don't know enough to be absolutely certain one way or the other. First, nobody saw the Pope's letter removing Wilibald Odo from the post of provost. Not even Agnes knows exactly what the Pope wrote, or what reason he would have for dismissing him. We ourselves cannot dismiss the possibility that no such document exists and the legate merely wanted to frighten the provost, again for whatever reason. And there's one more possibility here; that Agnes made the whole thing up about the document."

"The Pope's order is not the only thing in question, my lord. In my opinion, the threatening note which Agnes received on parchment from the Vysehrad chapterhouse actually attests to his innocence."

"What do you mean? To me, it is the only conclusive proof we have about Wilibald Odo."

"You said that no one else could have used this parchment. But has it not occurred to you that if Agnes could have gotten into the provost's trunk, then someone else could have also and stolen a sheet of the parchment?"

"It has, but I immediately rejected the notion. The provost would surely have noticed any such theft given that the parchment is rather expensive."

"You yourself have said that he despises books and learning. We can assume that he wouldn't notice the loss of a single sheet of parchment."

"Every prelate has to write a letter from time to time. Even one with no love of learning," Oldrich answered absentmindedly. Something else had just occurred to him but he kept it to himself. His squire noticed it but didn't press him further, knowing as he did that his master needed time to work these things out.

They put up for the night in Stockach, not quite a mile from the shores of Lake Constance. The city of Constance was now less than half a day's ride away. After dinner, as they prepared to go to sleep in a small chamber on the first floor, Oldrich asked the provost en passant whether by chance he had an empty sheet of parchment so he could write a letter to the King.

"Of course, I have a couple in my trunk," replied Wilibald Odo, belching at the same time. He groaned that he must've eaten something rancid or too fatty.

"But yours are quite expensive. I could easily do with something cheaper, even used," Oldrich humbly reasoned. "Surely you didn't bring these expensive sheets with you just to give them away."

"I'm glad to help if I can," the provost facetiously added.

"Am I the first to ask you?"

"Of course not. Two weeks ago I gave a sheet to Zdena Berkova. She wanted to write her parents. I have lots of parchment, don't worry. But if necessary, I can have my librarian Emmeram buy more. After all, we're Christians and should help each other." Not one to waste money, it was clear the provost didn't consider his parchments to be valuable.

Oldrich blew out the candle. He leaned back against the headboard with his hands folded beneath his chin. He was stumped. The case built by the abbess on the provost's paper was flimsy at best. What if it turned out that neither the Templars nor Odo had a hand in these murders? Why couldn't it be Zdena Berkova of Sloup? Oldrich had the blood of the lords of Duba on his hands and he trusted that clan far less than he did the provost.

Ota had obviously been right. Anyone could've stolen a sheet of parchment from the provost's trunk. And hearing his voice just a moment ago, so completely contemptuous of everything connected to reading and writing, Oldrich would have bet that the man had no clue how many sheets of parchment he had in his trunk. Of course, this meant that most of his reasoning over the past few days was probably wrong, the same as his mistaken belief that the provost wanted to kill him, Oldrich of Chlum.

Tomorrow they were supposed to reach Constance. If whoever wrote the note had meant to carry out such a vile act, tonight would be the last chance to do it. But what motive would the other pilgrims have to kill one of their own? Who was so desperate to keep the expedition from continuing?

Oldrich knew that Ota was right about one thing, which only served to make matters more complicated. It wasn't the perpetrator's desire to return to Prague, rather to deter the rest of them from their pious undertaking. All the pilgrims. There had to be some good, goddamn reason behind it, one Wilibald Odo was not likely to have.

Oldrich heard rustling nearby. He grabbed the hilt of the sword he took with him to bed and attempted to peer through the darkness. That's when he heard a tremendous belch, followed by footsteps.

"I have to go dump my innards," the provost announced in obvious discomfort. He hurried out into the hallway, forgetting to close the door behind him. The dim light of the oil lamps that burned all night above the staircase seeped through the half-open door.

Oldrich started wondering whether any crime would actually occur there that night. The wayside inn where they were staying was quite large, with enough rooms to give the pilgrims a break from having to crowd together in one large bunkhouse. Before they retired for the evening, he reiterated to all of them that they were not to leave their rooms by themselves. Anyone intending to do so had to take his or her bedfellow along. He was now chagrined to realize that he himself had broken this rule. He had become so accustomed to the idea that the killer was the Vysehrad provost that it didn't occur to him to accompany Wilibald Odo to the waste pit where, in all probability, he was heading.

He sighed and got up out of bed. With sword in hand, he walked out into the hallway. He went down the stairs, past the darkened tavern on the ground floor and entered the courtyard. The full moon made it easy to see his way around. Just behind the straw shed, in a corner by the fence, was the waste pit. As he headed in that direction, he nearly tripped over a body on the ground. It was Wilibald Odo lying in a pool of blood. He was dead, stabbed several times in the chest and gut. The killer had struck him from the front, meaning that the provost knew him. It was certainly no robbery, since the dead man's gold ring glittered in the faint moonlight.

* * *

The entire company of Czech pilgrims slowly gathered around the body of the murdered provost.

"How could the murderer have known that Wilibald was coming here of all places?" murmured Ota.

"He not only knew it, he planned the entire thing," answered a livid Oldrich. He was angry at himself for not guessing it might occur in this fashion. "We had porridge with meat for dinner. Everybody out of a single kettle. So why did Wilibald Odo get sick? He ate no more than usual and had the same thing we did. The killer had to slip him something in his food or drink. After that, it was only a matter waiting for him here."

"Lord of Chlum, I want to speak with you immediately," commanded Agnes, who had suddenly appeared. She stood for a moment and prayed over the body of the dead provost, then went back into the inn. Her lips were pressed tightly together and not a muscle twitched in her face. Her gait was stiff and erect, another clear sign that she was about to unleash her fury on him.

He had barely stepped into her chamber when she

thundered, "Sir Procurator, I warned you! If another pilgrim died on account of your negligence, I would have your head!"

"Venerable older sister, you said that I was to make sure the provost didn't kill any of the pilgrims. That was your explicit order."

"It stands to reason that..."

"I'm not finished," he shouted. Alarmed, Agnes fell silent. Looking at him askance, she could see that Oldrich was pale and trembling with anger.

"You forbade me to warn Wilibald Odo of the danger. You insisted he was the perpetrator, that your plan to protect the others from him was perfect. So how was the poor man to know what was lurking about? He had no chance to defend himself, all because you falsely accused him. His death is on your hands!"

"Enough! I refuse to listen to any more of this!" she shrieked. "The King will decide when we return who is at fault here."

"I have no idea when you're planning to return," he continued impertinently. "But I'm taking my squire and leaving for Prague tomorrow. All those who want to join us are free to do so. I've had enough of this charade. I will no longer be some fool for you to vent your anger on whenever you feel like it. Nor am I some toy for you to entrust me with the manhunt one day, then change your mind in the evening, and again in the morning. You're the abbess, you're leading this pilgrimage, but if you don't care that the killer takes out one pilgrim after another, so be it. I'm not a pilgrim. The King gave me a task to fulfill but I can't do it because you treat me lower than the soldiers accompanying us. Their commander has your respect, but not me. I shall go back and ask the King myself to punish me. God be with you!" He stormed out of the room, slamming the door behind him so hard it was a wonder it didn't fall off its hinges.

His fury subsided once he was out in the hallway. He had instigated the argument with Agnes because he felt it was the only way to ensure the success of the pilgrimage. Either she would finally change her attitude and let him get on with catching the killer, or she would continue to act like a spoiled child and then it wouldn't make a difference in the world whether she had him punished then and there or in a week's time. After all, this case was more than just about him. He had no doubt that the killer would strike again.

Standing near the stairs only a few steps from Agnes's chamber was Svetlana. They were shouting so loud that she had to have heard everything through the closed door. Her eyes were full of admiration for him. Before he knew it, she threw her arms around him and kissed him. "No matter what happens, I'm behind you," she declared. "I will tell the King that none of what happened is your fault."

"You're a good girl," he answered guardedly as he tried to free himself from her grasp. It took some jostling before he was finally able to manage it. Still, he couldn't help smiling at her tenderly and stroking her cheek, albeit a bit stiffly.

"What's wrong?" she asked suspiciously.

"You know me," he said, trying to evade the question.

"Of course! That was just a scene in there! You weren't arguing with her at all. You were shouting on purpose. And you're not planning to leave tomorrow, are you?"

"If Agnes and I can reach an agreement, I'll stay. I can't stand letting criminals off with impunity. I'll do anything to catch this person and see to it that he feels the full weight of the law."

"I'm worried that he will hurt you and you just...," she cried, pulling away in a fit of despair. "The Lord gave you a legal code instead of a heart. Silly me, I keep forgetting that you would make the worst husband in the world. I would be miserable with you."

"Yes. A man can make only one woman happy in his lifetime. My wife was happy with me, but the Lord took her from me and with her a piece of my heart. Yes, Svetlana, you're right that all I have left inside me is a legal code. But...you're a good person. I will pray that someday you too will find the right one." He turned and quickly walked down the stairs.

Svetlana silently watched him go, her eyes welling with tears. She sighed and lamented, "Your prayers will really help me!"

At that moment the door creaked open and Agnes's pale face appeared. Her eyes were also filled with tears. When she saw Svetlana, she asked her in a quavering voice if she didn't want to join her in her chamber for a while. It would do them good to pray together since they were both obviously suffering on account of the same man.

CHAPTER XVII

In the morning Abbess Agnes convened all the pilgrims in the courtyard. The Minorite Gregory went from chamber to chamber, bidding the others not to linger since it concerned an extremely important matter.

"What do you think Agnes is up to?" asked Ota. He had moved back in with his master after the murder of the Vysehrad provost.

"How should I know? She's not used to anyone standing in her way. But she is a devout believer and I think she won't do anything to endanger the pilgrimage. There's also her commitment to Clare of Assisi to consider. I just hope she cares the same about the other pilgrims. Of course..."

"Of course she's only a woman," Ota added, but Oldrich shrugged off his presumptuousness. "Of course, it's possible," he went on impatiently, "she has decided that her Christian faith makes it right for her to continue to Compostela alone. Or at least without the two of us."

"If she does indeed have a secret mission there, it

would look suspicious if she continued alone. Even if the Pope and Templars are trying to stop her."

"That's true..." Oldrich began, but then backtracked. "Yes, you're right. She's only a woman, and a princess at that. How are we to know what's going on inside her head? Come on, let's go see what she has to say."

Everyone had assembled in the courtyard, only the abbess was missing. Suddenly she appeared in the doorway of the taproom wearing the long white shirt of a penitent over her clothes. There was a noose made out of frayed rope around her neck and she was barefoot and bareheaded. She held a lit candle in her hands.

"The Vysehrad provost died on account of me," she announced. "I therefore must complete the pilgrimage to St. James. I love all of you and that is why I am releasing you from the vow you have given me. None of you must continue the pilgrimage. Indeed, I am begging you with all my heart to go back. It is too dangerous. I alone cannot protect you."

"We left Prague together and shall return to Prague together, sister," firmly declared Gregory. He left the others and went to stand next to her.

"Our brother provost died yesterday," chimed in librarian Emmeram. "I cannot say I loved him, but he was my brother and the only way I can pay tribute to his memory on behalf of the entire chapterhouse is by completing the pilgrimage to Compostela." He also went to stand alongside Agnes. Chaplain Wolf was the next to insist that he must finish the pilgrimage in order to win absolution for his sin. Friar Hyacinth declared that he too would continue but without offering an explanation for his motives. Peter of Rosenberg, however, had no intentions of keeping it brief. He boasted that every Templar must be ready to die at any time for the faith, and that's why it was totally out of the question to even consider canceling the pilgrimage. He wasn't afraid of death. Annoyed by his self-serving speech, Jost of Landstein said that if it were up to him, he would probably turn back. But he had to go on to show that he was truly sorry for the crime that had been committed at his father's castle and was hoping the Pope would offer him forgiveness. Svetlana then made it obvious that where her brother went, so did she. Blushing slightly, Jana of Blatna added that she had decided not to become a nun, but would instead always be at Jost's side. Prech of Michalovice grumbled that his assignment was to accompany the abbess with his soldiers and only the King could relieve him of that duty. Until that happened, he would continue on to Compostela with all his men. Katherine of Gutstein turned to Agnes and asked her for permission to continue. Zdena Berkova fixed her gaze on Ota before declaring that she didn't want to go back since she was sure the honorable Ota of Zastrizly wasn't going back either.

"What about you?" asked Agnes turning to Oldrich. There was gentleness in her voice now, not a sign of pride or schadenfreude from the victory she had just won. "I would be most grateful if you continued with us on the pilgrimage. But the decision is yours."

"I shall continue," he answered calmly, bowing politely.

"In that case I have a great favor to ask of you," she went on with tension in her voice. "Nobody can protect us as well as you can. Sir Prech shall command our soldiers, but you yourself shall lead the expedition in my stead. From this moment forward I shall devote myself only to spiritual matters. Please accept this challenge! I hereby declare in front of the others that I shall stand by my decision until you have safely led us back to Prague."

Oldrich looked her firmly in the eye and noticed fear, fatigue and trust amidst all the wrinkles. He silently nodded. He then quickly scanned the pilgrims, all of whom he was charged with protecting from that moment on. All of them, that is, except the killer.

"Shall we saddle up?" asked Prech.

"What? No, we have enough time. Why rush? We can leave after lunch. It's enough to get to Constance before dark. I want to question everyone this morning and decide the best way to proceed without anyone else coming to a violent end. We mustn't delude ourselves into thinking our tribulations have ended. The killer is still among us."

* * *

Oldrich sketched a layout of the wayside inn on one of

the sheets of parchment remaining in the trunk of the dead Vysehrad provost. In each of the rectangles representing the bedchambers he wrote the name of the pilgrims occupying that space. He wanted to determine who could have been in the courtyard just after dark when Wilibald Odo was slain. He had hoped it wouldn't be difficult since it was agreed that they should always move around in pairs. Fear, he was sure, would make the pilgrims accept this uncomfortable precaution. He soon realized just how wrong that assumption had been.

While it was the nature of the knight not to be overly worried about his life, the noble maidens were naïve and carefree, and the prelates were of the opinion that the hand of God watched over them. Oldrich finally abandoned his efforts. Practically nobody was where he or she should have been. Making matters worse, they weren't even in the company of the pilgrim they were supposed to be with for their own protection. There were only four people he could exclude from suspicion of killing the provost. Jost, as was now the norm after dinner, was with Jana, and Agnes spent the evening with Gregory discussing the theological importance of poverty. The others went about their own affairs after the meal. And that's the way it always was with the nobility. Insubordination marked the life of the knight and prelate just as much as courage and piety did.

As Oldrich sat down to put his futile efforts on paper, Friar Gregory appeared in his chamber.

Wearing a grave expression on his face, he informed him that older sister Agnes had to speak with the procurator immediately. Something extremely serious had happened.

Oldrich hastened to her chamber, where he found her kneeling under a cross and praying with trembling hands. She pointed to a table and a sheet of parchment on it, unfolded. It was bleached and very smooth, clearly from the same stock carried by Wilibald Odo. She bade him to read it.

He picked it up and read three sentences, written in brief and in the same handwriting used in the threatening note. It stated: "The heart grieves because you failed to heed wise counsel. If you cross the river in Constance, another pilgrim will die. Turn back before it's too late!"

"That was to be expected," he intoned gruffly, putting the note back on the table. "He's in a hurry."

"So it isn't over?"

"It would only be over if the killer wanted Wilibald Odo dead for personal reasons and tried to cover it up with the first threat. He would leave us alone now that he got what he wanted; only now it seems he really doesn't want us to continue to Compostela. We're obviously not heeding his warning, so he's threatening us again. If he's killed once, he'll surely do it again. There's no going back."

"Everybody declared in the courtyard that they wanted to continue the pilgrimage."

"The killer lied. To do otherwise would be

tantamount to a confession."

"Do you think you can prevent any other Christians from dying?"

"I think so, if you help me."

"What more can I do? I gave you complete authority. I can contribute nothing else except my prayers."

"But you can, venerable older sister. For starters, you can tell me the real reason for our pilgrimage. It holds the answer to why these Christians accompanying you are dying. But if you refuse to be sincere with me, then others will also die and I won't be able to stop it."

She sighed wearily. "It's terrible when one must choose between two evils." She made the sign of the cross and rose from where she was kneeling. She walked over to the table and gestured for Oldrich to sit down in the chair opposite her. "You are a wise man who studied in a monastery. Perhaps you'll understand what I am about to tell you. On one side you have devout pilgrims, on the other your faith. If you had to choose, which of the two would you save?"

"What you are asking, venerable older sister, is a sophism which has no answer. Faith without believers is an empty concept. The same goes for believers. They cannot be believers without faith. It's impossible to separate them. Is it your suggestion that the secret behind these murders poses a danger to the Christian faith? The reason you have been silent about it up until now?"

"Your estimation is correct. I was certain before last night that God wanted me to protect the faith. Now I am not. It's so difficult...," she sighed and clasped her hands as if she wanted to pray again. Oldrich let her be, didn't try to urge her on. This struggle with her conscience she had to endure alone.

"Can you guarantee me that if I tell you everything, the killing will stop?" she asked after a moment of silence. She did not look into his eyes, rather stared at the floor. She waited, and when no answer was forthcoming, she raised her head and murmured, "I see. Why to draw it out any longer? I already told you that it concerns Clare of Assisi. The object that she promised to return to the Pope is a small metal box. The Templars once used it to hide a papyrus scroll they found in the underground of Solomon's Temple. Supposedly this scroll contains some terrible secret. I swear I don't know what it is, but I can tell you that our pontiffs were afraid of the Templars because of it. But the Templars lost the box and through God's hands it fell into the possession of St. Francis of Assisi. Why do you think the pontiffs had other devotees of poverty burned at the stake, but declared Francis to be a saint for holding the same belief? As much as it pains me to say it, the Christian church is motivated by more than just pious intentions. But it was God's intention to deliver this box into the hands of Francis. He wanted all Christians to return to the humility of Christ's original teachings. He strove for this revival. He and us, his followers. Even though the mendicant orders have been a thorn in the side of the Roman curia, they dare not oppose us. Were it not for this scroll, Francis would have ended up on the stake and our orders persecuted by the Inquisition. That scroll is the future of the church, there's no doubt about it, because it provides protection for everyone who seeks to rid it of its pride and excess."

"But where does Clare fit in this story, not to mention you, venerable older sister?" Oldrich asked. He had been following her account with keen interest.

"St. Francis began to go blind toward the end of his life. Then the stigmata appeared on his body. He realized he had to entrust the box to someone who would not abuse its power over the Pope. The only person he truly trusted was Clare. The two of them lived together as brother and sister in a spiritual bond. So he gave it to her and Clare watched over it until her death. She never wanted to hand it over to the Pope. She wanted only one thing: For him to recognize her order to the greater glory of God. Her promise to return the box to the Pope was perhaps the only lie she ever told in her honorable and pious life. She wrote me the truth about it and asked me to hide the box."

"So why do you fear the Templars?"

"That box gave them unprecedented power. For decades they have been searching for it. They committed their entire fortune to finding it, but it was only until a few years ago that they learned it had ended up in Clare's hands. At first they tried to buy it from her, then resorted to threats, but she never gave it up. They even once hired a band of thieves to raid the monastery in Assisi to look for the box. Naturally it was in vain. I know what you must be thinking about our orders. But Clare was neither naïve nor foolish in this matter. She hid the box many years ago in a safe place. There's no need to mention that it's Compostela."

"Do the Templars know that?"

"Yes."

"Does anyone have a chance of finding the box in Compostela before we reach there?"

Agnes shook her head, but there wasn't much conviction in it. She reluctantly went on. "Actually I'm not exactly sure where Clare hid it. There were a couple of vague hints in her letter, but I can say nothing for sure until we get there. I have told none of this to a single living soul. Everyone probably thinks I know where the hiding place is."

"A somewhat dangerous game here. What role did the papal legate play in it? Did he really come to Landstein to remove the Vysehrad provost from his post?"

"As things are in life, I had to choose between two evils. I felt some help from the Pope was safer than making an agreement with the Templars. The sisters and I have found ourselves in a precarious situation. There exists a scroll that protects us from the Inquisition, but it isn't in our possession. The Pope promised not to move against the Minorites or

Klarites and I agreed to let a cardinal accompany me to Compostela. That's why he sent the one responsible for protecting the faith. God will certainly judge me for these words, but I was relieved when I saw him dead in Landstein."

"And you have no idea what secret is contained in this scroll? Perhaps it will help us identify the murderer."

"Only the Grandmaster of the Templars knows it. Probably the Pope too."

"Of course, Clare also knew it. Did she ever mention it? Perhaps she left some hint behind," suggested Oldrich.

"You are mistaken. I am certain that she did not know the contents of the scroll."

"She never once looked inside the box? Or Francis? How were they to know what they were actually safeguarding?"

"No one can look inside it. The box is locked. When the Templars lost the box, they lost the key to it as well. Francis got only the box. It's small and made of strong steel. It was forged in Damascus, where the best metalsmiths in the Orient work. Such a box can only be opened with fire, but then you will destroy whatever is inside. Believe me, it's better not to know some secrets. It's enough to simply fear them."

"So in your opinion nobody knows what's in this box, and still everybody is after it. Does that not strike you as strange?"

Abbess Agnes merely shrugged her shoulders. She

looked extremely tired, as if she had aged many years during the course of their conversation. Oldrich felt sorry for her, but he couldn't leave her with more open questions. "I still don't understand one thing which directly affects us. Why is the killer intent on stopping our pilgrimage to Compostela? What does he know about this box?"

"I've been pondering the events over the past few days," she sighed, "but can still make no sense of it. Originally I thought that both the Templars and Holy See would let me safely reach Compostela. They need my help. Even if they find the box, it would be useless to them without me. That's why I assumed they would wait until we got there before going after me and my retinue. So I decided to turn to Alfonso, the King of Castile, to provide me with protection. Compostela lies in Galicia, which is in his domains. I thought it would be absolutely safe this way and that was the reason I declined Ottokar's offer to have you accompany me. I was worried that your presence would only complicate things. I was mistaken."

"Why would this box be useless to the Templars and Pope without your presence?"

"That's not important. What is important is they don't find it."

"I still don't understand why any of them would go to so much trouble to hinder us on our journey to Compostela? I would think they would want to help us if it can't be found without you. Who doesn't want us to reach Compostela and why?" asked Oldrich impatiently.

"Neither the Templars nor the Pope would gain anything from me returning to Prague. That's why I'm afraid the killer is working for somebody else. For the King of France, perhaps, for the Johanites or the Inquisition? I have no idea." Agnes had come to the end of her strength. Sweat was accumulating on her forehead and her eyes gleamed feverishly. She was pale and shivering. "This is terribly painful for me. Please, leave me now. But I implore you not to let this criminal strike again!"

Oldrich bowed and left her chamber. He knew he had finally made some progress even if Agnes was still keeping something from him. He had the feeling she was concealing some tiny detail in this story. A tiny detail of the greatest importance.

Thanks to her confession, he finally understood why the pilgrimage was taking place during the wintertime and under such haste. But it had brought him no closer to catching the murderer. In fact, he had the sneaking suspicion that the case had only gotten colder.

CHAPTER XVIII

This time Oldrich was taking no chances. Knowing he couldn't rely on any measure of discipline among the pilgrims, he assigned one soldier to each of them to serve as a bodyguard. Peter of Rosenberg haughtily refused any such escort. Every Templar had a sword, he declared, and knew how to use it better than any guard.

Oldrich's response was harsh and to the point. "This concerns both your safety and that of the others. The soldier will not only make sure nothing happens to you, but that nothing happens to the others because of you."

"Are you accusing me of being the killer?" bellowed Rosenberg, drawing his sword.

"The killer could be anybody," Oldrich continued calmly. "Of course, I will be extra vigilant in your case precisely because you are a Templar. And don't waste your time playing sublime games with me here. Whether or not you're on a mission for your order, I'll see to it that you lose your head if you break the law. You're dismissed!"

Firmly gripping the hilt of his sword, Rosenberg turned pale as indecisiveness overcame him. Finally he mustered up a smile of contempt and put the sword back in its sheath. "If you take any action against our order, I'll see to it that you lose *your* head. I'm not afraid of you!"

Meanwhile Zdena was complaining to Ota. "I don't like the idea of a soldier always looking at me from behind. Can't you be my bodyguard?"

"I'm afraid not. My lord wants me to watch over all of you noble maidens," Ota explained with a look of gravity. "He's worried that you will argue and be jealous of each other if I devote all my attention to just one of you."

"Is that supposed to be a joke? Ha-ha," she mumbled peevishly and turned to leave. Ota caught her by the arm. "Wait a moment. We're alone and need to talk."

"Yes, completely alone. With the exception of that soldier there breathing down my neck," she scowled. "What a shame my father didn't give me a similar bodyguard at home last spring."

"Shame for whom?" he asked provocatively but not at all playfully. "My dear, there's something I need to know." He winked at the soldier and tossed him a silver piece. The soldier nodded and sauntered into the taproom for a beer.

"So that's how you do it," she laughed, a bit forced. "But why now all of a sudden? You had plenty of opportunities before."

"The provost gave you a sheet of parchment two weeks ago. What did you do with it?"

"How do you know? And why do you want to know?"

"Allow me to ask you this question. I care for you in my own way and don't want my lord to have to ask you it officially. If you tell me the whole truth now, then everything will be all right."

"So now it's my turn to become a suspect! You have nothing to go on so you want to blame everything on an innocent and defenseless girl. How pathetic!"

"Oh, girl, when will you ever learn to be reasonable?" he reproached her.

She stared at him angrily for a moment, then burst out laughing. "If only you could see how important you look!"

"You should know. What became of the parchment?"

"I wrote a letter home, that's all."

"No post has left our company since we departed."

"Well, remember that flea-bitten flophouse we stayed in? It was called Kaiserweiden or something like that. We joked that it had all the dignity befitting an emperor. We met a merchant in the tavern there from Bohemia. On his way home. You also spoke with him."

"I remember. So you gave him the letter?"

"I paid him to deliver the letter to my parents before the start of Advent. His name was Vanek, from Pisek. I made sure I got his name in case I needed to lodge a complaint against him when I got home. Anything else, sir investigator?"

"Yes. Who wrote the letter for you? You can't read or write if I remember correctly."

"The provost. When he gave me the parchment, he offered to do it himself."

Ota nodded. It was the answer he was expecting to hear. Too bad there was no way to verify it. Zdena drew close to him and put her arm around his shoulder. She looked deeply into his eyes and asked, with a slightly comical edge, "So, are you satisfied?"

"Yes, satisfied." But there was little satisfaction in his voice. "Satisfied once you tell me where you were last night after dinner. You said that you were in your chamber. Alone, because Jost came for Jana."

"Yes, I did," she nodded and stepped back. As much as she tried to smile, her eyes were cold and piercing.

"But that isn't the truth. The librarian Emmeram was looking for you because the day before yesterday you ripped your leather belt and he promised to mend it for you. He came to your chamber to give it to you but didn't find you there. It was just before my liege discovered the body of the provost."

"I wasn't feeling well. I went for a walk!" she snapped.

"As I recall, you were one of the first in the courtyard after my liege started shouting that there had been another murder."

"I was just coming back."

"Yes, only a coincidence," Ota nodded, clearly not

believing her.

"I can see that any reason you find to get rid of me is a good one for you," she sneered. "Don't worry. I won't try to impose myself on you any further. And when you go to ensure the safety of us noble maidens, please don't bother with this one!" She abruptly turned and walked into the taproom.

"She's hiding something," Ota heatedly told his master when he relayed their conversation.

Oldrich agreed. "Keep an eye on her, but discreetly. I distinctly remember that she walked into the courtyard from the stable, not the gate. She wasn't coming back from a walk."

"What could she have been doing in the stable?"

"I went to look for the provost immediately after he left our chamber. I saw no one in the hallway and the killer would not have had time to get back to his chamber in the inn. He was probably hiding in the stable."

* * *

As the pilgrims reached the massive gates to the city of Constance, the church bells rang out summoning the faithful to the evening service. Oldrich told the sentry who they were, showing him their safe conduct pass. The sentry thanked him with all due courtesy and allowed them to pass.

They walked along a wide road lined with tall, narrow houses with tapered roofs and windows glazed with small dots set in lead. Even though dusk was falling, a fair amount of traffic was still moving about. Craftsmen were putting the final touches on their wares and marketers were trying to unload the rest of their goods for that day on passersby. The party walked around a huge building that was both storehouse and silo and continued along the river to a stone bridge connecting Constance to the other part of the city lying across the river.

When they reached the bridge, the entire company came to a halt. Agnes anxiously looked at Oldrich, knowing that only the two of them knew about the killer's threat to slay another member of their party if they crossed the bridge. Oldrich merely sighed. There was nothing he could do but lead them across. With a slight nod of the head, he was the first to set foot on the bridge.

There was a fish market on the other side, full of hustle and bustle and haggling between buyers and sellers, not to mention the occasional heated argument. Tomorrow was Friday, and the homemakers were out in force carrying fresh fish home in baskets. Prech asked the market caretaker for the nearest wayside inn offering comfort and a good cook.

Practically every pilgrim who sought out the caretaker did so for the purpose of asking this same question. He informed him there were two such inns in the vicinity, both with outstanding reputations, and easily pointed out the way to them. Prech thanked him and was on the verge of leading the company along the meandering street when the sound of horse hooves resonated from the bridge. A swarthy man in immaculate silver armor rode up to them on a beautiful black stallion. Ota instantly recognized him as the stranger who had given him the pouch of silver coins in Old Town and then disappeared without introducing himself.

The stranger stopped in front of Agnes and politely bowed. He addressed her in polished Latin. "Venerable older sister, I am the son of the King of Jerusalem and emissary of King Louis of France. My liege and lord has sent me to accompany you on your pilgrimage to Compostela. My task is to ensure that your journey through the realm of the King of France is safe and comfortable. My name is Guy of Lusignan."

Ota quickly whispered to Oldrich that this was the same stranger who had approached him in Prague.

"He looks familiar," Oldrich replied under his breath. "I believe I saw him at the monastery in Melk among the other nobles and then again in Ulm. I kept telling myself I'd seen him somewhere before. Either he's making the same pilgrimage as we are or he's following us." He noticed that Friar Hyacinth was giving the emissary a most curious look.

"I appreciate the concern of your lord," said Agnes softly. "But we have our own armed guard and I would not want to abuse the kindness of the King. I can manage without your escort if you give me his gracious consent to cross through his lands."

"My lord welcomes you pilgrims from Bohemia, especially on account of your piety, venerable older sister Agnes," said Guy of Lusignan, bowing again. "On no account would my services be an abuse of the King's favor. Unfortunately I have no authority to give you his consent because then I would have to personally ensure your comfort and safety. Now if you please, follow me. We shall spend the night at the homestead of some French merchants. Their home will be entirely at your disposal."

Oldrich moved up alongside the abbess. He knew they couldn't refuse an escort sent by the King of France. To do so carried the implicit threat that their safety would not be guaranteed within his domains. He introduced himself and thanked him on behalf of the Czech pilgrims, declaring they were ready to follow him.

He waited for the others to catch up before turning to the Premonstratensian monk and quietly asking him, "Brother Hyacinth, do you know this emissary? I noticed the way you were looking at him."

After some hesitation, the monk shrugged. "I have never seen him before, but I would swear that I know him. He reminds me of someone, but it can't be that person because he's been dead for a long time now."

"May I ask you to tell me the name of this person Guy of Lusignan reminds you of?"

"It won't mean anything to you," grumbled the moody monk. He again shrugged and added that if the distinguished procurator insisted on knowing the name of the dead man, it was Arnold de Fournier.

The homestead of the French merchants lay in the harbor section of the city along the lake. It was surrounded by stone walls, with massive towers in each corner, making the homestead look more like a castle. Guy of Lusignan wasn't lying. The sleeping chambers inside the immense fortress were large and comfortably furnished.

Before dinner Oldrich, accompanied by Ota, went to seek out the emissary. His squire was carrying a large pouch filled with silver coins, which he handed to Guy without offering any explanation.

"What should I do with this?" marveled the French nobleman.

"I'm simply returning that which you gave me in Prague," replied Ota courteously.

"I have never been to Prague in my life. I have been in Languedoc all autumn, fighting the heretics. You have mistaken me for someone else. I cannot take this pouch. It's not mine. Now please excuse me!"

He politely bowed and left.

"Well, we'll have to wait and see what kind of strange game he's playing," growled Oldrich. "There's nothing about this pilgrimage that surprises me anymore." That conviction, it turned out, barely lasted the night.

* * *

In the morning the pilgrims slowly began gathering in

the ground floor hall of the homestead. Agnes was among the first there and eagerly followed the others as they walked in. She kept her hands concealed beneath the table, counting off each member on her fingers until all were accounted for. She had hardly slept a wink the whole night, praying and begging God to prevent the killer from carrying out his threat. They had crossed the bridge yesterday and now she was shuddering at the thought of what might happen now.

"Every pilgrim has a personal guard," Oldrich reassured her. "Nothing can happen. The soldiers are on alert. They're everywhere, next to the doors to each chamber and in the courtyard." Neither he nor his squire had slept at all either. They kept walking around the courtyard, checking on the guards. Ota offered to personally make sure each of the maidens was in the bed assigned to her. Oldrich would have normally upbraided him for such a comment, but this time he nodded and dryly added that it was a good idea. He himself would check on the prelates and knights. In the end the night passed in peace and silence.

The ground floor hall gradually filled with people. There were baskets of crispy cumin hotcakes on the table and the smell of baked ham emanated from the kitchen. The last to arrive were Emmeram and Hyacinth. Upon seeing them, Agnes crossed herself and sighed with relief. "Thank God, everyone is alive."

All of the pilgrims were a bit edgy. They didn't know what was happening, but couldn't fail to notice all the precautions taking place during the night on their account. Only when they were all sitting around the table did their good humor finally return. It had become Ota's habit to reserve a place next to him for Zdena, but she walked past him this time without even looking at him. She went to the end of the table instead and sat down next to Prech. It was Hyacinth who took the place beside Ota. He looked morose and in no mood for conversation. He excused himself by saying that being here again among the French brought back the terrible memories of his boyhood in Languedoc.

A girl with red hair and freckles brought them bowls steaming with hot onion soup. Agnes declined, saying the hotcakes were enough for her. As she reached for a napkin to wipe her lips, she froze. A small bit of parchment slipped out from the folds of the white cloth. It was bleached and uncommonly soft. Oldrich noticed it. He got up and stood behind her chair so he could read this latest missive from the killer over her shoulder.

Her hands shaking, Agnes unfolded the letter. It read: "Another innocent Christian has died. With tears in my eyes, I beg you to go back. This is my last warning!"

She angrily tossed the letter on the floor and turned around to Oldrich. "But we're all here! How can it be?"

"The killer must have stuck this note here before we arrived. He probably planned to carry out another murder, but didn't do it in the end," Oldrich explained unconvincingly. He began stroking his bearded chin. He looked over at the table in the corner where the soldiers were eating. He quickly counted them. There should be twelve, but one was missing.

He quickly walked over to Prech. Bowing, he whispered for him to join him outside. He didn't want to create any unnecessary panic.

"What's wrong? Did you lose somebody?" Zdena sneered. Oldrich got the sense she was drunk.

Once in the courtyard, Oldrich hastily informed the guard commander of his suspicions. It didn't take long to find the missing soldier, in the servants quarters where they were supposed to sleep but didn't because they were guarding everybody. He was underneath a gray woolen blanket. When they lifted it, they discovered a grisly sight. The soldier was dead, his throat slit. It had to have happened sometime during the night because the blood was already dry and the body cold.

"So he carried out his monstrous threat!" Oldrich exploded. He immediately left to inform the abbess, his mind wrestling with the thought that the killer was always one step ahead of him. He had made yet another mistake. He had put guards on all the pilgrims but forgot to make sure the guards guarded themselves too.

The abbess was sitting at the table and praying. He led her over to a window and whispered to her what he found. "The perpetrator did not explicitly say in his last note that one of the pilgrims would die. Of course, everyone just assumed that was the case. That was a mistake. It didn't occur to me he would kill one of our soldiers," a shaken Oldrich apologized to her.

"It didn't occur to you?" she asked with tears in her eyes. "It should have, Oldrich, it should have! Who will be next?"

"I fear that this time I won't be wrong," he answered, looking at the floor. "The killer has been stalking us the entire journey in order to make us go back. It's clear from his latest missive that this is his final warning. He knows what he's doing! Logically that means he has only one possibility left if he really wants us to turn back from Compostela. He must kill you, venerable older sister!"

CHAPTER XIX

They buried the body of the slain soldier in a small cemetery behind the homestead were other French merchants were reposed in peace. The abbess hired the nearest church to perform three requiem masses for the salvation of his soul and the Czech pilgrims left Constance before noon. No one mentioned anything about going back to Prague. Oldrich got the impression from the snippets of conversation that he overheard that continuing the pilgrimage had now become a matter of honor for many of them. In battle knights preferred to throw themselves at the enemy wherever he was strongest, and most members of the Christian clergy would rather be disemboweled, their innards torn asunder, than go astray from a holy mission. A martyr's death was the surest way to achieve salvation. When Oldrich spoke about this with his squire, he expressed his mystification that the noble maidens were being every bit as stubborn as the others in this pursuit.

"It's not so hard to understand," replied Ota grinningly. Apparently he wasn't suffering nearly as much as his master was from their worries and concerns. "A knight rushes headlong in pursuit of glory, a prelate for faith, and a girl for love."

"Are you trying to tell me that all these girls here are in love with someone?"

"Practically. Jana of Blatna has her Jost; Svetlana, whether you like it or not, has you; Zdena Berkova has me despite all the recriminations she levels at me. It's only Katherine of Gutstein I'm not sure about. But I have the feeling she's angling for somebody. Maybe even me," he added lightheartedly as he wiped his tunic free of some wet leaves that had fallen on him. They were passing through a dense forest at that moment.

"You think too much of yourself," Oldrich chided him. "This morning two of the girls were looking at you as if wishing you had been dead and buried a long time ago."

"You clearly have no understanding of a woman's soul," Ota informed his master. But he then turned serious and added that there was something wrong with Zdena. She was acting even more volatile than what was normal for her unstable nature. One day as soft as a kitten and the next hissing like a wounded panther.

"Could she possibly be the killer?" Oldrich asked matter-of-factly. He couldn't care less whether Zdena was a kitten or a panther.

"Women don't ordinarily have the stomach for slitting somebody's throat," said Ota expressing his doubts. "You saw for yourself what that dead soldier looked like. That was the work of no woman. And there's one more thing. She can't write. She couldn't be the one sending those notes to Agnes, and it would be very difficult to get somebody else to do it for her."

"You're right," Oldrich said. "I just keep wondering what she was doing on the night when the provost was murdered. She had to be in the courtyard. I will speak with her about it."

The Czech pilgrims continued on horseback along the river Rhine. The wide and comfortable road wound through some pleasant countryside full of conspicuous villages and carefully harvested fields. Herds of cattle were still grazing on the stubble and some of the fields had already been plowed by the farmers. Although the Feast of All Saints seemed like long ago, there was nothing in the weather to suggest that winter was arriving.

"Did you want to speak with me?" asked Zdena, who had suddenly appeared alongside Oldrich.

"Sure! And thanks for your willingness," he bowed courteously.

"There's nothing to thank me for," she scoffed. "I'm tired of listening to my pious companions. If I was the murderer, I would kill them all first."

"But you're probably not since they're still alive, thank God" replied Oldrich, taking care not to provoke her. He studied her closely. She had thrown up after breakfast but not because of drink. He continued in a kind, almost trusting voice. "I would like to ask you about a couple of things, Zdena, but first, what would you say if I asked an older, experienced woman to check you over?"

She scoffed again. "That would be a waste of time and effort. No, I'm not a virgin. I'm just surprised Ota didn't brag to you about it."

"I believe you yourself have told everyone you met about your sin," rejoined Oldrich. "But I'm thinking about something other than your chastity here. This woman would probably discover that you're pregnant."

"Who told you?" she recoiled in horror, but quickly regained her composure. "You needn't worry. The child isn't Ota's."

"I know how to count," he countered. "Your night together was in spring. Now it's nearly advent. Of course, you're not showing but even if we didn't take your mood swings into account, you're still sick sometimes. Totally normal for the first months of pregnancy. It was the same with my wife too. Who's the father of your child?"

She shook her head and looked off to the side.

"I don't think it's anyone in our party," he continued in a soothing manner. "And he doesn't know about the child. Not even you knew when you left North Bohemia. Otherwise you wouldn't have set off on this pilgrimage. The letter you wrote home wasn't for your parents. It was for him, wasn't it?"

"Why ask me if you already know everything?" she hissed and spurred her horse to get away from him.

But easily caught up and grabbed her horse by the bridle. "I'm not asking you for my own pleasure," he barked. "I want to know what I can get in return for my silence. Or would you like everyone to find out what I know?"

She bit her lip and, starting to sob, she blurted out, "He's married!" She lowered her head and quietly asked what it was he wanted.

"The truth, Zdena," he said softly. "The truth about two things: What were you doing on the night the provost was murdered? And what do you know about the death of that soldier during the night?"

"With Wilibald Odo you might as well know. I don't care. I didn't go for a walk. I was in the stable, with our commander, Prech. I happen to like him and since I'm pregnant, I don't have to be particularly cautious. Who knows how long I have left in this world? My aunt and cousin died in childbirth. If only they could have enjoyed life a little longer. Because, no offense, but your squire is hopeless. He's been flitting around me for a week and nothing."

Oldrich silently nodded. He knew Prech of Michalovice to be an honorable knight. And he didn't quite believe Zdena's claim that she was with him only because she wanted a quick roll in the hay with someone. She certainly wouldn't have told Prech she's pregnant. All of a sudden Oldrich realized a glorious wedding would be in the offing after their return to North Bohemia, which hardly thrilled him. The lords of Duba were sure to gain another powerful ally from her marriage. But he decided not to let it bother him now and bade her to tell him more about that night.

Somewhat surprisingly, she shook her head and said, "I know nothing about it. Why should I?"

"You were not completely sober in the morning. You smelled of wine," he reproached her.

She gazed at the floor and admitted that she had drunk a pitcher of wine laced with strong spices because supposedly it induced miscarriage. It made her terribly sick and nothing more. She then looked at him. "You are knight, I believe. I trust it will go no further than the two of us?"

"You have my word," he nodded.

"But you must promise me not to tell your squire."

"I will if you promise to let Ota be. I don't much like how you are always flitting around him."

"Me around him?" she erupted. "I wouldn't even notice him if he would only leave me alone." She bowed and reined in her horse, intending to wait for the other girls who were at the end of the column.

* * *

Before leaving Constance, Oldrich took several measures to ensure Agnes's protection. Looking pale and frightened, she readily agreed to them. She claimed not to be afraid of death as long as it was the work of the Lord. But she still had one more task to complete while walking among the living and she couldn't allow it to be thwarted by the evil intentions of someone who was worse than a heretic, pagan and non-Christian all rolled up into one.

Four soldiers now permanently accompanied the abbess, two riding in front of her and two behind her. Friar Gregory galloped along at her side. Agnes agreed to let him move into her chambers and sleep next to her. Although he was her spiritual brother, she insisted that they not lie next to one another and that there be two beds in her chamber. Oldrich arranged to have a simple folding cot made of polished wood purchased from a carpenter outside of Constance. It was tied to the back of one of the horses carrying their baggage. Anyone now wanting to approach Agnes of Bohemia had to do so in the company of Oldrich of Chlum. He didn't think the other pilgrims were in danger anymore, but he had soldiers riding alongside them just to be sure.

He was slowly starting to get a picture of the killer. He wasn't a cruel or evil man and probably took no pleasure from the act itself. His crimes were more likely to bother him. He had one single purpose in mind and that was to turn the Czech expedition around. He always killed someone in the hope that he would achieve his goal. The killer obviously liked Agnes, in his own way. He could have slain her first, but didn't. He simply wanted to force her to return. Only when his first course of action failed did he resort to the last. All this confirmed Oldrich's belief that the murderer was after some twisted, higher goal.

Usually it was prelates who thought like this, but he

couldn't rule out the Templars either. This meant that all the Czech knights were suspects, because the power of the Templars loomed large and they could compel anyone to do their bidding, including Jost of Landstein or Oldrich's friend Prech of Michalovice. Of course, both of them had alibis for the last two murders, but he had certain reservations about believing the girls who were with them. No, he had to take everything into consideration for this manhunt. He was actually hoping to find the killer from among the ranks of the church, because then he stood a better chance of finding out the true meaning of the pilgrimage to Compostela.

They put up for the night in Waldshut, where the local Benedictine monastery offered them shelter. It was none too comfortable. Only Agnes had her own room, which the abbot had personally made available to her. The others had to make do with cots in a large and inhospitably cold hall on the ground floor of the poorhouse.

Dinner was just as meager, consisting of porridge and wrinkled apples. "We are very poor here," explained the downcast abbot. "You cannot believe how many pilgrims pass here every year. We have to take care of all of them. But the money we receive is wretched. Sometimes we go to bed hungry because there's nothing left for us in the pot." He looked careworn and withered, like one of the apples he gave them for their meal. Oldrich was moved by his lamentations.

After dinner most of the company stayed seated in the dining room reserved for pilgrims. Now the kitchen of the monastery may have been modest, but the cellar was stocked with plenty of wine. The monks offered them several varieties, one better than the other, and all of them coming from the famous vineyards of the Rhineland. Mugs filled to the brim quickly lifted their spirits and allowed them to forget the events of the past couple days. Friar Hyacinth borrowed a hurdy-gurdy and began to sing. He was not so shy in front of the maidens anymore.

The emissary of the French king, Guy of Lusignan, sat together in a corner with Emmeram of Greifsfeld and Chaplain Wolf. They were having a heated discussion. Oldrich could hear their voices getting louder and got the impression it had nothing to do with scholarly disputation. He grabbed his mug and went to sit with them, curious to know what it was about.

"You cannot deny that some of the graves of saints actually contain the bones of someone entirely different," said Guy. The Czech prelates were absolutely outraged by his assertion.

"It is heresy to doubt the sanctity of their remains," argued Wolf.

"I never said I doubt their sanctity," the emissary said in his defense. "I'm only claiming that some of them are not the right ones. Unlike you, I was in the Holy Land. I know what the merchants there are capable of. Muslim and Christian. And because I was there, I can claim that Apostle James the Greater is not buried in Compostela."

Emmeram trembled with rage. "Every Christian authority has confirmed that he is buried in Compostela. Do you know nothing of the story of how the apostle's body was put in a boat and the angels guided the boat all the way across the Mediterranean?"

Guy disrespectfully waved him off and declared that he saw no reason why he should believe this particular legend and not any others. Because the legend going around in Jerusalem was different. Nor was it true that all Christian authorities spoke about a boat sailing to Hispania. Some claim that James was buried in the Holy Land. Shouting down Emmeram's objections, he continued, "It is said that the first Christians built a church on the site of James's martyrdom. From there his remains were transferred by the Byzantine Emperor Justinian to a monastery in Raith. I have seen the tomb."

"And how can you know who's buried in it?" chafed Wolf. All of them had had enough to drink, but while there was little sign of inebriation in the swarthy face of the emissary, Emmeram's was red and moist with sweat.

"The same can be said about the grave in Compostela," answered Guy provocatively. "How can *you* know who's buried in it?"

"All of your nonsense is befitting your king," shouted the Vysehrad librarian. "You want to turn the grave of Saint Martin in Tours into a major pilgrimage site. That's why you are challenging the authenticity of the grave in Compostela. You're a liar!"

"If you were a knight, I'd kill you forthwith," replied Guy smoothly.

"I was a knight," said Emmeram. "I will meet you anytime you want."

"Well, even if you were to kill me, which is complete nonsense, you cannot refute the irrefutable truth that James is buried in the Holy Land."

"No he isn't! No he isn't!" screamed Emmeram almost hysterically. He got up, swaying a little, and with his finger raised to the heavens declared that he could prove his claim. Wickedly, almost cunningly, he announced, "I have seen Lucius Aemilius's book on the Acts of the Apostles."

"How can you use a heretic's book for your argument? You're not by chance a Waldensian, are you?" sneered Guy, spitting on the floor. "I'm finished with you!"

"I'm right!" Emmeram insisted stubbornly before staggering to the poorhouse.

Oldrich turned and walked slowly back to his place beside Agnes. He noticed that Hyacinth had stopped singing and was carefully following their argument. From that night forward, Hyacinth began avoiding the scrawny librarian.

CHAPTER XX

The breakfast in the Benedictine monastery in Waldshut was just as meager as the dinner. Oldrich sat next to the emissary and told him how captivated he had been listening to his argument with the Czech prelates over the burial place of James the apostle.

"I don't even remember it. We were quite drunk," Guy shrugged with a smile. He had pearly white teeth which, set in his leathery face, looked like the fangs of a predator.

"That's too bad. I wanted to ask you to tell me more about Lucius Aemilius's book. I've never heard of this work on the Acts of the Apostles and have been to most libraries in the Christian world. I guess I'll have to find out somewhere else."

"Wait a minute!" the emissary stopped him short. "I happen to know a little about this work and it would be better if you heard it from me rather than make inquiries. You could be accused of heresy, and here in France, we deal with heretics in a quick and merciless manner."

"Yes, last night I gathered it deals with a heretical work."

"So why are you interested in it? Christians should only read books that convey devotional thoughts."

"Are you a knight or an inquisitor?" grumbled Oldrich. He did not like the emissary's superior attitude, but such were the French.

Guy of Lusignan laughed. "You are not going to find his book in any library in the Christian world. I also doubt there's anyone who can tell you more about it. There were only two copies and both were successfully destroyed. Lucius Aemilius was a Roman philosopher who lived in Jerusalem during the prefecture of Pontius Pilate. He saw Jesus crucified and knew James the apostle. He wrote many lies about both of them in his book. That's why it had to be destroyed."

"There are a lot of books written by pagan philosophers that contain lies and nobody destroys them. You can also find kernels of truth in these books. What was so terrible about this book that it had to be destroyed?"

"A wise man can still learn something from a book full of lies, which I happen to personally doubt. But there are many people who can read who are not wise. This book ended up in the hands of Peter Waldo. He was a merchant in Lyon who gave up everything he owned to begin preaching poverty."

"Just like Francis of Assisi. Yes, I know the name, but I believe Pope Alexander III gave Waldo his permission to freely preach his thoughts," Oldrich observed matter-of-factly. He was instantly intrigued by this connection between the two preachers of poverty.

"Verbally, yes, but not in writing," Guy frostily pointed out. "Waldo went too far. In his pride he even proclaimed himself to be the new King of Jerusalem. He denied the importance of the church and led thousands of people down a false path. His sect had to be wiped out with the sword of our King. And the root of all this evil was Aemilius's book. Everyone who defends it deserves the stake."

"Aemilius couldn't have denied the church, vestments and mass. Christians didn't have any of them during his time. They didn't even know about them. The rejection of luxury did not come until the Waldensians. What terrible thing did the Waldensians take from his book?"

"You're wasting your time," warned the emissary, shaking his head and crossing himself. "You will get nothing more out of me. Make inquiries for yourself, and question your faith and God!"

"I thank you nevertheless. And just one more thing: This monastery is quite poor, but the monks here have a good heart and deserve the benefaction of those who can share their wealth with them. My squire has decided to give them that fat pouch full of silver coins which someone stuck in his hands on the streets of Prague."

"Why are you telling me this?"

"I just thought you might be interested. If that

money winds up in the coffers of the monastery, then the hands of my squire are completely clean. And free!" smiled Oldrich faintly. He turned to leave.

"One moment," said Guy. He no longer looked quite as cold as he did a minute ago speaking about the Waldensian sect. "I've just remembered that rich people sometimes hide valuable objects at the bottom of a pouch full of silver coins. A ring, for example. Perhaps it occurred to your squire to see if in fact there is something like that there."

"No, it certainly didn't occur to him," replied Oldrich. "So it would seem the local monks have acquired a ring in addition to the money."

"I, of course, cannot be sure if something like that is really there," continued the emissary. There was the same sort of spark in his eyes that Ota had whenever he joked about girls. "I haven't been to Prague and didn't give him the pouch. But it has occurred to me that there are rings etched with a monarchial coat of arms, like that of our own King Louis the Pious. Such rings are priceless. If you showed any of them to a crown official, he would let you proceed without questioning and help you wherever he could. I know nothing, but I repeat it's possible to find such a ring at the bottom of a pouch. And now if you will excuse me, we are leaving momentarily. I must go and get the horses saddled."

Before Oldrich gave the silver coins to the Benedictines, Ota had poured out the contents of the pouch and discovered a silver ring with a royal coat of arms consisting of three lilies set with small pearls. Oldrich carefully hid it in his own pouch.

"The more the better," he said, shaking his head in amazement. "I should like to know what wickedness lies behind this little gem."

* * *

The party reached Basel after a comfortable journey through serene countryside. Oldrich rode alongside the librarian, whose face was marked by wrinkles and feverish eyes. He swayed on the back of his horse, his hands wearily placed on the pommel of the saddle. He had been drinking too much lately.

"Would you mind telling me what you were arguing about with that Frenchman last night?" Oldrich politely asked him.

"You heard him yourself. Their king Louis the Pious gladly persecutes the heretics but instead of burning all of them at the stake, he takes some of them into his service. Pious nothing! To claim that James is not buried at Compostela! It's...it's as if you would..." gasped Emmeram, but he wasn't able to finish his sentence and settled instead for spitting in disgust.

"I understand," Oldrich nodded. "You've known me for many years and know that I value books. Just like you do. You can therefore understand when I say I would like to know more about Aemilius's book, the one you were talking about, even if it is a heretical work. Is it really about St. James?"

"Well, first of all, it's not a heretical work," the prelate answered a bit stiffly. He swallowed hard and asked Oldrich if he didn't have some wine to share with him because he could barely speak, his throat was so parched. Oldrich untied a ceramic jar from his saddle, uncorked it and handed it to the suffering librarian. He drank from it with gusto but did not return the jar. He held the reins to his horse in one hand, the jar in the other, and sipped between utterances.

"In the literal sense of the word, a work is heretical if the author is a Christian who doubts the tenets of faith set forth by the Christian church," he explained in the tone of a master lecturing his student. "It's a work of heresy if it deviates from dogma. Aemilius's work on the Acts of the Apostles is godless but in no way heretical. The author was a pagan who was not trying to disprove dogma in his work. He didn't even know it, so his hand was not being guided by God, as in the case of the Gospels, but by the devil."

"I understand. And have you read this work?"

Emmeram swilled from the wine and thought for a moment. Reluctantly he went on. "I had the opportunity to leaf through it. I can't say I read the whole book. I didn't have much time, but what I read was enough! It was then that I understood my destiny in this world is to write a defense of James the Greater. As you know, I have been working on it ever since."

"Did Aemilius doubt the importance of James as an

apostle?"

"I told you he was a pagan. He understood nothing surrounding the crucifixion of Christ, so it makes no sense to repeat his lies. As soon as my own work is ready, you can read it. There you will find all the answers that relate to this story."

"I would be most appreciative," Oldrich bowed politely. "Just one more trifle. You spent some of your youth in southern France, didn't you?"

"I once spent several weeks in Carcassonne. A good librarian has to spend a lot of time in the saddle in order to get to know the treasures of Christian knowledge. Now I would like to ask you something since we're talking in this manner. Who killed our provost?"

"I still don't know," replied Oldrich. "Do you suspect anybody?"

"Certainly," nodded Emmeram. He finished the wine and gave the container back to him. "Young Rosenberg. Brother Wilibald Odo told me that he was afraid of him. Or rather I should say he confided his fear of the Templars in me."

"Why?"

"That he didn't tell me, but on the night he was murdered, I brought something to the maidens' chamber. You probably know none of them were there. Suddenly I heard you shouting in the courtyard. As I opened the door to go down, I saw Rosenberg running in the hall. Not towards the courtyard but from it. I don't think he saw me."

"Thank you," Oldrich smiled. "Your testimony is valuable."

The Vysehrad librarian hiccupped and muttered that his thirst still wasn't quenched.

* * *

In the afternoon it was just their luck that Rosenberg's horse injured its leg. It was nothing serious but would take some time to tend to it. The company decided not to wait for him because darkness would soon be falling and the Czech pilgrims wanted to reach Basel before the city gates were shut. Oldrich said he would stay behind with Rosenberg, stating that in view of their recent misfortunes, it was better for none of them to be left alone. Peter rejected his offer, whereupon Agnes severely rebuked him. Oldrich of Chlum, she declared, was the leader of this expedition. Rosenberg crossed himself and submitted, saying that the Knights Templar were not only brave but also humble believers in the faith.

Together they mended the horse's injury and set off after the others. Slowly, so as not to aggravate the animal's condition. Oldrich deftly started things off by talking about the struggle with the infidels, about the Holy Land and the courage of the Templars. The normally aloof Rosenberg quickly warmed and spoke with youthful enthusiasm about the bravery of his order. Oldrich was surprised to see him smile. He hadn't looked so happy in a long time.

Oldrich discreetly brought up the scroll that was found in Solomon's Temple, followed by the secret box that was later lost, but Rosenberg was unresponsive to these and other cues. Either he really knew nothing about Templar secrets or was perfectly adept at concealing them. It was the conviction of the Templars that it was nobody's business what went on in their affairs.

They quickened the pace after they reached a gorge where the Rhine fell with a muted roar and continued through a wide, peaceful channel. Rosenberg pointed to the waterfall and sneered, "I wonder how that fool Prech was planning to go by boat here?"

Rosenberg's horse was now able to gallop freely. In the distance they spied the tops of the cathedral towers. Oldrich switched the conversation to the events of the past couple days.

"Very unfortunate," said Rosenberg, piously crossing himself. "Of course, the fate of the believer is to suffer and die for his faith. Who can say whether the suffering that accompanies us in the end is not the work of God?"

"The provost was a pious and virtuous servant of the Lord," Oldrich pointed out.

"You say that because you are a courtier. Just like he was," he shrugged disapprovingly. "But I know that the Holy Father was planning to remove him from office. Wilibald Odo was using the chapter to enrich himself. He was even siphoning off the tithes he sent to Rome. A pious servant of the Lord shouldn't behave in such manner!"

"How do you know this?"

"It was the commendatore of our order who uncovered the provost's vice. He charged me with bringing the list of his sins to Rome. In return, I was accepted among the Templars."

"Did Wilibald Odo know this?"

"Why do you think he killed Commendatore Jacob de Vries? To avenge himself."

"You're sure he's the one who killed him?"

"Who else?"

"Let's say that he did. It brings up the question whether or not you wanted to avenge yourself on the provost?"

"Sure I wanted to," Rosenberg nodded in all seriousness. "But I didn't kill him. The order avenges itself in another way. When the Templars want to exact revenge, we kidnap the person and hold a court. Only then do we execute him. We don't murder people, Sir Procurator! We are servants of God."

"Perhaps, but on the night the provost was murdered, you were seen in the hallway running towards your chamber from the courtyard."

"Emmeram told you that, didn't he? He was trying to hide behind the door to the maidens' chamber. The fool! He thinks I didn't see him. Yes, I was running down the hallway. I had gone to the wine cellar because I was thirsty. Just as I was returning, I heard your cry. And because I didn't have my sword with me at the time, I ran for it. What good would I have been at that moment without my sword?"

"Quite logical, but you could've told me that when I asked you that night. A shame," said Oldrich not altogether unfriendly. "Did you notice anyone about when you went to the wine cellar? Who do you think killed the provost?"

"It's obvious," Rosenberg retorted angrily. He was clearly tired of talking about it. "Chaplain Wolf. He was sitting in the taproom when I went to the cellar, but wasn't there when I returned. And he wasn't in our chamber either; just so you know we had the same room that night."

"And the reason? Why would he kill Wilibald Odo?"

"You're the investigator," scoffed Rosenberg. They were approaching a wooden bridge across a moat. Before them stood two massive square towers flanking the gate. A guard with the coat of arms of the city of Basel on his tunic was preparing to close the gate. They galloped ahead into the dark vaulted entrance. The iron grille of the gate fell with a hollow thud just behind them. The sentry carefully secured it with two bars.

"If you're interested in knowing why Chaplain Wolf killed the provost, I suggest you ask Jost. He will do anything for his father, and the chaplain obeys all of Jost's commands. Didn't the two of them falsely accuse Friar Hyacinth? There you are! Supposedly, the provost was trying to get the King to remove Vilem of Landstein from his post as burgrave," Rosenberg added. He galloped off despite the narrowness of the street ahead and nearly ran down a mother and child. They managed to jump out of the way at the last second.

Oldrich followed him until he was out of sight. He himself had sat on the King's council for a couple of days and knew all about the scheming that went on there. Everyone against everybody. And Wilibald Odo had been the biggest schemer of them all. But Oldrich didn't believe that somebody wanted him dead for that reason alone.

CHAPTER XXI

They spent the night at the palace of the local bishop. In the morning Agnes surprised everyone by announcing that she didn't feel well. Even though she was getting on in years and riding in the saddle was quite tiring, they were worried some illness was coming over her. It was therefore decided that she would continue on to Besançon in a wagon. The Bishop of Basel promised to lend her his wagon, which was comfortably furnished and enabled her to lie down in the event she was seriously ill. But the wagon would make much slower progress than the others on horseback. So it was also decided that the other pilgrims would proceed ahead to Besançon and wait for her to arrive at her own pace. Most of the other members of her company immediately offered to accompany her, saying they would be glad to ride slowly alongside her wagon, but she adamantly refused.

"Only Friar Gregory will accompany me," she insisted. "And also Zdena Berkova of Sloup. I think the wagon will be more convenient for her. I'm sure we'll have something to talk about. I'm an old woman and need company." Oldrich instantly noticed a slightly frightened look on the face of his squire Ota.

"I will keep four soldiers for protection. That should suffice. Sir Oldrich of Chlum will lead the rest of you," Agnes continued. "He will ensure that none of you arrives late or becomes separated from the company. There's no need for me to point out that one of you is the killer. If any of you tries to leave, I will consider it an admission of guilt. And one more thing: I will use this time to also consider whether we will all proceed on the pilgrimage, or only some of us, or perhaps myself alone. I will tell you my decision in Besançon."

The main entourage had barely ridden through the city gates of Basel when Ota rode up to his master. "How could Abbess Agnes know about Zdena? You know how much she delights in arranging weddings for the children of noble families. But even if the King imprisoned and tortured me, I would still never get married!"

"It won't reach that point, Ota," smiled Oldrich. "I shouldn't tell you this now because you deserve to suffer for a while on account of your sins. But don't worry! You're not the only knight to succumb to the charms of Zdena Berkova. I'm sure their talk will be more about him. Or...perhaps them. There are at least two others," Oldrich added. It all depended on what Zdena's true intentions were. But he completely understood why Prech was acting even more nervous than his squire.

"Right now I'm worried about something else," Oldrich continued. "Agnes was fine yesterday, complaining of nothing. And did you see her in the saddle? She galloped along better than most of the soldiers. She's a princess of the blood and grew up on a horse. I don't think she's being forthcoming with the real reason for this change."

"Perhaps she fears for her life. You did warn her that she would most likely be the next target of the killer."

"I don't think so. She's stubborn and like most nuns relies too much on God for help. She constantly repeats that she's a bride of Christ. Still, I've noticed she's now carrying a dagger around with her. She's not so naïve anymore. Our actions over the past few days have virtually made it impossible for the killer to get near her unobserved. But if she continues alone, she will put herself in greater danger. Do you know what I'm afraid of? That she will persist in this bizarre game of Clare's secret and this mysterious box that was supposedly lost by the Templars."

"Why supposedly?"

"Because what could make it so important? I have the feeling that everything here is about Apostle James and the heretical sect of southern France. The Templars and some scroll from the vaults of Solomon's Temple have hardly anything in common with either of them. How many untruths about Christ and his crucifixion have been written and passed down over the centuries? Remember the Arians and their claim that Christ wasn't the son of God! And what about these incessant quarrels among theologians over the immaculate conception of the Virgin Mary? No, I think the situation here is much more prosaic. I would wager we're dealing with some compromising information about some major figure today. The Pope, the Emperor or King of France, perhaps even St. Francis himself. That would make much more sense than some communication from long ago."

"Do you think Agnes will send us home from Besançon and continue on alone?"

"That's one possibility. Do you know what worries me even more? Last night Guy of Lusignan paid her a visit. They spoke together for more than two hours. And now, in the morning, Agnes announces that she isn't feeling well and will journey alone. Doesn't that strike you as suspicious?"

"But the French emissary is still with us. I know, stupid argument," a chastened Ota immediately excused himself.

"I got the impression that maybe she wants to give me more time to find the killer. Did you hear her repeat that he's one of us? It's almost like she's trying to provoke him. Or at least draw him away from the expedition, which would be tantamount to a confession. If he truly wants to stop us, his only choice now is to kill Agnes. He would have to disappear and carry out his deed somewhere along the way. I only hope Agnes knows what she's doing. If she thinks setting yourself up as bait for a predator is smart, then she's dumber than I thought," growled Oldrich.

"Straight from the horse's mouth," nodded Ota. "I say that all the time whenever you set yourself up as bait, but do you ever listen to me?"

"Quiet!" snapped Oldrich. "Or else Zdena and I will say you're the..."

"So it's true then," Ota cut him off. "I thought so."

"What's true?"

"That she's pregnant," shrugged Ota with feigned indifference. "Forgive me, my lord, but we've been together long enough for me to learn a thing or two from you. In fact, we learn from each other, but now I can say, with all due modesty, that I'm a much better pupil than you are."

"Good heavens, you don't know when to quit! Now what are you on about? Svetlana again?"

"Just in general," he smiled good-naturedly. "Haven't you noticed the way Katherine has been looking at you admiringly over the past few days?"

"Of course. Usually whenever we two are together. And that's why I would be willing to wager that it isn't me she's looking at. I've also learned something from you, namely don't trust every glance that comes your way from a girl in love. Look, she's staring at us again. Or I should say...at you."

Ota shrugged as if unaffected by the news. Oldrich watched him, knowing as he did that it wouldn't take long for Ota to raise a hand and run it through his carefully coiffed wavy hair. Four clops of the hooves, to be exact.

Ota noticed his master's grin and realized he was on display. He quickly gripped his reins with both hands and asked whether they would continue their manhunt during the journey to Besançon.

"Of course," Oldrich nodded. "Even if it will be a complete waste of time and we end up going in circles. We have lots of contradictory evidence but no chance to verify what's true and what's not. We sleep in a different place every day, and as soon as we learn something, we're already somewhere else before we can check it out. At every tavern we stop at we're surrounded by barkeeps, servants, merchants and other guests. Our killer can easily get lost in the crowd. Nothing is worse than conducting an investigation during a pilgrimage. And now nothing is going to happen on the way to Besançon to draw attention to the killer. Unless he actually does disappear from our party and tries to murder Agnes. But the chances of that happening are the same as Archangel Gabriel visiting us tonight bearing a scroll with the name of the killer on it."

* * *

And nothing really did happen on the way to Besançon. None of the Czech pilgrims disappeared, nor did Gabriel appear, as Ota snidely pointed out. Once they were in the city, they immediately headed for the harbor in Doubs. Guy of Lusignan said the

King had a ship ready there to ferry them south. Indeed he did.

The boat was completely different from the crafts they used on the Danube. It was much longer, with a raised stern that included two lavishly furnished cabins. Another was located below deck but was also relatively large. It was furnished with benches attached to the walls and two long tables.

"We shall, of course, sleep on shore. These cabins are only in the event of poor weather," the King's emissary explained. He then added, upon noticing the sour looks on the faces of the soldiers as they gazed none too happily at the long, heavy oars, that the ship had its own crew and therefore they wouldn't have to bother rowing. There weren't enough of them anyway for all the oars.

They spent the night at a harbor inn called At the Deaf Chanticleer. They could see the moored ship directly from the windows of their chambers on the first floor of the large and elaborately built accommodations. They were anticipating a few days of rest. No one could guess how long it would take Agnes to make the trip there by wagon. Prech organized a betting pool. Those interested in playing handed him a silver coin with an estimation of the time when the wagon should arrive. Whoever came the closest would get all the money. Gradually everyone joined in, even the prelates and soldiers, with the exception of Rosenberg. He declined, declaring that gambling was a sin.

Emmeram was studiously avoiding the emissary. They had not spoken since their argument at the monastery in Waldshut. The librarian even neglected to greet him. He simply walked around as if he didn't exist. Guy ignored him in turn, and once even spat behind his back. And for the first time since they set out, Jost quarreled with his sister Svetlana. The bad mood seemed to be everywhere, and on top of that it began snowing that night. It was more like flurries, simply the first tentative touch of winter, but it did nothing to improve the general feeling.

"It's completely normal that we should start arguing with one another," explained Rosenberg in the morning. "It was the same when I was on a crusade. After a couple of weeks you start to get on each other's nerves and think the heathens would make better company than your neighbor in the tent. We need some distraction. What about organizing a small private tournament? There's enough space on the lawn behind the inn and we have just the right amount of knights among us to hold a decent jousting."

"I'm against it," said Jana. "What's the point of inflicting injuries on one another? You call that fun? I prefer music and dancing."

"You should know that my brother is such a lousy dancer that you would get more fun from a knot on his head than from him stomping on your toes," observed Svetlana. There wasn't much good humor in her voice. She was still upset from yesterday.

"Do whatever you want," said Emmeram

dismissively. "But count me and Chaplain Wolf out. The local Cistercian abbey has a couple of books worth reading. We're going there together just in case someone decides to say that one of us tried to disappear."

"I promised Katherine that I would accompany her into town. There's a big crafts fair taking place in the market today. Merchants are coming there all the way from Flanders," announced Ota. Svetlana and Jana were nicely angry at him for not saying anything sooner so that they could join them.

"I'm not leaving the maid of Blatna in the hands of Ota of Zastrizly," declared Jost good-naturedly. "I'll go to."

"And you, Oldrich, will you leave me in the hands of your squire?" asked Svetlana. He himself hated tournaments, derived no pleasure from personal combat. He would prefer to join the two monks in the Cistercian library, but knew it was better to keep an eye on the others. He agreed and in the end the tournament consisted of him, Rosenberg, Prech and Guy. Only Hyacinth remained behind in the inn. He had stumbled yesterday and fell down the stairs. Complaining of a sore back, he decided to spend the day in bed.

The company set off immediately after breakfast. It stopped snowing, the clouds dispersed and the sun came out. The remaining coat of snow on the ground quickly melted. The alleyways around the harbor were covered in mud, but the streets around the marketplace were paved. The crafts fair was indeed splendid, something completely different than the markets in Prague's Old Town with their vegetables, cattle and coarse cloth for sale. Here, covering the entire square, were carefully aligned wagons displaying the finest goods available in the Christian world. The girls went from one merchant to the next, admiring delicate fabrics, bottles of perfume, jewelry, tulle veils, silver belts, headbands and assorted makeup.

"We are on a pilgrimage," Rosenberg admonished them, but he might as well have tried to stop a herd of wild cattle with the same exhortation.

The pilgrims had lunch in a comfortable inn there on the marketplace and spent the afternoon shopping. They didn't return to the harbor until sunset. They were merrily hollering at one another, the excursion to the city having done wonders for their mood. After storing their purchases away, they gathered around a table next to the fireplace, where a beech log was crackling. The librarian and chaplain were there waiting for them. Only Friar Hyacinth was missing. Ota went to his chamber to fetch him but found it empty. His bed was made and his things were gone. The monk had disappeared.

Oldrich and Ota hastily devoured a few potato cakes and some fruit while a groom saddled up their horses. They left Besançon before the city gates were closed and galloped off in the direction of Basel, whence the wagon carrying Agnes of Bohemia was supposed to arrive. It started snowing again.

* * *

It was as if Hyacinth had vanished into thin air. Oldrich and his squire rode nearly throughout the night. They stopped at each wayside inn and by dawn had come upon the bishop's wagon in the courtyard of a cozy-looking tavern. In front of the doors to the chamber where Agnes was staying they found a soldier sitting on the floor. His lance was propped up against the wall and he was playing some kind of children's game with stones in order to keep awake. Oldrich first verified that everything was all right with the abbess and then praised the soldier for his vigilance. He woke up another soldier from the small retinue accompanying the abbess and ordered him to watch over the window to the chamber in the courtyard. He and his squire then went to the ground floor to lie on benches next to the fireplace, where several cinders were still glowing. From there they could see the front door and the stairs to the first floor. They wrapped themselves up in their cloaks and went to sleep.

In the morning they explained to a surprised Agnes why they had returned. She crossed herself and asked if this meant the horror was finally at an end.

"It could be," Oldrich admitted cautiously. "But we cannot rule out that Friar Hyacinth didn't run for another reason. Perhaps he was afraid to return to southern France. He was most probably a heretic in his youth and his parents were burned at the stake in Languedoc. Maybe he was frightened by the addition of Guy of Lusignan to our company."

"I don't agree," argued Agnes. "He could have run anytime. Moreover, he was washed clean of guilt upon joining his order."

"The Inquisition has burned many monks," Oldrich pointed out, but quickly conceded that this reasoning was rather weak. "It's true that Hyacinth is the only pilgrim who could not have murdered the papal legate in Landstein. If someone is truly committing these murderers in order to prevent this pilgrimage from reaching Compostela, he gains nothing by fleeing. And now he would just give up? I don't think so."

"Of course, he could be setting a trap for us," noted Ota. "The journey from Besançon here goes through several abandoned villages. He could collect a band of brigands and waylay us on the way."

"We'll take a detour," Oldrich decided. "The wagon will continue on the trade route as if our venerable older sister Agnes is in it. In the event someone really wants to waylay us, it will buy us time before he discovers the ruse. Venerable older sister, would it be too much trouble for you to join us on horseback?"

"My whole body aches from journeying in a wagon," the elderly abbess faintly smiled. "It will be a blessing from God for me to continue in the saddle."

As they prepared to leave, Ota walked up to Zdena and quietly asked her how she held up at the side of the venerable Agnes for so long. And whether everything was all right.

"She's a wise woman," she answered guardedly. "You needn't worry. Not a word about spring was mentioned. You can consider yourself free once and for all." When she noticed a hint of resentment in his face, she leaned forward and lightly kissed him, adding in a whisper that she would invite him to her wedding if he so desired.

Like the previous day, the snow stopped that morning and the skies cleared up. The innkeeper sent his brother and a small party of riders to accompany them on the side paths to Besançon. They made good time and reached it early in the afternoon.

They found the other Czech pilgrims sitting around the table next to the fireplace. They were hunched over a wooden board and arguing over which move would be the best. Oldrich could see over their shoulders that Rosenberg was playing chess with Lusignan and was, of course, losing. Sitting at one of the corners of the table was Friar Hyacinth, pointing at the chessboard and whispering something to Katherine.

Agnes began coughing the moment they walked in. Acrid smoke was hovering around the ceiling after someone had tossed a damp piece of wood into the fire. Since it was freezing outside, no one felt like letting in some fresh air. Jost shouted to the innkeeper to prepare some mulled wine for the venerable older sister. He then crossly informed them that Hyacinth had reappeared and explained everything to them. An ugly, emaciated bar girl brought her a cup of wine and set it down on a corner of the table without a word. She then turned and fled.

"Wait, you still have a chance to win," Prech shouted and grabbed Rosenberg by the arm. "But not that one. Take the rook..."

The whole company was bent over the chessboard. The guard commander had been right. Even though the French emissary had more pieces on the board, this one move had put his king in a position of no escape.

"Checkmate," announced Rosenberg, rubbing his hands like an excited child.

Oldrich noticed the cup unnoticed on the corner of the table. Svetlana was trying to worm her way through the others in order to get a better look and just about sent it crashing to the floor. "Drink, venerable older sister, before the wine gets cold."

Agnes gladly lifted the cup and held it in her cold hands. It felt delightfully warm. She then saw that Zdena was looking pale. She was leaning against the wall and appeared ready to either vomit or faint. She knew the girl was in the family way and even though she had conceived in sin, it was Christian to forgive. Plus, she had a plan for dealing with this particular situation. She herself never had children, but could imagine what it was like to carry one in the womb. She smiled kindly at the girl, huddled against the cold, and handed her the cup.

"Drink first, my dear, you need it more than I do."

Zdena gratefully took the cup and drank from it eagerly.

"More. Don't be shy," Agnes urged her on.

She drank again and then handed the half-empty cup back to her. Suddenly she was overcome by painful cramps and the cup fell to the floor. With foam coming out of her mouth, the girl collapsed on the floor. She cried out in agony, her hands clutching her abdomen. She beat about like an animal in its death throes.

"Quickly!" screamed Agnes. "Help her!"

Oldrich rushed into the kitchen with the cup, filled it with plain water from a vat and poured salt into it. He hurried to the girl's side, lifted her head and tried to force the water into her mouth.

"Drink! You must swallow and throw up!" he implored her. But it was too late. Zdena Berkova of Sloup jerked with one more painful spasm and expired.

Oldrich wiped some of the foam from her mouth with his hand, sniffed it, and then very carefully touched the tip of her tongue. He looked up at the horrified people who were still gathered around the dead girl.

"I know this poison. Somebody put it in the wine while we were all focused on the game. It was one of you. And it was meant for Agnes of Bohemia!"

CHAPTER XXII

The Czech pilgrims were locked up inside their rooms while the body of Zdena Berkova was carried to the nearby church, where Agnes of Bohemia went to pray over it. Only Friar Gregory was with her. Jost, who was in charge of the party Oldrich had left behind in Besançon, quickly explained to him the situation with Hyacinth.

"Someone sent a letter to the town hall denouncing him," he fumed. "It said that Hyacinth was no Premonstratensian, rather a heretical preacher in disguise secretly preaching the Waldensian heresy in the countryside. They immediately came here and arrested him. They warned the innkeeper not to say anything under pain of death. In the morning the local inquisitor arrived with an armed guard to interrogate us. The French emissary quickly straightened things out and brother Hyacinth was released. As for his things, they were bundled up in some cloth and tossed under the bed. Someone wanted it to look like he had disappeared."

"I don't suppose we know who denounced brother

Hyacinth?"

"No. The letter was received anonymously. They have such a stupid custom here, supposedly to protect honest Christians with a heavy conscience. Anyone who wants to denounce a heretic can slip a note into the box at the town hall gate."

"Really smart," sneered Oldrich. "If we tried to introduce something like that in Prague, there wouldn't be a box big enough to hold all the denouncements. It's hardly any way to seek justice and no law justifies encouraging the base instincts in people. But we are, after all, in France."

"I gather you don't much like this place," said Jost with a grin.

"I like all Christians. But I don't like any country that burns women and children on account of faith, as if that was somehow a monument to their piety."

After Jost left, Oldrich summoned his squire. They sat at a table and quickly deliberated what to do next.

"The killer is smarter than I originally thought," he sighed.

"Or he bloody well learns quickly," added Ota. He shouted to the innkeeper to fetch them a pitcher of hot wine. Spiced, if possible, but not laced with anything lethal. The innkeeper, dismayed by what had happened, now personally sipped from every pitcher in front of the host as a sign that the wine was harmless.

"It was an incredible twist of fate. Maybe Abbess Agnes is right when she claims that the hand of God watches over the pious individual," Oldrich shrugged and took a drink.

"Nonsense! Zdena Berkova wasn't so bad that God would punish her like that," Ota burst out. There were tears in his eyes. "I'll find whoever did it and kill him, I swear!"

Oldrich shook his head but Ota would not be swayed. After a moment of silence, Ota asked what next.

"No matter what I do, I can't protect Agnes when we're all grouped together like this. We're too confined. Curse this pilgrimage! We have only two possibilities to keep the killer from striking again. But before that, forget any thought that we know who this person might be. We still have absolutely nothing to go on. We cannot subject any of our pilgrims to trial by torture. And no one is going to confess anything freely. Our killer is smart and always knows how to manage everything so that no one sees anything. Which, frankly speaking, isn't all that difficult. But even if someone noticed somebody, what's so strange about members of the same party encountering each other in the hallway or tavern? Each would immediately forget about it. And I won't even mention the fact that none of them is willing to obey the measures we put in place, so they're for nothing. We are living in very cramped conditions where you can kill someone faster than a blink of the eye. The only thing we know is that the killer does not want us to continue to Compostela. And this is precisely the motive that tells us absolutely nothing. I thought that I was able to protect Agnes, but the truth is you can't be expected to protect anyone on a pilgrimage. So our only choice is she either continues while the rest of us turn back, or perhaps stay here under armed guard to keep whoever it is from setting off after her, or we all return together. There is no other possibility."

"There is perhaps one more," Ota added hastily, giving Oldrich the impression that his squire had already worked out another plan but was waiting for a moment like this to present it. "What if everyone continued on to Compostela and the killer is led to believe that Agnes is with us, but in fact she takes a shorter way there? With you as her escort, of course. She would be safe and I would stay with the others and try to find our man."

"Hypothetically it's a possibility, but I don't see it in practical terms."

"One of our noble maidens can start hysterically shouting that she can't take it any longer, that she wants to go home now. Agnes will witness it along with the others; she will grudgingly agree that it must be and angrily add that the best escort for her home will be you. Since you were not able to protect her and the other pilgrims, at least you might be capable of protecting one young girl. She will also add that she's determined to continue on. You two will argue about it for a while until you finally back down and promise to deliver the maiden safely to Prague."

"It's not the most glamorous role, but what should I

expect with you in charge of this theater," laughed Oldrich. But it was clear that the plan intrigued him. "What after that?"

"You leave this evening and secretly return sometime during the night and the girl will change to look like Agnes, who you will then spirit away."

"That's crazy! Everyone will know it!"

"Why?" objected Ota. "Before you leave, the abbess will retire to her cabin on the ship and spend the entire time in prayer and meditation. She will explain that as a sign of repentance she will surrender the worldly life and retreat into monastic solitude and so forth. She will certainly be able to explain it more piously than me. Naturally the girl will be there instead of her. She will be wearing her monastic habit so that anyone trying to catch a glimpse of her in the window won't notice the change. Meanwhile, you and the abbess will gallop as fast as you can for the sea. If you go through Clermont-Ferrand, you will reach the harbor in Bordeaux much earlier than we will. I found out that it's the quickest way, if less comfortable. Going by boat does have its advantages. Once you get to Bordeaux, take the first ship to Compostela and Agnes will have fulfilled her mission. After our boat reaches Montpellier and we saddle up, the girl will reveal herself. By that time it will be too late for our killer to reach you. Presuming, of course, that he's still alive. I will do everything to catch this bastard. It's only logical that he will try to murder whoever he thinks Agnes is."

"He's not stupid. I wouldn't underestimate him," warned Oldrich. "Let's assume that we try your plan. It's not bad. Of course, the one condition is that Agnes is able to make the shorter, more difficult way. She's no spring chicken. But she does everything for the glory of God and I've seen her in the saddle, so I don't think that should be any problem. But somebody will have to make sure that the girl doesn't leave the cabin while you're underway. And how will you convince the others that you're staying with them while I'm leaving?"

"That's the easiest part," smiled Ota. "Agnes will announce that everyone here has some reason to kill her. Everyone except me, and that's why she trusts only me to look after her. Not even her brother Minorite will be allowed near her. Everyone here knows well that Agnes has her whims. Such a declaration from any other person would seem suspicious, but not her. The thing is, I don't quite trust this Minorite, despite the abbess always referring to him as her brother. He is after all a prelate. And that cup was placed on a corner of the table where he was sitting with Emmeram and Hyacinth. Three prelates. One of them is the murderer. And standing next to them was Chaplain Wolf. Another prelate."

"This desire for revenge is not the best counsel. Especially if you're trying to uncover the truth," Oldrich mildly admonished him. "Jost handed the cup to Agnes. Even he had an opportunity to lace the wine with poison. And all three girls were standing behind our backs. Under certain circumstances, even the two knights who were playing chess could have done it. Remember how Rosenberg kept looking at the cup? The poison used was quite strong. Only two or three grains of it is enough. You can drop it into the wine unobserved even with a crowd of people around you."

"I wonder why the killer didn't use poison earlier. You yourself said that poison is used mostly by cowards, prelates and women."

"It's probably not true in this case. Poison was probably his last recourse after I put Agnes under heavy guard. Only this time luck wasn't with him. Since no one normally carries poison around with him, he certainly didn't plan to use any. So he has to go out and find it, but wayside inns normally don't carry it. When the murder of one of our soldiers didn't prevent us from crossing the bridge in Constance, he was resolved to kill Abbess Agnes and realized he would need poison with all the guards on alert. But he had no time to get it in Constance and so waited until we reached Basel, the next big town on the way. He probably got it there and decided to use it when Agnes still insisted on the pilgrimage going forward. Now it was either divine intervention or she sensed that Zdena Berkova was pregnant, because the wine was an opportunity for her to perform a Christian service. But before that, she wanted to be alone with the girl for a couple of days. An elderly pious woman and a young sinner. The killer probably wanted to use the poison at our stop immediately after Basel, but couldn't because of that first mischance. And this poison is special in that it loses strength over time. Since he has to somehow expedite the abbess's return to Prague, I would suggest that he denounced Hyacinth and hid his things to make it look like Agnes was in danger. He needed to get her here as quickly as possible, and he succeeded in that. After we left for her in the night, he gets the poison out and waits. When we arrive, everything looks ideal for him. There's all kinds of activity going on in the taproom, nobody has a chance to get their bearings, much less to think. But it's only more bad luck for him when the hand of Providence again intervened. Of course, it's possible that he will try and use poison again. Perhaps another type, because we don't know if he bought enough," said Oldrich, taking a drink. He thought for a moment and then nodded. "We can try your plan. I think it sounds good and could work. We have nothing better anyway. I'm sure Agnes would not be willing to go back even if it means paying for it with her life. She's constantly expressing her admiration for martyrdom. I take it you have already chosen the girl to play her in the cabin."

"There weren't many choices," said Ota. "If Jana declares she wants to go back to Prague, Jost will go too. If Svetlana says it, it's possible that both of them, Jost and Jana, will accompany her to Bohemia. Moreover, I don't quite trust either girl and therefore would be hesitant about entrusting them with the role. That only leaves Katherine. She's too simple a girl to be our murderer. She loves her fiancé and is meticulously saving her virginity for him, so there's no danger to her from my side. Which is a shame really, but I'll make up for it once we get home and all this is behind us. With your permission, of course."

"Spare me similar declarations," mumbled Oldrich. "Do you really expect me to sanctify your lascivious plans for the future? Will Katherine go along with this plan?"

"Why wouldn't she? Like I said, she's an entirely simple girl and won't realize she's in any danger. Plus, she will be eager to please Agnes. You can see how much she admires her. She may even want to join her order someday."

"You better see to it, at the cost of losing your head, that nothing happens to her," Oldrich advised him after briefly deliberating about it.

"If, by that, you mean the killer not harming her," said Ota, "then that I promise you."

* * *

As it turned out, Agnes of Bohemia not only knew how to maintain her self-control, but also, when necessary, how to act. Their performance in front of the other pilgrims in the taproom of the harbor inn was so convincing that Oldrich had the icy feeling that there, for a moment, the abbess actually despised him. And Katherine proved her equal in adroitness. Ota couldn't believe the tears he was seeing. The only part of her performance that seemed a bit far-fetched was breaking the pitcher of beer on the floor and stomping on the shards. But the others were quite amused. Oldrich and the young noble girl left the inn before nightfall. Several of the pilgrims accompanied them as far as the city gates. There the remaining two girls bade heart-wrenching goodbyes to Katherine while Agnes took up her quarters in the ship's cabin.

A slight difficulty arose during the night with the presence of two city guards watching over the royal ship in the harbor. But Oldrich overcame this problem by paying a rather plain prostitute to wander about the harbor in search of quarry, thereby distracting both sentries for a moment. As ordered by Agnes herself, only Ota was posted to watch over her. When Ota heard the part about how his master had managed to get past the guards, he reprovingly shook his head and reminded him of his own words that stipulated a good investigator never uses the sins of the flesh to search for the truth. Oldrich merely waved him off and promised to abide by it next time. He then embraced him.

"Take good care, my lord," Ota whispered to him.

"Who, me?" Oldrich whispered back. "I'll be traveling with a pious abbess. But you! You take care! I would be loath to lose you just because you're traveling with a charming young girl. Experience tells me that innocent girls tend to be more dangerous than depraved criminals. Especially for someone like you. Be careful!"

* * *

The next morning the entire company of Czech pilgrims boarded the ship. The crew, consisting of forty men armed to the teeth, appeared moments before the gangplank was raised. They took their places next to the oars, as well as on the bow and stern. Guy had the flag of the King of France raised and ordered the mooring lines cast off. Since the Doubs was not quite so broad at this point, the ship kept to the middle of the river, where there was sufficient draft.

Prior to departure, Ota had gone to the market to buy food, which he put in baskets under his watchful eye. He noticed that the French emissary was discreetly checking out the supplies. After he left, Ota went into the cabin where he found Katherine blissfully asleep on the bed. Hearing him enter, she opened her eyes and quickly fixed her hair. She beckoned him to sit next to her at the foot of the bed. They had agreed that if they were to speak together, it would only be in hushed tones. At that moment a shout was heard coming from the deck, where the ship had just grazed the shoreline.

"I was thinking about everything that has happened to us," she whispered. "I was glad to promise Abbess Agnes that I would do this for her." She was wearing the scent of a warm bed and it was most becoming to her. "It's my Christian duty. But I still think that I deserve some kind of reward in the end."

"God will certainly reward you and I don't doubt that Agnes will also. She knows how to be grateful and generous when she wants to."

"Of course. But I'm thinking about a different kind of reward. From you. And here, on the ship. You see, I'm not really speaking about a reward. Rather, I would be happy if you, as a knight, could demonstrate a certain service for me," she said, stammering with embarrassment. She looked crimson and adorably bewildered. She grabbed him by the arm and started to explain that she deeply loved Michal Kekule of Stradonice and hoped to become his wife someday. That's why she had never done anything in her life to displease him. She believed with all her heart that only with a pure soul, one unencumbered by sin, could she be happy in marriage.

Ota listened to her uneasily. He knew women and knew that similar assurances usually left his life more complicated.

"The problem here is...," she continued, becoming even more embarrassed, but having already decided to confide in him. "Two times we were lying together...so you understand...we were on the bed...and we wanted to..."

"I know what you want to say. You yourself reminded me of my poor reputation. Please forgive me for being bold...but are you trying to say that you have become man and wife? In that case congratulations!"

"I wish!" she sighed, looking demurely at the floor.

"You see, my parents never told me how these things are done. I wanted to show him my love, but it just didn't happen. We basically don't know what we're doing," she said hurriedly with tears in her eyes. She was tenderly stroking the back of his hand. Determined to soldier on, she quickly continued. "I asked Michal to go to a brothel and learn it there. He was terribly angry, shouting he could never humiliate me so. Of course, I was pleased to hear that. But the problem is he still can't manage in bed, and I don't know how to help him because I know absolutely nothing about it! So I thought if I knew exactly what to do and how to do it, then it will be all right. And that's the service I want from you. Teach me how it is properly done in bed."

"Is it enough to tell you about it or is a demonstration in order?" he asked, unable to mute the sarcasm. This was a first for him and he had to admit he felt a little offended by her offer.

"You're angry at me, aren't you?" she asked tearfully. "I knew you wouldn't be willing to help us. I meant to ask you at Landstein, but then I saw Zdena stealing all your attention. Well, God has punished her. I didn't want to impose, you understand."

"Yes, I understand," he nodded. He was now thinking he had overreacted. He had told his master that Katherine was a rather simple type and here was confirmation. She was not only unsophisticated in bed, but unsophisticated period. Why should he take this as an affront? She certainly wasn't meaning to demean him in any way. She was confiding in him something that surely required all the courage she could muster.

"Forget it," she said quietly, pulling away. "I have offended you. Or perhaps I just don't appeal to you?"

"What should I say? Love is not the same thing as learning to ride a horse or training for a tournament. You need to be consumed by passion. Your body must be burning with desire and it's difficult to learn something like that and still remain a virgin. Even if I wanted to teach you it, how could I possibly take that which you are saving for your betrothed? And I certainly don't want to betray Michal, because he's my friend."

"It wouldn't be a betrayal," she quickly replied. "I'm ready to lose my virginity with you. But if I don't do this for Michal, we'll both be unhappy, and maybe not get married in the end. And he...he won't know. Once you have shown me everything, I will show him and we will both be happy."

"Can I think about it?" he asked. He was completely caught off guard by her proposal and needed time to consider it carefully. Maybe it wasn't so completely absurd as it first sounded. Perhaps he really could help the two of them in the end.

"Of course," she said. "And please, don't be angry with me!"

CHAPTER XXIII

The ship flying the flag of the King of France sailed quickly downstream powered by two dozen oars. Guy of Lusignan was in command. He decreed they would keep going and not go ashore for lunch. It was cold out with a slight breeze, but the sky was clear and the river calm and he wanted to take advantage of the favorable conditions. Waves were splashing quietly up against the side of the boat while white foam was churning in the wake of their passage. On board were adequate supplies stored in wicker baskets. The cold lunch consisted of potato cakes, meat, cheese and pickled vegetables, served in the large cabin below decks.

Ota didn't leave his position in the rear of the craft. He sat next to the doors to the cabin presumably occupied by Agnes of Bohemia. Svetlana prepared two bowls of food and went aft to bring them to him. She sat down on the dirty planks of the deck next to him, leaned toward him and quietly began explaining that she had thought up a great plan. She knew how to find the killer. When he gave her an incredulous look, her demeanor grew stiff. "Don't forget our exalted King Ottokar has entrusted this investigation to your lord and me. And since Oldrich is gone, I am representing his interests in this matter. So hear me out."

"A rather bold presumption," he shrugged in amusement. Svetlana could look most becoming whenever she attempted to look important. But when comparing her to Katherine, the girl in the abbess's habit, at that moment on the other side of the door to the cabin, came off the better. He was warming to the prospect that, in all probability, he was going to see the would-be nun let her habit slip off, and the more he thought about it, the more excited he became. What's more, he was beginning to feel like a fish out of water. Here they were four weeks into their journey and his behavior had been as irreproachable as that of the monks.

Svetlana was saying something but he wasn't listening. Only when she poked him with her elbow did he snap out of his blessed daydreaming. She didn't take kindly to being ignored. "What in heaven's name are you thinking about?"

"You wouldn't believe me if I told you," he grinningly observed. "First, let's get something straight here. Sir Oldrich of Chlum turned over his office and authority to me before leaving. It goes to reason, then, that I'm handling the manhunt. Now tell me about your plan."

"You're lucky I had enough sense to refuse your master's offer to marry him," she snarled. She acted as if it were really the truth. Then, noticing the look of derision on his face, she quickly added, "I couldn't bear marriage with him because he gets on my nerves. And that was before I realized what a disagreeable squire he has. Well, as they say, the apple never falls far from the tree."

"Very witty indeed. Now, noble Svetlana, if you don't mind..."

"Well, I thought we could set a trap for the killer," she announced proudly. "After what happened in Besançon, his determination to stop us is probably greater than ever. Time is running out for him. He has only one way he can still kill Agnes. By using poison again. I saw you in the marketplace buying some supplies and taking them inside the ship. You're taking precautions and that's good, but you should give the killer a chance to get to the basket. We have to catch him right at the moment when he goes to try to poison some of the food."

"This kind of trap is very naïve but could work over time. Of course, presuming that we are able to keep a discreet eye on the basket, which won't be easy. There's also no guarantee he will jump for the bait. Let's wait until we reach Montpellier. Besides, trying to kill someone on board would be way too risky for him. Better to wait until we're back on shore. He'll try again then, believe me."

"It won't wait. I'm going to try to get him to do it tomorrow."

"How?"

"Oh, I know how. But first, I would like to know who's running this manhunt on board in your master's absence? You or me?"

"What is this, blackmail? It's a good thing you turned my master down. I couldn't bear to have you as his wife. I would have to go and seek service elsewhere."

"Nobody would take you," she snarled again. "So, are you going to listen to me are not?" He nodded like a condemned man. "So, I quietly spread the word that Agnes told me she saw the person who put the poison in the cup of wine. She's now consulting with God and tomorrow evening plans to leave her isolation in the cabin to lead the manhunt herself. Clever, isn't it? The killer will grow desperate. He will have to hurry and that's when we catch him."

Ota said nothing. His plan was now totally ruined because of Svetlana, not to mention Agnes would be in real danger if it got out that the abbess wasn't on board. He had no doubt that the Pope and Templars were involved, as was the King of France, judging by the superior attitude of the crew. If someone caught a glimpse of Katherine in her disguise too early, someone would be dispatched to catch up with Agnes before she could reach Compostela. The time she needed would be lost now thanks to Svetlana. Ota was anxious to catch the killer and punish him, but not at this price.

"What?" Svetlana asked, taken aback by his muted response. She was expecting him to answer with a joke or at least an objection, but this silence was unnerving. "Did I do something wrong?"

"Probably the worst possible thing you could have done," he sighed. "Now we have to figure out some way to repair the damage. It's no joke! You'd better listen to me or I swear I'll let you have it. Understand?"

Normally she would've protested, but the harshness in his voice was just as unnerving. With the expression of a girl caught in the act, she bowed and said, "Fine, you can lead the investigation. Now tell me what happened!"

He still said nothing, was all but ignoring her. She waited, then suddenly became furious. This was humiliating. He was treating her no better than a girl from the brothel. As she whirled around to leave, she cast a cold piercing look at him, and that's when she noticed his eyes. There was real fear in them. That's when she finally realized that something was indeed wrong.

Now more subdued, she sat back down next to him and pleaded with him. "Ota, what's wrong?"

"Have you ever tried to catch a squirrel in the wild? That's what it's like with you."

"Excuse me! Tell me what's going on!"

"No! But if we can't somehow stop this harebrained scheme you cooked up, it will be a catastrophe. I will explain everything to you later. All I can say now is you have put Agnes in real danger! Let me think for a minute."

Although not exactly convinced, Svetlana nodded and waited. Something no doubt had happened, but Ota surely had to be exaggerating the extent of the danger. If she had to, she would try to sneak in to see Agnes herself during the evening or night and ask her opinion whether her idea was as harebrained as Ota said it was.

"You will go out there now and tell everyone that you're delusional and in fact you're not sure at all whether Agnes meant it seriously or not. You understand?" Ota was speaking under his breath as if worried someone might overhear them. At that moment there were only rowers on deck. The others were down below eating.

She tried once more to get something out of him, even asking, incredibly, if he was worried he would not be able to guard Agnes against a possible attack. She offered, if he wanted, to guard the basket of food for him. The nasty look in his face eventually silenced her. All she could do was promise she would try to convince the others of her error.

She left to go back down below deck, amazed to find herself being so obedient. A rare thing that was whenever it happened. As she began to descend the stairs, she cast an inconspicuous glance at Ota, sitting in front of the door to the cabin. His master was a far more attractive man, but she had to admit that for the first time in her relationship with his squire, she was beginning to entertain impure thoughts about him. She gave her head a vigorous shake to let her blond hair fall across her face. Well, there was still a long way to go on this pilgrimage.

* * *

The skies grew overcast and a light drizzle began to fall, making the surface of the Doubs quietly ripple with raindrops. Wrapped up in his cloak, Ota was leaning against the door to the cabin and snoozing. When he heard some nearby planks creak, he opened his eyes and saw Guy standing before him. Ota put his hand on the hilt of his sword and stood up.

"I'm worried about the venerable Agnes of Bohemia," said the emissary of the King of France. "There's a rumor going around that she knows the name of this filthy murderer. I'm somewhat surprised that this whispering began among members of your own group, because if it is true, then she would be ill-advised to reveal the name. She could be putting herself in danger."

"The venerable Agnes of Bohemia never said anything like that. Her only contact now is with me, so I would know if it was true," Ota answered firmly.

"That doesn't change the fact that now she's in greater danger than before. Perhaps she has her reasons for deciding to have you guard her, but you are still only one. That's not enough. I have therefore decided to have one or two of my men assist you."

"No thank you. I can use our own soldiers."

"Take them, because from this moment on my men

are not going to move from the stern," he said, beckoning two of his armed retinue to join them. They were carrying lances with blue banners bedecked with gold lilies. "I sense a feeling of indignation from you. What a pity you didn't listen to me back in Prague. We could have had a friendly chat and you would have understood how important it is to my king that the venerable Agnes of Bohemia reaches Compostela safe and sound. We are both in the same boat. Both literally and figuratively. My head is also on the line for her safety, the same as your master's. That's why I will do whatever I think is best here whether this rumor going around that she knows the murderer is true or not. It makes no difference whether it was done out of evil intention or sheer stupidity."

He bowed in a gesture of departure and briskly headed for the bow. The two French soldiers walked past Ota and sat on the deck about three feet away. They leaned against the door facing the cabin and stretched out their legs. Their lances were propped up against the railing.

"What did he want?" asked Jost the moment Guy disappeared. He had been standing beneath the stairs that led below deck, interested in what they were talking about but not able to hear anything. "Svetlana asked me to come help you guard Agnes. Apparently something has happened and now she's in some new danger."

Before Ota could answer, Gregory rushed up to them. He sat down on the deck, crossed himself and mumbled that nobody could stop him from being here, as close to his older sister as possible. Next came Prech, with one of his soldiers in tow.

"I think the venerable Agnes of Bohemia is truly and finally safe," Ota told Jost. In his head he was also thinking the same of Katherine's virginity, for he had no doubt that this lot would still be here even throughout the night.

"I pray you're right," Jost said quietly and politely bowed to Ota. "I hope the abbess will reveal the murderer tomorrow."

"But she doesn't know who it is," snapped Ota. He made sure the others heard him as well.

"Sure, sure," said Jost, winking at him. "If you'll permit, I will also stay here with you. Besides, what else is there to do?"

* * *

Before nightfall, Ota collected some water out of the river into a big pitcher and carried it into the cabin. Katherine was sitting on the bed in her monastic robes with the cowl thrown over her head, dangling her bare feet above the deck out of boredom. The moment Ota was inside, he closed the door carefully and barred it. He poured most of the water into a bucket that was tied to the wall to keep it from tipping over. The rest he poured into a cup, which he gave to the girl to drink. He then sat on the bed next to her.

Katherine leaned toward him and kissed him, a bit

clumsily, on the cheek. Blushing, she asked, "What's happening out there?"

"I'm afraid we'll have to forgo our lesson tonight," he said softly. "Not because I don't want to. Believe me, I want to satisfy you. I've decided to do it for my friend. I will show you how a man and woman make love together. But not today. A rumor has been going around on the boat that Agnes knows the name of the killer. And now this cabin is being guarded by practically everybody out there wearing tights and carrying a sword. It's simply out of the question to lay down together under these circumstances."

"Why not? What would be so strange about you keeping the abbess company? You don't have to stay here the whole night. Maybe just till midnight is enough. I'm a quick learner."

"My dear girl, this cabin has wooden walls. What we're going to learn is not the quietest of lessons. It simply wouldn't work!"

"It's a pity," she moaned. "But if it can't be, so be it. But will you stay with me for a while at least? What am I supposed to do here all by myself? I feel like I'm in prison. Do you know what? Maybe you can at least tell me about it! What's it like to make love to a woman, Sir Knight of Zastrizly?"

"All right, but call me Ota," he said, adopting an intimate tone. He caught a glimpse of Katherine smiling ever so slightly before resting her head on his shoulder. Ungainly, as if she were nervous. "Of course, I won't describe exactly what happens in bed. I hope we'll be able to try it together next time. I'm really looking forward to it, believe me! But today I'll simply tell you about love. It's like when two people are in love, the rest just happens. Do you know the legend of King Arthur?"

"No," she replied somewhat disappointingly. "I don't care much for stories about knights and kings."

"This one you will. You see, Arthur's wife Guinevere was seduced by his best friend, a knight named Lancelot. This Guinevere was a lot like you. She loved Arthur, but at the same time she wanted to be held in Lancelot's arms," Ota began. He put his arm around Katherine's shoulder and continued with the telling. The rain outside the window grew ever stronger and soon they were immersed in darkness.

CHAPTER XXIV

That evening the ship was moored in Dole, not far from the channel where the rivers Doubs and Saône met. It was a lively river port town where, despite the late season, many laden merchant vessels were still anchored. There was practically no vacancy in the local inn, so even the two maidens had to spend the night in a large bunkhouse with the other pilgrims. Remaining on board the ship, outside the cabin where Agnes of Bohemia was supposed to be sleeping, were Friar Gregory and several French and Czech soldiers. They took up positions along the railing at the rear of the ship, wrapped up in their cloaks. The wind intensified as the sun set and the rain gradually turned into snow.

Katherine didn't want Ota to leave. Her head was resting in his lap as she religiously followed the legend of King Arthur. She had heard it before, but in different versions. She had heard the *Knight's Song* sung at home several times, had heard about the Knights of the Roundtable, the Holy Grail, Arthur's bravery, Merlin. But nothing about Guinevere's unfaithfulness. She could be that Guinevere now, the one whose love for Lancelot was pure, at least according to Ota. He was stroking her hair now and taking an occasional liberty or two, but always unintentionally, so it seemed. Michal's hands also wandered in secret, but never so sweetly. Her eyes were half closed as she dreamt the hand caressing her belong to her fiancé.

"That should do it for today, Katherine," said Ota, gently pushing her head to the side and getting up. "If you get hungry, my angel, there's potato cakes, cheese and fruit in the basket. There is also a jar of wine. I'll just take a bit of this food here for myself so I don't die of hunger. I can't leave the boat, but there should be enough for you. Feel free to eat as much as you want; tomorrow I'll buy some fresh food. And sleep in peace. I'll be right outside the door. Once I'm gone, make sure you latch it securely."

"Couldn't you stay a little longer?"

He shook his head, then hugged and kissed her, but this time making it count. After releasing her, he took a couple of cakes from the basket and quickly walked out onto the deck. There was shouting and singing coming from the tavern onshore. The sound of a church bell reverberated somewhere in the murky distance. He waited until he heard the creak of the latch before making himself comfortable on the deck. After wrapping himself up against the cold, he leaned back and sluggishly began to eat.

He had hardly finished when Svetlana appeared

with a bowl of millet porridge. It was still hot, with large strips of fried bacon floating on top. His mouth began to water. This was much better than stale potato cakes. Svetlana quietly told him that she had made a fool of herself but managed to convince the other pilgrims that nothing was amiss. "I hope someone will reward me for my efforts. I also hope that you will get around to explaining what's going on," she added, a touch irritably. She turned and began to walk towards the narrow gangplank that connected the ship to the wooden pier. Ota observed the silhouette of her slender figure with interest and pleasure.

He slowly scooped up some porridge in the wooden spoon and wondered whether it would be quiet that night. Despite all of Svetlana's blustering, he didn't quite believe that the killer had been discouraged from making another attempt. Oldrich always said that a murderer is usually more afraid than his victim. The longer a manhunt goes on, the more the perpetrator is consumed by panic. Even when an officer of the law has nothing realistic to go on, the criminal over time begins to fear his own shadow.

"A conscience, Ota, is a terrible thing. You know what I mean," Oldrich once said, while they were discussing justice over a goblet of wine. "If you can lock up a criminal with his conscience, it's a worse punishment than lopping his head off." Ota thought about all the members of their party and tried to imagine each of them as a criminal. Strangely enough, it worked for practically all of them. Nearby he heard monotone whispering. Gregory was kneeling next to the rear railing, beating his chest with his fists and praying, as if the world around him didn't exist. The last thing Ota remembered before falling asleep was thinking this was the troubled conscience of a killer in action.

He dreamt about Katherine. She was lying on the bed and when he went to lie down next to her, he discovered that the place was already occupied. At first he thought she was with her betrothed, only to indignantly realize that she was in the embrace of Lancelot himself. He was livid at all the knights of Arthur's Round Table, but before he could do something about it, he was awoken by a scream. With his eyes still closed, he grabbed his sword and jumped up. There was a tremendous commotion coming from the shore. The night sky over the inn was lit up by a frightening yellow and orange glow. Flames were raging high above the stables and an adjacent structure. People were dashing out of the inn and tavern with buckets in hand, dumping them in the river and returning to the courtyard to help extinguish the fire. The soldiers who were sleeping on board leapt to their feet and raced for the gangplank. One of the Frenchmen shouted at Ota and Gregory to go and lend a hand.

"I'm staying here," the friar duly announced.

"Don't you know the law, fool? Anyone who sees a fire but doesn't help put it out faces execution," the soldier informed him and left. Gregory crossed himself, clasped his hands and started to pray. It was clear he had no intention of leaving the ship. But Ota shouted to the soldiers that he would be right behind them. The fire meanwhile had engulfed the two structures and their thatched rooftops were gradually giving way. The flames by now had reached the neighboring cow barn. The innkeeper and his family were leading the cattle to safety, hard to do with the frightened animals in a panic the whole way. People were darting to and fro in the darkness; the air was filled with shouts and screams and the alarm raised by the church bell. Ota left his place in front of the cabin door and ran below deck as if intending to race to the fire. As soon as he was sure the Minorite monk wasn't looking, he quickly hid behind the mast and sail.

For a moment nothing happened. Then a figure appeared on the pier running towards the ship. Ota couldn't tell anything more about this individual in the glare of the flames. The person had already crossed the gangplank and was standing on deck before Ota was able to distinguish more. He was tall with a gray cloak, bearing the Templar cross, thrown over his narrow shoulders. He was wearing a knight's helmet with a hood over it. One hand was concealed beneath his cloak while the other gripped it around the neck to keep it from opening. Ota couldn't make out his face.

The man in the Templar cloak hurried up the steep steps to the rear deck. Gregory stopped praying. He produced a dagger out of nowhere and barred the way to the stranger. He then put the weapon away and Ota heard the apparently relieved friar ask how it looked with the fire. What the presumed Templar answered Ota couldn't hear. He gripped the hilt of his sword and waited for the next move. It was obvious these two men knew each other, but he couldn't be sure if the Templar was Peter of Rosenberg.

The Templar pointed off to somewhere in the dark and the monk turned to look. Everything then happened incredibly fast. The man with the helmet on pulled out the hand he was concealing under the cloak, and with it an ax. He brutally struck the Minorite with it, who fell to the deck. He axed him again and then turned to the door of the cabin where Agnes of Bohemia should be. He tried to force it open but when he realized it was firmly secured on the inside, he immediately struck it right above the lock with the back end of the ax. The latch held, but barely.

Ota dashed up the stairs with his sword in hand. The man in the Templar cloak struck again. This time a muffled crack could be heard and the door flung open. The attacker bolted inside with Ota a couple feet behind him, but he wasn't able to stop him from reaching the bed and letting the ax fall on the pile of blankets with all his might. Ota swung at him but the man deftly dodged out of the way in time with only a scratch on his shoulder. It was dark inside the cabin, lit only by the glare of the flames from the shore. Ota couldn't see his face.

The Templar threw the ax aside and drew his sword. Ota swung again but his opponent skillfully parried his thrust. He obviously had had combat training. Ota took a quick look around the darkened cabin. Katherine was nowhere to be seen. She certainly wasn't on the bed. There were only crumpled blankets in the wake of the murderous attack.

The edges of their swords clashed again. There was little space inside the cabin for maneuvering and Ota had to be careful not to trip over something. But he was stronger and didn't doubt he would come out on top. Suddenly the assailant let out an unexpected and painful cry. He stumbled and the sword fell from his hand. Ota quickly rushed up and put the tip of his sword against the man's neck. He then realized what had happened. Katherine had managed to hide under the bed but at one point during their struggle, she clambered out and sunk her teeth into the man's leg.

The attacker tried to kick Katherine in the face but he lost his balance and tumbled to the floor. That's when he recognized that she wasn't Agnes of Bohemia. He cried out something in Latin and folded his arms against his chest in a sign of surrender. Katherine took out a flint and lit a candle. Ota bound the man's hands and removed his hood and helmet. There before them was the face of the librarian, Emmeram of Greifsfeld, his emaciated face contorted with a kind of demonic creepiness, while his lips and eyes were shut so tight that he resembled a man possessed.

"You're no longer in any danger. It looks like we

have the pilgrim killer here!" Ota said to comfort Katherine, who was shivering and crying. He stroked her cheek. "Thanks for the help! But I'm worried it's still not over with! He didn't come here for us but for Agnes. That means you will still have to impersonate her. I only hope I can convince the other pilgrims that the venerable abbess, despite what just happened, insists on remaining shut up in here to meditate."

"You fool, do you think I will be silent?" shrieked Emmeram.

"Why did you kill all those innocent Christians?" Ota demanded to know.

"Not all of them!" the librarian answered in a dignified tone. "I killed only our provost Wilibald Odo. And he deserved to die more than any other person. Of course, I also had to kill that soldier in Constance, even though that bothered me. But what could I do? If only Agnes weren't so stubborn! I prayed to God to relieve me of this cross to bear but he didn't. Agnes just goes on and on. She's to blame for all of this. She should have turned back!"

"So you've made up your mind to kill her," concluded Ota. There wasn't an ounce of emotion in his voice. "You poisoned the wine and therefore you are also responsible for the death of Zdena Berkova of Sloup."

"I didn't want her to die. I prayed for her soul!"

"And now you've just killed that defenseless monk," Ota firmly declared. The librarian shrugged his shoulders before suddenly laughing out wildly. "It wasn't me! It was God. Why did he let older sister Agnes go on?"

"But what's so terrible about our pilgrimage?" blurted out Katherine, crossing herself. She was pale and looked like she could faint at any moment.

"Why?" raved Emmeram. "Because it threatens every decent and pious Christian!"

"Nonsense! You're lying, because you're nothing more than a filthy criminal," Ota snapped, all the while still carefully observing him. "You're blaming everything on faith, but you act like Judas! You're just doing it for yourself and whatever you get out of it!"

"Me? Judas? I'm protecting Jesus Christ," lamented Emmeram. There were tears in his eyes and his whole body was trembling. Ota was sure the librarian had lost his mind. He sternly reprimanded him. "Jesus protects those who protect Christianity!"

"Jesus protects those who protect his legacy," Emmeram quickly corrected him. He was obviously trying to unload all the suffering that had been tormenting him for weeks. "Lucius's book on the Acts of the Apostles means nothing to you. But to me yes. It's a book full of heretical lies. In my youth, God sent me to persecute the Waldensian heretics. That's when I got a hold of this book. It was I who lit the fire under Peter Waldo at the stake. And with him this book went up in flames. Would you believe that this heretic still had the nerve in his pride to proclaim himself the new King of Jerusalem?"

"I understand that there's still one more copy in

existence. Maybe several," Ota remarked dismissively. "Just because you burn a book, it doesn't mean you destroy the words and thoughts in it!"

"Fool! There's nothing in other books like there was in this one. Someone stitched a couple of faded parchments with Hebrew on them behind Lucius's text. They contain testimony that goes by the name of the Gospel of James. Do you understand? A fifth Gospel!"

"There are lots of writings out there that go by the name of Gospel. Supposedly there's even a Gospel of Judas. All were condemned by the church and the matter settled. There's no reason to kill on account of it!"

"You understand nothing!" the librarian sneered at Ota. "Nothing! Everything is the fault of Apostle James! For years I've been conducting my research and have finally revealed the most horrible conspiracy against our religion which you can imagine. Hah, in fact you can't imagine it! What's more, there is proof that the Gospel of James is right. Do you understand? Right!"

"But that's how it should be. The purpose of the Gospel is to preach the truth," interjected Katherine. She was huddled on the bed, shivering from the cold.

"Not like that! I thought if I burned Lucius's book, then this godless work would be consigned forever where it belonged. In hell! But I was wrong. The devil wants to subvert the Christian world. That's why God gave me this heavy cross to bear so that I might protect the legacy of his son Jesus Christ! Me and me alone. I implored Agnes, tried to explain to her why she should not leave in search of this secret. She laughed at me. She felt duty bound to Clare of Assisi. She wants to destroy our religion all on account of some stupid woman! I have to find her and kill her. And you two will help me! It concerns you too, for Christ's sake."

"I understand. But why did you kill the others? Why the Papal legate in Landstein? And the people in Prague?" asked Ota.

"I didn't kill them," Emmeram shrugged indifferently. "They didn't know a thing about the Gospel of James! Perhaps our provost killed them. He was a villain worse than Judas. He's already frying in hell. I did the entire Christian world a service by killing him."

"You keep speaking about this fifth Gospel. Why is it so godless? If James really did write it, then it had to spread only good tidings that captivated others," said Ota, trying to understand the insinuations being dropped by the librarian. Emmeram shook his head and with downcast eyes explained further. "He was on Calvary, but not his brother John. Why do you think John the evangelist doesn't mention a word about James even though he was his brother? Do you know what the most important thing about religion is? That you believe! So believe and don't ask. The time has come! Let's mount up and set off after Agnes of Bohemia. We have to stop her. At any price," he coolly said and tried to stand up.

But Ota wouldn't let him. The librarian kept trying, jerking himself upward, even injuring himself on the point of Ota's sword. Foam had appeared from his mouth, he started shrieking and wailing that they were on a mission from God and mustn't let him down.

"What do we do with him?" asked Katherine, now a bit more composed. "He's gone mad. He'll warn the others that I'm not Abbess Agnes. We can't let him."

"Don't worry," said Ota with an encouraging smile. "The main thing is you must securely close the door behind me and don't let anyone in!"

With his sword, he ordered the librarian to get up and leave with him. He led him below deck, where he forced Emmeram to get on his knees and pray. The Vysehrad prelate did as told. With a blank look on his face and trembling like an old man, he moved without any spirit or willpower.

"Do you confess before death that you're telling the truth?" Ota asked him coldly.

"You're no judge," retorted the librarian. With the last of his courage, he lifted his head and started spewing that no man on earth could judge one sent on a mission from God. Only the Lord of the heavens could, for only he knew that which was executed in his name was just. He tried to stand up again, proclaiming with an air of importance, "You can't judge me, understand? I'm on a divine mission! I must stop Agnes of Bohemia."

"We all have our missions," Ota cut him off. "I

swore I would avenge the death of Zdena Berková." He raised his sword and with one swoop lopped the librarian's head off.

* * *

Immediately after Oldrich and Agnes left Besançon, they headed for the first wayside inn. Even though it was dark and the tavern quiet, the innkeeper was still up. At first glance he was happy to see he had guests because his small tavern was otherwise empty. He wasn't equipped to handle merchants with large wagons and pilgrims usually stayed at home in winter.

They slept in a cold chamber on plank beds with musty blankets. In the morning they quickly ate and continued on their journey. Oldrich knew there was a bridge just passed Dole and he wanted to be on the opposite side of the river before the French ship bearing the other pilgrims got there. From that point on, the pilgrimage would split up. The others would sail south while they crossed the breadth of France heading west towards the sea.

The road was wide enough to allow them to comfortably trot along beside each other. The sky was overcast and a light drizzle falling, but nothing by way of actual winter was upon them.

"You are going to keep asking me what awaits us in Compostela," Agnes ventured to begin. "I should probably clear up a few things for you."

Oldrich nodded and waited patiently. He was

hoping the abbess would oblige him so, because he considered her to be a reasonable woman, and if they were to have any chance of success, she would have to confide in him sooner or later. The fact that she offered to fill in the blanks the day after they left the others was a sign that she knew what he expected of her.

"You already know most of it," she began in a calm voice. She had removed her habit for the ride on horseback. Without it on, she seemed much more fragile and less dignified. But younger. She had to have been a beautiful woman in her youth. She galloped along with the ease of an experienced rider.

"It involves two little things you should know about. I myself don't know much about the first one because most of it I had to infer from hints. But because it is a little thing, it can be very important. The box I spoke to you about, the one that Templars used to have, came into the hands of Francis of Assisi most probably in Lyon. He came from there, in case you didn't know."

"I admit I never showed much interest in his life," Oldrich apologized. Agnes gestured with her hand that it didn't matter. She had been in a good mood all morning, probably because, with their departure from the others, the feelings of responsibility and guilt had been lifted from her shoulders. With a teacher's kindness, she continued on. "Originally his name was Giovanni. His father was a merchant in Assisi named Pietro di Bernadone. He often traveled to France on business and it was there that he met his wife, Francis's mother. I needn't add that she came from Lyon, the same as Peter Waldo. Back home in Assisi, they nicknamed the boy the little Frenchman, Franciscus in Latin, and that's where we get Francis. This will be important later on. When he was young, Francis fought in the papal army against the Emperor and that's how he came to southern France. He had to have met Peter Waldo there. I know for certain that Waldo was the one who originally had the box. That's why the Pope permitted him to preach. Even if only orally. And therein was the problem. As soon as Waldo was no longer in possession of the box, the Pope declared him to be a heretic and started persecuting his followers, the Waldensians. Francis knew this and didn't make the same mistake. He held on to the box. That's why the Minorites didn't end up at the stake despite advocating poverty just like the Waldensians. That's the first important thing."

"Did Clare tell you this?"

"She hinted at it. But I have other sources," Agnes replied, significantly. She sighed and crossed herself.

"As for the second thing, it is much more painful for me to relate this. It involves my dear older sister Clare. But even this I know only from hints. Nothing was certain until I received the letter she wrote to me on her deathbed. I already told you that at one time Clare also went on a pilgrimage to Compostela. She was there for several months. While there, she secretly gave birth. She was quite young at the time and gave the child to someone to raise. That much I'm sure of. The rest is only speculation but I think important for us. And that is that I believe the child's father wasn't Francis. He truly was a saint. He was also very weak and suffered from various afflictions. I do believe that he lived with Clare as brother and sister. Their love was pure, and that's why I'm convinced that the father of her son was a different man. And Clare entrusted her son with the secret box. The box which prevents the Pope, Templars, and it would seem even King Louis of France from sleeping peacefully at night. And which has set someone on the path to murder."

"And how do you expect to find Clare's son, venerable older sister?" Oldrich asked incredulously.

"I think this box connects my sister Clare to the actual father of her son. The name Waldo is not so common in Galicia," Agnes answered quietly. "Clare's letter contained a secret code which we used to communicate the name of her son. His Christian name is Peter. He is an altar server at the church of St. James. Clare and two men, connected by a box with a secret document in it, love for poverty, and most of all love for Clare. All three are now dead and the box is in the hands of the one individual connected to all three of them: her son Peter Waldo."

"But he's not just going to give you the box! He most likely doesn't even know you."

"He will give it to me," Agnes calmly nodded. "And now you know everything."

She galloped on ahead. Oldrich followed her

intently, knowing very well that it wasn't everything.

CHAPTER XXV

They were able to extinguish the fire so that only the stables and an adjoining shed burned in the blaze. The flames had scorched the rooftop of the cow barn, but nothing more. Ota arrived on the scene as the fire began to fade, encountering people dirty from soot, their eyes bloodshot from the smoke but happy to be putting their empty buckets aside. The innkeeper grew emotional as he went around thanking them and inviting each into his tavern where they could eat and drink to their hearts' content.

Ota rubbed some soot on his face and sought out the royal emissary. "Someone should get back to the boat. Agnes is there..."

"You didn't stay behind with her?" Guy of Lusignan heatedly shouted. "That was most careless of you."

"Of course, I left the Minorite friar with her to guard her in my place. It's enough."

Guy shrugged evasively and shouted to two of his men to get back to the ship immediately and take up their positions outside her cabin.

"Someone set fire to the stables," Jost could be heard declaring behind their backs. "It's been empty since yesterday's vespers, so it couldn't have been started from carelessness. The shed was also empty. The innkeeper swears people go there only occasionally. What if the killer was trying to divert our attention away from the ship?"

Before he could speculate further, one of the French soldiers came running up towards them from the river. He was waving his arms and shouting that they found two dead bodies on board.

Horrified, Guy shouted back, "Is the Czech abbess one of them?"

"No," said the soldier. He stopped to catch his breath. "Just two of the prelates."

Along with the royal emissary and Jost, Ota dashed out of the courtyard and headed for the ship. They crossed the rickety gangplank and discovered the body of Emmeram of Greifsfeld, his severed head lying near the railing. Next they found Friar Gregory lying in front of the cabin door.

Ota pounded on the door with his fist and cried out: "Venerable older sister, it's me, Ota of Zastrizly. Something horrible has happened. I must speak to you."

For a moment it was quiet, then a sound could be heard coming from inside. Ota realized that Katherine had barricaded the door with the trunk. The door had barely begun to open when Ota squeezed inside. Guy tried to follow him in, but Ota barred him the way. He literally slammed the door in his face. Using his finger to tell Katherine to keep silent, he started recounting in a loud voice how two more members of their party had been found murdered on the ship. Also that they were able to put out the fire, but it had probably been started by the killer as a way of sneaking onboard the ship unobserved.

"I will pray for their souls," said Katherine, able to do a good job imitating the voice of Agnes of Bohemia. "Stay with me, we shall pray together," she added with a mischievous wink at him.

"I would be honored to do so," Ota bowed before opening the door and slipping outside. Meanwhile Guy and Jost were on the stern deliberating who could have murdered the two men.

"The killer tried to break into the abbess's cabin," Ota announced. "There are ax marks on the door. Probably from the one lying next to the dead friar there. Something happened then, because Agnes says she heard him give up and flee. But then she heard an argument ensue on the rear deck, followed by a shriek. Almost right after that we showed up. We probably interrupted him before he could carry out his godless deed."

"Praise the Lord," said Jost, crossing himself. "Could she make out the voice of the killer?"

Ota shook his head and added that the abbess asks to be allowed to spend the night in prayer. She's quite shaken, you understand. Her conscience is nagging at her on account of these latest murders."

"I will keep my guards posted here," Guy promised. Knitting his eyebrows, he looked at Ota inquisitively, like he wanted to add something else, but then shook his head as if he thought better of it. Before Ota disappeared inside the cabin, he heard Jost shouting over the railing toward the shore for two of the Czech soldiers to get there on the double and join the Frenchmen in guarding the abbess.

Ota closed the door behind him but since the latch was half broken, he propped it up with another trunk. It was practically dark inside the cabin. When Katherine doused the candlelight, he could see only the outline of her figure. He fumbled about trying to reach her. She met him halfway and embraced him. Putting her lips up to his ear, she whispered, "I promise to be quiet as a mouse...I really want to...I want you!"

He picked her up and carefully put her on the bed. First he removed her habit, which was made out of some unpleasantly prickly coarse material. With that, he began the lesson, which continued all the way till just before the sun rose.

* * *

Ota was awoken by the sound of the church bell. The moaning tone penetrated the shutters of the cabin, beseeching the faithful to come to mass. Ota's shoulder felt stiff, but he was afraid to move it because Katherine was blissfully asleep on it. They were both naked. Despite all the blankets on top of them, he shivered a bit from the cold. He carefully slipped his arm from underneath the girl's head and got out of bed. He managed not to wake her. The last time he felt this sore was after an intense jousting tournament. He noted to himself, a little sarcastically, that he did everything he possibly could for Michal Kekule of Stradonice.

He got dressed, opened the shutters and looked out through the narrow window. The first thing that struck him was the blanket of white snow everywhere. The sky was gray and a light snow falling. He went back to the bed and gently shook the girl awake. She opened her eyes, stretched and quietly whispered: "Is it morning already?"

"I'm going ashore for breakfast. You have to get up and secure the door."

"Will we continue this evening?"

"You already know enough," he grumbled.

"I want to know everything," she replied, meekly lowering her eyelashes. "And then, there are so many things I forget. You know what they always tell pupils. Repetition is the mother of wisdom." She then stuck the tip of her tongue out at him and pulled him close. She kissed him and whispered, "And besides, I really enjoyed it with you. Thank you very much!"

"It's been a long time since I had such a good pupil," he said softly and stood up. He picked up her habit, which was lying on the floor all wrinkled up, and helped her to put it on over her head. Then he left her.

The guards, both Czech and French, were sitting on the lower deck, squeezed together underneath a small shelter and rolling the dice. There wasn't much snow out, but it was wet and heavy and would most likely melt away during the day. The clouds were beginning to disperse and the snow was gradually tapering off. It was slippery on the gangplank, so Ota crossed it very carefully. Once he was on shore, he bolted for the tavern. Practically all the tables inside were occupied. The fire burning in the furnace made the place nicely warm inside. He could smell the aroma of fried bacon, vegetable soup, potato cakes and wine.

All who were left of the Czech pilgrims were sitting around the table next to the furnace. Three knights, two noble maidens, and two prelates. Guy was also sitting with them. The soldiers from both companies were sitting on benches against the wall of the tavern. Each was slurping from his morning bowl of soup.

"I can't figure out why the librarian was wearing Rosenberg's tunic and helmet," said Prech. "Why did he want to look like a Templar knight?"

"It's obvious," growled Rosenberg. "So if somebody saw him, they would accuse me."

"If that's what he really intended, then it means he didn't have a clear conscience," Jost pointed out. "So the fire starts, and in order for him to grab the things from Rosenberg, he had to know it was going to start. That means he started it. It's clear he's the murderer we've been looking for. What was he even doing on the ship while all of us were putting out the fire?"

"He was trying to kill Agnes of Bohemia!" screamed an exasperated Wolf, the Landstein chaplain.

"It's very probable," concurred Guy. "Of course, what I don't understand is who killed him. It was no ordinary murder. Somebody chopped his head off, like he was a condemned man. Sir Ota of Zastrizly, would you know something about that?"

"Why would I? I was putting out the fire like the rest of you," Ota replied in his defense. He gestured to the innkeeper to approach and asked him to prepare a basket full of food for the entire day.

"One of my soldiers standing guard on the ship remembers that when the fire broke out, you left behind him. Only the dead friar remained on board," said Guy with a nod of the head. "It seems that was so. The only thing is, the soldier isn't sure he saw you at all on shore. And I remember noticing you had blood on the hem of your tunic. I can see that you still have it there. Where'd it come from? It was you who executed the librarian, wasn't it?! Why did you do it?"

"I probably got it on me while on deck. There was blood everywhere," Ota shrugged. "And your soldier didn't see me on shore because he ran ahead of me and didn't look back. Nothing more to it."

"But somebody killed those two men," chafed Rosenberg. He too fixed a stern gaze at Ota, as if reproaching a servant. "Someone chopped Emmeram's head off with a sword. There are only four knights here among us. The gentleman from

Landstein and Sir Guy here I saw at the fire, but not you!"

"I saw Sir Ota of Zastrizly there, but none of you," Svetlana suddenly spoke up. Even though her expression was grave, Ota sensed the slightest of grins on her lips. She went to stand by his side, understanding that everything that had happened was connected to the manhunt. Above all, it was connected to the trap she herself had laid for the killer. She was proud of her work. She knew Ota naturally didn't want to speak about it in front of the others, so she felt obliged to speak up in his defense.

"I saw the gentleman from Rosenberg," said Jana.

"But I didn't see you," Friar Hyacinth interjected.

"This is pointless," Guy snapped, standing up. His hand was resting on the hilt of his sword. "Somebody saw someone, that's for sure. But that isn't important here. Only one thing is, and that's whether Abbess Agnes is all right. So I have still one more theory. What if our murderer is Ota of Zastrizly here? He killed both prelates and her. And to make good his escape, he claims that the venerable Agnes refuses to leave her cabin. He doesn't want to let anyone inside to see her."

"My soldiers heard two voices in her cabin at night. Male and female," said Jost, dismissing his theory. Of course, he didn't add what the soldiers also told him. They said that if they didn't know it was Ota in there with the venerable abbess, they would've guessed, judging by the noise inside, that there wasn't exactly praying going on.

"Anyone can imitate a voice," insisted Guy. "I say I go there now to have a look at the venerable Agnes of Bohemia. The King has made me responsible for the safety of all of you, but primarily for hers. I have to see for myself that she's all right, even if I have to break down her door."

"I'm with you," chipped in Rosenberg.

"You will not disturb the venerable abbess!" shouted Prech angrily. "If you insist on making sure she's safe, I will do it myself. I will ask her to allow me to come into her cabin, and if she refuses, there's nothing we can do about it! And you have no right to use force to invade her privacy! She is the aunt of our exalted monarch, King Ottokar. She deserves our respect!"

"She also deserves to be safe," countered Guy and he got up to head for the door. Ota jumped up and blocked his way. Their eyes met. The royal emissary of the King of France haughtily smiled and smirked, "I don't believe a word you say, Zastrizly! I'm going to get to the bottom of this. I want to see her with my own eyes even if I have to kill you. You are a very stubborn sort. You should know that anyone who declines to take silver usually ends up with iron! If only you had understood that back in Prague, things might be different today."

Ota didn't reply. He merely stepped back and drew his sword. Guy did the same. Everything happened in a flash after that. The French men-at-arms sitting on the benches grabbed their lances and leapt to their feet. They turned the tips of their weapons against their Czech counterparts and the last of the pilgrims. The only one able to draw his sword in time was Prech, who managed to get in one good lunge that injured one of the Frenchmen in the hand. But the Czechs were still outnumbered more than two to one.

"I will spill blood here if I have to," Guy of Lusignan called out. "We are in the kingdom of France and I shall decide how to proceed. You are going to wait here while I go to make sure the venerable Agnes of Bohemia is all right. Nothing more!"

"You will have to kill me first," Ota challenged him. "You just said you would do it a moment ago. A knight should keep his word!"

"The French emissary didn't say that," Svetlana countermanded him. She paid no notice to the lance being pointed at her and walked up to both knights. "Do you really want to draw blood over something like this? I suggest that we all go to the ship. All the pilgrims, I mean. No soldiers. Violence has no place on a pilgrimage! Aren't you aware of that, Sir Guy? You are, after all, in the service of the king named Louis the Pious. Conduct yourself, therefore, like a servant of a Christian monarch."

The emissary frowned and put his sword back in its sheath. "All right. The soldiers and your commander will stay here. Also the two prelates. This is a matter for us knights."

Svetlana cast a brief, uncertain look at Ota, as if

apologizing for not being able to do more. Ota knew she was right. Since it had come to this point, there was really nothing more they could do. So he put his sword away as well. Guy would be alone on the ship with the pilgrims. But even if he had Rosenberg on his side, Ota could still count on Jost. Two swords against two swords. Including the two girls, they would have the superior numbers.

Ota took the basket full of supplies from the innkeeper and all of them left the tavern. The snow on the ground had changed to slush. Two merchant vessels were just then leaving the dock. They could hear the shouts of the seamen and the oars smacking the river surface. The minute they were on board, Guy ordered the soldiers to go back to the tavern. Puzzled, the Czechs looked at Jost for guidance. His nod indicated they should follow their French counterparts.

Jost attempted to open the door to the cabin, but it was firmly barred from the inside. He called out to Agnes for permission to enter her chamber with the maidens. There was a moment of silence followed by a muffled, "No!"

Guy stood next to Jost and strongly insisted on permission to enter. When the voice inside again refused, he stood back, and with all his might, rammed his shoulder into the door to try and dislodge it. Ota drew his sword and raced for him, only to find young Rosenberg blocking his way. He too had a sword in his hand. The fight was on.

In an instant Guy had drawn his sword and had Jost in his sights. Caught off guard, the young knight wasn't prepared to defend himself. He managed to dodge the blow but stumbled on a pile of rope rolled up on the deck next to the helm. He still tried to get his sword out as he staggered but it was too late. Guy jabbed him with the tip of his weapon, coolly warning him to drop his sword and not to resist because he didn't want to have his life on his conscience. But he wouldn't hesitate to slay him if he had to. He forced Jost to kneel and keep his hands behind his back. He quickly tied them and went to help Rosenberg.

Ota was getting the best of their fight and already had Rosenberg on the deck when Guy came to his aid. The speed of the clash sent both girls below deck to seek cover underneath the stairs. There was very little room on the stern and to stand there amidst knights in combat would have been blatant stupidity.

Ota kicked Rosenberg and was able to knock the sword out of his hand with such force that it skidded through the railing and fell into the river. He now turned to repel the thrust from Lusignan.

Each was holding his sword with both hands, blade crashing against blade, each propelling his body against the other in an attempt to corner him against the railing and thereby gain the advantage. Ota was the stronger of the two and eventually had Guy backing up. Ota pressed home his attack, but the emissary was a skillful swordsman. He parried his thrusts, ducked and extricated himself from an otherwise hairy predicament. He managed to glide past the railing to reach the open space next to the cabin.

Ota then spotted Rosenberg creeping up behind him with a concealed dagger. Guy's dash for the stern bought him a little time. He tossed his sword from the right hand to the left, grabbed it by the blade, and struck Rosenberg in the head with the hilt. The helmet saved him from serious injury but the blow was enough to stun him. It was hardly any respite for Ota, however, for the emissary was again on the attack. He had just got the sword back in his right hand in time to fend off a sharp blow aimed at his neck.

The duel continued with fierce tenacity, the clash of swords filling the air with the horrid screech of metal. Both knights were practically winded, but Ota was slowly gaining the upper hand. He noticed that Jost had rolled his body toward the railing and managed to wedge a metal hook behind the helm between his hands and the cord used to bind them. Pushing with his hands against the wheel post, he struggled to free himself. It was only a matter of time before he would succeed. Ota again started beating the French emissary back toward the railing. Lusignan was running out of room to maneuver.

At that moment Ota spied Jana running up from below deck carrying a dagger in her hand. He figured she was planning on freeing Jost. He turned his body so that she could use the cover of his back to safely reach the helm. He then charged at Guy to make sure he didn't hurt the girl. His eyes were totally trained on his French foe when he suddenly heard Svetlana cry out. Thanks to his training as a knight, he immediately reacted by ducking and dodging. He felt a sharp pain in his right shoulder, even though it was only a scratch. The whole thing was so unexpected that he had no idea what was happening.

He put his hand with the sword in it on the deck in an attempt to push himself up and out of the way of his approaching enemy but found he couldn't move his sword. The leg of a charming young woman had slammed it to the deck. Jana was standing there holding a dagger with Ota's blood on it. At that moment Guy could have killed him but didn't. He merely placed the tip of his sword on his neck and ordered him in no uncertain terms to surrender. Jana turned and ran to the helm, where she pointed the dagger at Jost as an indication he should lie still. She checked the cord on his hands. She then shouted to Svetlana to remain below, else she would kill her brother.

Several French soldiers bolted through the door of the tavern and raced towards the wharf. They crossed the gangplank, tied Ota's hands and firmly retied those of Jost. Rosenberg meanwhile came to. He leaned up against the railing and puked. He had a huge welt on his forehead that was quickly turning blue. Jost looked at Jana in disbelief. She had betrayed him! The French allowed Svetlana to come up and treat Ota's injury. But they watched over her with their lances ready to strike.

Guy ordered two soldiers to smash through the cabin door. He walked in and then almost immediately returned dragging Katherine, still in her abbess's habit, behind him.

CHAPTER XXVI

"What's this supposed mean?" yelled Guy almost beside himself. He pushed Katherine so hard she fell to the deck. The royal emissary menacingly turned his sword on Jost.

"Let him be," said Ota. His shoulder hurt, but he had endured similar wounds in his life. "Nobody knows anything about it except me."

Guy turned and walked up to him, playing with the sword in his hand. Grinning, he said, "I suppose you're going to play the hero now and tell me you have nothing to say."

"On the contrary," Ota said cordially. "I'll tell you everything...if you let the others go."

"Dumb condition!" scoffed Guy. But before he could continue, shouts and the clang of weapons could be heard coming from the tavern. The emissary ordered his men to keep a tight guard on their prisoners while he and several other soldiers rushed ashore.

Katherine got up and went over to Ota, who was

being attended by Svetlana on one side. Giving her a rather dismissive look, she sat next to him on the other and asked whether his wound was serious. She also apologized for ruining everything.

"It's not your fault," said Ota, shaking his head. He cast a reproachful look over his shoulder at Svetlana and added, "Stupid coincidence. Our chaplain was right when he claimed that the best Christian is he who simply listens to the voice of the Lord. The Lord usually doesn't like anyone who tries too hard, because faith isn't his guide; ambition is."

Katherine nodded and fell silent. It was clear she was trying to figure out what he just now meant and how it related to her. She had the nagging feeling that he was angry at her for something and for that she was sorry.

Guy appeared at the door of the tavern with sword in hand and yelled to his soldiers to bring their captives there. He then disappeared.

When the Czech pilgrims walked into the large ground floor room, they could see that a tremendous struggle had taken place there. Several tables and benches were smashed, two shutters ripped away, and a servant girl was sweeping shards of broken pottery into a pile. The Czech soldiers and Chaplain Wolf were sitting on the floor next to the wall with their hands tied. A few of them had bloody gashes and welts. The French soldiers as well. Prech of Michalovice was standing next to the furnace, his face bloodied and hands tied. A glowering Guy of Lusignan was pacing next to him.

Go sit there by the window and listen," he snapped at them angrily. "Where is Agnes of Bohemia? I shall not repeat the question. It depends on you whether you live or die."

"You may have more soldiers than we do, but not intelligence," Prech retorted insolently. "Don't you know, my good sir, that to assault pilgrims on a pious undertaking is a mortal sin and the Pope will cast you into hell for it? And I won't mention the other stuff. The King of France will have to pay the church a fine so high that Louis the Pious will have you flayed alive. My lord, the King of Bohemia and Moravia, will not keep silent about this."

"And how will the church find out about it?" snarled Guy coldly. "So many people have drowned in that river that there'll be nothing suspicious about five or six more joining them. You fool, do you really think I'm going to let any of you just walk out of here?"

"Your words are for nothing. As I said, not even an ounce of intelligence," scoffed Prech, shaking his head provocatively as if upbraiding a dimwitted page. "Why do you think my soldiers attacked yours? Do you think we're after glory? You must think I'm a really poor commander if I can't even recognize that we had no chance of winning. Or maybe you think we started brawling with you just for fun? Look around you and tell me if anyone here is missing? Weren't there two prelates with us?"

Guy suddenly realized that the Premonstratensian

friar had disappeared. Only the Landstein chaplain was sitting next to the captive soldiers. He drew his sword and ran out into the courtyard. He returned after a while, panting as if he had been running. He was shaking with anger, which he took out on the first of his soldiers in line by kicking him so hard the man fell to the floor, breaking the shaft of his lance in the process. He screamed at his men for letting the skinny monk get away.

"It's not their fault," said Prech. Even though he was bound and bloodied, he was clearly enjoying himself. "Our monk slipped out the back through the kitchen. We arranged it. He and my men. We all know what he has to do. You see, our advantage is your men don't understand Czech but we do French. Our King Wenceslaus, bless his memory, always said that he who understands his enemy wins the battle. And you know what's interesting? Most German and Austrian knights understand Czech, as do the Poles, Hungarians, Prussians and even Bavarians. But you French understand nothing except French."

"Kindly spare me the lesson for another time," Guy responded glibly. He was letting him rant so he could think for a minute. He was an experienced knight and knew how to cut his losses. Now, quickly revising his plans, he smiled at the Czech pilgrims and announced, with an almost sinister silkiness, "You just heard for yourselves that your commander is an idiot. He attacked troops of the King of France for no reason at all and is now threatening me with a curse. This is a dangerous area, and if anything happens to the monk, it will be his fault and his alone. It's also true that I did not assault you. No one has greater respect for pilgrims than my lord, the King of France. That's why he has earned the name the Pious one."

"That's news to me," said Ota. "And this claim that you didn't attack us...what was that skirmish on the ship all about then?"

"On the ship?" replied a surprised Guy. "All I know is that we went there to make sure the venerable Agnes of Bohemia wasn't in any danger. As you yourselves can see, she clearly is. Somebody kidnapped her and locked this wretched girl in her chamber. Several members of your party have already come to violent ends. That's why I took you under my protection. And under our protection you shall remain until we have managed to free the captive Agnes of Bohemia and return her to among you."

"Nobody kidnapped her," declared Ota. "She left by herself and on her own free will. You didn't see the maiden Katherine here leave with my lord? All of a sudden she's here and the abbess is gone. Don't you know how to count? One plus one is two, isn't it?" Ota realized his plan had failed; he was just happy that Prech had risen to the occasion.

"I've had enough of your stupid insinuations," retorted Guy, flushed with anger. He was beside himself because he despised it whenever someone suggested he was smarter than him. "I don't need you or your prattle! I can count much further than you can imagine. A good knight has to know how to play chess. So the monk has fled. What of it? Agnes of Bohemia and Oldrich of Chlum are making the pilgrimage to Compostela in secret. Taking some shortcut in order to get there before we do. Surely they are doing it out of praiseworthy devotion. They simply can't wait to kneel before the tomb of a saint. Which way they took, I suspect none of you knows. But you wouldn't tell me in any case. So it seems you think you have outwitted me."

"Haven't we?" asked Ota, trying to provoke him as a means of learning as much as possible about his intentions. "You will catch neither my lord nor the venerable Agnes. If there's one thing you can learn from Oldrich of Chlum, it's shrewdness."

"Me learn from him?" laughed Guy affectedly. "Your Wenceslaus wasn't right when he said it was important to understand your enemy. More important is to triumph over him. Perhaps we French don't understand everything, but we are victorious! What has become of that ring in the pouch, the one you were so stupid enough to refuse back in Prague?"

"What's so important about it?" asked Ota a little uneasily.

"So you haven't got it," the royal emissary grinned triumphantly. "You gave it to your master. I suspected as much. He will obtain help wherever he shows that ring, that's the divine truth. He will be able to travel in relative comfort. But it's also true that I will quickly find out where he has shown it. And there's one place where he will have to show it. There's no way of getting to Galicia over the mountains during winter, so they'll have to go there by sea, and he won't be able to sail out of any French port without first showing that ring."

"That's enough!" barked Rosenberg. "Why tell them all of these things, brother? Especially if we have to let them live...for now anyway. You had better pray we don't catch your monk."

Guy growled, ready to put him in his place, but checked himself. He knew that Rosenberg was right. He ordered the innkeeper to bring him a pitcher of wine and then, with supreme calm, turned to Prech. "You have carried out an act of violence against troops of the King of France. I could easily sentence you to death for that and no one throughout Christian Europe would be able to say that I acted unjustly. But I will show you mercy. You and your entire armed company will return immediately home. The chaplain too. And just to make sure you don't cause any problems on our soil, I shall confiscate your weapons and have an armed guard escort you to Basel. I wouldn't try to come back. Anyone we catch trying to do so shall be executed without mercy."

"You're sending all of us home?" asked Jost angrily.

"Not all of you," the emissary replied. "You, Sir Ota of Zastrizly and the two maidens shall remain here. You will be the guests of the King of France on his ship. As my lord had always wished. That ship, of course, is not going south. What would you do there now that the venerable Agnes of Bohemia has left you? The ship shall remain moored here. Feel free to move around on it. But as I said, it's dangerous here on shore, and since your weapons will be confiscated as well, I will assign an armed guard to oversee your safety. And I must reluctantly point out that any attempt to escape will be taken as an unfriendly provocation. If one of you tries it, I shall be forced to punish all four of you. I will set off for Compostela so that I can be of good service to the venerable Agnes, and as a demonstration of good will, I shall take part of her retinue with me. Peter Rosenberg, knight of the Templar order, shall accompany me, and to accompany the abbess when we meet her will be the honorable maiden Jana of Blatna."

* * *

Before the Czech men-at-arms set off for home, Ota and Svetlana managed to get in a word with Prech. Ota was curious how the guard commander came to decide it would be a good thing for Hyacinth to escape.

"I not only told him to flee," related Prech proudly, "but I explicitly ordered him to make his way to Compostela and the abbess as fast as possible. To warn her about the emissary and our fine young Rosenberg."

"Excellent decision that was, but you couldn't know that the abbess wasn't in her cabin."

"You underestimate me, my friend. Of course I knew. I know both you and Oldrich, and there were a couple of details I couldn't fail to notice. First, he would leave while you stayed behind, as if nothing in the world had happened? Second, he would leave Agnes of Bohemia while there was a murderer after her? And third, you would spend an entire night in a cabin with only an abbess as company? The soldiers on guard mentioned that there were signs of other things besides prayer going on in there between you two."

"Soldiers can think of only smut and nothing else," Svetlana sternly reproved him. "Katherine of Gutstein is a virtuous maiden in love with her betrothed Michal Kekule. And we're on a pilgrimage. Katherine would never dream of such sinful behavior!"

"She accepted the difficult role of Agnes of Bohemia," Ota added with a dignified expression. "I stayed with her because someone tried to kill her. She was terribly afraid. She slept on the bed and I in the chair which I used to block the door. If your men heard anything, it was me snoring. I think I'm coming down with a cold, which isn't surprising in winter."

"Like I said, I not only know your master, but you as well, Ota," Prech nodded in agreement. "I thought it was something like that. I admonished my men not to dream up such rubbish or to slander Katherine when they get back, for she certainly doesn't deserve it. But in any case their wrongheadedness helped me uncover the truth, so thanks to them Hyacinth is free and heading to Compostela. I gave him two bundles of silver coins so he wouldn't have to linger anywhere and beg."

As soon as the Czech commander and his men were gone, Guy had the pilgrims brought on board. He himself set off with his detachment, taking the shortest route west towards the sea. A sullen Svetlana inched up to Ota and asked him to explain what that night on board was all about.

"How should I know?" Ota replied defensively. "You know soldiers. They would even slander the virgin Mary."

"Sure. You can't trust anything that comes out of a soldier's mouth. Nor yours. Fortunately, Katherine is a chaste girl. We're going to be imprisoned on this ship and it's not so large that we won't be stumbling into each other. So I promise I will be at her side to prevent any temptation from occurring."

"You're afraid that a virtuous maiden like Katherine will find herself in a moment of temptation? Aren't you more afraid of being tempted yourself under the same circumstances?" Ota laughed, but Svetlana could sense there wasn't much sincerity in it.

"Aha, so the soldiers were right," she declared dryly. "Well, it's not going to happen again, you can be sure of it! The King asked me to help your master with his manhunt, but also to keep an eye on the entourage of noble maidens. Now we are only two, but I will see to it that nothing distracts Katherine from her virtuous intentions." She impishly winked at Ota and headed for the cabin.

* * *

The innkeeper brought them lunch directly to the large cabin below deck. He placed a metal pot filled with a hot meat porridge on the oblong table, then stretched out a hand and said they owed him one silver piece. He was ready to cook for them every day if they wanted, but of course it would cost them.

"Prisoners are supposed to get free food," protested Svetlana.

"Sure," said Ota. "Moldy bread and pond water."

Katherine reached into the pouch that hung from her purse and paid him. She then noted that tomorrow was the feast day of St. Martin and asked the innkeeper to roast a goose for them. He politely bowed and started calculating all the ways he could prepare it so that it met their satisfaction. In the end they all agreed the goose should be baked in honey and served with a plum stuffing.

While Ota and the two girls were absorbed with the innkeeper and all the details for preparing the meal for tomorrow's feast, Jost sat quietly, almost apathetically. When anyone said anything to him, he merely nodded absentmindedly and remained silent. Finally Svetlana couldn't take it any longer and tried to urge him, with rather excessive solicitude, to forget all about Jana. She may be from a noble family, but showed that she was worse than a slut off the street.

"She betrayed me," he whined. There were tears in his eyes, completely at odds with the coarse features of his knightly expression. "Do you know the worst part of it? She's not just some slut, but a murderer too! I embraced a murderer. I even told her I loved her. Why can't women be as true and faithful as a knight? They're nothing but snakes!"

His proclamation caused an immediate storm of protest from the girls. But Ota shouted them down, demanding that they be quiet for at least a moment, because if they had any sense at all, they would realize that what Jost just said was about more than whether women come from basilisks, scorpions, snakes and locusts, basically a collection of everything that will accompany the Apocalypse.

Katherine tried to kick him under the table, but it was too wide for her to reach him. So she settled for rolling a piece of potato cake into a ball and throwing it at him.

Ota deftly ducked his head and continued in a serious tone. "You said, Sir Jost, that Jana of Blatna is a murderer. Who does she have on her conscience?"

"Who?" he wailed, throwing up his hands in a gesture of despair. "Why, the Papal legate! Jana went to visit him the evening he was killed. He was still alive when she left him. She spent the night with me and later confirmed that I had not left my chamber for even a moment. Which was true. But Sir Oldrich didn't think to ask if the opposite was also the case. Jana left me sometime during the night, saying she had to go relieve herself. She said she was too ashamed to use the chamber pot in front of me. She added she would also run down to the Great Hall for some sausages. Never in my dreams did I think to suspect her. I had forgotten all about that little detail until this morning. Then it hit me. I went to accuse her of his murder before she left with the French emissary, and you know what she said?"

"She laughed at you," snarled Svetlana.

"Yes," murmured Jost, hanging his head. "But not because I accused her. She admitted she killed him. No, she claimed they couldn't allow anyone from the Holy See to stick their noses into this matter."

"They couldn't allow? Who did she mean besides herself?" Ota asked.

"She didn't tell me. Maybe the Templars. I don't know. She said I was a fool to think she could ever one day belong to me," he confided bitterly. He grabbed the wine pitcher and nearly emptied it.

CHAPTER XXVII

Oldrich and Agnes reached Bordeaux two days after the feast day of St. Lucia. Even though it was halfway through Advent, they were lucky not to have felt the brunt of winter yet. Only once did they encounter any snow. A strong wind was blowing in from the sea, but it was warm, and if any clouds gathered in the sky, it simply rained. Nowhere were they held up for long and they often spent morning till sunset in the saddle.

Usually an entire day would pass without talking. Abbess Agnes was morose and often snapped at Oldrich on account of some trifle. He sympathized with her, knowing that such a journey would be exhausting even for young person. She was moreover bothered by the deaths of the all people who had accompanied her from Bohemia on a holy pilgrimage. But no matter how worn out she was after a full day of riding, she never missed a long night of prayer for the salvation of their souls. Her fatigue had been making a marked impression over the past few days, but with the characteristic stubbornness of the Přemyslids, she refused to rest anywhere longer than necessary. They even spent the feast days of St. Katherine and St. Nicholas in the saddle.

Only once, when they stayed the night at a Cistercian monastery near Limoges, was she in a more talkative mood. She did not go to sleep after prayers, rather offered to join Oldrich for little wine. They were sitting in chairs next to the fireplace. The flames cast a flickering glow on the tired face of the aged abbess, revealing the fine lines around her lips and eyes. She took a sip and then quietly asked if he ever realized just how much God tested the faithful. She didn't wait for him to answer. She needed to unburden herself.

Taking another sip and staring at the flames in the fireplace, like looking into her own past, she quietly continued. "It was exactly thirty-five years ago today that Emperor Frederick II announced he was canceling our engagement. I had to return home to Prague from Naples. I was so unhappy at the time, but later I thanked God for rescuing me from the bitter fate of living side by side with an Emperor under interdict for his impiety."

"That's why you have devoted your life to serving Christ," Oldrich replied understandingly. Much to his surprise, she firmly shook her head in denial.

"Next I was betrothed to Henry Plantagenet, King of England," she recalled. "When he broke it off after three years, I wasn't too upset. I had never even seen him. The engagement took place in Prague only with the participation of his ambassadors. Henry turned out to be an even more faithless sort than Frederick. No, I certainly didn't despair over him. Didn't pray either. But believe me, even if young Frederick loved me once, and perhaps I loved him as well, it wasn't because of him that I chose the path to humility and repentance."

Agnes lifted her goblet and waited for Oldrich to fill it. He said nothing, realizing it was pointless to either ask or answer anything at this point.

"Sometimes I hesitated whether I chose the right path. Every Christian has doubts about his fate. Even the mother superior of a convent. But the older I became, the surer I was that I made the right decision. Now I'm finally sure it was the right one. Yes, this journey to Compostela is a mission that God has entrusted to me here in the earthly world. I have to redeem my sins. I cannot disappoint him!"

"Only Jesus Christ can redeem the sins of mankind, venerable older sister," he tried to comfort her. He could never remember her expressing such feelings of regret before.

"This is not about mankind, Sir Oldrich! It's about us, the Přemyslids. The sins of our blood."

"Every royal house in Europe has someone who the pope excommunicated or who killed his father or brother for the throne or violated his oath and did not behave like a true Christian knight. To rule is a difficult chore. I'm not making excuses for anyone, but why are you so troubled by it? The Přemyslids are no better or worse than other rulers."

She nodded and finished the entire contents of her goblet. As he refilled it, she sighed, apparently plucking up the courage for something rather difficult to say. She hung her head and slightly shook it. "Sir Oldrich, this is about a much worse sin. I must atone for the terrible shame that has befallen us. It doesn't concern our Přemyslid forebears. It's about the blood that came into our family from my mother Constance of Hungary. In her youth she was the most beautiful woman in all Christendom. Her veins flowed with the wild blood of the beautiful women of the East and the bravest knights of the Christian world who liberated the Holy Land. My maternal grandmother was Agnes of Antioch, the daughter of Renaud de Châtillon. Now of course, you will find countless knights who have robbed, murdered and betrayed their allies. But this Renaud de Châtillon was responsible for the infidels conquering Jerusalem. The Muslims have the Holy Land again because of my great-grandfather. And if only that were all!"

Agnes took a sip and shook her head violently. She was quiet and Oldrich didn't try to encourage her to continue. He waited.

She suddenly stood up and announced that it was late. They had a long journey ahead of them tomorrow and it was time to go to sleep.

She would never return to the subject.

* * *

Bordeaux lay at the end of a long and narrow bay that cut deeply into the French coastline. It was here that the river Garonne flowed into the ocean. The city was surrounded by massive walls with dozens of towers and a wide moat. As soon as Oldrich and Agnes crossed the bridge and gateway to the city, they headed straight for the harbor.

Several merchant vessels had been hauled ashore, their bulky hulls propped up by enormous beams. Around them were workers busy caulking the seams between the planks with oakum and hot pitch. Others were scraping algae and barnacles off the blackened sides. The air was filled with the stench of rotting fish, moldy wood and dirty seawater. Other merchant vessels were moored alongside long piers. Some men were hauling bundles of goods from their holds while others were reloading them with cargo. A little further on, opposite the stone fort that guarded access to the harbor, were four large military caravels at anchor.

Even though everything had gone according to plan, Oldrich felt a special anxiety. It was the first time he had ever seen the sea. Its infiniteness was something that surpassed any Christian understanding. There in the distance, where the ocean disappeared beyond the horizon, was the end of the world. The idea of this end, however, disturbed him far more than the void which scholars attributed to infinity. What was at the end of the world? Every sensible person knew that open countryside lay beyond the walls that guarded the city. But what was beyond the borders of the end of the world?

He was conscious of just how little he had learned at the monastery. He grew livid at the thought of the papacy forbidding Aristotle's works on nature. Perhaps for the first time ever he was wandering into heretical territory by pondering whether it was right for the church to order people how to think. A Christian was supposed to believe in the tidings of the Gospels and think at the same time. If the word of God was correct, belief was not in conflict with reason. But if it were... Here he broke off, because he had forbidden himself such musings. He was a knight and the procurator, nothing more. Let the scholars of higher learning trouble themselves with Aristotle and human reason. He sighed and looked away from the never-ending expanse of the ocean.

He led Agnes to a more upscale inn not far from the harbor so she could rest up. He went alone to find out about any ships leaving for Galicia. Luck was with him on the second merchant vessel he came to. The crew said they were heading for Porta in Portugal and it would be no problem to stop off in Muros, close to Compostela. They had shown similar service to many pilgrims. All he had to do was reach an agreement with the captain. A scruffy seaman who reminded Oldrich a little of his squire Ota cheerfully told him that the captain often took pilgrims to Muros because he had some nice girl there.

He found Captain Santander in a nearby tavern. He was sitting at a table with his helmsman and another maritime captain and drinking some foul-smelling oily liquor. Oldrich had tried it once during his travels in southern France and knew that it was much stronger than mead or wine and was produced by the Moors. It couldn't be drunk in large quantities because it went straight to the head. Fortunately, all three at the table were still sober. Perhaps it was only their first bottle.

Oldrich of Chlum introduced himself and made his request, adding that he was ready to pay well. Santander diffidently rubbed one of his meaty gray palms over the stubble on his chin and asked if he really was from Bohemia. When Oldrich nodded that he was, the captain sadly shook his head and started explaining that maritime travel was dangerous during winter. He didn't want to have the lives of any pilgrims on his conscience if his ship were to founder and sink. Only with the harbormaster's permission could he take him on board, otherwise he was out of luck.

Although Oldrich had no experience with the way things worked in seaside ports, there was something suspicious about the captain's explanation. Withal, he had no other choice but to head straight for the fort overlooking the caravels flying the flag of the King of France.

The harbormaster was a baron something-or-other. He repeated his title twice but Oldrich still didn't understand him. The man spoke Latin with such terrible pronunciation that the Czech barely managed to catch every third word. The Frenchman simply made no effort to be understood. He was no doubt convinced that if somebody wanted something from him in France, he should kindly learn French.

The argument went on so long that finally a clerk appeared who could speak excellent German. In clear, intelligible language, he explained to Oldrich that it was forbidden from the start of Advent to carry any foreign passengers from France unless they had a safe conduct pass from the King. He sheepishly added that he didn't know why such an ordinance had been issued, he was only a clerk. But he informed him that it would be useless to try in other ports because the regulation applied up and down the coast.

The harbormaster assumed an air of importance and not even an offer by Oldrich to pay handsomely would mollify him. He had the face of someone who welcomed such offers, only in this instance he didn't dare. He had his orders.

The harbormaster told him that was that and pointed to the door. "Tell him," Oldrich ordered the clerk, "that I don't have a safe conduct pass, but I bear a message from the King. Have him kindly look at this." He grabbed the leather pouch tied to his belt and pulled out the ring given to Ota by Guy of Lusignan. He was sure his squire hadn't received it merely out of kindness from the French emissary. It was clear the moment he showed it, the harbormaster in Bordeaux would send a messenger to Paris, or thereabouts, to report that a man had appeared with this ring. But he had to risk it. Time was of the utmost now.

The harbormaster took the ring and studied it carefully for a moment. He then nodded his head and added politely that the situation, of course, was different now. If the gentleman from Bohemia would come back in a week, he would be glad to have the necessary documents ready for him.

"I have to leave today. Tomorrow at the latest," Oldrich shouted imperiously. He presumed the harbormaster had instructions to report any man bearing this particular ring. He certainly didn't know more than that; probably only that he was supposed to delay him there. Since he obviously had no idea what it was all about, Oldrich hoped that if he acted haughtily enough, he would get what he was after. It turned out he was right. After arguing for a minute, the harbormaster had the clerk draw up a document with his consent for departure.

Later that evening, Oldrich and Agnes came on board Captain Santander's ship. His caravel was called *St. Michael* and was heading to Portugal with bags of dried lavender, textiles and wine. Thanks to its cargo, the ship didn't smell nearly as repulsive as most others. They received a small cabin below deck and during low tide that morning, the ship pulled up anchor and left.

Agnes had arrived in the comfortable traveling apparel she wore the whole time on horseback, but once in the cabin she changed into her gray habit. When the sailors saw her in that outfit, an argument immediately broke out whether the presence of a nun onboard meant bad luck or not. The helmsman even suggested they turn around and put both of them ashore. Finally the captain himself had to step in. According to his experience, passengers like nuns were an omen, but if the honorable Sir Oldrich of Chlum would pay him an extra twenty silver pieces, he would be happy to run the risk.

This matter turned out to be the only disturbance throughout the entire voyage. Despite the late season, the weather was still superb and many of the sailors even began to declare loudly that having nuns onboard in fact brought good luck. Finally Captain Santander had to step in and scold them for saying such drivel, because in this case he would have to return the twenty silver coins. Oldrich overheard him and ironically observed that he would not only have to return the silver, but also pay extra for the luck they had brought with them. The sailors did an immediate about-face. As soon as they caught sight of the tiniest wisp of cloud in the skies, the entire crew declared that luck on the seas was something entirely different from, say, the luck of a nun. Even that tiny wisp could turn into a full-blown storm.

It took one week to reach Muros. The ship didn't head into port, rather dropped anchor at the entrance to the wide harbor. The captain and crew exchanged friendly farewells with Oldrich and Agnes and brought them ashore in a launch manned by two oarsmen. They were now only one day's ride away from

Compostela.

They put up for the night in a comfortable almshouse that King Alfonso himself had built for pilgrims not too long ago. While there were still three more days until the feast of the Nativity, practically all the beds were occupied by pilgrims. Even in winter time, hundreds of pilgrims descended upon Compostela from all over Europe. Finding two horses in this harbor town was no easy matter, despite the fact that the city basically lived off providing services for pilgrims.

A businessman who owned an imposing farmstead not far from the pier apologized that all his horses were gone, but he could offer them a pair of donkeys. In his opinion, they were much more appropriate for making the pilgrimage to the apostle's tomb, because the donkey was the animal St. James had used during his wanderings in Hispania. It was the same elsewhere. In summer time pilgrims usually walked to Compostela, but preferred to hire out horses in winter.

The local magistrate came forward and advised them to ask around the peasants in the surrounding villages. They were also in the horse trade for pilgrims because it earned them a decent income during the summer and their prices were lower than the merchants in town. He then added amicably, "Don't let yourselves be talked into taking a donkey! Sure, it's the animal of the Old Testament and the apostles, but pretty darned stubborn too. You would get there faster on foot. Forgive my curiosity, but where do you come from?"

"From Bohemia," answered Oldrich. The magistrate of Muros was a talkative and likable sort.

"I thought so," he nodded. "I was speaking to a man this morning who's looking for you."

"Nobody knows we're here," countered Oldrich.

"You are mistaken, noble sir," replied the magistrate, shaking his head in the affirmative. "He gave me an exact description of you. You are Oldrich of Chlum, are you not?"

CHAPTER XXVIII

"We should find out what this man wants," Agnes decided when Oldrich informed her of this latest unsettling development. "Perhaps he's a pilgrim who needs our help!"

"I greatly doubt it," said Oldrich. "How would he know my name? I will go to look for him and find out. Very quick and formal like. Who he is and what he wants from us. He certainly doesn't need our help. There is one more possibility here. While in Landstein, I brought you a letter from your relative King Alfonso. Did you inform him that I was accompanying you? And that we would be coming to Galicia by ship?"

"I asked him for protection," she replied formally.

Oldrich nodded and said nothing further. Trying to get any information from this group of pilgrims was like carrying water in a sieve. The King of Castile had to at least suspect that Agnes of Bohemia was not coming to Galicia merely to kneel at the tomb of James the Greater. If this secret was of such value that the Pope, the Templars and the King of France were all eager to get their hands on it, why shouldn't the King of Castile be in on the act too? And the fact that he was a relative of Agnes only made him more suspect. Oldrich knew that among the ruling families it was safer to trust strangers than relatives.

He went back to Muros. There were perhaps fifty dwellings in the city and a third of them provided accommodations for pilgrims. He went from one to the other making inquiries. As he walked into the seventh or eighth one, he noticed a monk in the white habit of the Premonstratensian order sitting at a table in the corner. He recognized Hyacinth immediately and walked up to him. Once Oldrich was sure he was the one asking the magistrate about him, he breathed a sigh of relief. Not that he completely trusted Hyacinth, but it was better him than some new antagonist. This entire situation had become so complicated, so interwoven with plots and intrigues, that Oldrich had absolutely no clue how the whole thing was going to end up.

He took a seat next to the monk and ordered some mulled wine to warm up a bit. It had been unpleasantly cold in their cabin during the voyage and it didn't get any better once they reached the shore. An icy wind was blowing in from the sea and the snow began falling intermittently. Hyacinth gave a calm and systematic recounting of all the events that occurred after he left their party. Oldrich listened intently, the expression on his face becoming one of rage as he learned of the betrayal of Peter of Rosenberg and Jana of Blatna. He was also quite astonished to hear Hyacinth relate how somebody slew Friar Gregory and Emmeram of Greifsfeld on board the ship. Unfortunately there wasn't time to go into more details.

"Of course, the French emissary couldn't be trusted from the beginning," stated Oldrich when Hyacinth finished. "But to be betrayed by your own people is a bitter blow. If you remember when we met Guy of Lusignan back in Constance, you said that he reminded you of somebody. Somebody long dead. Is that all? I don't trust this man, because I'm wondering if his name really is Lusignan. I certainly don't believe he's the son of the King of Jerusalem, as he claims."

"Why not?" asked the monk. He finished his mug but declined to have another one.

"Guy of Lusignan was already a middle-aged man when the Muslims defeated him at Hattin and seized Jerusalem. That battle took place nearly eighty years ago. He had to be really old to father a son who would turn out to be this French emissary?"

Hyacinth nodded but otherwise didn't show much interest in what Oldrich was getting at. He wasn't like Ota. He was used to receiving orders and fulfilling them. He was a monk. Then, suddenly, his expression changed and he grew hysterical. He quickly crossed himself. But when Oldrich asked him what was wrong, he replied with feigned calm that everything was fine. Oldrich was convinced otherwise. Hyacinth had remembered something, something involving Guy of Lusignan. He most likely knew who he was, but for unknown reasons didn't want to talk about it. So he changed the topic and asked the monk instead how he was able to get there so quickly. More importantly, how he was able to board a ship in France.

"I'm only a man," replied the monk. For a moment he paused and blushed slightly. His eyes started darting to and fro in a puzzling manner, as if he had said something inappropriate. But he regained his composure and said that he was able to travel faster than them because he could stay in the saddle longer than Agnes. Sometimes he rode on even after sunset.

"So when I got to the coast and found out I wouldn't be able to board a ship without the royal authorities knowing it, I knew I had to find another way," he said proudly. "As a monk, I'm able to obtain a safe conduct pass in any port, but they would have followed me and I didn't want to unwittingly lead them to you. That's why I decided to seek out the help of smugglers."

"How did you know where to find them?" Oldrich asked hesitantly. He had to carefully consider any information he now received from a member of their party. He couldn't be sure if Hyacinth's account of the events that took place on the emissary's ship were completely true. Perhaps they really happened as he claimed, perhaps not. He could easily be the one who betrayed them, not Rosenberg, and was sent here by Guy. All he could do for the time being was hope the monk was telling the truth. But he would be on his guard in any case. Since leaving Landstein, Hyacinth always seemed to be present anywhere something suspicious was happening. The last incident occurred in Besançon, when he disappeared supposedly because somebody had denounced him for heresy. As a result, Oldrich had to bring Agnes back into their party, where someone didn't waste any time trying to poison her. It took divine intervention to spare her life and take Zdena Berkova's instead.

"Don't forget, noble sir, that I come from southern France," smiled the monk with bitterness. "The locals trust me because I speak Occitan. If I were to speak French with them, they would be wary. But there are lots of smugglers on the coast. It wasn't any problem at all."

"At all?" asked Oldrich, noting the special emphasis he placed on the last words.

"The Lord constantly places obstacles in our path," said Hyacinth. "Of course, the smugglers did not bring me ashore here in the harbor. They have their own little harbor set up in a cove well hidden among the rocks. These rocks are so high and the surf so strong that no one unfamiliar with the place would ever find it. We landed at night and I proceeded to Muros in the dark. Suddenly I heard horses approaching. I don't know why but I decided to hide. As the horsemen passed me, I could see they were Templars riding out of Muros."

* * *

The magistrate was right. Oldrich found three horses in the first village he came to and just after daybreak they set off for Compostela. The road was covered with a blanket of snow, but the skies were clearing underneath the winter sun. The flatland in front of Bertarimans looked as smooth as bleached linen. They were the first to ride this way that morning. The hooves of their horses completely disrupted the sparkling, powdery surface.

The way to Compostela was lined with shrines. Agnes insisted on stopping at each one for a moment of prayer. Her mood that morning was solemn and somber. She knew that the point of their long journey would most likely come to a head that evening. She prayed to God that the heavy burden that had been placed on her shoulders by the dying Clare of Assisi might finally be lifted. Beggars with outstretched hands were sitting at the entrance to each shrine, beseeching the incoming pilgrims for handouts. Agnes gave them a handful of small copper pieces. Even though she had a specific mission to accomplish in Compostela, she couldn't forget about the original purpose of her pilgrimage, which included charity for the poor and miserable.

As the sun continued to rise, the snow quickly turned into mush, shallow depressions into puddles of dirty water. Yet they managed to ride on quickly and by early afternoon they could see the towers and high roof of the Church of Santiago de Compostela. The entire cathedral was covered with copper plating that reflected the sun off its viridescent surface like a golden waterfall. A large courtyard enclosed by a stone wall, reinforced at the corners by massive towers, stood in front of the entrance to the cathedral. There was a lively trade going on in the courtyard. Shopkeepers in a long line of colorful stalls against the wall were offering potato cakes filled with vegetables and meat, hot wine, candles, and amulets with the remains of St. James. On the opposite side stood a sizable shelter with a thatched rooftop, under which the pilgrims could tie up their horses next to a stone trough. The traffic in the courtyard included people wearing threadbare smocks and several knights in splendid armor. Wending their way among them were beggars carrying poles with leather pouches fastened to the end of them. They used them to thrust home their urgent appeals.

As soon as the tomb of James the apostle came into view, they stopped and dismounted. All three knelt and bowed their heads in prayer as a sign of thanks to the Lord for bringing them there safely. The shadows were growing as the sun slowly began sinking towards the horizon. Oldrich was a little impatient, because unlike Abbess Agnes and Friar Hyacinth, he didn't think now was the time for excessive piety. It quickly grew dark. It was the winter solstice, the shortest day of the year.

They stood up when Agnes finished her prayer but

didn't get back on their horses. Leading them by the reins, they proceeded to the cathedral on foot. Once they passed through the high gate of the courtyard, Hyacinth took control of the horses and brought them to the shelter. He tied them up next to the others. They were foaming at the mouth after the long journey and needed straw and water. A marketer with curly black hair stood at the entrance to the shelter selling fodder.

Oldrich walked behind Agnes, looking around warily. If someone was stalking them, here would be the place to strike. It was certain to happen sooner or later. He thought the open space of the courtyard represented the greatest danger to her. She walked slowly, her hands clasped in silent prayer. It was quiet all around them. They continued unobserved.

They ascended a long marble staircase and entered the gloomy church nave through a wide, magnificently decorated portal. The hips of the vaulted ceiling were lost high above their heads and the smell of incense and aromatic spices permeated the air. Directly in front of them on a stone grade was the grave of the apostle James the Greater. Dozens of silver candlesticks with scores of burning candles stood around it. Pilgrims were kneeling before it with their heads bowed to the floor and praying. Agnes paused with tears in her eyes. She was deeply moved.

"Please, Sir Oldrich, allow me a moment to myself," she asked him and headed to the apostle's grave. She knelt among the others and clasped her hands.

Oldrich approached a young, swarthy prelate who was standing next to one of the side altars and cleaning a silver box on a stone communion table. "Please, brother, help me," he said in cultivated Latin. "I'm searching for an altar server here. His name is Peter Waldo."

"I don't know him," answered the prelate. "There are quite a few of us here. I've been here only three months. Ask brother Orenseus. He's the older man there next to the window. He knows all the monks here." He then turned and went patiently back to his work.

Friar Orenseus shook his head when Oldrich asked him. "I'm sorry, venerable brother pilgrim, but I cannot help you. Brother Peter Waldo left us six months ago. He's no longer in Compostela. They say he went to the tomb of Jesus Christ in Jerusalem."

Oldrich thanked him and walked towards the crowd of pilgrims. He kept a constant eye on Agnes, even though he wasn't afraid of something happening inside the cathedral. It was unhallowed ground he had to worry about the most. He walked around the slender columns supporting the vaulted ceiling and noticed a deep apse separated from the nave by silver bars. There was a stone slab inside which held gifts left by more eminent visitors to the tomb of St. James in the past. Each contained a card with the name of the donor. They included an outstanding gold reliquary in the form of the apostle's head, donated to the Church of Santiago de Compostela by Emperor

Frederick Barbarossa. There were other fabulous gifts from the Castilian, French and English monarchs. Among the papal gifts to the church was a cross studded with rubies, symbolizing the blood shed by Christ to redeem the sins of mankind. There was also a gift from Pope Innocent III. Poignant among these gems was a withered bouquet of roses left there at one time by St. Hedwig, and next to it a large pink candle from Clare of Assisi. It had been turned so that only the end of the inscription could be read: "...of Apostle James."

As Oldrich looked to see if any of the cards contained the name of a donor from Bohemia, someone tugged him on the sleeve. It was a hunchbacked man with only one arm. He was skin and bones. Before Oldrich could grab the pouch hanging from his belt to give the man some alms, the wretch asked him quietly, "Where are you from, Sir?"

"Why do you ask?"

"It's important. Please, tell me. And speak the truth; we are in the house of the Lord."

Oldrich hesitated for a moment before saying, a bit resentfully, that he was from the kingdom of Bohemia, and if that was all the man wanted to know, he could now kindly leave him in peace.

"Excellent!" the wretch rejoiced. "In this case, please come with me."

"Where to?"

"I heard that you are looking for the altar server named Peter Waldo. He is aware that someone from

Bohemia should come here. He asked me to immediately bring this person to him."

"Supposedly he left for the Holy Land."

"Not true," the man answered impatiently. He grabbed Oldrich by the hand and started pulling him towards the exit. "He's in hiding. Afraid for his life. It's not far. Please come!"

"I'm not here alone," said Oldrich, but the man was insistent. "I cannot bring more of you," he told him. "Only one person. Brother Waldo is afraid. Maybe after he speaks to you, he'll want to see the others too. For Christ's sake, come already! I told you he fears for his life. Pretend like nothing is happening. And be careful not to draw attention to us. Especially from any of the local prelates. Brother Waldo is afraid of them the most!"

CHAPTER XXIX

Agnes of Bohemia was praying at the tomb of James the apostle and took no notice of what was going on around her. When Hyacinth saw Oldrich leaving the church in the company of the hunchback, he immediately ran up to him.

"Stay here with the venerable abbess," Oldrich told him in a low voice. "If possible, don't let her leave the church until I come back."

The monk nodded and sauntered over to one of the side altars, where he began praying. Oldrich noticed it was dedicated to St. John the Baptist, he who had baptized Jesus Christ and was the inspiration to the Waldensian heretics as the symbol of the poverty and humility of the first Christians.

It was dark outside, but the entire courtyard was lit up by dozens of candles and several fires burning in the corners. The stalls were still doing a lively business. Oldrich felt there were more pilgrims outside than inside the church.

"It's not far," said the wretch, quickly leading him through the gateway. They walked amidst the twisted trunks of olive trees, now completely bare, and headed for a nearby village. Everyday life in Compostela gave no indication that it was one of the places where thousands of pilgrims turned their heavenly thoughts to. Homemakers were preparing their evening meals, and farmhands were feeding the cattle while the farmers themselves were sitting and chatting on doorsteps. They passed a row of low houses, turned between some gardens, and found themselves in front of a small shanty that looked like it belonged to an old peasant. The wretch tapped a signal on the door. A latch could be heard moving inside and the door creaked opened. Standing in front of them was a burly man of about forty with a good-natured face. He glanced around and hastily motioned Oldrich to enter. He thanked the beggar and gave him a few silver coins.

There was a single large room inside. It was simply furnished but nicely warm. The man politely introduced himself as Peter Waldo. He gestured for Oldrich to take a seat. He studied him carefully before asking, almost sheepishly, "Do you really come from Bohemia?"

Oldrich nodded. In the light the man looked even younger than in the doorway. There was no hair on his temples and his eyes had a special blue-green tint. He moved with the slow deliberation of most prelates.

"I've been expecting someone," Waldo continued hesitantly. "If you are privy to what it's all about, then you understand I must be careful. I will tell you one name. If you answer correctly, I shall praise the Lord that we have met. If you do not, we are only two people whose paths crossed by chance and who will now depart and forget about this completely insignificant episode. So...Clare of Assisi."

Oldrich nodded, but hesitated. He didn't like to be received under such circumstances. He was especially bothered by the fact that Waldo had left the Church of Santiago de Compostela, reportedly to go overseas, but in fact was living nearby. He was also supposedly in hiding out of fear of the other prelates, but this shanty certainly didn't provide much protection and he could meet any number of prelates anytime in Compostela. It was, however, true what the young man had said to him back at the altar. There were lots of clergymen in the Church of St. James and not all of them knew each other.

He explained that his brethren had stopped paying attention to him after he removed his robes. Few of them were so observant that they would even recognize that the man in the peasant smock used to be one of their own. But even if Oldrich's reservations were unfounded, he didn't have much choice. The longer they were there, the greater the danger that Guy would appear in Compostela. Assuming, of course, he wasn't already there, since he could travel faster than Agnes. And so Oldrich said, "The name you are probably looking for is Agnes of Bohemia."

Waldo smiled, stood up and embraced him. "Welcome to Compostela, brother. I was beginning to fear you wouldn't make it. What kept you?"

"Long history," he answered evasively. "What now?"

"We have to fulfill our mission," Waldo replied gravely. "But first I must speak to the venerable older sister. Just a few words, but in confidence."

Oldrich wasn't happy to hear that, but nor was he surprised.

"Do you dare enter the church?" he asked Waldo.

"Why not? I'm no criminal, nor am I under interdict. Of course, there are a couple of the brethren who cannot know that I'm here. I will change into the robes of a Minorite monk. If I wear a hood over my head, not even Friar Hybernius, whom I share a common cell with, will recognize me. Wait a moment."

He went to a trunk and pulled out a dirty gray habit and an equally dirty, torn and crudely stitched together cloak. It was precisely the kind of outfit the poor monks were walking in around there. He put it on over his smock and together they left for the church.

When they got there, the activity in the courtyard had abated and most of the people were inside in preparation for Vespers. Agnes was still kneeling in front of the tomb while Hyacinth was a few steps behind her with clasped hands, as if he was praying, but in fact he was keeping a careful eye on her. Waldo asked which one of the women was Agnes and then begged Oldrich to give him a few minutes alone with her.

Oldrich regretted the fact that he didn't have Ota with him. Together they knew what to do without speaking. He didn't know if Hyacinth was as clever, but it was worth a try. As Waldo turned his back and started for the tomb, Oldrich gestured to the Premonstratensian to verify if this was the man they were looking for. Also, he should try to overhear what they were saying without the abbess knowing he was doing it. But Hyacinth looked completely oblivious. He merely stood there impassively, moving his lips in silent prayer.

Peter Waldo walked up to Agnes of Bohemia and knelt. He leaned close to her and started whispering something. At first the abbess flinched but then leaned close to him and a discussion ensued. Suddenly Waldo crossed himself, stood up and started back towards Oldrich; only Hyacinth by that time had darted from his place and intercepted him.

Before Oldrich could join them, he noticed Hyacinth making some gesture of disapproval. He decided to put his faith in the monk's judgment. He leaned against a pillar, as if nothing at all were happening, and waited. They spoke only a few words, then embraced and Waldo headed for the exit. When he reached Oldrich, he told him that everything had been agreed to and they would see each other tomorrow. Claiming he needed no escort home, he bowed politely and disappeared.

The mass started just as Oldrich walked up to Agnes. He knelt on the cold, tiled floor, clasped his hands and together with the other mass of believers extolled the glory of God. It was a celebratory mass given there were only two days remaining until Christmas.

Once it was over, they left the church. Speaking only in monosyllables, Agnes declared that her mission had finally been accomplished. However, she declined to divulge what had passed between her and Waldo.

"Let's find some shelter," grumbled Oldrich. He was beginning to like the whole matter less and less. It wasn't just the fact that he had to know what this secret involving Clare was all about, aside from being naturally curious, but when thinking about everything that had happened on their pilgrimage, as well as all the signs involving the secret box, the burned heretical writings, Clare's son, the Waldensians, Templars and that vicious crusader Renaud de Châtillon, he was certain something was amiss. Something they still had to worry about, and all because Agnes wouldn't tell him everything. And by now declaring that her mission had been fulfilled, she was still showing this same old unwillingness to follow his advice.

"I asked around," grinned Hyacinth. "Finding accommodation here is the easiest thing in the world. We only need to pay somebody in the courtyard to lead us to a nearby inn and there's sure to be some beds available. But it's a little like throwing the dice. Sometimes they bring you to a decent inn, sometimes to a stinking flophouse."

Oldrich stopped and announced out loud that he was looking for a place to sleep. He was immediately approached by three men, each one trying to shout down the other two, each claiming he knew of nice and cheap accommodations while the other two were mere swindlers.

"Which one should we choose?" asked Hyacinth, who then came up with his own suggestion. "I have an idea. There are three of them. The skinny one looks like a scoundrel, the fat one like a rogue. What do you say we choose the one in the middle?"

"A very wise idea," said Agnes, smiling for perhaps the first time since they arrived in Compostela. "If we must roll the dice, then let it be by Christian principles. The gluttony of the fat is just as much a sin as the greed of the skinny."

The choice appeared to be a good one. The middle man led them to a small but clean and pleasant wayside inn not far from the market. Even the price wasn't too high considering this was Compostela, where everything was more expensive than in other pilgrimage destinations. They took a seat next to the fire and ordered something to eat.

Only after a black-eyed servant girl had brought them bowls of soup, a basket of potato cakes and a slice of roasted meat on a tray did Friar Hyacinth say anxiously, "I must tell you something. I believe the situation is extremely serious!"

"I do hope you are not going to try to talk me out of tomorrow's meeting with Peter Waldo," Agnes asked sternly. "I saw you two talking together in the church and I couldn't help noticing the evil look you were giving him."

"Forgive me, venerable older sister, I certainly do not want to talk you out of your meeting with Peter Waldo," the monk humbly answered with downcast eyes. Elderly abbess or not, he was forever shy around women. "It is the reason we came to Compostela. I only want to talk you out of meeting this particular man. He is not the son of the merchant of Lyon, Peter Waldo. Most probably not even of Clare of Assisi."

"How do you know?" snapped Agnes, laying aside her spoon as if she had just lost her appetite. She was trembling slightly due to the tension of the past few days. She was an old woman and everything she had had to endure up to that point would be too much for most young noble women, let alone a nun.

"Of course, you both know that I come from southern France," Hyacinth continued softly and with emotion. "My parents knew Peter Waldo. They also came from Lyon. Waldo used to come to our home to preach. I knew him too. I was quite young at the time but I still remember what he looked like, and this man who spoke to me in the church looks nothing like him. Peter Waldo was small, skinny and had sharply cut features in his face."

"So he doesn't look like him. What of it?" Agnes was becoming upset. "Many sons don't look like their fathers."

"Does he at least look like the venerable Clare of

Assisi?" The monk was obstinate.

Agnes shook her head, adding that her older sister was of smaller stature and darker. Still, he was her son because he had the same eyes as she did.

"Maybe," said Hyacinth, holding his ground. "I told him that I knew his father and that he reminded me of him. I was lying, of course. I said Peter Waldo was just as tall as he is, the only difference being he had a thick black beard. And you know what he said? He agreed and added that he had often seen his father in his youth. What do you think of that?"

"He was confused, or maybe he's ashamed of the fact that he never knew his father," Agnes said in his defense and stood up. She said she was tired and going to sleep. But she reiterated that tomorrow she was going to meet Peter Waldo whether they liked it or not, because he had the box they were after.

"He confirmed that?" asked Oldrich a tad sarcastically. He didn't like the man either.

"No!" retorted Agnes in an official tone. "He had it with him and gave me a peek of it." She walked through the door next to the furnace and to their quarters for the night.

"He's not the son of the merchant of Lyon," the monk remarked quietly and without the slightest movement. He looked at Oldrich apprehensively.

* * *

The Czech pilgrims being held captive on the ship had

made an attempt to escape at the beginning of Advent, so their French captors forbade them to come out even on deck. From that moment on they were stuck in their cabins. They slept in the rear of the ship, the girls in one cabin, Ota and Jost in the other. They were allowed to spend their days together in the large cabin below deck, where they could buy plenty of food and drink, but that wasn't enough for the life of knights and noble ladies. They were all terribly bored and getting on each other's nerves. They fought over every little trifle.

The sour mood even affected Ota, who ceased enjoying the company of both girls. Only once did he ask Katherine if she wanted to continue her lessons, but he did so more out of obligation than anything. She angrily replied that he should forget about such nonsense and think of a way to get them out of there. But it was Svetlana having the hardest time of all. Her captors tried their best to stay out of her way. She broke a mug over the head of one of the French soldiers and deliberately stomped on the foot of another one so hard that he limped around for a week.

"This can't go on," growled Jost after he and Ota were again locked up inside their cabin. "Either Guy is going to catch up with Agnes, kill her and then kill us so that there are no witnesses, or else he's going to come to an agreement with her and will let us live, only by then we'll all be dead because these soldiers will have had enough of my sister and kill us anyway. What can we do?"

"Nothing! We didn't prepare that first attempt well. We have to be patient now and hope a second chance presents itself," Ota sighed crossly. He undressed, splashed some water from the bucket on him and went to lie down.

"Svetlana insisted on it and dug in her heels," mumbled Jost. "She's acting like a caged animal right now. Ota, can't you try to calm her down somehow? You know how it works with women. I have this idea that if you went to her and Katherine to me..."

"Absolutely not!" Ota cut him off. He had observed Jost taking more than a passing interest in Katherine over the past few days. "Of course, I'm not worried about me. I'm ready to sacrifice myself short of Svetlana scratching my eyes out or doing something even worse to me. But I have to protect the interests of my friend Michal Kekule of Stradonice. How can I look him in the eye if I have to verify a certain unpleasant development in their relationship?"

"Why all the sudden change of heart?" sneered Jost. "Are you planning to enter a convent, oh guardian of maidenly honor? Why do I waste my time with you? You're the same as your master. I warned Svetlana to avoid you. Your conduct is unbecoming for a knight. The same goes with Oldrich of Chlum."

"So I don't conduct myself as a knight because I don't want to dishonor your sister?" fumed Ota. It was the swipe at his master that infuriated him most.

"As soon as we get our swords back, I trust you'll be ready to take up this matter again. Honorably, face to face. With sword in hand!" sniped Jost threateningly. He lay down and turned his back in a sign that he was finished with him for today. Ota did the same. There was only one bed in the cabin, but fortunately it was wide enough for both of them to fit on it.

It was freezing outside and snowing heavily. A thin layer of ice was forming around both the riverbank and the hull of the ship. Thick clouds hung in the sky. Not a single star could be seen and the darkness was nearly impenetrable. They hadn't been asleep long when a muffled shriek, followed by a hollow thud, could be heard outside the door, as if something heavy had hit the deck. Both knights immediately jumped up. Somebody outside removed the latch and opened the door to their cabin. A dim light from a lamp revealed the figure of Prech of Michalovice standing on the threshold, sword in hand.

"You two still like it here?" he grinned. "Quickly, we haven't got much time!"

They said nothing, only got dressed in a flash and tossed their things into a leather pouch. They found their swords and weapons in a trunk on deck where their captors had hidden them. It took the two noble maidens much longer to get all their things in order. Prech kept hounding them to leave a couple of the more superfluous items behind lest it held them up.

"Nothing is superfluous," declared Svetlana defiantly.

Prech had the bound and gagged French guards taken to the cabin on the stern. One of the Czech soldiers remained behind with them to make sure they didn't try to escape and summon their companions, who at that moment were nicely asleep in a nearby roadside tavern.

At last they were ready to go. They crossed the gangplank and started walking along the riverbank. The way was icy and slippery. "The horses are just outside of town," whispered Prech. Before leaving the harbor, Ota noticed several men casting off the lines and the ship sailing away into darkness.

"Guy's men are going to be surprised in the morning," Prech chuckled. "They will give chase to the ship because they're idiots. They will think that you have commandeered it and are heading south. We'll be over the border by the time they figure it out."

"What about the crew on board?"

"Only one of our men is there and he can take care of himself. The rest are locals whose services we hired for a pretty penny. They will beach the ship somewhere after one or two days and vanish. But before that, I suspect they will strip it clean. They are thieves, very good at their trade."

"How were you able to pull this off?" asked Ota, slapping the guard commander on the back. "I owe you one."

"I hope so," said Prech good-humoredly. "I knew Guy would send a party to make sure we returned home. So we left Basel and headed for Constance. After spending a few days there, we took a detour back and started staking out how they were guarding the ship at night. I saw to it that the French soldiers on shore got drunk senseless in the tavern while we easily took out the three guards on board."

"You deserve a reward. The King will be grateful," Jost announced. The snow was still falling heavily, but Svetlana looked up at the night sky with the eyes of deliverance. She then leaned towards Prech and whispered that he did indeed deserve a reward, and if someday he were to be equally brazen inside her sleeping chamber, he might find her a willing accomplice, because she admired courageous knights.

"I assure you, noble maiden, that I will be so brazen," he bowed politely.

As soon as they reached the horses, they mounted and set off. It was a three day's ride to the border assuming the weather didn't get any worse and they were able to travel from morning till evening.

They decided to go to Basel. Ota had agreed with Oldrich that they would meet there after the matter in Compostela had been settled and he was on the way back with Agnes. Realizing it could take some time, they asked the Bishop of Basel for shelter. He freely made one of his farmsteads, which lay along the Rhine just outside the city walls, available to them.

Their first night there, Katherine stole into Ota's chamber. She threw off her clothes and slipped under his covers. Hugging him, she excitedly reminded him that he had offered to continue their lessons.

"But you refused," retorted Ota.

"That's not true. I only conditioned it on you

getting us free. Now we are free and nothing is standing in the way of more instruction."

"But I have nothing else to teach you."

"So let's think up something together," she laughed under her breath. "It was terribly boring in captivity, so I thought about the art of romance and came up with a few ideas, but I want to try them out with somebody before I introduce them to my fiancé. That makes sense, doesn't it?"

"Completely," he agreed in earnestness and began to passionately kiss her.

CHAPTER XXX

In the morning, Agnes ordered Oldrich to wait for her in the taproom while she took care of their little matter by herself. He adamantly refused, saying he couldn't let her out of his sight even for a moment.

"How dare you disobey me!" she hissed, angrily stomping her foot. "I am a Přemyslid!"

"Exactly," he shrugged as a sign of apologizing for his impertinence. "But I have explicit orders from our exalted majesty. My lord and your lord. It doesn't matter that you are his aunt and I am only his procurator for North Bohemia."

"I am not here as a subject of the King but as a servant of the Lord," she protested sharply.

"We don't have time to play these word games. The moment Christians start babbling instead of doing something will spell the end of Christendom. Our strength lies in our determination to pick up the sword and wage battle. You can win with learned disputation in the refectory maybe, but not in life.

When facing the enemy, knights and not nuns should decide. Forgive me, venerable abbess, but you will now do as I say. And for starters, I want the truth!"

"Leave me be!"

"I'm waiting!" Oldrich demanded, forcing her to take a seat in the process.

She was shaking with fury, but knew this knight wasn't going to back down. Her nephew, King Ottokar, had warned her so. He said no one was as capable as Oldrich of Chlum and she couldn't be in better hands. But he was also extremely stubborn and even ready to disobey the King himself if it came to that. "Forget about an abbess," moaned Agnes to herself. She clasped her hands and quickly prayed in order to assuage the wrath in her soul. Important here, she knew, was to fulfill the mission entrusted to her by Clare.

It took a moment to fully regain her composure. Then, icily and full of spite, she declared, "So be it! You will know the truth, even though you already know practically all of it already."

"Thank you for your trust," he bowed politely.

She flashed a disagreeable look at him and continued. "I didn't tell you the whole truth. Clare did ask me to find the box, but her dying wish was for me to open it and destroy the scroll inside. I don't know what it says, but I do know it somehow represents a threat to the Christian faith. Our religion could disappear forever as a result of it!"

"But you yourself told me, venerable older sister,

that the box is locked, and any attempt to open it will destroy whatever's inside it."

She nodded, then tugged at the edge of her cowl and pulled out a small key hanging from a chain around her neck. "This will open the box," she said quietly. "I already told you that I am the great-granddaughter of Renaud de Châtillon. He's the one who stole the box and key from the Templars and it was his son who took them away from the Battle of Hattin. Renaud had two daughters, and after the death of their brother, they divided up the relics he had collected. The older one got the box and her son went on to become the Count of Lyon. The other was my grandmother, Agnes of Antioch. When she died, the key went to her daughter, Constance of Hungary, and it was from my mother that I got the key. Now you really know everything. The Pope and Templars know what's in the box. That's why they are trying to get their hands on it. They also suspect that I have the key. That's why it was important that I come to Compostela personally, because I'm the only one who can open it."

"Then you're in even greater danger. They already tried to kill you once," he noted firmly. He had to think, and quickly. Agnes had finally told him everything she knew. If she had been more forthcoming earlier, so many things could be different today. But there was no sense grieving about it now. It was sufficient to let the abbess do the grieving. And yet Oldrich still had the nagging feeling that there was a missing link in this long chain of events. Minor perhaps, but still missing.

"You said that the man who claims to be Peter Waldo showed you the box in the church. But how can you be sure it's the right box?" They had to be certain, because the last hurdle of their pilgrimage to the tomb of St. James consisted of the contents in that box.

"Sister Clare wrote to me that the box was marked. There's a nick in the corner at the bottom. No one else knows about it. The box I saw yesterday had this nick and so it is undoubtedly the right one. And that man is Peter Waldo! No one else could know that I should meet the son of Clare of Assisi here. Nor does anyone know that her son is named Peter Waldo!"

"No one," Oldrich said hesitantly. "That's true. The Pope doesn't know it. Not the Templars. Otherwise they would have found him themselves. But someone does know it. There's no other way to explain it."

"No, no one!" Agnes insisted. "Only the real Peter Waldo could know about Clare's true legacy."

"Of course, only the real Peter Waldo," Oldrich repeated slowly, as if weighing the value of this information on a pharmaceutical scale. If the man who met Agnes yesterday wasn't the real one, then who was? He was stroking his chin when it hit him. He turned to Agnes with a new theory. "Venerable Abbess, please try to remember. It's very important here! Peter Waldo, the merchant of Lyon and later the preacher who ended up on the stake, wanted to return to the faith and life of the early Christians. He strove to reform the kingdom of Christ. Do you have any idea what he said on the stake?"

"That heretic?" she asked in disbelief. She didn't like talking about him, but had heard a lot about his sect. "He said he was the King of Jerusalem. Such impudence!"

"Of course, that's what I thought!" nodded Oldrich. He had heard something like that not long ago. "Now it's clear why this man is passing himself off as Peter Waldo. It's a trap. Now the only thing is how to get ourselves out of it."

"You're talking like Sibylla. Now I would like to know the truth for a change!" Agnes protested sternly. "Who could have the audacity to keep me from fulfilling my mission for my sister Clare? Perhaps your task is to protect me, but you certainly have no right to hide anything from me. Does it concern the Christian religion or not? Well?"

"I will tell you everything, venerable older sister, but first allow me to ask you one more question. What did you agree to with this man posing as Peter Waldo? Where to give you the box?"

"After lunch we should meet on the road to the city of La Coruňa. He gave me an exact description of the place. There are ruins of an old Moorish fortress not far from Compostela. He will wait for me there. Alone."

"He could have easily given you the box in the church yesterday. He had it with him, you saw it for yourself. Why make it so complicated?" Oldrich asked.

"He was afraid someone might see us. He knows about the danger involved," Agnes explained. She was still not convinced that Oldrich's fears were warranted.

"Sure, it will be much safer outside the city in some abandoned ruins," he smirked. "First, let's try to figure out who the actual son of Clare of Assisi is. I agree with Friar Hyacinth that the real Peter Waldo should look at least something like his heretic father. His father was smaller in stature and had a thin face. The man we met yesterday looked completely different. But the French emissary, Guy of Lusignan, is of smaller stature. He has a thin face, and when Hyacinth first laid eyes on him back in Constance, he swore that he knew him from somewhere. He was mistaken because he had never met him before. But because he remembers the features of the heretic from Lyon, he subconsciously thought he knew Guy of Lusignan."

"Mere speculation! There are small men by the thousands everywhere," scoffed Agnes, shaking her head reproachfully at what she considered utter nonsense. They were only wasting time, but she was powerless to do anything about it. She was in his hands and he was stronger.

"Sure, lots of small men," he agreed and began to carefully stroke his bearded chin. "Only Guy of Lusignan let something slip if you remember when he introduced himself. He said he was the son of the King of Jerusalem. If he does come from the family of Guy of Lusignan, who lost the Battle of Hattin and with it Jerusalem, he would have to be about ninety years old. To me, he looks at most forty, so the King of Jerusalem would have to have been around a hundred years old when he had him, and as far as I know he didn't reach that age. Both possibilities don't pan out. But there is a third one here, and that is Guy is the son of the man who proclaimed himself to be the King of Jerusalem. I mean the heretic Peter Waldo!"

"If you're right, why is he playing this nasty little game with us? He would know about the dying wish of his mother, and Guy of Lusignan has been doing everything to keep me from fulfilling that wish," Agnes retorted weakly.

"That's not entirely true," Oldrich corrected her. "Someone else has been trying to keep us from reaching Compostela. From what Hyacinth told us, it seems that Emmeram of Greifsfeld was out to kill you. The true son of Clare of Assisi – let's say for clarity's sake it's Guy of Lusignan – was not involved with him. My belief is he was planning to bring you here and steal the key to the box at some opportune moment. Only you escaped and all his plans were thwarted. So he had to come up with a different plan, but frankly speaking one not as good as the first one. I believe he's already here, but I don't believe he left the box in Compostela. He's had it with him the whole time, and now that he's back and ready to draw you into his trap, he lent the box to the man pretending to be Waldo so he can lure you to this Moorish fortress. And that's where Guy of Lusignan will be waiting to relieve you of the key."

"It doesn't sound totally stupid."

"Thank you, venerable older sister!"

"Of course, I must ask again why he's doing all this. I don't understand his motive! He presents himself to us as the emissary of the King of France, which is certainly true. But why would he want to help Louis the Pious when he was the one who destroyed the Waldensian sect and ordered that his father be burned at the stake? And where do the Templars and Rosenberg fall into this story?"

"Here I can only guess. When Guy learned of the death of his mother Clare, he devised a scheme of his own. I'm gathering this from what he might have done after leaving Compostela. He probably went to offer his services to the King of France, but Louis at that time was still campaigning in the Holy Land. And according to one of the prelates at the Church of Santiago de Compostela, Peter Waldo left for there, where he probably made a deal with the King and changed his name. He came back, only to discover that the Templars and, of course, the Pope had become involved in this matter. That complicated things. But as for why he's going to all this trouble, I cannot say. Maybe for money. A scroll that could be used to blackmail the Pope might prove useful to a King who calls himself the pious one."

"I admit that your theory sounds plausible," said Agnes. "If you're right and Guy of Lusignan is the real son of Clare of Assisi and is in Compostela, where are the others? Peter of Rosenberg and Jana of Blatna?"

"I'm not a seer," grumbled Oldrich. "But there are only two possibilities here. Either Guy of Lusignan has betrayed the King of France and sold his services to the Templars for a higher reward. In this case the other two are with him. Or I would venture that he was only using them to get what he wants, so he may, in fact, have already killed them. I would also dare say that Guy killed Jacob de Vries, the commendatore of the Templars in Bohemia. I haven't told you this before, but my squire Ota met Guy by chance in Prague right before our departure."

"But I must fulfill Clare's last wish even if it costs me my life," Agnes cried out heatedly. "What if we visit this Waldo pretender and force him to give us the box?"

Oldrich was pleased that Agnes accepted his opinion that the man she spoke to yesterday wasn't the Peter Waldo. He now proceeded carefully so as not to infuriate her again. "That's not a good idea, venerable older sister. First, I suspect we will not find this man in his shanty. He's probably hiding somewhere now. And even if we do find him, he has surely given the box back to Guy. He had it with him only as bait. The only thing we can do is go to the planned meeting in the ruins."

"He ordered me to come alone. He will certainly be watching the entrance and if he sees there are more of us, he will disappear and I will never see the box again."

"Of course, only one person will go to the meeting," said Oldrich. "Me! I will disguise myself in your habit and take my sword with me. If I'm right and Guy of Lusignan has killed the others, he will be alone. And if this other man going under the name of Waldo shows up too, I'll be able to handle both of them."

"And if you're not right? What if he comes with Peter of Rosenberg and other Templars?"

"Then I will lay down my life for the King, you and Clare of Assisi," replied Oldrich gravely. "We must proceed wisely here. Before Guy of Lusignan appears, the man playing Waldo will surely want to see the key. They are not going to act rashly, because this is their only chance and they know they won't get another one."

"I refuse to give it to you!"

"Keep it, venerable older sister. I will buy one from a locksmith. I simply must have any key in hand to show him. If I don't return, you should go and seek protection from the King of Castile."

Agnes blessed him in a dignified gesture and promised that she would pray for him. She went to her trunk and pulled out a habit to give to him. Oldrich bowed and started to leave.

"Wait a moment," she ordered. She walked up to him and kissed him in the fashion of sisterly love among the nuns of her order.

CHAPTER XXXI

The ruins of the Moorish fortress were not at all extensive. All that remained were the battered ramparts, the crumbling gateway, the elongated oval courtyard of the former palace, and the lower floor of the tower. Wearing his habit disguise, Oldrich stopped on the road and tied the reins of his horse to the trunk of an olive tree and proceeded there on foot. He walked with his head bowed to the ground so his face wouldn't be visible. For extra surety, he wrapped himself up in the white veil of a penitent woman.

He walked into the courtyard and looked around. The large man who had passed himself off as Peter Waldo was standing amidst the palace ruins. As soon as he saw the figure in the habit, he shouted for the venerable abbess to come closer and show him the key. Oldrich grabbed a chain with a key from around his neck and quickly approached the man. As he passed by the ruins of the tower, he heard the rattling of stones. He jumped to the side and turned around. Standing at the opening that used to be the entrance to the tower was Guy of Lusignan with sword in hand. With one hand, Oldrich undid the lace of his habit and cast it aside. With the other, he removed the veil from his head. He was wearing full knightly armor. He reached for his belt and drew his sword.

The man playing the part of Waldo had barely realized something was wrong when he clumsily took off along the ramparts towards the gateway. He stumbled onto the road and fled.

"The key!" said Guy coolly as he stretched out his hand. "Otherwise I will kill you. I should have known you would see through my ruse."

"Then you probably also know that I am not going to give you the key," Oldrich shrugged. "But I have an idea. Let's settle it like two honorable knights. I have the key and I suppose you have the box. We shall lay both aside on the ground, then have at it. The winner takes it all."

"A respectable proposal," agreed Guy. He grabbed his belt and untied a leather pouch from it. He then opened it and took out a small, cylindrical box, carefully placing it on a flat rock. The whole time he carefully watched as Oldrich laid the key on a broken remnant of the gateway.

They lifted their swords, submitted to the code of knightly honor, and commenced combat. Guy of Lusignan was more of a prelate than a knight and while he had a certain amount of training, he was no match for Oldrich of Chlum. All it took were a few lunges and thrusts and Oldrich had forced him on the defensive. Guy steadily retreated. At one point Oldrich had to go around a pile of fallen masonry. Guy decided that now was his chance and leapt on top of the crumbly brickwork in an attempt to assail his opponent from above. Only he stumbled on the loose rock and fell forward, right into Oldrich's sword. He let out a shriek, dropped his weapon and collapsed. Blood gushed out of the wound in his chest.

Oldrich left his sword in Guy's body. He knew pulling it out would only accelerate his death. He kneeled next to him and declared, "It's over! The time has come to unburden your soul!"

"Why?" he asked, gasping and coughing.

"You are going to meet your mother Clare of Assisi. Why didn't you want to fulfill her last wish?"

"My mother!" he answered with such hate and contempt that Oldrich shuddered. His dying words were a bitter diatribe. "Surely you had parents. Do you know what it's like when your mother gives you up as an infant? In a Christian world, they give you to nuns. They should be happy to have you, but they're not. They only think about themselves. They're resentful of their fate and only chatter about serving God. And they forget about you. What's a small child to them? No one holds you, comforts you…"

There were tears in the dying man's eyes. He clenched his fists, more out of regret than the pain he was in.

"My mother wanted to be a saint. Her desire was to be honored by all Christians. A mother should care more about her children. Later she wrote me many letters. She never apologized to me, never told me that she loved me. She only wrote how much she loved Jesus."

"So you decided to take your revenge out on her?"

"What do I care about a Christian world! Why should I care about Christians when they let me suffer? I was hoping to take what's in that box and announce it to the entire world. My father knew what's in it. That's why he renounced the church. If only I could have done so too... You think that you've won? You have only killed me. But sooner or later someone will tell the world what it's about. And that will be the end of your hypocrisy. The hypocrisy of all Christianity. Love of God has replaced love of people! What a world!"

"And why Apostle James?"

"Why? Because Jesus Christ never rose from the dead! It's a lie, you understand, a lie! That means that even if I had lived a God-fearing life, there was nobody to redeem my soul after I died. My mother gave me up for that ideal! And she had to know that it was all a lie!"

He could no longer control his emotions. The tears were streaming down his face. His eyes seemed oblivious of Oldrich; they were looking off somewhere where others couldn't see.

"What about the Templars?"

"Nothing would change if they got it back. They would protect it for the power it gives them. But they discovered me and I had to swear that I would help them. But I'm smarter! Rosenberg and that noble whore are dead. I didn't need them any longer."

He started gasping again as blood trickled out of his mouth. His face was covered in sweat, his breathing became labored, he was close to suffocating.

"He didn't rise from the dead, you understand," he repeated. He began shivering feverishly. "You must tell everyone! You must..."

His head sunk. He tried to say something but couldn't. The son of Clare of Assisi, who had been named after his father Peter Waldo but called himself Guy of Lusignan, was dead. Oldrich drew his sword out of his body, cleaned the edge of it on the dead man's cloak, and put it back in its sheath. He left the key on the rock. He carefully picked up the box, put it back into its pouch, and left the ruins of the Moorish fortress.

He hopped on his horse and galloped with all due speed back to Compostela. The celebratory Christmas mass was set to begin in a moment.

Agnes was nervously pacing back and forth in her room. When he entered, she breathed a sigh of relief and crossed herself. With trembling hands, she took the small box from him and pulled out the key from around her neck. She inserted it into the slit on the side. She lifted her eyes and looked uneasily at Oldrich. She hesitated for a moment and then quietly said, "You deserve to know what this secret is! But you must swear never to tell anyone!"

Oldrich nodded and approached for a better view. His curiosity was stoked by the dying man's claim that Jesus did not rise from the dead.

Abbess Agnes turned the key. It turned freely, without any click. Apparently this key did not belong to the lock on the box. Her hands still trembling, she took the key out of the lock and looked miserably at Oldrich. "What do we do now?"

"Let's go to mass and there we will pray for God to show us the way," he replied wearily. "Somewhere I made a mistake in my reasoning. Either you don't have the right key, or this isn't the right box."

* * *

For centuries the day before Christmas had been referred to by ordinary people as Christmas Eve. Eventually the church began doing so as well. The services that evening were particularly opulent. The Christians were rejoicing with sincere and boundless enthusiasm. Their tables seemed to almost buckle under the amount of food being consumed and few went to bed that evening sober. Young people in mischievous masks were frolicking and singing on the streets. All the pilgrims who had trekked to Galicia that year were congregated in the Cathedral of Santiago de Compostela. They were shoulder to shoulder.

Oldrich, Agnes and Hyacinth found a place a couple of feet from the saint's tomb. They knelt with the other pilgrims, their heads hung humbly as they worshiped in praise of their Lord. But gnawing away at Oldrich's prayers were the heretical words uttered by the son of Clare of Assisi. He was greatly vexed by what this man had told him in such bitterness.

Did his saintly mother have the right to leave him to despair just so she could preach the faith to others? He knew he was unable to solve such a dilemma. He himself was constantly burdened by the excruciating uncertainty that always accompanied the search for truth and justice. On the one hand, there was the order of the Christian world, on the other a real person who had committed an offense or injured someone. The order of the world had never been universal in the sense of being able to satisfy everyone. Truth was for everyone on the face of it, but in reality only some people lived in a just world. The same held true for religion. It helped Christians find joy and happiness in the suffering and hardship that plagued the world and which no one was able to advert. Life was unbearable without faith, as harmful as it was at the same time. And it had brought many a believer to grief, some who ended up on the stake just for having a different opinion about the holy Trinity. Guy had come to grief so that his mother might be a saint. So it was and there was nothing anyone could do about it.

Of course, Oldrich was more troubled by the box and key. He again mulled over everything he knew, all the people involved; what they said, what they did, and whose hand they died by. Of the people who had set off on the pilgrimage to Compostela, barely a handful survived, and most of them were far away now.

The box he had taken from the dying Peter Waldo had to be the right one. It had a nick at the bottom precisely where Clare said it would be. Because Waldo believed that he was going to the ruins to get the key, he certainly didn't have a copy made to bring with him. Who did he need to deceive in that case? He had no reason to fear anyone and would have been eager to get the box open once he had the key.

In terms of this logic, the key worn around the neck of Agnes of Bohemia had to be a phony. But this logic also had its weak points. Who could have swapped it and when? The key had been passed from hand to hand in the family of Renaud de Châtillon. And if someone had changed it, why didn't he use it long ago and removed the contents from inside the box? Everyone with knowledge about this special secret had done everything to make sure Agnes of Bohemia reached Compostela, so none of them certainly had any shadow of doubt that this key was the right one. It's true they had little choice but to believe it, yet there was also no one who could have made the switch. Logically speaking, this dilemma was a real dilemma. Almost as if someone wanted to have a good laugh at everyone's expense.

The devotional singing of the faithful, thankful for the birth of their Savior, rose to the heights of the vaulted ceiling. Oldrich noticed none of it. He wasn't praying to God for help. Whenever he had the feeling that things in his life were not going well, he did not beseech Jesus Christ, rather he searched his own conscience. He was convinced that everything he did ultimately depended on his reason and ability. Now, perhaps for the first time in his life, he despaired that he had lost the case despite finding no weaknesses or chinks in his arguments. He was so close to revealing the secret of the abbess of Assisi, but failed in the end.

All of a sudden he was aware that his neighbor was offering him his hand in a sign of symbolic reconciliation that was a part of every evening service. He quickly took the man's hand and realized, to his shame, that he had also failed to say a single Lord's Prayer during the entire time of the mass. While most of the other believers were standing around him, he was still on his knees and quietly praying. He never believed that prayer could help him. It didn't help his young wife when she was dying. But he did discover that with time prayer brought a certain peace of mind. It bonded him not to heaven, but to other Christians.

He stood up and looked around. Suddenly something grabbed his attention. Unable to focus his thoughts, he couldn't quite discern what it was, but it seemed as if some strange, higher power was directing his gaze, until he found himself looking straight at the answer in front of him. There was no mistaking it. He had finally figured out what secret lay in the box hidden by Clare of Assisi in Compostela.

* * *

They returned to the inn after mass, where they quickly had supper and went to their rooms. Agnes was disappointed and grumpy. Before she went to sleep, Oldrich came to her and asked to see the key again.

"Why?" she asked distrustfully.

"I would like to try it one more time. If it doesn't work, then no harm done. It will still be the wrong key."

She thought for a moment and then pulled out the small chain from around her neck and handed it to him. But before giving up her cherished relic, she said, "Promise me that if you are successful, you will be guided most of all by the last wish of Clare of Assisi."

"I swear," Oldrich nodded and quickly left.

He walked out onto the street. Despite being dark out, there was a lively scene going on. The people were still celebrating the birth of Jesus Christ. The crowd included naughty bands of young boys and girls, and at one point Oldrich was forced to join a group of merry well-wishers in a dance before they would let him through. It took a while for him to reach the courtyard of the Church of St. James, where he found more dignified peace and calm. The shopkeepers had left their stalls and were doing business on the street. Even the inside of the church was empty. All the prelates were probably in town dancing and drinking with their flocks.

Oldrich went straight to the apse and all the precious gifts left behind in it by affluent pilgrims. As expected, the silver bars separating the apse from the rest of the church were in no way firmly fixed. After all, who would dare commit an act of thievery in such a sacred place? He easily managed to pry two of the bars far enough apart to slip inside. He grabbed Clare's gift of a candle and quickly left. He straightened out the bent silver bars as much as possible to keep anyone from noticing the damage.

He just made it. He heard footsteps coming from the entrance. Oldrich edged up against the wall and around a column. He walked around the tomb, dropped to his knees and began to pray. An elderly sexton passed by. The man in the brown monastic habit observed him apathetically and continued on with his rounds. As soon as he was gone, Oldrich stood up and, using the nearest candle, lit the wick of the candle he had stolen from the apse. He placed it on a metal tray with the charred remains of other candles set alight that day. He knelt next to it, prayed and watched how the wax slowly trickled down from the top of the candle. He knew he had a long wait in front of him. The sexton passed him two more times before Clare's candle had burned down sufficiently enough to reveal the glint of something metallic next to the wick. Apparently the inscription on the candle – The legacy of Apostle James – had been no lie.

A moment later Oldrich drew out his dagger. He extinguished the flame and started carefully flicking away the soft, pinkish wax around the object until he was holding in his hands a metal box, looking exactly like the one he took away from the ruins that afternoon. Even though the metal casing was still hot, he eagerly inserted the key given to him by Agnes into the slit on the side. He turned it and the lock quietly clicked. He removed the key, unscrewed the top of the casing and put it aside. There inside he saw a delicate, yellow papyrus scroll. He took it out, closed the box and locked it. He stuck the box and key in a pocket on the inside of his cloak. With the scroll in hand, he walked to the nearest stand with burning candles.

He gently unrolled the fragile scroll. It had to be extremely old, because its edges had crumbled to dust. The text was written in Latin, in classically rounded capital letters, as was the norm in ancient Rome. It stated: "We, the disciples of Jesus Christ, confirm to the Roman authorities, as represented by Pontius Pilate, that we took the crucified body of the said Jesus Christ at dawn on Sunday from Golgotha so that we might bury him." It was followed by three signatures – James, Peter and Andrew.

Oldrich felt as if someone had just thrust a sword deep into his body. He instantly recalled the words of the Gospel of Matthew, who suggested that immediately after the Crucifixion, the Pharisees began spreading the word that Jesus hadn't risen from the dead, rather his body disappeared because it had been stolen by his own disciples. That itself brought to mind the illumination by Heribert of Graz, which

Oldrich saw in one of the codices at the scriptorium in Melk. It depicted the Resurrection with a coffin, over which hovered Jesus Christ, while crouching next to it was a figure in a Roman toga identified by the small inscription as Pontius Pilate.

If the scroll was right, it explained many contradictions in the Gospels. Andrew and Peter were brothers, as were James and John the evangelist. While Andrew and Peter remained very close after the Crucifixion, John had nothing to say about his brother James in his Gospel. A drunken Emmeram of Greifsfeld had pointed this fact out to Oldrich. The librarian clearly suspected what was in the box and tried to keep Agnes from opening it. He could only speculate the reason behind the rift between John and James. Perhaps it was indicated somewhere in the scroll he held in his hands. But the candle could also be a fake. How many lies have been written about Jesus and his Resurrection by everyone, and not just the heretics!

Oldrich knew what he had to do with the scroll. Not because it was Clare's last wish, but because, despite his views of the Christian world, he knew people needed religion. Living with religion was sometimes difficult and painful, but to live without it was much worse. He placed the edge of the scroll against the candle flame. The dry papyrus immediately caught fire. He let it fall to the floor. Once the fire was out, he used the tip of his boots to crush the blackened cinder underfoot and vigorously scattered the remaining dust. He then turned and headed for the exit.

He walked outside and was greeted by the new dawn. He didn't realize he had spent the entire night in the church. Weary, he stretched and walked across the courtyard to the gateway. He had barely reached the road when a number of men on horseback appeared out of hiding. Each was wearing a gray tunic with the red Templar cross emblazoned on the chest. At their head rode a dignified-looking knight. The insignia on his helmet indicated he was the Grandmaster himself.

They surrounded him and one of the Templars dismounted with sword in hand. Oldrich calmly observed him. He gave no sign of trying to reach for his sword.

"Search him, brother," the Grandmaster ordered, casting a very disagreeable look at Oldrich.

The knight didn't have long to search. He discovered the box and key inside his cloak. He raised both triumphantly and handed them to the Grandmaster, who opened the box with trembling hands, only to cry out disappointingly, "Empty! What did you do with the scroll inside it?"

"Naturally, I opened the box. But there was nothing inside it," Oldrich answered firmly. "By all means, search me again!"

Despite it being winter, the Templars performed another, more thorough search. They stripped Oldrich of Chlum naked and fingered every little fold in his garments. They had to report to the Grandmaster that they really found nothing on him.

"Watch him," the Grandmaster ordered two of the Templars who were searching him. He and the others walked into the church. They were in there for a long time, determined to make sure that Oldrich hadn't hidden the scroll somewhere. They returned only after they were convinced they weren't going to find it in the church or the courtyard.

The Grandmaster looked into Oldrich's eyes inquisitively and sternly announced, "We found some charred ashes on the floor. What do you know about them?"

"If you are suggesting, venerable Grandmaster, that I burned this scroll, I would have to be the biggest fool and lunatic in all Christendom," he replied. "I needn't tell you what riches I could get from it? Moreover, I had no idea you were stalking me. Why would I hide it here if I'm never planning to return? It's a pity. I could leave this place a very wealthy man."

"How did you know there was supposed to be a scroll inside it?"

"I don't know anything for sure, but I received a number of hints that told me there was something of enormous value inside it. But since it's not in the box, it must be elsewhere. I plan to keep looking for it."

The Grandmaster thought for a moment, and then ordered his knights to release the man. He turned to him once more and added, "If you ever do find it, we'll offer you the highest price in the Christian world. Remember that. With it, you'll always be welcomed in

Acre!"

He then turned his horse around and headed for the coast, with his knights behind him. Oldrich watched them until the silhouettes of the knights with the red cross on their tunics slowly dissipated in the fog.

Oldrich of Chlum felt his knees shaking. But at last it was behind him, and through the twisted features of the olive trees, he could hear the joyous voices of people emanating from the nearby town proclaiming the birth of their Savior.

www.ingramcontent.com/pod-product-compliance
Lightning Source LLC
Chambersburg PA
CBHW060218030726
47499CB00004B/1098